NEW WORLD

J†M†J

Published by Snowy Wings Publishing
www.snowywingspublishing.com

Cover designed by Najla Qamber Designs.
Model photos by Mosaic Stock Photography.
Interior graphics by [adj] Millennial.

Definition of asexuality quoted from the Asexual Visibility and Education Network (asexuality.org). Quoted with permission.

ISBN (Hardcover): 978-1-946202-19-2
ISBN (Paperback): 978-1-946202-98-7

FOR THE ONES WHO WAITED

NEW WORLD

the iamos trilogy , book two

LYSSA CHIAVARI

Snowy Wings
PUBLISHING

DEAR READER,

The Iamos Trilogy is designed to be a single story broken into several parts: three full novels and a novella. Because of the way the story is structured, each installment is not intended to be read without the foundation of the previous books before it. In order for you to best enjoy the series, this is the recommended order to read the books in:

Book 1: *Fourth World*
Book 1.5: *Different Worlds*: An Iamos Novella
Book 2: *New World*
Book 3: *One World*

This novel contains a number of references to the events of both *Fourth World* and *Different Worlds*, and will be understood most fully if you read both those books before starting this one.

Thank you for reading!

LYSSA CHIAVARI

I CLOSED MY EYES, BREATHING IN DEEPLY THROUGH MY NOSE. Each breath was difficult, but with practiced skill, I managed to keep my inhalations and exhalations steady, refusing to allow my breathing to become labored. I'd known what I was getting into, coming here. Simos' gravity was much stronger than Iamos', and in the weeks before we stepped through the postern, my body had undergone rigorous training in preparation. Adjusting to the added body weight was difficult, but not impossible. The other colonists were relying on us to get them through this transition period—they couldn't see their *geroi* struggling. Eristin and I had to be strong.

Breathe in. Breathe out. That's all there was to it.

"*Geros* Achillios," a man's voice called out.

I didn't permit my eyes to snap open. I inhaled one last time before lifting my lids calmly. I could hear the way the man struggled to regulate his breathing as he pushed his way past the jungle plants to approach me. He needed a calming influence.

"Tirios," I said. "Deep breaths. Slow movements. Don't tax yourself."

Tirios tugged his earlobe, placing his hands on his knees and panting. I watched silently, allowing him to catch his breath. Tirios was one of the System experts on our expedition. He knew the intricacies of our interlinked minds better than any man or woman on Iamos. He'd been selected for this expedition in the hopes that that knowledge could save us. Every colonization party that had made the journey to Simos had disappeared. They'd lose their connection with the System soon after arriving on the planet, if not immediately after. The *gerotus* blamed the magnetic field for the disruption, but Tirios had assured me that the new refinements he'd made to our earpieces would counteract the disruptive signals of the planet.

I confess that I didn't exactly have a technical mind. The inner workings of the System were beyond me. But I trusted Tirios. If he said his modifications would work, I believed him.

But then we got here. Unwavering belief meant little in the face of harsh reality.

"Have you made contact with Iamos?" I asked him when he straightened.

"No, *kyrios*. I am still receiving the same error as before—a blank signal. We can connect to the System, but we receive no response to our communications."

I breathed out, steepling my fingers and closing my eyes again. Inhale. Exhale. "Keep trying."

"Yes, *kyrios*. But that's not why I'm here. *Gerouin* Eristin is asking for you. She's up on the ridge."

I opened my eyes. "I'll be right there."

I felt my way down the dark jungle path, weaving between enormous trees and brushing past tall plants that reminded me of *fraouloi*. I'd been briefed on what to expect, but I still hadn't been entirely prepared for the abundance of greenery Simos had to offer. If Iamos had ever held life this verdant, it had been generations before my birth. I was five years *enilos*, and by the time I was old enough to walk, see, remember, all of Iamos had been a barren desert. This rainforest was more of a shock to my system than even the stronger gravity.

The trees thinned the farther up the hill I climbed, and then they broke apart, revealing a rocky ridge that looked down over the coast. Waves broke roughly over the shoreline below, and the air was heavy with the smell of salt and water, greenery and *life*. The sky above my head was black, cut in two by the thick band of galaxy and a small sliver of white—Simos' moon. That crescent of light illuminated the fair, sandy hair on my partner's head, while the rest of her form was drowned in shadow.

"Eristin. Tirios said you were asking for me."

She turned to face me. "Yes. Look at this."

I came to stand beside her at the edge of the ridge. Eristin was more than just the *gerouin* on this mission: she was our leading astronomer. Her knowledge of the stars was unmatched. She'd been eagerly waiting for the sun to set so she could get her first glimpse of the constellations from this new world. I hadn't expected her to move from this perch all night. But what she wanted to show me, I couldn't imagine. The stars were beyond my realm—my expertise lay in mundane political dealings.

"I ran the charts before we left Iamos. I calculated the seasons of this world, the position of the stars from this hemisphere. At this time of year, Oryos should not be visible from here. But there it is." She pointed to a triad of stars in the northwestern sky. "These stars are all wrong."

"Is it possible you calculated incorrectly?" I asked her.

She frowned, the movement of her lips shadowed in the starlight. "Maybe, but... there's more." She looked at me. "You might want to sit down, Achillios."

I glanced around myself. "Where? On the ground?"

She let out a humorless chuckle. "Suit yourself." She gestured into the sky. "There. Do you see that star?" It was small and dim, but still prominent in the sky alongside the stars. It glowed with a faint red hue. "That's Iamos."

I didn't understand what she was getting at. Seeing our homeworld from such a distance was strange, humbling—but it was to be expected. We knew how far we were going when we undertook this mission.

But then she moved her finger across the sky, gesturing to a larger, brighter, yellow star that I didn't recognize. My mind struggled to recall the different names of celestial bodies, and I once again found myself cursing, wishing that our earpieces were receiving transmissions from the System. My brain was still not accustomed to having to hold its own information, to think and recall unassisted.

"What is that, Eristin?"

"That's Hamos," she said.

I stared at her, uncomprehending, before looking back to the star. "Hamos?"

She tugged her earlobe.

"But... why is it so far from Iamos?" Our worlds were twins, our orbits tightly interlinked as they sped through the solar system, circling the sun in a calculated dance.

"I don't know," Eristin replied. "Something has happened."

"Is this why we can't contact Iamos?" I asked, horror unfolding in my chest. "Was there some kind of... disaster after we left?"

"This couldn't have happened in the twelve hours we've been gone," Eristin said flatly. "A cataclysm of this scale would have massive repercussions on the planets around us. It wouldn't be peaceful like this. The sky would be on fire. Everything would be destroyed. There could be no life here."

"So, in order for this to have happened, and this planet to be unaffected...?"

She made a tiny noise in the back of her throat. I glanced at her, and for the first time noticed the odd way the light from the moon and stars was making her eyes shine. She blinked, and then I saw the telltale streak of tears on her cheeks.

"Ages must have passed," she said at last.

"There must be some mistake," I protested.

"There is no mistake, Achillios. The stars don't lie."

My legs felt shaky, and now I knew why she had told me to sit. But I wouldn't let my legs give out on me. I wouldn't let that weakness show. I was a *geros*. I was in control. I stood, though the weight of this world dragged at my bones every second, calling me down to it.

At last, I spoke. "So, all the colonists who came to Simos before... who disappeared..."

Eristin swallowed, looking up at the stars. "The question isn't *where* they went. It's *when*."

PART ONE
MARS

Tierra Nueva, Aeolis Province
Martian Colony
2075 C.E.

CHAPTER 1

- n a d i n -

THE SKY WAS BLUE.

I couldn't believe it at first. I blinked several times to make sure I wasn't seeing things, but the image remained unchanged. Brilliant, bright, cloudless. An unblemished azure color arcing over my head, taking the breath from me. I'd never seen a sky like this, even as a child, even before the atmosphere on Iamos had thinned so much that we were no longer allowed outside the citidome. I was used to a hazy yellowy-purple that turned more and more red as the sea had evaporated beyond repair. But this...

This was beautiful.

The awe I felt at the sight, however, was quickly jolted out of me. After an instant my mind caught up with me, and I realized where I was, how I had come to be there—lying on my back, my chest constricted and bruised-feeling. The postern. The explosion.

Ceilos.

I sat up in a panic, disentangling myself from Isaak, who'd stumbled to the ground when I fell into him. I'd lost my balance when Ceilos let go of my hand, and I'd staggered forward, bringing Isaak and his father down with me. I looked around myself frantically for the others: Ceilos, Gitrin and Emil. We were all supposed to come through the postern together. That had been the plan. The six of us were to come here, to Mars—to the future—to try to reason with the rulers here, the ones Isaak called GSAF. To tell them the story of Iamos, my dying world.

But something had gone horribly wrong. We were alone.

Isaak's father muttered something in English that I couldn't quite understand. I could barely even hear his words over the roaring in my ears. *What happened? Where are they? Where is he?*

I tried to say something, but terror trapped my voice in my throat. I cleared it and tried again. "He let go," I managed at last.

Isaak struggled to his knees and stared at me in confusion. "What?" But I'd already turned my back on him, whirling around, searching.

"Ceilos!" I shouted, hoping beyond reason that maybe he was here, that we'd just gotten separated. We were in a small trench or a crater of some kind. It was possible that they'd landed just above us, out of my line of sight. But though I called again, no response came.

"Where are the others?" Isaak asked, finally seeming to understand what I was trying to tell him: that we were alone. "Emil? And Gitrin and Ceilos?"

I looked at him, wild-eyed. "Isaak, he let go."

"Who let go?"

I swallowed down the bile that was burning my throat. "Ceilos. He had my hand as we were stepping into the postern, and just as I passed through, just when I heard that noise... he let go." His hand must have been torn from mine by the blast. My ears were still ringing from the sound of the explosion, and the force of it had knocked me off my feet. What could have caused that? I felt so frantic I wanted to pull my own hair out. *What had happened?*

"What's she saying?" Isaak's father asked in English. I started to answer him, but Isaak interrupted me, speaking in Iamoi.

"What does that mean?" he asked. "Where did they go?"

"I don't know," I said, my voice breaking. "If the postern closed before they made it through, they'll still be back in Elytherios. But if Ceilos let go of my hand after they were already in the postern..." Nausea overwhelmed me again, and I had to squeeze my eyes closed and breathe in through my nose to keep from vomiting. Panicking this much was not going to help anyone. "*Guard your emotions,*" Gitrin had once told me.

Gitrin. Panic engulfed me once more.

"We have to go back," I burst out, snatching the posternkey Isaak still gripped in his hands. I had to know what had happened, had to make sure they were all safe. That they hadn't been...

"How are we supposed to do that?" Isaak asked. "First we have to get to that cave that my dad and I—"

"Then let's go!" I grabbed Isaak by the elbow, dragging him up to his feet.

"It's not going to be that simple," he argued. "Emil said that GSAF—"

A voice speaking in English cut him off. My eyes flew up to see a man standing at the lip of the crater, towering over us.

The man was tall and reedy, with receding brown hair peppered with gray and shorn close to his scalp. Reflective glass covered his eyes, preventing me from truly seeing him. It was unsettling. Two other men stood beside him, brandishing instruments I didn't recognize but knew, instinctively, must be weapons. My mind hurriedly scrambled to understand what the first man had said, but in my panic the meaning wouldn't come.

Beside me, Isaak and his father froze, slowly lifting their hands, showing the men their palms. I quickly did the same.

"Well, well. Isaak Contreras. Just the person I've been looking for all this time. And if there was ever such perfect timing, I've never seen it," said the man with the glass eyes. His mouth twisted up into a grin. He spoke slowly enough now that I could understand his words, but I still didn't grasp their meaning.

Isaak blanched. Wordlessly, he trudged over to a rusty metal ladder bolted to the hard rock side of the trench. His father trailed behind him, and I nervously followed, tucking the posternkey into the silver reticule at my waist. My knees shook as I reached the top of the ladder, and one of the men shouldered his weapon and grabbed my arm. I wasn't sure if he was trying to support me or if he was taking me prisoner, but his fingers clamped my flesh tight enough to bruise. I winced, but he didn't loosen his grip.

The three men led us down a dirt path that wound between various pits and trenches like the one we'd climbed out of. We were in some kind of canyon that reminded me of the route we'd taken to Elytherios, but the features of the rocks were unfamiliar. A loud voice echoed off the stones around us. An oration of some kind?

We followed the path as it curved around a tall sandstone formation, and I stopped short. The canyon opened out to a wide clearing filled with people. I stared in shock at the crowd before me. Hundreds of men and women were squeezed shoulder to shoulder in the tight space, and all of them looked *different* from one another. Tall and short, heavy and thin, with different variations in skin tone and hair color. A girl with bronze skin and hair as orange as a sunset glanced over her shoulder at me, before murmuring something to the person standing next to her, a narrow, pale boy with hair that was two different colors: cropped short and dark on the sides of his head, long and straw-colored on the top. I saw a girl with straight, black hair that was cut bluntly above her shoulders, and a fair woman with light hair that waved loosely down her back. A tall man with dark skin and even darker hair in long braids, and a short, stubby man with a woven cap covering his head. Every single person was an individual.

I had never seen anything like this on Iamos. The inhabitants of the citidome all looked alike, matching their region's chosen traits. Even in Elytherios, where people from every citidome had come together, I had still recognized every trait grouping. This diversity was unfathomable.

Was this what Iamos was like before? I thought weakly. A century ago, before the eugenicists had molded us, choosing only the best traits to maximize our chances for survival—had we looked like this? Had everyone been *different*?

At the front of the crowd, a man stood on a platform. I realized that he must be the orator just before he broke off mid-sentence. I followed his gaze to where Isaak stood, his own arm gripped tightly by the man with the glass eyes. Isaak was staring at the person on the platform in shock, his mouth slightly agape.

His face had gone pale, even more so than it had in the crater.

"Isaak?" I whispered through the silence. The men and women closest to us in the crowd turned, watching us in confusion. "What's wrong? Who is that?"

The man with the glass eyes smirked as Isaak struggled for a response. "It can't be—" he started.

Then the man on the platform shouted, "Isaak!" His voice resounded through a speaker system which shrieked with feedback, making me wince. But the crowd didn't seem to mind. When he said Isaak's name, the people roared in response, whirling around and rushing toward us. I shrank back, and the man who'd been holding my arm released it, stepping in front of me and brandishing the weapon once more.

"That's enough!" the man with glass eyes shouted, but the crowd was unstoppable.

Abruptly my brain thrust me back to Iamos, to the riot in the citidome the day we found Gitrin missing. Masses of bodies shoving against one another, shouting, threatening to trample anyone in their path. Screaming "*Death to the* geroi!" The only thing that had kept the rioters from violence that day was the adherence protocol, but there was no System here. Nothing to control this. No way to stop them.

I couldn't breathe.

My heart beat erratically, and my hands and fingers tingled like grains of sand ran through my veins. The edges of my vision burned white until I squeezed my eyes closed. "Nadin!" I thought I heard Isaak call, but his voice sounded muffled over the ringing in my ears. My mouth was dry, and when I licked my lips, it tasted sour and acidic.

"Back off! Give her room, she needs air!"

I did need air. I so desperately needed air. I couldn't draw a breath. I couldn't hear. I couldn't see.

Darkness swallowed me.

I opened my eyes slowly, my head reverberating. It felt like the ground was moving beneath me. I realized after a moment, as I gathered my bearings, that in a way it was—I was in a transport vehicle of some sort. We had some of these on Iamos, though they'd become increasingly rare since travel by postern had become most common. Now they were only used when a large number of people had to travel between citidomes, rendering postern travel impractical.

The man who'd held my arm before the riot was seated next to me, still holding his weapon. Isaak and his father were nowhere to be seen.

I swallowed, my throat feeling dry and my head spinning slightly. I was getting tired of waking up with a headache. It had become far too frequent over the last few weeks. I thought for a moment, trying to remember the words; then I said in English, hesitantly, "Where is Isaak?"

I think the man must have understood me—I know I pronounced the words correctly—but he didn't answer. He merely smirked.

I glowered and looked out the window of the vehicle.

Despite the ominous presence of the man beside me, just being away from that crowd made me feel more calm. I could breathe again. As the vehicle rolled silently forward, I began to pick out more details. The city we were passing through was unlike anything I'd ever seen. It was vast; the whole of Hope Renewed would fit easily inside just the portion I could see out the window. The buildings were tall, some even seeming close to the height of the pyramid in my citidome, though they were nowhere near as wide. Here and there, I caught the silver glint of water between the buildings. Rivers and creeks seemed to run throughout this city, winding between buildings and meandering under bridges. Unremarkable features to the citizens here but a wonder to my eyes. So much water—enough to sustain a population of this size.

This was Isaak's Tierra Nueva. This was Mars.

And it was Iamos, too. The *geroi* believed we could never make the planet like this again. But these people had. I squeezed my eyes shut for a moment, wishing. *Please let them accept us,* I thought. Despite Isaak's assurances, I don't think I ever completely believed that his world could hold us. But now that I was seeing it with my own eyes, I believed. Maybe there was hope for the Iamoi. Maybe soon we would be returning through the postern with impossible, wonderful news.

But will Ceilos and Gitrin be there to hear it?

My stomach lurched, and I focused my mind on calming it. I wasn't going to worry about it anymore. It would do me no good to keep panicking, not after what happened back in the canyon. I had to concentrate on my task. The posternkey was designed to return us to just three minutes after we'd left. Whatever had happened, we could help them when we returned. In the meantime, I had other things to think about.

I had to deal with GSAF.

The vehicle came around a corner, revealing some of the

largest buildings I'd seen yet. On an island in the center of the river, a massive tower seemed to cut the sky like the dorsal fin of a *psara* slicing through water. The buildings on this side of the river weren't much smaller. We were approaching one that was rounded on its sides like a dome, with two matching towers jutting from the center. Another crowd of people was gathered in front of it. The vehicle was soundproofed enough that their voices seemed to be a muffled hum, but I could see by their faces that they were shouting. My pulse quickened again involuntarily. I hoped that this was not our destination.

That hope was dashed when the vehicle began to slow, pulling to a stop in front of the building.

The man beside me said something in English that I didn't understand and opened the door on his side. The roar of voices poured in, deafening. He slid out, gesturing for me to follow him. I shrank back in my seat.

He looked at me impatiently. "Come on," he said slowly, and this time I did understand.

"No," I said. I thought for a moment, then shook my head the way I'd seen Isaak do.

The man took a deep, irritated breath through his nostrils and shook his own head. He slammed the door shut and stormed away from the vehicle, disappearing into the crowd. A moment later he returned, a woman by his side. She had fair, straight hair that just brushed the top of her shoulders, and skin almost as pale. I winced at the thought of what solar radiation must do to that complexion.

She opened the door and smiled at me. "Hello," she said. I could barely hear her over the shouts of the rioters. "We need you to come inside. I can't talk to you here. Will you come with me?"

I squared my shoulders and shook my head again stubbornly. It didn't matter whether my guard was a gruff, armed man or a smiling woman. I wasn't going out into that crowd again.

Someone whistled loudly, and the woman looked over her shoulder. "Gerald, would you please get these people out of here?" she snapped. At her word, the man who'd been guarding me began waving people back. It annoyed me that he'd listened to this woman and not me, but I had to remind myself that I wasn't a *patroin* here. I was no one to these people. I unconsciously reached for the medallion around my neck and rubbed it between my fingers.

Several other men in dark clothing emerged from the building, and the group of them parted the crowd. The people were still shouting, but there was a wide path through them now.

The fair-haired woman looked back in the door at me. "It's safe now," she said, smiling again.

I took a deep breath and slid across the seat, stepping out of the vehicle.

The woman led me into the building, her hand on my elbow. Unlike the man earlier, she didn't seem to be trying to hold me prisoner—her touch was more reassuring. Inside the building was a large, cavernous space with a vaulted ceiling. It was brightly lit, with tile floors that gleamed. There were windows everywhere, even on the ceiling, letting sunlight stream in. It was a stark contrast from the darkness of the citidome, where even the glass-faced pyramid had stone walls on the inside to shield the *patroi* from radiation.

I looked around, taking it all in. There were a number of people here as well, but they didn't approach us. They seemed to be preoccupied with their own work, and only glanced occasionally in my direction. Relief washed over me.

As the doors slid shut behind us, a middle-aged man strode across the room toward us. I expected him to address the woman, but to my surprise, he looked directly at me and inclined his head, placing three fingers on his brow.

I stared at him in confusion. How did he...?

"*Kyrin* Nadin," he said in nearly unaccented Iamoi, "it is an honor to meet you."

I took a step back, my eyes wide as I looked back and forth between the man and the woman who'd escorted me in. "How is this possible?" I breathed.

The woman smiled. "We've been expecting you, Nadin."

CHAPTER 2

- i s a a k -

TICK. TICK. TICK.

I stared down at my hands as the clock on the wall counted away the seconds. They looked dirty. Even after spending a week in Elytherios, I still hadn't been able to get the grime out from under my fingernails from our long journey through the caves and dusty Iamos wilderness.

It felt surreal. This morning I'd been on another world, thousands of years in the past. And now I was back home, in my own time. *Home.*

Well, sort of. For one thing, I wasn't *home,* I was in some empty office in the GSAF building waiting for Joseph Condor to come back in and probably haul me off to a dark prison cell. And for another thing, this wasn't exactly my time. Everything was different. Every*one* was different.

I still couldn't believe that had been Henry earlier, but I knew it had to be. You can't be best friends with a guy for half your life and then not know him when you see him. But he'd definitely aged. And he'd *cut* his *hair.* That was possibly the most mind-boggling thing of all, seeing a short-haired Henry standing at a podium giving a speech like a torquing politician or something. His mom had never been able to get him to cut his hair. His dad was Sikh, but Henry was an avowed atheist. Religion had never been a part of his long-hair phase, it was one hundred percent rebellion. His mom had lived in America until she was in high school, when her father died and the family moved to India to be near relatives, and she had American sensibilities through and through. As far as Mrs. Sandhu was concerned, good boys had short hair. And when I left—just a couple weeks ago, it felt like to me—Henry had been anything *but* a good boy.

How long had I been gone? I remembered how Dad had thought he'd only been gone for a month when he'd been missing for more than two annums, and I felt sick to my stomach.

If I'd been gone as long as Dad, what had happened to everyone in that time? I'd seen how Henry had changed, if only from a distance. What about everyone else? What about...

What about Tamara?

Did she remember what had happened between us the last time we'd seen each other? What had she thought after I vanished? Did they assume I'd been kidnapped? Or did they think what we'd all thought about Dad—that I'd abandoned everyone?

Tick. Tick. Tick.

I felt fidgety and wired, like I'd downed a bunch of coffee or something. Just waiting here was driving me nuts. Joseph Condor had left me in this room with barely a word, just telling me he'd be back shortly. And then what? He knew I'd stolen government property when I took the posternkey from the dig site. Whatever he was planning for me when he got back, it couldn't be good.

And I had no clue where they'd taken Dad, or Nadin—

My stomach knotted again as I remembered the way Nadin had collapsed, slumping against that suit who'd been holding her arm. Was she okay? Had the postern travel made her sick, or was it the stress of not knowing what had happened to the others? And that crowd... She didn't do well in crowds. I'd seen it back on Iamos, in the citidome when there was that riot. She'd been pale and irritable for hours afterward. God only knew how she was feeling now. After she collapsed, it had been pandemonium. Joseph Condor shoved me into a black SUV and we'd peeled out. He wouldn't speak to me at all, other than to tell me that Nadin would be "taken care of," whatever that meant. And then he spent the whole car ride over here glued to his palmtop, silently tapping away.

Nadin had to be okay. She had to be.

Tick. Tick. Tick.

Out in the hallway there was the sound of muffled voices. My hands clenched on the table, and I sat up straight. The door opened, and Joseph Condor stepped inside. He leveled those ice blue eyes on me for just a second, just long enough for my heart to stop for a couple of beats. Then he moved aside, and someone behind him came through the door. Another familiar-but-not person, just as gut-wrenching as Henry.

My jaw worked soundlessly for a moment as I stared at her. "Mom," I finally managed.

Time seemed to freeze, Mom's gaze locked with mine, neither of us speaking. I couldn't believe my eyes. Once again, I found myself wondering how long I'd been gone. There was so much gray in her hair, and deep, dark circles under her eyes, like she hadn't slept in months.

I'd done this. I'd caused this.

She stared at me for just a moment longer; then she rushed toward me. I started to stand just as she collided with me, almost knocking over the plastic chair I'd been sitting in. "Isaak," she cried, her voice breaking. Her shoulders shook as she buried her face in my chest. Hot tears soaked through the worn fabric of the Iamoi clothing I was still wearing. I probably looked like a reject from a sci-fi flick. What must she think, seeing me here like this? What had she thought the whole time I'd been gone?

I swallowed, trying to blink away tears of my own.

Finally, she pulled away, running her thumbs across my cheeks, peering into my eyes. "Where have you been? What's happened to you?"

"I—That is—" I didn't know where to begin.

"We'd all like to know those answers," Condor said, still standing in the doorway. "But we'll save our questions for another time. Right now, it's important for Isaak to be reunited with his family."

Mom nodded tearily. "Thank you, Mr. Condor," she said.

I gaped at the two of them. "Wait, seriously? You're just letting me go?"

Condor quirked an eyebrow. "Are you saying I shouldn't?"

"No, no," I blurted. Of course I wanted to get the heck out of there. But I was supposed to buy that Condor was just going to let me go, after everything he'd put me through before? What was his real game here?

Mom threaded her fingers through mine, and I let her pull me toward the door, my eyes never leaving Condor's. His expression was unreadable. As we passed, he cleared his throat.

"Professor Garcia," he said. She turned to face him, and he folded his arms. "Before you go, there's someone else you need to collect as well. Do you want to tell her, Isaak, or shall I?" He almost sounded amused when he said it.

Mom looked at me quizzically. *Crap.* I'd forgotten about this part.

"Uh, Mom," I began, shifting uncomfortably. "This might be kind of a shock, but... I, uh..." I swallowed. "I kind of found Dad."

Hours later, I sat at the foot of my bed, looking around my room with a sense of surreality. Everything was the same as it had been when I left it. Untouched. The room was dusty—not as much as I would have expected for two annums, but enough that I could tell Mom hadn't been in here all that often. I knew she'd come in at least once, though, because my bed was made. I hadn't bothered to make it before I left for school that last morning.

Two annums. My fingers clenched the bedspread involuntarily. That's how long I'd been gone. A month to me, two Earth years to everyone else. And Dad? He'd been gone almost five by now.

Mom had not been pleased, by any stretch of the imagination.

"You brought Raymond back?" she'd said when she at last found her voice. "*Why?*"

"I couldn't exactly leave him there," I'd said awkwardly. "We weren't on Earth, Mom. We were... somewhere else."

"Oh, really? Where were you, then? Where have *the two of you* been for so long?"

I'd glanced uncomfortably at Joseph Condor, who was

watching us both with his eyebrows raised. "I'll tell you when we get home."

She'd stormed down the hall, her heels clacking noisily against the tile floor. "He's not coming home with us, Isaak."

But he'd had to, in the end. There was a great big argument about it when we got to the parking garage, where Erick was waiting in the car with Celeste. Seeing my little sister again might have been the hardest thing of all—worse than Henry, worse than my mom. She'd grown so much, she genuinely was unrecognizable. Her missing front teeth were back. Her long, wild brown hair had been cut to her shoulders, with a clip pinning back what had once been her bangs. I realized with a jolt that she'd gotten so tall she didn't even need a carseat anymore. Who was this kid? She couldn't be my sister.

She stared at me with wide eyes, like she was terrified. Like I was a ghost.

Every time I'd ever been annoyed with her—every time I'd told her to go away, to not bother me; the irritation I'd felt when she was clinging to me and Tamara at the dig site the day before I found the posternkey—slammed into me like a freight train. How could I have been such a jerk to her? She was my sister, and I'd lost *years* with her. I felt like I had seeing Mom again in that empty office, all gray-haired and broken. My eyes burned. I had to squeeze them shut before anyone saw me on the brink of tears.

What had I done?

While Celeste stared at me from the backseat of the car, Mom and Dad argued. Erick had gotten out of the car and stood awkwardly to the side as they yelled.

"You cannot come home with us, Raymond. It's absolutely out of the question," Mom snapped.

"Where else am I supposed to go?" Dad snapped back. "It's my house, too!"

"Oh, no," Mom said, waggling her finger. "That house was in my name, remember? Since I was the one with the steadier job—does that ring a bell? It does not belong to you in any way."

Dad made a noise in the back of his throat. "I can't go to a hotel, Jesica. I don't have any money."

"You never do."

"Will you get off your damn high horse for one minute? Isaak said I've been gone for years. There's no way my credit cards still work. My accounts have got to be closed by now. How am I supposed to pay for a hotel?" He crossed his arms, looking slyly at her. "Unless you want to pay for it."

Erick stepped forward then, starting to say something, but my mom cut him off. "We're not giving you a cent, Raymond."

Dad glanced past her at Erick. "Who's this guy?"

"This is my husband," Mom snapped.

"What?" I gasped, almost losing my balance. I grabbed Celeste's open door to try to steady myself. Mom had gotten remarried? She and Erick had only just started dating when I left! But I looked at Celeste again and the time difference slammed into me once more. I gripped the car door until my knuckles turned white.

Dad looked back and forth between them incredulously. "I'm your husband!" he sputtered.

"Oh, no, you're not. I got an annulment."

"Nobody asked me!" Dad protested.

"How were we supposed to do that?" asked Mom. "Considering you've been gone four and a half years with no word. That's called abandonment, Raymond."

Four and a half years—I knew she had to mean annums. Most people used the terms interchangeably, still thinking in Earth terms. That's when I'd realized I'd been gone for two of them. Two annums. A whole Martian orbit. I struggled to take a breath.

"I'm talking to a priest!" Dad shouted, his voice echoing off the roof of the parking garage.

I groaned and squeezed my eyes shut. "Will you give it a rest, Dad?"

When I opened them again, he was looking at me, considering. I knew he was thinking about what I'd said to him in Elytherios: "I *saw what you left in that box in the garden. Where's your wedding ring, Dad?*" He'd flat-out admitted he was planning to leave Mom regardless. So what was he complaining about now?

Erick took advantage of the quiet to step forward. "Why don't we discuss this later, Jesica? Celeste is stressed, and"—he glanced over at me—"I'm sure Isaak is eager to get home."

"What about me?" Dad asked.

"You can go f—"

"Mom," I interrupted. "Can Dad at least come back to the house for dinner or something? Just so we can all tell you what happened? Then we can figure out somewhere for him to stay." She frowned, deep creases forming around her mouth. She was really skinny now, I realized. On top of everything else. Her face was lined from it. "Please," I went on. "I'm just... I'm really tired."

She and Erick looked at each other, in silent conversation for a moment. Then she sighed. "Fine. But then he goes."

Dad and I squeezed into the backseat next to Celeste, who looked at us like we were strangers. I sat between them, and she scooted as close to the window as she could, giving me a wide berth. Guilt twisted my stomach once more.

Erick and Mom rode in the front, and Erick drove rather than relying on the self-steering controls. I didn't think I'd ever seen anyone actually drive this car before. We sat silently until he pulled the car onto the Santos Creek bridge. Then Mom caught my eye in the rearview mirror.

"Okay, Isaak. Ready whenever you are. Are you going to tell us where you've been?"

I took a deep breath through my nose. Here's the part where they wrote me off as crazy.

And I told them. About the artifact I'd found at Erick's dig site, and its connection to the coin we'd found among Dad's possessions in our backyard. How I'd used it to track down a disgraced scientist who turned out to be none other than Dad's former coworker at the factory. How I'd run when GSAF tracked me, and it led me to the postern in the caves.

"But *why* did you run?" my mom demanded as we pulled into the garage. "Why didn't you just hand it over to them? Isaak, I've always taught you to cooperate with the police, not *run* from them! Running only makes things worse."

I gritted my teeth, scooting out after Celeste and slamming the car door shut. "Mom, they're up to something! They've been covering all this up!"

She rolled her eyes. "I don't believe any of that nonsense, Isaak. That's just Henry Sandhu talking."

"And Henry's right, Mom!" I snapped.

A weird look crossed over Mom's face. She started to say something, but my dad interrupted.

"Look, Jess, would you just let the kid talk?" he said.

Her nostrils flared. "Do *not* call me Jess."

"I've always called you Jess."

"Not anymore."

"*Anyway*," I said pointedly. I didn't want to be this irritated with my family so soon after coming back from Iamos, but they were making it incredibly difficult not to be. "So I used Dad's coin to open the key…"

I told them about how the key unlocked the postern to Iamos as my mom led us all into the kitchen. Celeste drifted away from us, going to sit in the living room on a large, unfamiliar armchair in the place of our old faux-leather one. I could see her peeking surreptitiously around its winged back, like she still wanted to listen but didn't want to get too close.

Erick began to brew a pot of coffee. He poured himself, my mom, and—after a minute's hesitation—my dad each a mug while I told them about what the citidome was like, about meeting Nadin and Ceilos, about the totalitarian nightmare that was the *geroi* and the System. He sank into a chair next to my mom, a concerned look on his face. They glanced at each other, and I trailed off, realizing how I probably sounded.

"Look, I know this must sound insane," I said hesitantly.

"Of course not," my mom responded woodenly.

"It's not that, Isaak," Erick added in a more convincing tone. "It's just that this sounds an awful lot like what Henry—"

"We're not going there, Erick," my mom broke in firmly.

I looked back and forth between them. "What about Henry?"

"Forget about Henry," my mom said. "Tell us the rest of your story."

I refused to be distracted. "What's going on with Henry, Mom? What was he doing at the dig site today, anyway? If it's really been two annums—"

"Two annums on the dot, actually," Erick said. "You disappeared on this day in 2073."

"Oh," I said, looking down at the table. "So, what, that crowd was there for some kind of memorial or something?" I wasn't sure if I was moved or weirded out. I started scratching at a dried-out coffee ring with my fingernail and said, "I probably ought to get a hold of Henry later and let him know I'm okay. I didn't get to talk to him earlier."

"No," my mom said abruptly.

I blinked at her. "What do you mean, no?"

She crossed her arms. "I'm sorry, did all that time on 'Iamos'"—she made air quotes with her fingers, which I found kind of offensive—"make you forget how to speak English? Let me give it to you in Spanish, then: No."

"Cute, Mom," I scoffed.

"I'm serious, Isaak. I don't want you speaking to that boy. Tamara, either."

"But why?"

"How can you ask me that question? Isaak, those two led you astray. They got you involved in something you should never have been involved in. Something that made you *disappear* without a single trace for two years. I just got you back, I'm not going to let you vanish again." She stamped her foot firmly. "I don't want you hanging around them anymore."

"You've got to be kidding me, Mom. *They* didn't get *me* involved in anything, it was the other way around! Our family was already embroiled in this ages ago. Or did you forget that Dad's the one who went to Iamos in the first place?"

That was a mistake—it turned her attention back to Dad. "As a matter of fact, I did. Tell me, Raymond, how did you manage to wind up on an alien planet, and then drag our son there as well?" Her voice was dripping sarcasm. She didn't believe me. How could she have not believed me?

"I was so desperate to get away from you, I didn't care how far." My dad glowered, sinking into his chair and crossing his arms. "Is that what you want me to say, *Jess*?"

I groaned. "Are you two going to keep this up all night? And I've been trying to explain to you, Mom—Iamos isn't an alien planet. It's *Mars*. It's Mars from the past. Thousands of years ago, when there was still life on the planet. But their time is running out. The planet's dying. It's going to wind up how it was when we found it. We have to do something, or all those people are going to die."

She stared at me, her expression unreadable.

"I'm telling the truth, Mom!"

"He is, Jesica," my Dad put in. "I know it seems impossible, but it's true. It's all true." I glanced at him in surprise, but he stubbornly refused to meet my eyes.

My mom sighed and slumped back in her chair. "Okay. All right. I just... need time to process this, I suppose. Why don't we call it a night? You can tell me more about it tomorrow. For now, I just"—she pinched the bridge of her nose between her fingers—"I just want to appreciate the fact that you're home."

We wound up ordering pizza, and while we waited for the delivery drone, Erick went into the bedroom to make a couple calls. I watched him disappear down the hall, a weird hollowness eating away at my chest. He lived here now, too. That was going to be an adjustment to say the least.

When he emerged, he approached my dad, who was still sitting next to me at the kitchen table, staring at his empty coffee mug. "One of my colleagues at Kimbal rents a room to professors on sabbatical. He doesn't have a lodger right now, since we're coming up to the end of term and most intersessions on Earth have started already. He said you can stay there for the time being. No worries about rent."

I thought that was surprisingly generous, but Dad just scowled.

"Great. Super. Kicked out of my own house—but my wife's new man found me accommodations."

Erick's face hardened. "You've been gone a long time, Raymond. You can't hold the world hostage because of your own reckless actions. I want to help you because I realize not all of this was your fault. But if you're going to spit on my hospitality, I think you know where the door is."

Dad stared at him for a long minute. Then he stood. "Your friend lives in Curiosity Bay?"

"Yes."

Dad pulled his wallet out of his back pocket. It was, as usual, void of cash, but he did have his ADOT pass still. "We'll see if this still works," he said. Erick led him to the door. He glanced at me one last time over his shoulder before disappearing.

I wasn't sure if I was sorry to see him go.

No one talked much during dinner. After we finished eating, I went to the bathroom, splashing water on my face and scrubbing at my fingernails with soap to try to get the rest of the red dirt out from under them. Then I went to my room, changing out of the silver Iamoan bodysuit into a comfortable t-shirt and jeans. My clothes smelled a bit musty from all that time in the closet, but they fit fine. Of course. They hadn't changed, and neither had I.

I tossed the bodysuit into a corner, unsure of what to do with it, and sat sullenly at the foot of my bed. That's where I stayed, watching out the window as the world outside grew darker. Mom's garden had different plants growing in it now, but it was as neat as ever. There wasn't a spider weed to be seen. Knee-high green stalks swayed in the cold breeze that had kicked up as the sun started going down. Everything was different, but I was the same. How was I ever going to catch back up?

I wondered if Tamara knew I was back yet. Had she been part of that crowd earlier, and I hadn't seen her? What was she thinking? And Abuelo—Mom hadn't mentioned anything about him or Abuela. Were they both okay still, back on Earth?

I drew my knees up into my chest, resting my forehead against them. And what about Nadin? Was she safe? How was I going to find her again?

When it got too dark to see, I stood and walked over to my dresser, picking up my Speculus headset and wiping the dust off it with the hem of my shirt. My palmtop was long gone, so I couldn't text Henry, but Mom apparently hadn't thought to take this away. I could still go on chat with him, and we could figure out how to find Nadin. I placed it over my head and pressed the power button. Nothing. I sighed. I hadn't plugged in the set after I'd used it last, since my battery was almost full. No one else had plugged it in, either, so the battery had run down completely. It would probably need overnight to charge. I fished around for the cord, which had slipped partially behind the dresser, and plugged it into my headset.

I sank down on my bed again, overwhelmed. How had everything gotten so messed up? I wished there was some way I could go back in time, without causing a paradox or any of that crap Emil had warned me about. I wished I could make it so I'd never gone to Iamos in the first place.

But what about Nadin and the other Iamoi? What would have happened to them if you hadn't?

Everything was such a torquing mess.

I heard a small sound through the wall behind my headboard. I frowned, listening carefully. There it was again.

Oh, Cristo.

Slowly I stood, brushing off the knees of my musty jeans, and went out into the hallway. The noise was a little louder from out here. Crying. I went to Celeste's door and knocked.

Sniffles, and then a phlegmy "Come in."

Celeste was lying on her bed with her face buried in her pillows. Her room looked different. Her furniture had been rearranged, and she had a new bedspread with cartoon characters on it that I didn't recognize. Probably a new Disney flick or something that had come out while I was gone. Matching curtains framed the window. It was so dark outside that the glass became a mirror, reflecting the light from the lamp and my hazy

26

form back at me.

"Hey," I said, sinking onto the bed next to her and putting a hand on her back. She didn't roll over to look at me, but she didn't flinch away, either. "Are you okay, Celeste?" I said it like Abuelo always had—"Ce-lest-eh."

She nodded her head against the pillows. Finally, she rolled over and looked at me. Her face was red, her eyes bloodshot. I leaned over and grabbed a tissue out of the glittery pink box on her nightstand. She wiped her face off and blew her nose.

"Is it really you, Zak?" she asked.

I nodded. "Yeah. It's really me."

She nodded back, trying to fight the resurgence of tears. "Bianca said you were dead. She said I was stupid to believe you weren't."

"Bianca has always been a jerk."

She giggled stickily. "She really has," she agreed. For just a second, I could see the old Celeste on her face. My kid sister. Then she sobered once more. "Are you going to go away again?"

"No," I started to say, but I broke off. It wasn't all over yet, despite the fact that Joseph Condor had been weirdly accommodating. We still needed to help the Iamoi, and Emil...

Celeste watched me knowingly. "If you have to go again, you'll tell us this time, right?"

"Yes. It was an accident before. I never would have gone without telling you guys if I'd known."

"I know," she said softly. Her eyebrows scrunched again, and she squeezed her eyes shut, putting her hands over her face.

"I'm sorry, Celeste," I said quietly. "I'm so, so sorry."

She nodded and crawled awkwardly over to me, curling up

against me. I put my arms around her and squeezed her tight.

"I missed you, Zak," she said into my chest.

"I missed you, too, Celeste," I whispered.

Finally, she pulled away, looking up at me with red-rimmed eyes. "Zak," she said, almost shyly. "Could you... could you tell me the rest about Iamos? I want to hear it."

I blinked at her. The corners of my mouth turned up involuntarily. "Sure thing. This is going to be quite a bedtime story, though. Hope it doesn't give you nightmares."

She giggled. "It's okay. I don't need a bedtime story. I'm not a little kid anymore. I just want to know. I want to hear the truth, even if Mom doesn't believe you."

She sounded so grown up when she said that, my voice caught in my throat for a minute. "All right," I said, swallowing. "Buckle up, then. What would you say if I told you I'd ridden a dinosaur?"

She gasped. "No way!"

"Well, you'd better believe it, because it's an important part of the story."

I told her everything, while outside the window a cold wind blew.

CHAPTER 3

- n a d i n -

MY MIND WAS STILL REELING AS THE WOMAN LED ME INTO A large, square office with a window that took up the entire wall across from the door. Pots with green plants were scattered throughout the room, large ones in the corners and a smaller one on the center edge of a big desk. My eyes lingered a moment on the bright, rounded leaves. I had to force them away. "I don't understand," I said as the man who spoke Iamoi closed the door after us. "How could you be expecting me?"

"Well, not you, specifically. But we were hoping a representative for your people would appear at some point," the man said with a smile. He gestured to one of three plush chairs across from the desk, while the woman sat behind it. "Please, *kyrin*, have a seat."

I sat, keeping my shoulders square and my back straight as I'd often seen *Gerouin* Melusin do. The thought of my mother sent a pang of guilt and a small stab of anger through my chest, but if this man knew enough of the castes to address me as "*kyrin*," I needed to act the part.

"You know my name," I said to the man in Iamoi, "but I cannot say the same of you. Who are you?"

Rather than respond, the man translated my question to the pale-haired woman. She smiled and looked directly at me. "My name is Kate Ponsford. I'm the governor of Aeolis Province, which is where you are right now. This is Stephen Moyer. He's a linguist who's studied your people's language."

Stephen Moyer began to translate this, but I waved him off. "You are GSAF?" I asked in English.

She raised an eyebrow. "In a way, yes. I was appointed governor by the Global Space and Astronautics Federation on Earth. This building is their administrative headquarters for the province."

That I did not understand. Seeing my confusion, Stephen Moyer translated her words, but the technicalities were still lost on me. It was unimportant, I decided. Isaak had said that GSAF on Mars was similar to the *gerotus* on Iamos—that was enough for me.

"How do you know about my people? Enough for this man to be able to speak our language? I was told that the Iamoi were..." A lump in my throat caught my voice. I swallowed and tried again. "That we had..." I couldn't do it. I couldn't say the words out loud.

That we were all dead.

"It's true that when our people came here this planet was uninhabited," Kate Ponsford said gently, her eyebrows furrowed in concern. "As we've lived here, we began to study the planet more, and we uncovered some of the artifacts of your people. That's how we came to understand that there were humans here before us."

Humans. She made no distinction between Iamoi and Simoi. It was such an important difference to us, though. The origin of the humans on this planet spelled the difference between my people living or dying.

I rubbed the bridge of my nose between my fingers. "But I do not understand. Isaak said that no one on Mars knew about us."

Kate Ponsford looked at Stephen Moyer. They seemed to share a silent conversation for a moment; then finally Stephen Moyer said in Iamoi, "Many things have changed since Isaak passed through the postern. How much did he—"

The door opened, and he broke off mid-sentence. A man entered, tall and lean with brown hair tinged silver. I recognized him as the man with the glass eyes, but now he had removed that apparatus, revealing irises an even lighter blue than my own. He closed the door behind him.

"Ah, Joseph," Kate Ponsford said. "Come in, have a seat."

I followed him with my gaze. "Where is Isaak?" I asked. The last time I'd seen him, this man had been holding him tightly by the arm. They'd seemed antagonistic toward each other. The fact that this man was here alone now made me nervous.

The man smiled coolly at me, sitting in the empty chair next to Stephen Moyer. "Isaak is fine. He's with his family now. They're taking him home."

Relief washed over me, and my shoulders relaxed, my spine slumping ever so slightly. Isaak had seemed so frightened of this man and of GSAF, but obviously his fears had been misplaced. "When can I see him again?" I asked.

Stephen Moyer and Kate Ponsford looked at each other again. "We'll arrange something," the blue-eyed man said, his cool smile unwavering. "In the meantime, we have many questions to ask you."

"Yes, I have questions for you as well." I hesitated, then turned to Stephen Moyer. In Iamoi I said, "I was hoping Isaak would be here to help me. He knows our situation, and he also knows the ways of your people better than I do. I thought perhaps he could help interpret."

"That's what I am here for, *kyrin*," Stephen Moyer replied. "I've been assigned to act as your interpreter."

I shifted uncomfortably. "I suppose that will do," I said. *For now.*

"We were just telling Nadin about our discovery of the Iamoi artifacts," Kate Ponsford said to the blue-eyed man. "Since you've worked more directly with the System, Joseph, I thought you might be able to give her some more information."

"The System?" I interrupted. "You know about the System?"

The three of them stared at me for a moment. "My goodness, she speaks English well," Kate Ponsford finally said with a laugh. "Did Isaak teach you?"

"Yes," I said slowly, my eyes moving between the three of them. I had the unpleasant suspicion that they hadn't wanted me to understand everything they were saying.

"The System was a discovery we made relatively recently, *kyrin*," Stephen Moyer said, turning the conversation back to where it had been before the blue-eyed man they called Joseph had entered the room. "We've been trying to decrypt it for some time, but only recently made enough headway to access small amounts of data. Most of these were the final video recordings stored on the System. Our scholars taught ourselves your language using these videos. You were in a number of them, which is how we came to recognize you. We suspect the System lost functionality shortly after those recordings were made."

My heart beat erratically. If some of the last recordings on the System were of me, what did that mean? That the cataclysm was coming soon? Within weeks of Isaak and me leaving Iamos? Days?

Hush, Nadin, I told myself. *Remember what Isaak said. This could be a sign. Our mission is destined to be successful. We will evacuate and shut the System down.* The thought calmed me.

"In a few of the recordings, we saw Isaak Contreras, a boy from our province who had been missing for some time. That is how we realized that your people had some means of time travel that he had inadvertently stumbled across," Stephen Moyer said. "We were hoping that meant if he could travel backward, he might also be able to travel forward. This is why we've been waiting."

"But you must understand, Nadin," Kate Ponsford put in swiftly, "this information was classified. Do you know what that word means?"

When I shook my head, Stephen Moyer translated. "Not all of this information had been passed on to the general public before Isaak left Mars. Like the *geroi* of your time, GSAF is responsible for the population. More than that—we're responsible for the welfare of the planet, including its history and culture. We wanted to wait until we understood everything about the System before we made the announcement. There are many unscrupulous people who have been known to raid archaeological sites to steal artifacts and sell them for profit. We needed to be able to conduct our studies without the threat of thieves."

"Unfortunately, some bad actors leaked the information," Joseph interrupted. "Hence the riot you witnessed earlier. They felt we were covering up what had happened to Isaak. The truth was, we've known for some months that he was with you, but without more advanced knowledge of the System, we were unable to reach him. We had to wait and trust that your people would be able to help him."

I narrowed my eyes, trying to process what he was saying. "So that's why the people were angry?"

"Yes. But now that you're here, things should settle down. I don't anticipate any more riots," Kate Ponsford said with a smile.

I exhaled, settling back into the plush chair. It was much softer than the woven copper chairs I was used to on Iamos. "That's good," I said. Then I sat forward again, squaring my shoulders once more. "But that doesn't address the purpose of me being here. *Kyrin* Kate Ponsford, I'm here on behalf of my people. If you have access to the System, then you must know the severity of our situation. Our planet is dying. If we do not evacuate, our population will be decimated. We need your help."

Kate Ponsford nodded, her expression grave. "Of course, we understand that your situation is dire. But I don't know how we could help you. In matters of time travel..."

I shook my head in frustration. I could see where her thoughts were leading her—as Emil warned, if events in the past were changed it could be disastrous. "The proposal we had is one that would not alter the course of events that have already been set. We... that is, Isaak..." I closed my eyes. It sounded so ridiculous to say aloud. I wished Isaak were here; I'd feel less idiotic if I had someone with me. Why had they split us up? "We were hoping that the Iamoi may be permitted to settle here. In this time."

Silence. I tentatively opened my eyes. All three of them were staring at me. Kate Ponsford's mouth was agape, and Stephen Moyer's was pressed into a thin line. Joseph, on the other hand, was giving me the same disapproving look I'd seen on the faces of the *geroi* time and time again throughout my life. My first instinct was to wish to disappear into the vacuum of space, but then a defiant anger rippled through me. I refused to let them condescend to me. I was here on a mission, and I was not going to let them deter me.

"I understand that this is a sudden request, but it is only made out of absolute need. On Iamos, our core belief is that all lives are one. Our people are different from yours, but as you said earlier—we are all human. The last several weeks I have spent getting to know Isaak, one of your people. From all I know of him, I know that to at least some extent, you share this core belief. You cannot leave us to die."

Joseph cleared his throat. I looked at him, but before he could speak, Kate Ponsford interrupted.

"Yes, Nadin. Of course we do," she said, her words rushed. She gave the blue-eyed man a severe look before leveling her gaze on me. "We would like to help you. But you must realize, I can't speak for all of GSAF."

"Then let me speak with the others. Your... your *gerotus*. Surely you must have one."

She hesitated, then nodded. "Of course. I'll arrange a meeting for you. But it will take time. It could be several months."

I squeezed my eyes closed. I had known, deep down, that this wouldn't happen overnight. The posternkey was programmed to take us back to just moments after we left, but Isaak had repeatedly said before we left that he had no idea how long it would take for us to secure GSAF's help. At that time, I'd thought I would have Ceilos here to help me, he and his mastery of persuasion.

But I was alone. I would have to accept it.

"I understand, Kate Ponsford," I said. "I am willing to wait."

She smiled. "Excellent, Nadin. You're welcome to stay in Tierra Nueva as our guest until a meeting with GSAF's delegates on Earth can be arranged. And we may have need of you in the meantime."

"Need of me?" I repeated.

"The System," Joseph said. His arms were folded across his chest.

I looked at him in confusion. Between us, Stephen Moyer chuckled hollowly. "Remember, our scientists have been trying to decode it for months now, but we've made very little headway. As a native user, you could help us understand it better and access the areas we've been unable to reach."

"Oh," I said. "I suppose. I am not as well-versed on its inner workings as some of our other people, though. My partner Ceilos would be able to help you more, but he was... unable to accompany me here." I swallowed down the lump that formed in my throat. "If you would be willing to wait—"

"We'll take whatever help we can get. I'm sure you're more capable than you give yourself credit for," said Joseph. His tone indicated that he was *not*, in fact, willing to wait. I furrowed my brows.

"We can discuss this another time, Joseph," Kate Ponsford added severely. "It's getting late, and I'm sure *Kyrin* Nadin is tired."

"Yes, please," I said, grateful for the opportunity to escape. The tension in this room was palpable, and the more he spoke the less I liked this Joseph man. I remembered the bitter way Isaak had talked about GSAF in Elytherios, and the hostility between them in the crater. I wasn't entirely convinced that this man was one I could trust.

Kate Ponsford stood, coming around her desk and taking me gently by the elbow again. Stephen Moyer jumped up to follow, but the man called Joseph stayed seated. "If you'll come with me, I'll arrange for a place for you to stay."

"Thank you," I said, glancing back at Joseph over my shoulder. He watched me with unreadable icy eyes.

I followed Kate Ponsford down the brightly-lit hall back toward the larger room we'd entered the building through. A younger woman with light brown hair approached us, holding a rectangular object in her hand. She looked down at it, swiping across it with her fingertips. "The state suite at the Plaza, ma'am?" she said, falling into step beside Kate Ponsford.

"Not this time. She's young and she's unfamiliar with our culture. I'd rather have someone looking after her."

"What about me, ma'am?" Stephen Moyer suggested. "I'm the closest thing to an expert on the Iamoi as we have."

I was to stay with Stephen Moyer? I pursed my lips. I appreciated his knowledge of my language, but the thought of having to be with him at all times for possibly months made me uncomfortable. Why couldn't they let me stay with Isaak's family? I already knew him and his father.

Kate Ponsford smirked. "Thank you, Stephen, but I already have someone in mind."

As we entered the large entrance hall once again, a fair-haired boy stood and began walking toward us. He was close to my own age, and at least as tall as Isaak, but he looked more like Kate Ponsford in every other way.

"Hey, Mom," the boy said. "You needed something?"

"Yes. Wyatt, this is Nadin. Nadin, this is my son."

Her son. The resemblance was clear now. "Nice to meet you, Nadin," he said, sticking his right hand out. I remembered Isaak doing this back in Hope Renewed, when he'd said he, Ceilos and I were to be a team. Hesitantly, I reached out my own hand and he took it, moving it up and down.

"Wyatt, would you be able to take Nadin over to Bryn and Delia's house?" Kate Ponsford said when he released my hand.

The brown-haired woman made a *tsking* sound. "Are you sure that's a good idea, ma'am? Mister Condor won't like that."

Kate Ponsford sighed. "I know he won't. But Mister Condor isn't in charge here, even if he likes to think he is. Wyatt?"

Wyatt nodded and gestured for me to follow. I glanced at Kate Ponsford.

"Go ahead, Nadin. Would you like Mister Moyer to come with you?"

"No, no," I said quickly. "I think I will be fine." I hoped. Though I was pleasantly surprised with my English capabilities so far, especially without the assistance of the System. Isaak had been a good teacher, and we'd had ten full days' ride to Elytherios with nothing to do but practice—and I'd continued to do so once Emil had joined us in working on the posternkey, since Isaak had had to stop and translate just about everything we'd said to him. Besides, we wouldn't be separated much longer. I'd make sure of it. If there was anything I had trouble understanding, Isaak would be able to help.

I expected Wyatt to lead me back out the doors I'd entered from, through which the huge crowd of people was still visible. But instead he led me across the large room and down a hallway. "My car is in the parking garage," he said by means of explanation. I just nodded my head, hoping his words' meaning would reveal themselves once we reached our destination.

The hallway opened up into a dark, cavernous building filled with vehicles like the one I'd ridden in earlier. Wyatt led me up a ramp and over to a large white vehicle. So this must be what he'd meant by his *car*. I committed the word to memory. He opened the door for me, then went around and got in the other side himself. Once seated, he pressed a button and a screen lit up. He swiped and tapped a few times, and the car came to life. Bright lights on the car's nose illuminated the wall in front of us. As it began to roll backward onto the ramp, Wyatt turned to me and smiled.

"So, Nadin. What brings you here to Tierra Nueva?"

I couldn't think of what to say. I was drained, tired, and thinking in English so much was starting to make my head hurt. Plus, I didn't want to go through it all again—especially since I was going to have to wait for answers regardless. I tried to remember what I'd heard Isaak say when he didn't want to answer a question. "It's a long story."

To my relief, Wyatt nodded agreeably and didn't press the matter. "I know you're probably tired. This day was crazy. I couldn't believe it this morning when I turned around and there was Isaak. He's been gone so long…"

"You are friends with Isaak?"

"Ahh"—he made a face I couldn't read—"not exactly. He's more of a friend of a friend."

"Oh," I said quietly.

"Anyway," Wyatt went on, "Bryn and Delia will make you feel right at home. They're nice ladies. Bryn has been one of my mom's best friends for years, and their daughter—oh!" He broke off, seeming to remember something.

"Is anything wrong?" I asked.

"No. It's nothing. It's just… their daughter is a good friend of Isaak's, actually. Or was." He pinched the bridge of his nose between his fingers. "This is complicated."

I looked out the window as the car crossed a bridge. The water was wide and sparkled in the late afternoon sun. "I know," I murmured.

Wyatt filled the silence for the rest of the trip by pointing out different areas of Tierra Nueva to me. This city was so vast, I could scarcely comprehend it. Isaak had said there were more people in Hope Renewed than in Tierra Nueva, but we were crammed tightly together, with most of the city underground. Here there was no need for that. There was room to sprawl. This city spilled over the whole valley and even climbed into the hills.

The sun was close to the horizon, and the sky was changing from its bright blue to a vibrant orange, the clouds streaked yellow. It reminded me of home. But I'd never seen this much water on the whole of Iamos. The sun's rays glinted off the rivers, reflecting colors to rival the phosphorescent mosaics of the underground.

The car turned off the main *vi'in*—no, *street*, that is what Isaak had said the word was—and began to ascend a narrow, winding road into the hills. Here, sprawling villas began to peek between the green foliage of trees so tall they embraced the sky. The car climbed higher up the hill until we reached a building that was smaller than many of the others around it, but still very grand. The smooth, light-colored stone front and tile roof reminded me of the *geroi*'s villa at home.

No... What it really reminded me of was the ancient villa Ceilos and I had found in the ruins of the old capital, years ago. So long ago I'd nearly forgotten. The building the *geroi*'s villa was meant to recreate. I reached for my medallion and rubbed it between my fingers, remembering.

The car came around a circular drive and stopped. "Well, we're here," Wyatt announced.

Before I could respond, the front door opened and a tall woman with curly hair the same color as the sunset above us bounded out. Her skin was pale as death, but the smile on her face was full of life.

She opened my door for me. "Hello, love. Wyatt, thank you for bringing her here. Tell your mother she's not to worry, we'll take good care of her." The words flew from the woman's mouth so rapidly, it was difficult for me to keep up with what she was saying. She spoke differently than Isaak and the others, which compounded matters. Where their Rs were crisp and hard, hers were softer and they rolled off her tongue. Her words blended together in a different way than how Isaak had taught me, and I struggled to comprehend. Finally I gave up, only catching bits and pieces of what she said as she led me up the walk to the villa.

As she chattered, I glanced over my shoulder at Wyatt, who was lingering by the car. He grinned at me and made a gesture I didn't understand, placing his fingers against his forehead and swiping them away. "I'll see you around, Nadin," he said.

He was leaving, then. I swallowed the urge to beg him not to go. Everyone I encountered here—except Joseph—was so friendly, but they kept passing me off to new people. Wyatt was my age at least. I wished he would have stayed. "Goodbye," I finally managed as the sunset-haired woman swept me into her home.

Just inside, a small, lithe woman with short hair was waiting for us. She smiled at me as the taller woman closed the door.

"Now, my dear," the tall woman said, guiding me into the room, "I'm Delia Randall-Torres, and this is my wife, Bryn."

I smiled tightly, struggling to remember all these strange names. "It's nice to meet you, De-Delia"—my tongue tripped over the syllables, and I rushed, face burning, to get the rest of them out—"R-Randall-Torres."

She laughed congenially. "Oh, love. It is a mouthful, isn't it? You can just call me Delia. Or Mama D, if you prefer. Randall-Torres is my surname. That is, my family name," she clarified when she saw my look of confusion. "Do you have those where you come from?"

I paused for a long moment, my brain trying to process what she was saying. She spoke so accursedly fast. "No," I replied finally. "We are all family on Iamos."

"Well, no matter. I'm sorry if things are a bit confusing here." Those were the last words I caught. She prattled on, her sentences running together more and more quickly until my head felt like it was spinning. Now I wished I had gone with Stephen Moyer after all. I'd thought I would be fine, but I clearly had overestimated my English skills. Kate Ponsford—or should it be just Kate? Was Ponsford her *surname*?—had spoken much more slowly and deliberately than this woman did, which had made it easier for me to follow. I wondered if she always talked that way, or if she'd been doing it for my benefit. Oh, why had they split Isaak and me up? How was I supposed to survive here on my own when I couldn't understand what anyone was saying to me?

"Delia," Bryn interrupted, the first word she'd spoken since I'd entered the villa. "You're overwhelming her. Slow down."

Delia broke off mid-sentence, her cheeks turning a vibrant pink. "Oh. Sorry," she said, chagrined.

I felt my own face warm. "No, I am sorry. I'm still learning..." I trailed off. Not just learning English. Learning *everything*. This was so frustrating.

Bryn smiled and came over to me, stretching her arm around my back without touching me, a hesitantly protective gesture. She said, speaking slowly and carefully, "It's not just on you. We also have a lot to learn. More than I ever thought was possible, honestly," she added softly. "The universe is changing. What we know about it, anyway. Our worldview has to change with it." I glanced down at her. Her face was wistful. Then the moment passed. "But you must be exhausted. If you want to lie down, I can show you our guest room. There's also a bath if you'd like..."

Bath—that was a word I recognized. I nodded eagerly. I needed to wash this day away.

Bryn smiled and led me to a large, sweeping staircase across from the door. Delia followed, chattering again but enunciating much more clearly. "I'll get you some fresh clothes. You're a bit taller than our daughter, but you look to be about the same build as her otherwise. She has some tops and skirts you can use, and if you're cold you might be able to wear some of my pants if you wear a belt with them."

At the top of the stairs, Bryn opened a set of double doors and led me inside while Delia bustled down the hall, still talking to no one in particular. "The bathroom is just through there," Bryn said, gesturing to another door. I hurried over, opening it and finding a bright room with light-colored tiles across the floor, cream and pink and sea-foam green, and smooth, white walls embossed with a swirling design. A huge mirror took up an entire wall. As I stared at my haggard reflection, Bryn appeared behind me.

"Sink, toilet, bathtub. Shower through there, if you prefer," she said, gesturing.

I nodded. Cosmetic differences, but not terribly dissimilar from what I was used to at home. The bath was much smaller, and the toilet was more rounded, but otherwise the same. "I'd prefer a bath, please," I said softly.

Bryn smiled and nodded. "I'll get it running for you." She pulled something out of her pocket, a small, rectangular tablet like the one the woman at GSAF had been using. She swiped her fingers across it, explaining, "You could just use the tap, but Delia installed a system that lets us control the water temperature.

That will keep it from getting too hot or too cold."

Water began filling the tub, and Bryn put her tablet back in her pocket and moved over to a cupboard on the opposite wall from the mirror. Inside were a number of fresh white towels, neatly folded. A robe hung on a hook beside the towel shelves. She pulled this and a folded towel out and set them on the stone countertop beside the bathtub.

"Call me if you need anything. When you're dressed, feel free to come downstairs to get something to eat." I nodded, and she turned to leave, but she paused at the door. "You doing okay?"

I swallowed. "Yes," I finally managed. "I am fine."

Bryn closed the door, and I stood there for a moment, looking at myself in the mirror. My filthy silver bodysuit, my wan, dirt-smudged face, my disheveled hair. Resolutely I unfastened my reticule, stripped off my clothes and tossed them in a pile on the corner of the floor. I hesitated a moment before pulling off my medallion as well, setting it gingerly on top of the pile. Then I stood, naked, watching the tub fill with water. I shivered, though it wasn't cold in here by any means—the steam starting to waft off the water was quickly warming the already-comfortable bathroom.

My shoulders shook harder, and a sob tore from my throat, catching me off guard. Once one escaped, I couldn't hold the rest back. I crumpled in on myself, sinking to my knees onto the cool tile floor. I'd been carrying on automatically, almost detachedly, but now it was hitting me with a force greater than even that of a tesseract. In the weeks since my *enilikin*, my world had been shattered, put back together, and shattered again, over and over and over.

I wanted to go home. But there was no home for me anymore. I couldn't even picture what the home I yearned for would be. With Gitrin in Elytherios? With Ceilos in Hope Renewed? Truly, I'd never belonged in either of those places to begin with. The Elytherioi didn't know me and didn't trust me. I was not one of them and I doubted I ever could be. I was *geroi's* blood. But the *geroi*, that whole world I'd so longed to be a part of for so many years, considered me a fool. A pawn to merely be manipulated. Not an equal, not a person with my own assets, not someone who could be trusted. Nothing.

It was irrelevant, regardless. Iamos was falling apart. My world was coming to an end. I had no home—not anywhere, not in any time.

I knelt there, naked and filthy and sobbing, until steam filled the room and obscured the mirror before me. The bath was filled with water, and the tap had turned itself off. Wiping away the mess from my eyes and nose with the back of my hand, I climbed into the tub and sank into the water.

I scrubbed and soaked and cried some more. The water was hot, just the right temperature, and slowly I felt the aching in my joints begin to melt away until all that was left was the headache I was sure would remain until I fell asleep tonight. Finally, when my fingers had become wrinkled to the point where it was almost painful, I crawled out of the tub. I dried myself off with the towel Bryn had given me and put on the robe. It was soft and pink.

The bedroom was empty when I emerged from the bathroom. As promised, Bryn and Delia had laid various articles of clothing out on the bed for me to change into. There were so many different colors and fabrics that I began to feel overwhelmed again. I'd never had to make choices like this about what to wear before. On Iamos, everyone dressed the same. Gitrin had a few loose-fitting woven tunics that she'd sometimes worn over her standard silver bodysuit, an eccentricity afforded her by her position as a scholar, but she was the only one I knew who'd broken from conformity.

I picked through the pile uncertainly. There were some smaller pieces that I eventually deduced were undergarments. I selected a set at random and pulled them on, then eventually settled on a soft blue shirt that stretched as I pulled it over my head. A silvery pattern was printed on the front of it, flowers with intertwining vines that reminded me of the verdant clearing beside the creek in Elytherios. I felt my face grow hot as thoughts of that night in the clearing came back to me—the night Ceilos had returned. His jealous reaction to seeing me talking to Isaak.

Just talking.

The memory of Isaak's warm arms around me made my cheeks flush again. I closed my eyes for just a moment, then pushed the thoughts firmly out of my head and started sifting through the pants on the bed.

The first pair I tried on must have been Delia's. They were long enough, but too large through the waist and seat. I remembered she'd said I could try them with a belt, but I didn't feel up to figuring that setup out. I grabbed a smaller pair, made of the same soft, stretchy material as the shirt. These must have belonged to their daughter. They fit much better apart from the fact that the bottoms of the pant legs only reached halfway down my calf. It was warm enough inside that I didn't mind this, so I decided to leave these pants on.

I considered staying in this room for the rest of the night and just going to sleep, but the growling in my stomach had become painful since getting out of the bath. The hunger seemed to be making my headache worse. I couldn't ignore it any longer. I was going to have to go back downstairs and accept Bryn's offer of food. I turned to leave the room, then paused, returning to the bathroom to retrieve my medallion and the reticule with the posternkey from the pile of clothes on the floor. I set the reticule on the table beside the bed, then fastened the medallion around my neck, tucking it under the neckline of the shirt.

I opened the double doors, peering hesitantly into the hall. There was no one in sight, but I could hear distant voices drifting up from downstairs. I crept out of the room and toward the staircase, but I paused partway down the hall. A frame hung on the wall, and inside it pictures appeared and then disappeared, as if on a visual indicator. Images of a young girl, then an older one. After a moment I realized it was always the same girl, but at different stages of her life. I watched as the images cycled every few seconds until it reappeared—the one I'd thought I'd seen out of the corner of my eye.

In it, the girl looked to be a year or two younger than I was now. She wore a lavender dress that sparkled in the light. Beside her were two boys dressed in black. One I didn't recognize, but the other...

The other was Isaak.

"*Their daughter is a good friend of Isaak's.*" That's what Wyatt had said. I'd already forgotten. This girl must be Delia and Bryn's daughter, then.

I stared at the picture, at Isaak's grinning face. His arm was around the girl, and the two of them looked like they were laughing. The second boy looked more subdued, but his eyes had a hint of mischief to them that made me wonder if he was the reason for the other two's laughter.

The image faded out, replaced by another. I stood there, watching as the pictures cycled back through until the group image reappeared. I watched it for three more cycles, feeling oddly hollow inside. There had been nothing like this in the *geroï*'s villa. No tribute to me as Antos and Melusin's daughter. After all, they couldn't be just my parents. They were responsible for the whole of the citidome. I had no pictures of myself at all, apart from what must be saved on the System—whatever GSAF found when they made their discovery. What had they seen of me? I doubted there was much laughter in my recordings. I wondered if there were even any smiles. I'd always saved those for Ceilos, and always when we were offline, where the System couldn't track us.

Finally, the growling of my stomach became insistent enough to tear me away from the frame on the wall. I descended the stairs, following the sounds of the voices.

I found them sitting in a large room with a high ceiling. Couches and chairs were grouped around a low white table, facing each other. Beyond, a big glass door opened out to an atrium. A fire burned in a white brick fireplace a short distance from the sitting area.

Delia and Bryn sat together on one couch, and three others across from them—two young women and a young man with short black hair. At the sight of me they all fell silent.

The young man stood, staring at me, his lips parted. I wanted to shrink beneath his gaze, but I kept my back straight and my shoulders square.

"You..." he said softly. "You're real."

I looked at him in confusion, not sure I understood him. "Yes?"

He swallowed, looking down at the girl seated beside him. I followed his gaze, and in an instant recognized her as Bryn and Delia's daughter. A moment later, I realized I had seen this young man before, not once but twice: he was the other boy in the picture with Isaak. But I'd seen him before that—this was the orator from this morning. Before the riot.

He looked back up at me, his face contorted with emotion, his eyes shining. "Isaak's alive," he said.

CHAPTER 4

- i s a a k -

I WOKE UP THE NEXT MORNING FEELING GROGGY AND CONFUSED. I'd slept deeply—the wonders of sleeping in your own bed after weeks in an unfamiliar place—but that just made me more disoriented when I awoke. That weird feeling of everything being the same but *not* overwhelmed me, and I rolled onto my right side, trying to steady my breathing and keep the contents of my stomach down. Maybe pizza last night had been a bad idea.

When I finally felt sturdy enough to stand, the first thing I did was go over to my Speculus headset on the dresser. The power button had turned from red to green. It was fully charged. "Yes," I said under my breath, unplugging it from the charger. I couldn't wait any longer to talk to Henry or Tamara—even Scylla, if I could get a hold of her.

I slipped the device over my eyes and saw that it had already powered itself on in the night. *Mandatory system update in progress*, it said on the home screen. *Nineteen hours remaining.*

"Are you torquing kidding me?" I tossed the headset back onto my dresser.

I pulled on a pair of jeans and a soft cotton t-shirt, relishing the familiar feel of normal clothing on my skin once again. Then I left my room, following the ever-present smell of coffee into the kitchen. My mom sat at the table in the breakfast nook, her old favorite chipped mug in hand. She had an earpod in and was staring down at her deskpad, a frown on her face. When I came into the room, she quickly removed her earpod and tossed it onto the table. The sound from whatever she was watching switched to the miniature built-in speakers on the deskpad, faint and tinny.

"Isaak, good morning!" she said with unnatural brightness. I wondered how long things were going to be forced between my mom and me, and that wave of guilt washed over me once again.

"Hey, Mom," I said, smiling as easily as I could manage. "Where's Celeste?"

"She's at school, *papi*. It's ten-thirty already."

My eyes widened. "Seriously?" I never slept in this late. I never had a chance—I had to get up super early to catch the train on school days, and the last few months I'd had to continue that even on the weekends in order to work at Erick's dig site.

Mom chuckled. "You were tired. You must have needed it. Do you want me to make you something? *Migas con huevo*? I have a carton of fresh eggs in the fridge. Erick got them from the ag department at work."

That sounded delicious, especially with real eggs. With most of our food still being shipped over from Earth rather than grown here, livestock still hadn't been brought over *en masse*. When it came to perishables, we mostly relied on canned or freeze-dried—fresh eggs, milk and meat were super expensive. But despite the tempting offer, my stomach felt queasy, and I wasn't sure I could handle anything more adventurous than corn flakes.

"I'll just have some cereal," I said. Mom nodded, smiling tightly, while I went about getting together the bowl and spoon, the box of corn flakes and the pitcher of reconstituted milk from the fridge.

As I moved past the kitchen window with my bowl of cereal, I paused. "Mom, there are people outside!"

It wasn't exactly a crowd, but there were at least six or seven people standing on the sidewalk looking at our house. A few of them held palmtops, and the rest were wearing headsets. Undoubtedly recording. They didn't seem to be planning to leave anytime soon. As I watched, our next-door neighbor pulled up in the same beat-up old sedan he'd been driving the last time I'd seen him, unchanged apart from the new oxidation spots on the hood and roof. It stopped in the street, auto-drive sensor lights flashing as the vehicle detected bodies in its way. He rolled down his window, glaring at the photographers, and yelled something I couldn't quite make out. They shuffled away from his driveway just enough to give him room to pass, and I heard his garage door go up through the shared wall before he and the car disappeared from my sight.

"Don't stand there," Mom said, coming over to the window and closing the blinds. "They want footage of you. They've been here on and off ever since you—left. Especially since Henry started causing all this trouble."

My eyebrow quirked at the mention of Henry's name. "What kind of trouble?" Henry had always been known for trouble, but from the weird way she'd been acting every time someone said his name, I got the feeling that this was more than the usual.

She shook her head. "It's nothing," she said.

I gritted my teeth. How long was she going to keep me in the dark about what was going on here? My torquing Speculus had better start working soon, that's all I could say.

Between the closed slats of the blinds, the flashing of red lights caught my eye. I shoved past my mom, lifting one of the slats to peek out. Now the cops were outside. As I watched, two uniformed men started waving people away, ordering them to disperse.

"Well, that's convenient," I said. I wondered if our neighbor had called them.

"The police don't like large groups of people congregating these days," Mom remarked.

I frowned and started to let go of the blind slat, but then my eyes fell on the plants in Mom's front garden. The leaves on them were shriveled and desiccated. I hadn't noticed last night in the dim twilight. "That tomato doesn't look good," I commented. "Do you want me to go out and water?"

Mom snorted out a small, humorless laugh. "Water's only part of the problem. But today's not a watering day, so we're going to have to leave them for now."

"What?"

She gestured to the fridge, where a small piece of paper hung by a magnet. My mom was always printing out digital notices from the city, from Kimbal, from the trash service—you name it. She was a bit of a Luddite, though of course you couldn't completely escape technology these days. Erick seemed to be the same way, with his refusal to let any vehicles drive themselves.

The paper read, "*Do your part to conserve! Only water your plants on the following days...*" This was then broken down by whether your address ended in an even or odd number, with one set watering on Tuesdays, Thursdays and Saturdays, and the other watering on Mondays, Wednesdays and Fridays.

I glanced over at my mom. "Are we in a drought?"

She shrugged. "It's an alien planet. We always knew life was going to be hard here."

I frowned. Yeah, but we'd been promised things would get *easier* the longer we were here, not harder. Maybe it had been naïve of me, but I guess I'd assumed that by the time I was born, these things had mostly evened out. We'd never had a problem with drought before, at least not as long as I could remember. It seemed like they happened every ten years or so in California where Abuelo lived, but Earth was much hotter than Mars, and California in particular went through regular dry periods between wet periods.

"Are your plants going to be okay?"

"We'll see." She smiled and looked up at me. "But don't worry about it, Isaak. It's not important. Especially not right now. All that matters is that you're home. We can deal with everything else later." She patted my shoulder and guided me over to the breakfast nook. I sat across from her at the table, taking a bite of my now-soggy corn flakes. I was considering dumping them and pouring myself a new bowl when my ears caught the tinny sound coming out of the speakers on her deskpad.

"*I'm here today to confirm that the rumors are true: we are not alone.*"

I jolted alert at the voice. It was barely audible, but I would have recognized that voice anywhere.

"What's going on?" I asked, my head jerking toward the sound.

"It's nothing," Mom started, but I reached across the table and slid the deskpad over to myself before she could stop me. Text in the lower left-hand corner of the screen said *Live Broadcast.* Joseph Condor was standing in front of the GSAF building. I could see the tops of people's heads in front of the cameraman—there was quite a crowd. A blonde woman who looked vaguely familiar stood to his left, a gold badge bearing the GSAF crest pinned to her lapel. I tapped on her, and a bubble identifying her as *Governor Kate Ponsford, Aeolis Province* appeared. The sight of her last name reminded me why she looked familiar: she was that tool Wyatt Ponsford's mom. She was governor now? That was new.

I tapped on Condor's image and the ID bubble informed me that he was *Lieutenant Governor Joseph Condor, Aeolis Province.* That was new as well. A lot had changed while I'd been gone. I didn't like that Condor had been promoted so high.

My eyes moved to the person standing in the shadows to Condor's right and I started again. It was Nadin. I hardly recognized her in the clothes she was wearing now, a light blue turtleneck with a crisp black blazer over it. Her hair was pulled back in the tight braided spiral she'd worn it in when I'd first met her. I'd already gotten used to seeing her with her wild hair falling loosely around her shoulders. Pulled back like this, it reminded me of the impression I'd had when I'd seen her for the first time—that she was an old woman. But her face was young, and her blue eyes bright, the nervousness in them barely visible.

"What's she doing with him?" I asked out loud. "What's going on here?"

"Press conference," my mom said blandly, avoiding my eyes. "Telling everyone... what you told me last night."

I gaped, then hurriedly cranked up the volume on the deskpad.

Kate Ponsford was talking now. "I understand this will be incredibly difficult for everyone to process. This changes everything about our understanding of our universe, and the repercussions will be felt everywhere—from our classrooms to our homes, from science labs to our faith communities. Humanity will have to relearn our own history, and we're going to have to cope with that. At the same time, this is a marvelous opportunity. The technology of the Iamoi is far beyond anything our own engineers have ever been able to create. By learning from their achievements, we will be able to revolutionize our own abilities to travel. Imagine being able to reach Earth in just a few moments rather than the two weeks it takes now. Imagine being able to ship goods, food, and other necessities instantaneously. Things that were once only dreamed of in science fiction are now within our grasp."

Before she could go on, someone in the crowd shouted, "Why the cover-up?"

She opened her mouth to respond, but Joseph Condor stepped forward then. Governor Ponsford gave him a sideways glance, and I thought I saw a spark of annoyance in her eyes. "There were a number of factors involved in our decision. This information, as you can easily see, is Earth-shattering. *Reality*-shattering. We needed to be sure we had the facts right before we released any information. We've seen in past months the damage that can be done when inaccurate information is leaked to the public." He arched a brow, his tone loaded, and my skin crawled. What had happened since I'd been gone?

"And since this case involved a missing person, it was especially sensitive," he went on. "It was essential that we acted cautiously in order to ensure the continued safety of Isaak Contreras. That was our number one priority." The sound of my name on his lips made my back stiffen. He was using me as his shield!

"I doubt he gave a damn about my safety," I muttered bitterly.

Mom shook her head. "Mr. Condor was very good to us while you were gone, Isaak," she said softly. "He checked in with us frequently while you were gone to give us updates on the case and make sure we were doing okay. He oversaw the investigation personally, even though he had a ton of other things he needed to take care of. He has to worry about the whole province, not just one family, remember," she added, lightly chastising at my incredulous look. "But he's a good man. He wanted you back just as much as we did."

I scoffed. I'll just *bet* he did. I looked back down at the deskpad sourly.

"But now that our boy is home, we can move forward," Condor said, and I cringed. *Our* boy indeed. "With *Kyrin* Nadin here, we intend to open up a dialogue with the Iamoi and discuss how best to move forward, in a way that's mutually beneficial for both our societies. And with full transparency to the Martian people, of course."

I rolled my eyes. "Of course," I said. Then I glanced sidelong at my mom. "So, do you believe me now?"

Mom shrugged. "I didn't *not* believe you last night. I needed a little bit to process things. But yeah. This helps."

I frowned, chewing on the inside of my cheek. I didn't like that Joseph Condor had gotten in with my mom while I was gone. She'd fallen for him hook, line and sinker.

A change in the voices coming from the deskpad made me look down. The livestream had ended, and now the screen was filled with the figuscan of Mom's favorite commentator, Nancy Ramirez, host of *Downstream*. She'd updated her avatar with a shorter haircut that I assume reflected reality, but otherwise she looked pretty much the same as she had when Mom was watching her show the last morning I was here, blearily munching my breakfast after barely getting any sleep the night before. One relatively unchanged thing, at least.

"That's the official word from GSAF," she said. "Now let's hear what the other side has to say. I'm joined now for a rebuttal from Henry Sandhu, known by many as the unofficial leader of the Free Mars movement. Henry, thanks so much for your time."

I choked, sitting straight up in my chair.

"Thanks for having me," a voice I recognized as Henry's said, but the figuscan that materialized in the stream sitting next to Nancy was completely foreign. Henry's old figuscan had sported his old, long hair, and was always dressed in chainmail, loot he'd picked up across years of gaming. This looked just like the guy I'd seen on the podium yesterday: short hair, tidy stubble, dark jeans and a neat t-shirt—not one of his faded pop culture tees, either, but an immaculate white v-neck—with an open suit jacket over it. Henry *hated* wearing long sleeves. He *hated* suits, too. I supposed this wasn't really a suit—more like the closest approximation he could stand coming to—but still. Who was this guy?

"As you may recall," Nancy Ramirez said, "Henry achieved notoriety earlier this year with his whistle-blowing revelations that GSAF was researching an ancient technology called the System, which he alleged had the ability to manipulate humans' minds."

"*What*?!" I exploded.

"Isaak," my mom said, pulling the deskpad away from me and folding it closed, "hold on."

"*Hold on*? Are you torquing kidding me? Turn that back on, Mom!"

"No."

"Mom!" I wanted to completely tear out my own hair. "You can't keep hiding this stuff from me! I have got to know what's going on! GSAF knows about the System?" Had they known all along? Was that the reason they'd always been so quick to close down Erick's dig whenever they found *anything* that had even the remotest possibility of being man-made? The thought of the likes of Joseph Condor having access to the Iamoi's technology made me sick to my stomach. If he had that kind of power, would our world be like Iamos before long? A totalitarian, dystopian nightmare?

But if Henry knew... if Henry was trying to stop them...

"Just don't worry about it, okay?" my mom said softly, in a tone I'm sure she meant to sound conciliatory but which came out more condescending.

"Mother!" I shouted. "Stop treating me like a kid! I know what I'm talking about here. Way more than you do." I flinched even as

I said the words. It was ingrained in me not to speak to my mom this way, down to my very bones. But she had to understand this. "We cannot let the government have access to the System!"

"So what are you going to do to stop it, Isaak? Join Henry's revolution?" Her brow was arched, and her voice had gone from warm reassurance to ice-cold cynicism. "Because that's what he's trying to start. That's why I didn't want you talking to him. Because of this. He wants war. Is that what you want?"

My mouth opened and closed soundlessly. "No, of course not, but—"

"That's what it's coming to. That's what this all boils down to. You want me to stop treating you like a kid? Then you need to be rational like an adult. You need to think about the consequences of your actions logically, not just lash out based on what you *feel* is right. The moral high ground means damn little to me when it comes to protecting my family." I stared at her, anger burning in my chest, but I kept my lips pressed tightly closed. "I know how you feel about GSAF, Isaak, but you have to pick your battles. Speculation is not worth bloodshed. Right now, any access GSAF has to the System is completely theoretical. You heard what Mr. Condor said—GSAF is committed to complete transparency. And I trust him. Over the past two years he's earned that trust." She held my eyes. My face flushed, but I refused to back down by looking away. More softly, she said, "They've stated repeatedly that they have no intention of doing anything more with this technology than studying it for scientific and historical purposes. We're going to have to believe them. To protect our family."

I shook my head bitterly, remembering how with a single word the Iamoi Enforcers had been able to bring a rioting crowd to their knees. How the *geroi* had used it to subjugate their entire world. "If you really wanted to protect us, you'd be out there with Henry, fighting to make sure the System can never come to Mars," I whispered.

Mom bristled, looking like she was going to argue with me again, but I turned on my heel and strode down the hall, slamming the door to my bedroom.

CHAPTER 5

- n a d i n -

"I THINK THAT WENT WELL," KATE SAID, FOLLOWING ME THROUGH the door back into the capitol building. "Better than I expected, considering the news we had to give them."

Joseph made a grunt in response. "It would have been better if we hadn't had to do it at all. But this was a boon, really, in the wake of the last six months. The perfect means of rebuttal against the accusations the Free Mars movement has been hurling at us."

"Yes, that should knock the wind out of their sails." Kate looked at me and smiled, placing a gentle hand on my shoulder. "Thank you for agreeing to be here today, Nadin."

I shifted awkwardly from one foot to another. I hadn't been aware I'd had a choice. A guard had been sent to collect me this morning—not the same man who had ridden with me yesterday, but dressed in the same way: dark clothing that opened around his collar to reveal white underneath, with a band of black tied about his neck, bisecting the white. Delia and Bryn had seemed nervous when he arrived, though they did their best to hide it. Surprisingly, Delia seemed better at masking her worry than Bryn

63

did. He'd brought me back to the GSAF offices, where I hoped Isaak might be waiting for me. But no. Kate had informed me that they were making a public statement about my arrival and that she wanted to introduce me to the public. The thought of having to face the Martian crowds again after yesterday had made my heart leap into my throat, but in the end it was not much different from what I'd had to do with the *geroi* many times before: stand there looking supportive while Melusin and Antos—or in this case, Kate and Joseph—did all the talking. And while the people today seemed disbelieving, shouting out questions in a quick barrage of English I couldn't hope to keep up with, there was none of the uncontrolled anger we'd faced yesterday. I'd managed—I hoped—to remain calm and poised as I'd been trained to be.

I stared down at my feet, foreign in the strange-looking shoes Delia had given me as she and Bryn scrambled to get me dressed in what was considered "business attire" here on Mars. In just one day I'd come to realize that that involved a lot of black.

I sighed, squeezing my eyes shut. The course of the last day seemed like something out of a dream. I wasn't sure yet if it was a good dream or a bad dream. Last night when I'd come downstairs to find a group of strange Martians scrutinizing me, I'd been convinced that coming here was a horrible, horrible mistake. But it hadn't been as bad as I'd feared. Henry was intense, but I'd soon come to understand why: Isaak was his best friend, and he'd spent the last year—or two? I didn't quite understand how these Martian *annums* worked—believing that GSAF had kidnapped or murdered him. And that I was in league with GSAF.

Tamara, Bryn and Delia's daughter, had quickly intervened,

running a hand along his forearm to try to soothe him. "Let her talk, Henry," she'd said gently.

"I-I'm sorry," I'd stammered, struggling to think of how to phrase what I needed to say in English. "I understand how worried you must have been, but you must realize, I had nothing to do with Isaak's disappearance."

"That's impossible," Henry snapped, leaping to his feet. "I saw you right there on that video footage. On the System. You were holding Isaak prisoner!"

Part of me wanted to shrink away from him, to run back upstairs and lock myself in my suite and not come out for the rest of the night—my growling stomach could just spend the evening complaining—but his anger made me angry in return. Regardless of his concern for Isaak, I had done nothing to cause his disappearance from Mars. "I helped Isaak escape, actually," I snapped back. "I'm the one who brought him back. If it weren't for me, the *geroi* would still have him."

Tamara stood, wrapping her hands around his elbow and pulling him back down to the sofa. "Henry, come on," she scolded. He glanced at her, the fire seeming to fade from his eyes when they met hers.

The third person who had come to the villa with them—a girl named Scylla with short, choppy black hair and dark eyes— watched them for a moment, her lips pursed thoughtfully. "Who are the *geroi*?" she finally asked, turning to me. "Are they some division of GSAF we've never heard of before?"

I shook my head in exasperation. "No, we have nothing to do with GSAF. We're not from Mars."

Tamara leaned forward, resting her chin on her hand

thoughtfully. "So he was back on Earth?"

"No, no." I squeezed my eyes shut, trying to fight my frustration and think—calmly—of how to say it in English, cursing GSAF once again for having separated Isaak and me. It would be so much easier with him here. I took a deep breath. "I am from Iamos. It is... Mars. But from another time."

"What?" the three on the couch all said at once. Across from them, Bryn and Delia watched silently, fretfully. Kate had told them some things, obviously, but how much did they really know, and what had and hadn't they shared with their daughter and her friends?

I reached to tug my earlobe, then caught myself and nodded instead. "Isaak used an item called a posternkey to activate a doorway to our time. He said he found the key here on Mars, in this time." I looked around at them, staring at me with unreadable expressions, and quickly added, "You activate it with this." I pulled my medallion out from under my shirt collar.

"That's the coin!" Scylla exclaimed, sucking in her breath.

"That's what Isaak called it as well. High-ranking members of my society have these, we use them to... access parts of the System that not everyone is permitted to use. Like the posterns."

"The System," Henry said, his voice low. "Your people built it."

"Yes."

He ran a hand through his short hair and slumped back against the cushions. "This is impossible. How are we supposed to believe this?"

I struggled to come up with an answer, and came up short. If they didn't believe me, there was nothing else I could do.

"I believe she's telling the truth," Delia broke in then, her voice quiet. I turned to look at her in surprise. Her face was flushed a bright pink. "I'm afraid I haven't been quite honest with you all for the last several months," she added.

"Honey?" Bryn murmured, her eyebrows furrowing in concern.

Delia looked sidelong at her, smiling tightly, but waved her away when Bryn tried to scoot closer. "Tamara," she said then, looking over at her daughter. "Do you remember a while back you caught me with a man at the door? You pretended you hadn't, but I knew you were there."

Tamara flushed now. "I didn't hear anything," she said. "I saw you talking to someone, but I honestly didn't hear anything else."

Delia snorted. "Right. It doesn't matter, though. The man I was talking to was Emil Hassan."

My jaw dropped. The man from Mars who'd come to Iamos?

Henry jumped to his feet. "You've seen Emil? He's been missing almost as long as Isaak!"

She nodded, looking chagrined. "It's been months. He approached me with a theory he'd been working on, about that object you lot had dug up in the hills. The one that Isaak liberated from our basement the day he disappeared. Oh, don't give me that," she said to Bryn, who'd opened her mouth—whether to say something or just in surprise, I wasn't sure. "I know you'd already guessed. But I couldn't tell you more. Whatever it was had my maker mark on it. I was involved with it whether I wanted to be or not, but I didn't want to drag you in as well. I'd thought it was a forgery. It was Emil who suggested that it may have been something else. He showed me all these notes he'd made, diagrams of artifacts he and Raymond Contreras had found in the hills. He suggested that the one way my mark could have gotten on something that was otherwise completely ancient was if the object itself had originated in this time and then gone back. It sounded absolutely barmy, but the more he talked to me about it, the more I thought—you know, this is the only thing that makes any sense." She shrugged. "So I said what the hell. I still had the original scans I'd taken of the thing before Isaak left with it. What would be the harm in printing out a copy? So I did, and I gave it to Emil. He said he was going to try to use it to find Isaak, and that he didn't know when he'd be back. It was a long shot, but if it meant we could bring him back..." Her eyes glistened now.

Bryn reached over, taking Delia's hand firmly between hers and rubbing the back of her palm with her thumbs. "You had to try. Isaak is too important to not have tried."

"Emil made it," I said eagerly, my mind whirling as the pieces of the puzzle fell into place. "You managed to create a working posternkey. The Elytherioi found him in the same place Isaak and his father had been. He was supposed to come back with us. But..." I frowned, biting my lip. "We got separated."

"What does that mean?" Scylla asked, brushing her choppy black hair out of her eyes. "Is he all right?"

"I—I think so. I mean, I'm not sure. We won't know for sure until we're able to establish a stable connection to Elytherios. But," I added hurriedly at all their worried expressions, "I'm almost certain we were separated before Emil and the others passed into the postern. I'm sure they're all right."

The others nodded, and Tamara breathed out a sigh. "This is unbelievable."

"Tell me about it," Scylla said. "A doorway between two time periods. Can you imagine? This is way better than any sci-fi flick. What's it like, Nadin? I bet Iamos is super fresh."

"Fresh?" I repeated.

"You know, stellar. Cool. Neat. Uh"—Scylla grinned at my bewildered expression—"really good?"

"Oh." I didn't know how to respond to that. Iamos may have been *fresh* at one point, but it hadn't been for any part of my lifetime. The *geroi* had seen to that—the planet had been dying, but the *geroi* had been all too willing to help it along if it meant they remained in power. Now it was just a place to try and survive, a place to escape. There was nothing about it that made it worth staying, to be honest. Nothing but the people. And most of those people wanted nothing to do with me.

But I wasn't going to leave them, regardless of how they felt about me. It was the best I could do to try to make up for my complicity in the *geroi*'s actions.

We'd spent the rest of the evening talking. When my stomach had finally growled loudly enough that the others noticed it, Bryn sternly interrupted to insist that I eat something. But Henry, Tamara and Scylla had followed me into the kitchen, asking more questions about Isaak and about Iamos, while I slowly ate the strange-tasting Martian food Bryn cooked for me.

When I managed to get a word in edgewise, I asked the question that had been hovering at the back of my mind all evening. "So... none of you have spoken to Isaak?" I was surprised at how quiet my voice came out as I asked about him, and for some reason it made my face grow hot. The three of them shook their heads, and I looked down, worried. "I hope he's all right. I haven't seen him since I—since this morning. No one at GSAF would give me answers about him. They only said that he was with his family."

Henry looked grim. Tamara watched him for a moment, then said, her voice almost unnaturally bright, "I'm sure that's true. They'll have had to have notified his mom, and she'll have wanted to see him right away. They have a lot of catching up to do. More than anyone could have expected."

"Of course," I said. "His family must have been very worried about him while he was gone." I wondered how the *geroi* had reacted when they realized I was missing from the citidome. Had *they* been worried? Or were they just angry with me? Did they know that the Liberator had taken Ceilos? Did they think he'd taken me, too? Or did they suspect the truth—that I'd betrayed them?

I frowned deeply, poking at my food with the metal utensil Bryn had given me. But I wasn't able to dwell on these thoughts, because Scylla quickly broke in, "Our food is probably really different than what you have on Iamos, right? What sorts of things do you eat?"

And they were off again, overwhelming me with questions about my world—some mundane, some that I struggled to answer, either because I didn't know how to word it in English or because they were things I'd taken for granted, that I'd never considered back home. They'd stayed late into the night, until my head was pounding in time with my heartbeat and I felt like I was going to fall asleep at the table. Tamara had stood then, announcing that they were leaving so I could get some sleep.

"You're leaving?" I asked, trying to stifle a yawn. "Isn't this your home?"

Tamara smiled, pushing in her chair, and shrugged. "It is and it's not. I'm at university right now, so I usually stay at the dorms. The school's just on Hershel Island, though, so it's not far. You'll see what I mean tomorrow."

I hadn't understood what she meant, but I did when I awoke this morning. I'd slept fitfully, awakening often, heart pounding at the unfamiliar sights and sounds. Strange dreams about the *geroi* and Gitrin and Ceilos and Isaak had plagued me, but every time I woke up, the memory of them would dissipate almost instantly, leaving me confused and disoriented. Finally, when sunlight began drifting through the sheer curtains over the window enough to light up my bedroom, I'd crawled blearily out of bed. I was uncertain what I should do with myself. As I debated whether I should emerge from this room to face Delia, Bryn, and who knew who else downstairs, I'd wandered over to the window and glanced out.

My breath had caught in my throat.

The villa was nestled in hills that bordered the sea. The ocean was visible from my window, wide and dark and blue, with the bright cloudless sky soaring over it. Gooseflesh broke out across my skin at the sight of it, and all thoughts of my fitful dreams fled from my mind. As beautiful as the sky had been yesterday, and the sunset off the rivers, nothing could surpass this. The last time I'd seen the sea, I'd been a small child. I drew back the sheer curtains framing the window and spent a moment figuring out how to open it. As soon as I did, the familiar sound of waves washing over the shore reached my ears. An involuntary giggle tore from me, and I flushed—though there was no one here to hear it. The sea. The *sea*. It had returned. It felt impossible, but it was real. All of this was *real.*

In the distance, I could see land emerging from the water, a small island dotted with tall buildings. That must be Herschel, where Tamara's school was located. Close enough to see from the windows of her home. What a place this was, overlooking a vast, deep ocean, a sky that wasn't *red.* As opulent as the *geroi*'s villa on Iamos had been, nothing could compare to this. Nothing in the world.

Ceilos will never believe this, I'd thought then, trying to ignore the pang of guilt gnawing at my chest. There was nothing to feel guilty about. He'd be seeing it soon enough. I knew he would.

The sound of Kate's voice dragged my attention back to the present moment. "I couldn't let her stay with me. She's a teenage girl, I have a teenage boy."

"What, you don't trust your son?" Joseph asked, his tone almost smug.

"Of course I trust him! But it's an issue of public image," she added, lowering her voice to almost a whisper. "It would be impropietous for her to stay with me."

"But it's not *impropietous* to have her staying with a family whose daughter is directly involved with the Free Mars movement?"

Kate shook her head. "They're also executives at the biggest corporation on Mars, Joseph. In case you forgot. AresTec is the biggest employer in the province, and their parent company financed most of the colonization of this planet."

"So we kowtow to private industry and ignore the fact that they're supporting a group of revolutionaries?"

At that, Kate made an aggravated sound in the back of her

throat. "That's exactly the point! That's what we want to *avoid*. The protests were centered around Isaak's disappearance. Now that he's back and we're giving the people answers, all of this will die down. But not if we treat them like criminals."

"Henry Sandhu *is* a criminal."

Up until this point, I'd been struggling to keep up with their rapid conversation, but the sound of Henry's name centered it. They were talking about me. Joseph didn't want me staying with Delia and Bryn—because of Henry? He was a criminal? My stomach turned. Henry was brusque, but he didn't seem like a *criminal*, and the women I'd met last night didn't seem like the sort who'd keep company with one.

"He's a whistle-blower. There's a difference. This isn't a revolution, Joseph. But it could become one if we treat those we disagree with politically as enemies rather than free citizens, the same as you and me."

Joseph scoffed, once again reminding me of the *geroi*. The castes. Kate had said, "*The same as you and me*," but it was clear that Joseph didn't think of them that way.

"Henry Sandhu is not a threat," Kate said firmly, her words leaving no room for argument. "I've said all I'm going to say on this matter." She turned to me. "Come on, Nadin. I'll make sure you get back home."

Home. My heart skipped a beat before I realized she meant back to Delia and Bryn's home, not my own. I'd been here one day and she was already treating me like I belonged here. Maybe that was a good sign, a sign that the Iamoi would be welcome here?

I started to follow her, but Joseph stayed me. "Don't forget about my request, Nadin. GSAF needs your help with the System."

"Oh," I said, frowning. "Yes. Maybe in a few days, when I've had a chance to get more acclimated to Mars?"

He stared at me for a long moment, his icy eyes unreadable. "All right," he said finally. "But please let me know as soon as you're ready. Oh, and Nadin—keep in mind how crucial this is. Not just for us, but for your people as well. GSAF are the ones who are going to be able to help the Iamoi. Not Henry Sandhu or his separatists."

I swallowed. "Of course. I'm aware of that, *Kyrios* Joseph."

His lips curled upward at the sound of the Iamoi title alongside his name, making me regret having used it. "Good. I just wanted to confirm with you, in case you'd received any alternative offers."

I nodded and pushed past him, eager to get away before he could see my face—see the way it blanched at his words. I *had*, in fact, received an alternative offer: from Henry, last night after I'd finished eating. The conversation had lapsed for a moment, Scylla sipping something that looked like *sokol* out of a ceramic mug, Tamara looking about as exhausted as I felt. Henry had been staring down at his hands, contemplative in the silence. Then he'd said, slowly, deliberately, "Nadin, if your people invented the System, you must know how to use it, right?"

I'd looked at him warily, my mind replaying Joseph's words from earlier in the day. His insistence that I help GSAF with the System even though it was far from my realm of expertise.

"Henry," Tamara said warningly. "What are you thinking?"

"I'm not thinking anything!" he protested. "I just want to make sure GSAF isn't planning on turning that knowledge against us, that's all."

Tamara rolled her eyes. "Don't you think you're jumping the gun a little? She's been here less than twelve hours."

"GSAF did ask me about the System," I said then, and the three of them stared at me.

"I knew it!" Henry burst out. "You can't trust those bastards for five minutes."

"I don't know what they're planning on doing with it, though," I added quickly.

"I can *guess*," Scylla muttered under her breath.

"You can't help them, Nadin," Henry said almost imploringly. "GSAF is just as bad as the *geroi*. They've made progress with the System, but they're not able to use it on ordinary people yet. But if they learn how? You'll just be moving your people from one shitty situation to a new one. They *can't* have access to that System."

I rubbed my temples with my fingertips, feeling overwhelmed. "But how am I supposed to stop them? They're in control here. They only way I'm going to be able to help my people is by cooperating with them."

Henry shook his head adamantly. "Don't, Nadin. There's got to be another way. Our group—the Free Mars movement—we've made major strides against GSAF, but we haven't been able to break free from the colonial government. But maybe if you joined us, if the Iamoi were on our side..."

"It could work," Scylla said eagerly. "This is their planet, after all. They should have sovereignty over it. This might be enough to win people over to our side."

I didn't know what to say. This was all so confusing, so overwhelming. It felt like what was happening on Iamos—the *geroi* versus the Liberator—had spread into this time, too, but I had no frame of reference for any of this. Committing to one faction or another could end disastrously for my people, but *not* choosing a side could be just as bad. My head felt like it was going to burst. I wasn't the right person for this job. I couldn't do it on my own. Why, *why* had Ceilos and Gitrin gotten separated from me?

"Okay, I think that's enough of that," Tamara had interrupted then, concern etched across her features. "She just got here. She has no clue what's going on. Let her figure this out in her own time, all right?"

I hadn't had words for how much I'd appreciated that intervention. But Tamara wasn't here now. She wasn't going to be able to help me when dealing with Joseph, apparently. I'd just have to keep trying to stall him, and avoid him to the best of my ability until I was able to make a decision. Whenever that would be... and *what*ever it would be.

"Nadin?" Kate called from the next room, and I hurried to join her, eager to escape the feeling of Joseph's eyes boring into my back.

CHAPTER 6

- i s a a k -

THE NEXT FEW DAYS WERE POSSIBLY THE WORST OF MY LIFE— and that included the time I'd spent on Iamos. Traveling through time, being held by the *geroi*, and being trapped in an unfamiliar place had been terrifying, but I'd barely had a spare moment to sit back and think about my situation. From almost the beginning, I'd been in motion. Helping Nadin unravel the secrets of the Liberator, escaping from the citidome, making our trek across the wilds of Iamos... there'd been too much going on to worry about anything.

But now I had nothing but downtime, nothing to occupy my mind but my own thoughts. Nothing to do but worry. Worry about Nadin, alone here without any friends and with Joseph Condor manipulating her. Worry about Emil, trapped back on Iamos, unable to speak the language—even though I knew, rationally, that next to no time would have passed when I saw him again. *If* I saw him again, that is. Worry about what Henry was up to, what Tamara must be thinking right now, what I was going to have to do in order to get in contact with them.

It didn't help matters that I had no way of communicating with the outside world. I was still without a palmtop, and Speculus was a bust. On Thursday morning, my second day back home, I'd grabbed my Speculus headset, slipping it on to check on its status. *Update complete*, it informed me.

"Torquing finally," I said, waving the notification away. Everything went black for a second, and then there was a loud beep in my ear. *System error: unspecified.*

"What?" I snapped. In frustration, I held the power button down for ten seconds, but when it booted back on, it just gave me that same system error. I hard reset it twice, but no go. It was fried.

"Why didn't it tell me this before I spent two days charging and updating the damn thing?" I snarled, hurling the headset across the room. It hit my closet door with a satisfying *smack*, but that satisfaction was short-lived. There was no way I was going to be able to get in touch with anyone until my mom showed mercy on me and got me a new palmtop. And the way things were going? That probably wouldn't be until next annum. I had some money in my e-pay account, but not that much. Certainly not enough for a new palmtop or Speculus system. With this one fried, I was stuck.

Ordinarily when things were this crazy, I'd just leave. Go somewhere to cool my head—usually down to Escalante Bay. But now there were a few things that kept me from going out the door.

The first was the fact that my mom seemed hyper-alert. She'd taken the week off work to spend time with me, but it felt more like she was guarding me. She appeared every time I'd emerge from my bedroom. She didn't physically block me from leaving the house, she just kept looking at me with worry all over her face, her expression saying it all: "*If you go out that door, how can I be sure you'll come back?*" A month ago—at least, a month ago to me—I would have just found a way to sneak out anyway, but now the guilt of two missing annums kept washing over me. I would say, "Mom, I'm not going anywhere," but the truth is that I hadn't *meant* to go anywhere the first time. I couldn't actually guarantee something wouldn't happen to make me disappear again.

Especially now, which was the bigger reason I didn't dare leave the house. Despite the near-constant police presence around our house, there were always groups of people congregating outside, trying to snap a picture of me when I got too close to the window or went out in the garden to help Mom with her plants. And there were more than just photographers. Hecklers shouted at me, demanding I tell them what I knew about the System, or about Nadin, or about GSAF. Some of them seemed to be part of Henry's supposed separatist movement, wearing *Free Mars* shirts or waving posters in favor of Martian independence. But it seemed like even more of them were mad at *me*. The worst one was an angry man who'd come up to the fence when I was in the backyard, demanding to know where I'd *really* been the last two annums. "You're the cause of everyone's troubles," he shouted, spittle flying from his mouth, enough that I could see it from three meters away, making me wince. "You're best friends with that Sandhu nutjob, and I'm supposed to believe that you conveniently vanished just long enough to stir everything up?"

When I'd called back that if I was lying, why would GSAF have confirmed it, the man actually started to try to climb over the fence. It was just a small picket fence, easily vaulted, and I'd scrambled to my feet to get away from him, but fortunately the police were out front and they quickly rushed over and grabbed him. That had been the last time I'd gone outside. Mom and Erick promised to install a privacy fence as soon as they could afford it, but I wasn't sure if even then I'd feel totally comfortable going out in my backyard alone.

Thursday afternoon I sat alone in my room in the dark, the blinds to my window drawn to prevent the crowds outside from looking in at me. Without my palmtop or Speculus, I'd been reduced to perusing Mom's collection of paper books for something to entertain myself. The small fiberboard shelving unit in her bedroom had been replaced with a tall wooden bookcase, and the collection had grown, I assumed to include Erick's as well. A couple of regular technophobes, though I supposed that worked to my advantage. I'd taken a copy of H.G. Wells' *The Time Machine* just for laughs, but I couldn't manage to get past the first two pages, so I gave up and just lay there staring at the ceiling.

A small knock came from my door, and I sat up. "Yeah?"

Celeste opened the door, smiling broadly at me. "I made you something in art today," she said.

I folded my legs in front of me and patted my bed. "Let's see it."

She hurried over and handed me a piece of red construction paper. Pieces of paper in other colors had been torn out and glued onto it, forming the rough approximation of a dinosaur. She'd layered strips of blue and green to form the scales, with yellow stripes across the creature's back, and a yellow belly.

"It's Tuupa," Celeste said proudly. "Do you like it? Does it look like her?"

"I love it," I said with a grin, admiring how much my sister's artistic talents had grown over the last two annums. "It looks just like her."

"I know you miss her," she said.

"Yeah. I think I missed you more, though."

She looked at me in surprise, but before either of us could speak again, another knock came at my door. "Hey, guys," Mom said, opening the door and peeking her head in. "Your grandparents are on chat, do you want to talk to them?"

Celeste squealed and scrambled off my bed, following Mom out the door. I hurried after her. Mom didn't like to use Speculus for chat—or anything, really; she got bad motion sickness—so I wasn't surprised when Celeste ran straight to Mom's desk in the living room. Her deskpad was propped up on its stand, the light on the built-in webcam flashing to indicate it was in use.

"Hi, Abuelita! Hi, Abuelo!" Celeste said cheerfully, waving at the small image on the screen. I came up behind her, leaning over the back of Mom's swiveling desk chair to look at them. I was used to talking to Abuelo on Speculus, in the private chatspace he'd designed to look like Laguna de los Cerros. His figuscan with its sun-browned skin and soft flannel shirt. Over the webcam, he looked smaller, and not just because of the size of the screen. He'd gotten thin and gaunt like Mom had. His shoulders had become hunched. Beside him, Abuela's formerly silvery-brown hair had turned pure white. With her short, curled hairstyle, she looked like she had a snowball on top of her head. Both of them looked... old.

That now-uncomfortably-familiar feeling hit me again, reminding me that I'd lost two years of my grandparents' lives. If I hadn't discovered the postern, I would have had two more summers visiting with them in California. Two more annums of chatting with Abuelo on Speculus, learning more Olmec and Mayan, hearing stories that he could have sworn he'd told me before but were always new and interesting to me. I wouldn't get that back. I would *never* get that time back.

"Isaak, *mijo*," Abuelo said to me once Celeste had stopped talking.

"Hey, Abuelo," I managed to mumble past the lump in my throat.

"You're really home," Abuela said, her voice thick with emotion. "We're so glad you're home, *chiquito*. We missed you so much."

"Yeah." I swallowed. "I missed you too."

This time, I couldn't quite stop the tear that squeezed out of the corner of my eye.

Saturday morning was the first time all of us were home at the same time without someone scrambling to leave for work or school. The house felt smaller, somehow, than it ever had when it'd just been the three of us. Like there wasn't quite enough room for us all. I wanted a quiet corner to escape to, but there wasn't one apart from my bedroom, so that's where I'd been holed up any time everyone was here.

That morning, Mom did make *migas*, to use up the eggs before they went bad. I could smell them cooking all the way from my bedroom, and my stomach growled. I definitely felt up to something more substantial than corn flakes now. I could hear Erick and Celeste talking loudly to Mom, which made me want to stay in hiding, but the scent of the hot food was too tempting to resist. I emerged reluctantly from my room.

"Morning, Isaak," Erick said brightly as I entered the kitchen. He handed me a plate. When I hung back, he prodded me forward. "Go ahead, get yours first."

I smiled awkwardly and went over to the stove. Mom gave me a big scoop of tortilla, egg and onion from the pan. "Salsa and hot sauce are on the table," she said.

Erick sat across from me, Celeste across from Mom, just as we'd done at dinner all week. I chewed my food quietly, expecting that Celeste would carry the conversation for the whole table as usual, but to my surprise, as he reached for the bottle of hot sauce, Erick said casually to me, "Any plans for today, Isaak?"

I stopped chewing for a second, taken aback. Then I swallowed. "Just sitting around the house staring off into space. You know. The usual," I replied.

Erick clucked his tongue. "That's no way to spend a Saturday."

"Well, I don't know what else I'm supposed to do. Not with that going on out there." I jerked my thumb toward the window, blinds tightly closed over it.

"How would you like to spend the day with me? I'm working on some stuff at the lab over at Herschel."

I blinked and then shoveled another bite of food into my mouth to give myself some time to think of an answer. On the one hand, an afternoon in the lab with Erick sounded about as much fun as a root canal. On the other hand, though, it would mean getting out of the house...

"You seemed to enjoy working at the dig site so much before," he added nonchalantly. "It would be a similar sort of experience."

I took a swig of water. "Grant won't be there, right?"

Erick laughed. "No, he finished his master's thesis last annum. He's onto his doctoral now, at a university in Tharsis Province. He's their problem now."

I snorted. Maybe a day out wouldn't be so bad. I *had* enjoyed working at the dig site, loath as I was to admit it. "Okay, sounds good. Uh—that's all right with you, right, Mom?"

"Of course," she said, though I could see from the way she was poking at her *migas* with her fork that the idea of me leaving the house made her nervous. But she couldn't exactly begrudge me going out with her—with my stepdad. God, that still felt weird to think. I wondered how long it would take for me to get used to this.

After we finished eating, I got dressed and brushed my teeth to get the onion taste out of my mouth. When I went back to the kitchen, Erick was waiting with the fob to his pickup in his hand. "Ready when you are," he said.

"Make sure you're back before curfew, okay, guys?" Mom said from over by the sink. She was washing the dishes in what looked like five centimeters of water. I frowned slightly.

"Curfew?" I asked as Erick opened the garage door.

"Yeah. GSAF's orders. No one's allowed out after nine o'clock on weekdays, eleven on weekends."

"Seriously? Why?"

"Riot control. Things got a little heated after Henry blew the whistle about the System," he added in a low voice.

Henry again. It seemed incomprehensible. He'd always been a rabble-rouser, arguing with the teachers at every opportunity and leaving anti-government graffiti around the Academy's campus. But I guess I'd never taken him that seriously. What would have happened if I hadn't gone through the postern? Would he have still become such a dissident? Or had it all been because of me? Was this all my fault?

Erick's beat-up old Ford pickup was parked in the driveway. I tensed as we came outside and the photographers jumped into a frenzy, hurrying to get a shot of me. Erick just waved at them like they were our neighbors or something and nonchalantly pulled out his palmtop to close the garage before unlocking the truck. I leapt quickly into the passenger side and slammed the door shut, manually pushing the lock tab down.

He backed out of the driveway and drove down our street toward the San Bernardino intersection. "Want to listen to some music?" he asked, gesturing to the pickup's archaic stereo.

"Uh, sure," I said. Since I didn't have my palmtop, I couldn't stream from my own music collection, though. I swiped my finger across the touchscreen on the console, trying to see if there were any names I recognized on the free-to-listen stations. Finally, I gave up and tapped randomize. The upbeat melody of a pop song crackled its way through Erick's crappy speakers.

"Hey, Isaak," Erick said over the top of the female singer. His eyes were riveted firmly on the road. "I've been wondering. What did you miss the most while you were gone?"

"About here?" I asked.

"Yeah."

I looked down at my shoes on the dirt-encrusted floor of the truck. I hadn't been gone that long, not the way it seemed to everyone here. Three weeks, a month at most. I hadn't really had a *chance* to miss anything. It had never really crossed my mind that there could be a chance I wouldn't make it home. Maybe that had been cocky of me. Even when Emil had tried to explain it, I'd just never really grasped how much I might have lost.

"You guys, I guess," I said finally.

"Us?" Erick said. He glanced over at me, his eyebrows raised. It took a second before I understood why he was surprised, and I rushed to clarify.

"I mean, not *you*, exactly." I colored as I realized that hadn't been very tactful, but there was no taking it back. "That is— everybody here, I mean. Mom, Celeste. My grandparents. Tamara, Henry, Scylla... everyone."

He nodded. "Of course."

The bridge over Santos Creek was predictably traffic-ridden, though it was moving smoothly. I looked out the window at the band of water winding between the familiar buildings of my hometown. I hadn't been that homesick while I was gone. But now that I was back... *now* I was feeling homesick. For the life I'd left behind, irretrievably, in the past.

The refrain of the pop song was playing now, and I found myself humming along, though I couldn't remember why I knew this melody. I hadn't heard this song before, I was certain, but for some reason it felt like I had. Not like this, though. Played on a piano, I think. And someone humming it to herself in class...

Then, suddenly, it slammed into me, so hard that for half a second I thought Erick's truck had collided with another vehicle. The girl singing—this girl, on the radio—

I lurched forward, staring at the track info on the screen. The singer's name was T-RT.

T-RT.

Tamara Randall-Torres.

"Holy shit!" I all but shouted.

Erick jumped in his seat. "What's wrong?" he asked, looking away from the road for just a second, alarm written across his face.

"Is this Tamara?" I demanded.

"What?"

"This song! Is this Tamara singing?"

He frowned, listening. "I think so."

"Tamara is on the radio?"

"Yes," Erick said in confusion. Then, his brows lifting, he said, "Did that happen after you left?"

"Um, *yeah*," I snapped. I couldn't believe no one had told me this. She'd been my best friend since I was eight. She was my— my—

My face was on fire.

"I'm sorry, Isaak," Erick said, seeming genuinely chagrined. "I couldn't remember. I know it must be important to you, but I don't pay much attention to popular media..."

I tuned him out, my head reeling. Henry was some kind of political figurehead now. Tamara was a pop star—at least enough of one to be on the radio. Wyatt Ponsford's mom was the governor of the whole province. What else had happened while I was gone? Had Scylla been made Pope?

Tamara had gotten her big break. The thing she'd been working for, dreaming for, her whole life. And I'd missed it.

I was so overwhelmed with my thoughts, I didn't notice that Erick had taken us westbound rather than getting on the freeway east to Curiosity Bay, where Kimbal Tech was located. I had no clue where we were until we were suddenly in the hills, his deathtrap truck *putt-putt*ing its way up the steep street.

"Wait a minute," I said, my eyes coming back into focus. "Where are we going?"

"I was wondering when you were going to ask that question," he said with a laugh. "I personally would love to spend an afternoon in the lab, but I somehow got the feeling that that might not be your highest priority right now. Like you said— you've been out of the loop for a while. Even with everything going on, it's not fair to keep you in solitary confinement." He pulled into the circular driveway and put the truck into park. "I'm rehabilitating you, Isaak."

My hands were shaking as the door to the house opened. I somehow managed to get my own door open and climb out onto the driveway without my knees giving way. I closed the door, leaning against the truck for balance, as one by one the figures emerged: Scylla, Henry, Tamara...

And Nadin.

CHAPTER 7

- i s a a k -

NADIN WAS THE FIRST ONE TO MOVE. IN THREE STEPS SHE'D crossed the gap between us and careened into me, her loose white hair flying out behind her. I caught her in my arms, squeezing her tightly with relief. She was here, and Joseph Condor was nowhere to be seen. Thank God. What was she doing *here*, though? How had they managed to get her away from GSAF?

"Are you okay?" I whispered, and she nodded, looking up at me in a weird way, almost shyly. She caught my eye for just a moment, and I could see her own eyes were shining. She was trying not to cry, and doing a good job of it. This week must have been hell for her, stuck on a strange and unfamiliar planet with no one she knew. I knew *exactly* how she felt, better than almost anyone in the universe. I held her close for a moment, my mouth next to her ear. "I'm so, so sorry Nadin," I murmured. "I won't leave you again, I promise."

Her breath hitched slightly, and she swallowed, trying to keep those tears from spilling over. She took a couple of deep breaths and then nodded and loosened her grip on me.

I let go of her, my face burning as my brain caught up and I suddenly remembered that we had an audience. I looked over at Tamara standing next to Henry, her eyes riveted on me, and it felt like the whole world crashed to a halt. What had I been *doing*? The last day I'd seen Tamara—before I'd left the Academy, on the sky bridge outside Tyson Hall—replayed in my mind, making the blood drain out of me. *Tamara.* What was I thinking? What must *she* be thinking?

Quickly I stepped away from Nadin, trying to ignore the second wave of betrayal that slammed into me as I did so. *Crap.* This was a mess. I didn't know what I was feeling anymore.

"Hey, guys," I said awkwardly, unsure of what to say next.

Scylla didn't give me a chance. In half a second she'd bounded over and pulled me into a bear hug. "You're home!" she wailed, her voice reverberating through my chest.

Tamara and Henry were right behind her. Tamara hugged me less intensely than Scylla did, the scent of strawberries wafting from her long dark hair. It had grown from just below her shoulders to all the way down her back, thick and wavy. When she released me, Henry grinned awkwardly, giving me a split-second one-armed bro-hug. "Glad you're back, man," he said, and I smiled back, both of us avoiding each other's eyes lest we catch a hint of mistiness there.

"I've been going nuts all week wanting to get in touch with you guys," I admitted. "I don't have my palmtop or Speculus anymore, and my house is surrounded by reporters and protestors day and night. How did you...?" I trailed off, glancing over my shoulder at Erick, who was leaning nonchalantly against the hood of his truck.

"I arranged it," Scylla said proudly, puffing out her chest. "Professor G is my advisor at Kimbal. I may have discussed a couple extracurricular activities when I was in his office planning my course load for next annum."

I looked at Erick, taken aback. Subterfuge against my mom? That was unexpected. He kept surprising me. "I... Thanks, Erick," I finally managed to say.

"No problem." He smiled. "All right, I'm going to head over to the lab now. Have a nice time, stay safe—Tamara, I trust you know how to handle photographers at this point."

She shrugged, looking embarrassed. "I'll do my best, Dr. Gomez."

"That's all I ask." He got back into the truck and turned on the ignition.

After Erick left, Tamara led us into her moms' garage, where a shiny, new-looking dark blue Tesla was parked. It seemed odd that we were taking a car—we always took the train everywhere before. But everything was different now. I couldn't exactly keep a low profile on public transit, I supposed. And, apparently, neither could any of the others, except maybe Scylla.

Tamara opened the driver's side door and got in. Henry started to open the front passenger door, but then he hesitated, looking at me with an odd expression on his face that I couldn't quite read. "Do you want to sit up here?" he offered.

I glanced at Tamara, then over at Nadin, standing behind me looking nervous. "No, I'll take the back," I said.

"I'll sit in the back, too," Scylla said quickly, with a broad grin. She bumped shoulders with Nadin, who flushed and smiled back.

A small wave of relief washed over me at the sight. Scylla had always been inordinately friendly. If she'd been looking after Nadin, that had probably been an immense help.

Henry nodded silently and climbed into the front seat next to Tamara. I took the seat behind him; Nadin scooted into the middle seat and Scylla got in after her.

"So, where are we headed?" I asked as Tamara hit the power button on the car and started programming directions into the drive console.

"I thought we might take my moms' boat out on Yellowknife Bay. Somewhere we can be private without being, you know. Here." She added in a low voice, "So we can talk without people overhearing."

I nodded in agreement. Yellowknife Bay was part of the greater delta north of Tierra Nueva. We used to go out there every summer—the water there was less choppy than in Escalante Bay, where winds from the Cimmerium Sea often led to high waves.

"I'm relieved you're all right," Nadin said softly to me in Iamoi as the car backed out of the garage. "The more days passed without GSAF letting me see you, the more I thought that I wasn't going to see you again."

"Me, too. But how were you able to get away from them to come to Tamara's house? And without a guard?"

"I have been staying here since the day we arrived on Mars."

"What?" I hissed.

Nadin looked surprised at my reaction. "Kate Ponsford sent me to stay with Bryn and Delia. They are friends of hers."

"Seriously? Joseph Condor didn't have a problem with that?"

She frowned, chewing on her lower lip. "I don't think he's happy about it. But he hasn't done anything to try to stop it... yet."

I scoffed. I could only imagine. I knew the Ponsfords were friends with Tamara's moms—Tamara hung out with Wyatt sometimes, and she always looked unhappy when Henry and I would rag on Wyatt for being an unbearable prick—but I wouldn't have expected this. I remembered the way Joseph Condor had talked over the top of Governor Ponsford at that press conference, and that glint of irritation in her eyes when he did. Maybe Condor didn't have as much control of GSAF as I thought he did. It would be a godsend if that were the case. Maybe the Iamoi would have a chance here after all.

"This is hilarious, incidentally," Scylla said.

"What is?" I asked.

"You two. I can't understand a word you're saying, but then I hear *GSAF* and *Joseph Condor*, and it all becomes crystal clear."

"Oh. Yeah," I mumbled.

Scylla laughed awkwardly but trailed off when Nadin and I didn't laugh with her, and an uncomfortable silence fell over the car. No one seemed to know how to break this ice that had built up around us. Why did I suddenly feel more at ease talking to Nadin than I did to my lifelong friends? How had so much changed in such a short time?

Because it wasn't short at all.

I felt bad that Scylla had made an effort and I'd dropped it. I didn't want to spend the entire afternoon in this unbearable silence any more than she did. In a desperate attempt to clear the air, I blurted out, "So, uh, what's been going on with you guys since... uh... since the last time I saw you?" But the question felt inadequate, like I was making small talk with a classmate I hadn't seen over the term break. Not the best friends I'd been torn from against my will, who'd spent two full annums probably thinking I was dead. Now here I was, back among the living—completely unchanged, while their lives had gone on without me. "*What's been going on?*" didn't seem to even remotely cover it.

"I heard your song on the radio earlier, Tam," I added.

"Oh?" Tamara said, looking over her shoulder, her cheeks tinged pink. "Did you like it?"

"It was stellar. I'm so happy for you," I said earnestly.

"Thanks. I met my agent—not long after you left. At, um, at the museum opening."

A small pang nipped at my heart. So she had gone. Everything had fallen into place for her at the event I was supposed to attend as her date. "That's great," I said, hoping my smile looked genuine. I meant it to be genuine. I was happy for her, truly. "What about the rest of you? Henry, I saw you on the news. The one thing I saw on my mom's deskpad before she snatched it away," I added with a laugh. "Guess you're famous now, too?"

"Heh. Yeah. With all the 'fun' that entails." He smirked, but something about him seemed off. The typical defiance in his eyes had dulled a little. I'd expected him to brag about it, but he seemed reserved for some reason.

Worried.

"Shit happened," he finally said, uncharacteristically quiet. And that was apparently that on the subject. The ice that had been splintering around us seemed to solidify once more.

Scylla frowned, leaning forward in her seat to look at me, then Henry, then Tamara. She pursed her lips and let out a breath that ruffled her bangs. "Nadin, have you ever been on a boat?" she asked, switching to the one person in the car who seemed willing to talk.

"I'm not sure. What is that?" Nadin looked at me hesitantly.

I thought about it, trying to guess the loanword that would be the closest to the Iamoi word for *boat* or *ship*. I must have guessed correctly, or close enough, because Nadin said, "Ohh. No, there... there wasn't enough water left on Iamos for *acalli* to still be in use."

"This will be exciting for you then, I think," Scylla said brightly.

We merged onto the freeway heading north toward Mount Sharp and the Gale Delta. I glanced out the window, watching the cityscape go by. We'd be passing the Academy soon. This part of town used to be on the outskirts of Tierra Nueva, without much apart from some of the more upscale homes and the school, but I was surprised to now see a number of new office buildings and a couple strip malls. Just off the freeway, a massive building was being constructed. All around it, giant cranes perching high on steel framework rose into the sky. It reminded me of when AresTec was building Sparta Island.

"What's that?" I asked, pointing.

Tamara turned to look. "Oh, those are the new Rainier offices."

"The Speculus people?"

"Yeah, GalaX bought them out several months back and decided to move their facilities to Aeolis. Mom's been working overtime juggling the transition—GalaX is transferring some personnel from AresTec over to Rainier. They wanted Mama to come over to work on their new Speculus Nano thing, but she wants to stick with AresTec at least until the next gen A-Top is out."

Beside me, Nadin was craning her head to look out the window. The Rainier building had disappeared behind the hills now, but she still was peering around with such interest that I felt bad about having taken a window seat.

"Where are we going, Isaak?" she asked in a low voice.

"Yellowknife Bay? It's a reservoir just west of the delta." I tried to think of how to describe the Gale Delta. "All the rivers that run through town stem from there. It's like a big network of rivers and lakes and marshes that kind of bisect each other. At the base of the mountain, north of Hope Renewed," I said, hoping that would make sense to her. She nodded thoughtfully, and I added, "You'll be able to see it soon."

Tamara's moms' boat, a mid-sized bowrider that Mama D had named the *Merrow's Jewel*, was moored at a private harbor in Yellowknife Marina. As the car pulled into the parking lot, Tamara leaned across Henry to open the glove compartment. She pulled out two baseball caps, a pink one and a black one. She handed the black one to Henry before putting the pink one on herself, adjusting the hat and her hair in the rearview mirror. Then she leaned over again and pulled a pair of sunglasses out of the glove compartment, with large round lenses that took up almost half her face.

I snorted as Henry pulled the cap on. Probably the only thing weirder than seeing Henry wearing a suit was Henry wearing a baseball hat. "You guys going incognito mode?" I joked.

Tamara looked over her shoulder at me in surprise. "Yeah,"

she said simply.

Oh.

The air outside the car was still but cold enough to make me shiver. It was absolutely cloudless out, but despite the sunny day it was cold as winter. It was May-II, wasn't it? If it was May-I, that would be one thing, but we were supposed to be coming into summer soon.

"Are you going to be warm enough?" I asked Nadin. She was wearing a long-sleeved t-shirt that I recognized as one of Tamara's, purple with a rhinestone butterfly appliquéd on the front. The jeans she was wearing didn't quite reach the top of her shoes, showing off a brown patch of ankle between her socks and the cuff of the pants.

She nodded, sliding out after me. "It's not as cold as Iamos," she said.

"I brought some blankets," Tamara said, popping open the trunk of the car. Inside were, indeed, a few folded blankets, a case of water bottles, and a cooler with sandwiches inside. Henry grabbed that and I took the water bottles. Scylla took the blankets, handing one to Nadin who trailed behind us, looking around at the marina with wonder in her eyes.

We followed Tamara down the dock to where her parents' boat was moored. I hung back, watching Nadin as she paused next to every boat we passed, staring down into the water or up at the mast on a tall catamaran. The breeze had picked up, playing at the loose tendrils of her hair, making them dance around her face. I smiled as she reached up to tuck the wayward strands behind her ear.

She quirked her head at me, noticing my gaze. "What?" she

asked.

"Nothing. I like your hair down," I said.

She looked at me in surprise. "You do?"

"Yeah. It makes you look... happier."

One of her eyebrows twitched, and she tightened the blanket around her shoulders, her face flushing. "We'd better catch up with the others," she said finally. "I don't know where we're going."

"I do. The berth is just around the corner, come on."

Scylla was still standing on the dock, handing the rest of the blanket stack to Tamara. She looked over her shoulder as we came down the dock beside her. "There you are. Dawdlers."

"I'm sorry," Nadin said. "I was looking at the boats. Isaak made sure I didn't fall behind."

"I'm just teasing," Scylla said, shooting me a grin. "Let's get you in. Here, hold on to me." She held Nadin's hand to steady her as she climbed aboard the boat, then hopped aboard herself.

"Here," Henry said, handing me a life vest after I'd followed them on board. "Can you get yours, Nadin?"

"Yes," she said stubbornly, putting her arms through the armholes and staring down at the straps, then looking at Scylla to watch how she fastened the vest before attempting it herself.

"Make sure it's secured tightly," Henry said before moving to loosen the mooring lines. The boat pitched slightly as he moved, and Nadin grabbed the railing beside her to balance herself.

"You okay?" I asked in a low voice. "People sometimes get sick from the movement of the water. It's different than being on land, or even moving in a car."

"It feels strange," she admitted, "but I think I'm fine."

"Okay. Brace yourself when we get moving."

Nadin nodded and we went to sit beside Scylla as Tamara turned on the motor and maneuvered the *Merrow's Jewel* out of its berth. I watched Nadin, looking around in amazement as we moved away from the dock and out into the open water.

"Incredible," she breathed in Iamoi. "Look at that sky. I don't think I'll ever get over how blue it is. What time of day will we be able to see Hamos?"

I jolted at her question. *Hamos.* How could I have already forgotten, in just a week's time? That huge, bright moon that had burned in the Iamos sky, making it feel even more like an alien planet. Like a larger, golden version of Earth's moon.

The moon we didn't share. Because in Nadin's time, Hamos—Venus—had been Mars' twin planet. And now it wasn't. And I had no idea how or why.

But whatever my answer would be, Nadin wouldn't like it.

"It's, uh... it's not as easy to see now as it was on Iamos," I said, choosing my words carefully.

"Because of the atmosphere?" she asked.

"Um, that's part of it."

She nodded, seeming to find that answer acceptable for now, and I let out a breath of relief. I couldn't keep hiding it from her forever, but the truth was, I had no clue how I was going to tell her. She'd want answers, and I simply couldn't give them. I didn't know what had happened, or how any of this was possible in the first place. I made a mental note to research this more once I had a palmtop or a Speculus set at my disposal.

The narrow channel that connected the marina to Yellowknife Bay was widening now, the signs of civilization disappearing around us. The shoreline was red, covered with scrubby brushes and spider weeds, like a desert landscape cut in half by a band of blue. Ahead of us, Mount Sharp soared into the cloudless sky, its slopes striped with white—though I was concerned to see that the white was only on the cap now. Usually the whole mountain looked snowy until into the summer months. The bare shoreline around us looked larger than usual, too, wide swaths of red unmarred by foliage. I remembered my mom washing the dishes in water barely deep enough to cover the sink bottom this morning.

"How bad is this drought, exactly?" I asked, raising my voice to be heard over the sound of the motor and the wind kicked up by the moving boat.

Tamara looked over her shoulder at me and shrugged. "They're not being very forthcoming about it. They keep saying everything's fine, but I'm sure you can tell..." She gestured at the dry shoreline that I'd been staring at.

Nadin poked me. "What does that word mean?" she asked in Iamoi. "*Drought?*"

"A water shortage," I said.

Her eyes widened and she looked around once more. "This is how a water shortage appears to you?" I could hear the skepticism in her voice.

"The beginnings of one." I turned back to Tamara and raised my voice again. "Isn't GSAF doing anything about it? What about the southern ice cap?" My heart skipped as I asked that. Part of my bargaining chip with the Elytherioi had been that our southernmost continent, Cimmeria, had remained unsettled. I'd been hoping that the Iamoi might be permitted to colonize it. But what if that phase had been started on while I'd been away?

"They're building another space mirror," Henry said, resting his forearms on his knees and leaning forward. There was a ragged red piece of yarn tied around his wrist, and he fiddled with it as he spoke. "Supposedly that will take care of it. I don't know about that. Some people in the Free Mars movement have been expressing some concern about our lack of a magnetic field. Without one, solar winds do some pretty nasty stuff to the atmosphere."

"That's all the more reason why you need my help," Nadin said eagerly. "The scientists in Elytherios know all about terraforming. Their technology had the power to renew our atmosphere. If GSAF, or"—she paused, looking distinctly uncomfortable—"or *your* people... if you would allow us to come to your time, we would be able to help. We know of ways to accommodate for the lack of magnetic field."

"Well, you already know you have my vote," Henry said to her with a meaningful quirk of his eyebrows.

"Yes," Nadin said softly, her voice almost lost to the wind and the noise, "I know."

I frowned, watching the two of them.

Some distance from shore, Tamara turned off the motor and we dropped anchor. Scylla bustled around, handing everyone sandwiches from the cooler.

"We have PB and J, and lunch meat for you carnivores," she said.

"Which one is better?" Nadin asked, wrinkling her nose and peering at the sandwiches in Scylla's hand.

"Well, I know what I think," Scylla answered with a laugh.

"You can have a bite of mine to see if you like it." She unwrapped her own sandwich and broke off a piece, handing it to Nadin, who chewed it thoughtfully.

"Sticky, but sweet... and salty." She swallowed. "I'll have this one."

Scylla handed her a peanut butter and jelly, and the five of us ate in silence. After we'd finished, Henry stood and moved to the bow, breaking off pieces of his crust and tossing them into the water, like he thought there were fish in there to eat it or something. Maybe there were by now. Though it seemed a long shot that they would have introduced marine life with a water crisis going on, apparently nothing was predictable these days.

Nadin took a sip from her water bottle and sighed.

"I understand where you're coming from, Henry," she said out of nowhere. He turned to face her, leaning back against the railing. I looked between them in confusion, but Henry's even expression told me that she was merely picking up a conversation they'd already started a while ago. "But GSAF are the ones with the access to the posterns. We need to be able to establish a secure link between our times for my people to pass through. If we can't access the posterns, we won't have any hope." She looked uncomfortable, but she sat with her shoulders firmly back, in that I'm-a-gerouin-don't-mess-with-me stance she adopted whenever other people were around. "You have to see my position."

"Yeah," Henry started, but then abruptly Tamara snapped, "Henry, get down!" I jolted alert. Before my brain could catch up with my eyes, Tamara had shoved Henry down in his seat and stepped in front of him. I jerked around to see what she was reacting to. Two men on a boat about thirty meters away from ours were watching us. A third had something in front of his face, black, with a long scope that glinted in the sunlight.

"It's a camera," Scylla announced, her voice trembling slightly. "Just a camera."

"Oh," Tamara said; then, "Dammit. I was hoping no one would recognize us."

"It's my fault," Nadin said in a quiet voice. "My hair. I'm the only person I've seen here with hair like this." She pulled at a coarse strand in annoyance.

"It's not your fault, Nadin," Tamara said earnestly. "I should have thought of that. I could have given you my hat, or brought extra. I was"—she bit her lip, looking over at the photographers—"preoccupied. I didn't think."

"Should we try to shake them? Go down the river?"

Henry shook his head, getting back to his feet. The boat rocked, and Tamara reached out to brace him. A bit of braided red yarn poked out from under the cuff of her long-sleeved shirt. "No point. That footage is probably already out there. We're busted regardless. Just ignore them." Tamara withdrew her hand, and I felt that pang again, smaller and duller than before, more like the ache of a bruise than the stab of a knife. I didn't know what kind of hell the three of them had gone through while I was gone, but it had made them closer. At least, whatever they'd gone through, they'd had each other. They hadn't been alone.

I just couldn't help but wonder where that left me.

Henry took a shaky breath. "Where were we?"

"The posterns," Scylla said, scrunching her mouth into a small, round shape, thinking. "GSAF controls access to them. No one gets anywhere near those hills without their say-so." She drummed her fingers on her knee a few times in rapid succession, then sat bolt upright. "But only the ones they *know* about."

Henry's eyes widened, a familiar spark flooding into them. "Right," he said, the corners of his mouth drawing up. "There are probably other arches all over the planet, right? Not just the one in the caves Isaak found. If the Iamoi used them so much, they must be out there. We just need to find them."

"Wait," I interrupted. "Are you guys saying we should go around GSAF? Try to get the Iamoi here without their help, without their permission?"

"That's exactly what I'm saying," Henry said, folding his arms. "Earth's control of this planet is tenuous enough as it is, and that was back when we all believed that this was an uninhabited planet without a prior claim to it. The Iamoi's existence proves GSAF's illegitimacy. Their days of running this planet are numbered."

My jaw worked soundlessly for a moment. "Okay, but what do you think is going to happen to you—your movement—all of us—if that's the case?"

He shrugged. "We'll have to work that out with the Iamoi. Negotiate, form a treaty. But I think it would be better for everyone that way, don't you?"

I wasn't so sure about that. The Elytherioi were one thing, but what about the others? What about the *geroi* and the *patroi*? How would they feel about sharing the planet with people from Earth? I wanted to argue with him, try to make him see reason; but before I could speak, Nadin nodded, seeming to make up her mind.

"We will make this work. We will find a way," she said resolutely. Then she frowned. "But first we need to find the posterns. And the trouble is, I'm not sure where to look for them. Everything looks so different here. I don't even recognize this valley, this... crater. I have no frame of reference."

I sighed, shoving my protestations to the back of my mind. At the end of the day, this was Nadin's call. These were her people. Whether they worked with GSAF or with Henry's group, there was always going to be this problem. There was no point worrying about it now. Maybe they were right—maybe it would work out better this way. "It would probably have to involve digging," I said. "From what I saw of it, most of the important parts of the citidomes were underground."

"Well, what about the one we dug up before? At Erick's dig site? Not that we've had much luck accessing that area, but it might be easier than getting into the caves," Tamara suggested.

"How big was that arch, Isaak?" Nadin asked.

"Like this," I said, gesturing with my hands to indicate about waist high.

Nadin shook her head and frowned. "I suspected as much. If it was close to surface-level, it was probably a goods transport. They're not designed for humans or other living beings to pass through."

"That's out, then," said Henry, folding his arms. "Is there anywhere else on Mars where there might have been an Iamoi settlement that we can access that GSAF doesn't already know about?"

We sat there quietly, thinking. "What about Elytherios?" I said finally. "The city was inside the caldera of Elysium Mons. There's a chance GSAF isn't aware of its existence."

Nadin stood, chewing her lip, and moved over to the railing by Henry. She wobbled a little, and for a panicked moment I wondered what would happen if she fell overboard—could she swim? I doubted it. But she steadied herself and leaned against the railing beside him, tossing her hair away from her shoulders as if daring the photographers to take her picture. She looked majestic, standing like that. At home.

"It could work. It would be a bit..." She trailed off, struggling to think of how to phrase what she wanted to say in English. She switched to Iamoi, saying to me, "How would I phrase this? It would be a strange coincidence if we established a stable link between the same postern in two eras."

"Ironic, I think," I told her in English. She nodded once, as if committing the word to memory.

Tamara looked up at the sky pensively. "It's too late to head over there now. Especially if your mom wants you back before curfew, Isaak. It's a good five-hour drive from here to Elysium."

"When would we be able to go?" Nadin asked, looking at me eagerly.

"I'm not sure. I'd have to see if Erick would be willing to sneak me out of the house again," I said.

"We're going to have to watch our step with GSAF, too," Scylla pointed out. "I can guarantee you that Joseph Condor's already gotten wind of this little day trip. He won't be happy about Nadin being out here with us, and with you, Isaak. We're going to have to watch our step."

Nadin's face fell. Quickly, I said, "Maybe next weekend? That should give us time to get a feel for how GSAF is going to react. Maybe if we lay low for a week, we'll be able to make it out there without a problem." It felt like a long shot, but I had to give Nadin that little bit of hope at least.

She nodded. "How long is one of your weeks?"

"Seven days."

She turned, looking down into the dark blue-green water. "All right. Seven days. I can wait that long."

The breeze picked up again, ruffling my hair, making Nadin's halo out around her. Seven days it was. Seven days until everything changed forever.

For better or worse.

"Did you have a nice day?" Mom asked as Erick and I came through the door.

"Yeah, we got a lot of work done," Erick said cheerfully, hanging his fob on the hook on the wall. "Isaak's a natural at this sort of thing." His smile didn't waver, but I stopped in the doorway. I recognized that look on her face, the sarcastic tone in her voice. Erick was walking straight into her trap. We were busted.

"Yes, he's always been right at home on a boat. I used to call him my little *Tritón*."

Erick looked genuinely mystified. "A boat?"

"Forget it, Erick," I said, rolling my eyes. "She's got us."

He let out a sigh of frustration. "But how...?"

He broke off as Mom held up her palmtop, revealing footage of all of us aboard the *Merrow's Jewel*. Then he groaned. "I thought Tamara said she could handle the paparazzi."

I shrugged. "She could, but Nadin and I couldn't."

He turned back to my mom. "Look, Jess—"

"Erick, I thought we were in agreement about this."

"You can't keep the kid locked up here forever," he protested. "You've got to go back to work next week, and who's going to watch him then? A security drone? Are you going to have the police guard our house?" He sighed at her dark expression. "I know you want to keep him safe—we both do! But you can't wrap him in bubble wrap. You can't keep him isolated from the world. Not when the world is already changing so much. He needs his friends, now more than ever."

I expected Mom to argue back with him, for this to turn into one of the epic rows she used to have with Dad, but to my surprise she just squeezed her eyes closed. "I know," she said in a surprisingly level voice. "But can't I at least keep him safe for one *week* without—"

I have no clue where she was planning on going with that, because just then the doorbell rang, making the three of us jump. For a panicked instant, I was certain it was Joseph Condor—after all, if Mom had seen those pictures, he was absolutely sure to have by now. Frowning, Mom went into the entryway. I trailed behind her, watching as she peered through the peephole. "*Dios*," she whispered contemptuously before pressing her thumb to the lockpad and flinging the door open. "What do you want?"

"And a good evening to you, too, Jess." My dad pushed past her, his arms laden with shopping bags. He was wearing new clothes: slim-cut dark rinse jeans and a burgundy sweater over an Oxford shirt, the sleeves pushed up just enough to reveal an Ares watch around his wrist. His hair had been cut and his stubble shaved, and he smelled strongly of cologne; it filled the house as soon as he came in the door.

"No, seriously," Mom said, closing the door and narrowing her eyes at him, "what do you want?"

"I just want to visit my children. Is there a problem with that?"

"Not until I talk to a custody lawyer," Mom muttered under her breath.

Dad turned his back on her, directing his attention to me. "Hey, kid. I got you something. And your sister, too. Celeste!" he yelled. "Where are you? Come out here!"

Celeste had been lingering in the doorway to her room, peering out at him suspiciously. I realized then that a lot of the reason she'd been hanging back the first night we got home was probably because of him. I wasn't sure if she even remembered him, to be honest—he'd vanished when she was three, and now she was... eight. Erick seemed to have completely filled the *father* void in her life, in a way he hadn't been able to for me. Dad was a stranger to her.

When he called out again, she shuffled out of her bedroom, her eyebrows drawn. "There you are, *mija*! Come here. I brought you presents." He set down the bags as she came down the hall. "This one's for you"—he pushed one bag toward her with his foot—"and Isaak, this one's yours."

I bent to open the bag and my jaw dropped. On top was a sealed black box with the AresTec ram logo. I pulled it out; it fit neatly in my hand. A new palmtop. And a larger box underneath...

"A new Speculus set!" I said out loud.

Dad chuckled. "I figured it's probably been a while since you got an upgrade, right?" I pulled it out of the bag, turning it over to look at it. This must be the newest model—the GalaX logo was now printed beside the old Rainier mountain in the upper left corner. A banner across the top of the box read, "*Now with Speculus Nano support!*" Tamara had mentioned that earlier. I flipped the box over for a description of the feature. "*More than VR —Speculus Nano technology provides a full sensory immersion experience.*"

Nanobots? I didn't think Mom would go for that particular accessory. To be honest, I didn't love the sound of it myself. Technology inside your body was too eerily reminiscent of what I'd just left on Iamos.

"Raymond, we didn't want her to have one of those yet!" Mom exclaimed. I looked up to see Celeste pulling a Speculus set of her own out of the bag. Mom had sometimes let her watch VR flix on the old set in her room, but she hadn't let me have my own set until I was thirteen, and I'd assumed it would be the same for Celeste.

"What's the worst she's going to do? Watch flix in her room?"

"I like it, Mom!" Celeste protested, holding the heavy box against her chest.

In a low voice, Mom hissed, "It's not good for kids to be plugged in all the time at such a young age."

Dad rolled his eyes. "Whatever. I did it when I was a kid. You're being melodramatic, as usual. Besides, that's not the only thing I got her." He stooped to pull the other object out of the bag, a large LEGO playset that matched the unfamiliar cartoon bedspread that I'd seen in her room.

"Rose Red's forest!" Celeste crowed, setting the Speculus set down and taking the LEGO box from him. It was one of those big, detailed playsets that take up the whole table when you assemble it. One of those *expensive* playsets.

"Dad, how did you afford all this?" I asked, my eyes moving from the pile of gifts on the floor to his new wardrobe. "I thought you said your accounts had been closed." Even if they hadn't been, I couldn't believe he'd have enough money to get Celeste and me these things. Any money he had should be going into living expenses, getting back on his feet—right?

"Fortune has been smiling upon me, Isaak!" He grinned at me, his teeth white in the dim hallway. I cringed. I'd heard him use those words before, and then two days later he and my mom would be yelling at each other about how they were going to pay the bills that month. "I'm back home, and everything is coming together again. The last couple months are going to be nothing but a bad memory before you know it." I frowned and he elbowed me. "And I couldn't neglect my only son and daughter! Come on, open that palmtop up. I want to see how they've improved while we were gone."

I tore away the plastic wrap on the outside of the box with my fingernails and lifted the lid. The device inside was a bit longer than my old one, a bit thinner. Its corners were more rounded. I lifted it out of the box, feeling the pliable material between my fingers.

"They said it's foldable now, like the deskpad. No worries about cracking it now," Dad announced as proudly as if he'd designed it himself.

"It's nice. Thanks, Dad."

"Leave it to your old man," he said, clapping me on the back. "I always take care of you. I'll make sure you get what you need."

I looked up as I saw movement in the corner of my eye. Erick stood to Mom's left, watching Celeste opening her playset. I frowned.

"Yeah. Thanks, Dad," I said again. "Listen, I really appreciate you coming over, but I've kind of had a long day."

He looked at me in surprise, his eyebrows raised. "Seriously? I thought maybe we could go get dinner and catch up."

"Catch up? It's only been a few days since I've seen you."

"A lot can happen in a few days," he said, his voice full of meaning. I nodded, looking down. *Truer words...*

"Maybe another day," I suggested.

He laughed. "All right, all right. I get the message. You enjoy your new stuff, all right? Get caught up with the world. Celeste, I'll see you later, okay?"

She glanced up from her LEGOs, the look of distrust in her eyes mostly faded now. When he bent to give her a kiss on the top of her head, she didn't shy away. He moved to the door, hands in his pocket, and met my mom's eyes. "And I'll see *you* later, too, Jess."

An odd expression crossed Mom's face. Without a word, she opened the door and Dad left.

"Well," Erick said, looking around at the mess of bags and boxes and plastic wrap spread across the floor, "never a dull moment, huh? I'll, uh... I'll get dinner started. My night to cook, right?"

He turned and went back into the kitchen. "Erick," my mom started, but he waved her off.

I looked down at the palmtop in my hand, feeling oddly guilty. "Mom, is it okay for us to have this?"

She sighed, sweeping her hair away from her face and looking at the ceiling for a minute. "Yeah. It's fine."

"Yippee," Celeste said, going back to unwrapping the LEGO figures in the middle of the hallway. I shoved the palmtop in my back pocket and bent to pick up the Speculus box.

"And Isaak," Mom said, her voice sounding pained. I looked up at her in surprise. "Erick's right. I can't wrap you in bubble wrap. If you want to be with your friends, it's... it's fine." She sighed. "Just let me know where you're going, okay? No more sneaking around."

"All right." I nodded.

"And be careful, okay?" I glanced at her and she looked away, but not before I saw that her eyes were shining. "Just be careful."

"I will," I murmured softly.

Back in my room, I plugged in the palmtop's docking station and nestled it inside to charge. Then I opened the Speculus box, disconnecting my old, broken set and setting the new one on my dresser.

I was back. I was connected. Things could go back to normal now.

But first I had something I needed to do.

I activated the palmtop, connecting it to my old account and waiting as it synced to the last backup that was miraculously still intact on the cloud. The home screen opened up, vivid and blue, and I tapped on the messages app.

Today had been awkward at first, trying to chip away at the ice between us, but it had gotten better as the day went on. The only way things were ever going to go *completely* back to normal was if I refused to let the discomfort eat away at me. I had to *make* things normal. I had to relearn how to be friends with them.

And... whatever else we were. That needed to be addressed as well. The kiss on the sky bridge still weighed heavily on my mind. I needed to know where we stood. I couldn't move on until I knew.

I typed her address into the new message bar quickly, before I could allow myself to chicken out. *Hey Tam*, I wrote, *it's Isaak. I got a new palmtop! Finally, lol.* I struggled for a moment, trying to think of a funny way to say that my mom was letting me have contact with the outside world again, but every time I came up blank. Forced, awkward, trying too hard. Finally, I just settled on, *Are u busy tomorrow night? Maybe we could get dinner.*

I hit send before I could change my mind and then shoved the palmtop into my nightstand drawer to keep myself from sending her a *Just kidding!* follow-up text. Henry had told me time and again that I needed to be proactive with Tamara or risk losing her. I'd already lost so much time with her as it was—if there was a chance things could still be salvaged, I had to act on it now. I just... I had to know.

I'd been two annums late for our first date. I wouldn't make that mistake again.

Unbidden, the memory of cool rain in a dark clearing rushed into my mind. Of tentative fingers hooked into the fabric of my shirt, and the look on her face when I told her she had me. Of the feeling I'd had when she whispered my name.

I pushed the memory away, flopping onto my bed and pressing the heels of my hands into my eyes. That wasn't the same thing. Not the same as years of unspoken feelings, of waiting, praying for a chance. Of a lifelong friendship yearning to grow into something more.

No. Not the same at all.

Chapter 8

- n a d i n -

IN THE DREAM, WE'RE BACK ON THE BOAT.

The sun shines above us, bright, and the air across my face is cool. Isaak, Henry, Scylla and Tamara are playing a game that involves dozens of small paper cards. I watch, trying to understand the rules, trying to decipher the patterns and symbols across the faces of the cards. They laugh as I take a bite out of my second peanut butter and jelly sandwich, making a face as the sticky sweet food clings to the roof of my mouth.

The boat rocks beneath us on the water, a strangely disorienting feeling, one that at first had made me feel like I was going to fall to my knees. But I've gotten accustomed to it. It isn't as bad as travel by postern, after all. I've learned to stand. I haven't fallen.

I lean back against the railing of the boat. The photographers have long since left us, and we're alone on the water now. The sun is setting, turning the sky fiery red. Red like the sky on Iamos. Red like the fire from an erupting volcano. Red like burning, like death...

"Ne'haoi ifaisteioi mesau elytherios."

I shake my head, the whispered voices in my ear dissipating. Isaak is watching me. I tuck a loose strand of hair behind my ear and he grins, making my face grow warm. "Something wrong?"

I smile back. "No, nothing. Will we see Hamos soon?"

"Yeah, any time now. Look—there it is."

I look up into the darkening sky eagerly. A golden orb appears on the horizon just as the sun sets. It rises quickly, far more quickly than it should. It cuts through the sky like this boat cuts through the water, and then it is above me, right over my head. Huge. Much larger than I've ever seen it before. Close enough that I can see its features, and they are wrong. All wrong. Yellow and gold and orange and fiery, fiery red, burning and screaming and dying...

I can see mountains on its surface erupting, spewing rock and lava, and my blood runs cold. Ascendant Dawn. The *gerouin*—Ceilos' mother. There'd been no warning. Why hadn't the early warning protocol worked?

The System's been tampered with.

I hear her voice echoing from the surface of the planet, reaching me here, far, far below. Clodin's screams of agony.

"This is your fault —you knew —"

"I didn't know!" I protest.

"You didn't know what?" Isaak is looking at me oddly, seven playing cards in his hand, splayed like a fan.

My eyes sting. I can feel hot tears slipping from the corners. "I didn't know."

"Nadin, what are you talking about?"

He can't see it. Can't hear it. Can't hear *her*. My partner's mother screaming accusations at me. I flinch as she shrieks again and again.

"Nadin—"

I'm on my feet, barreling into him, burying my face in his chest. "Make it stop, please," I beg.

And like that, the screaming stops.

And then another voice comes.

"So Isaak can comfort you when your partner cannot?"

I open my eyes in horror.

Ceilos stands there at the bow of the boat, his arms folded casually. "So this is what happens when we're separated for a few days? You forget all about me?" he says.

"I haven't forgotten you," I protest. "I think about you every moment of every day! What happened, Ceilos? Why did you let go of my hand?"

Ceilos ignores me, looking instead at Isaak. Isaak's arms fall away from me and he steps back, facing Ceilos.

"Answer me, Ceilos!" I cry.

Now he does look at me. And he laughs. "It was all part of the plan, of course."

My heart falls. It feels like the boat just drops out from under me, leaving me suspended in empty space. "What plan?"

"You don't seriously believe I meant to come here with you, do you?"

I shake my head, an almost instinctual gesture at this point. How quickly it's permeated my subconscious. "I don't understand."

"*Yachin*," Ceilos says, but his voice doesn't carry affection. It carries pity. "You never belonged in our time. It's clear you belong here."

"No. I'm coming back for you," I say firmly.

"Forget about us. Forget about the Iamoi. Just stay there."

My eyes are burning again. "I won't. I won't leave you behind, Ceilos. You're my partner. I... I love you. I won't leave you behind."

"Love," Ceilos scoffs. "Please. How could you love anyone when your heart is made of stone?"

I try to argue, try to protest, but I can't move my mouth. I can't move any part of myself but my eyes. I look down at my hands and find them cold, solid, gray as the carved rock in the deepest part of the underground.

"You're as lifeless as a statue," Ceilos says.

I wake up screaming.

I sat up in bed, my heart pounding, looking around myself in terror. Light was streaming in through the sheer curtains at the window. My hands were shaking uncontrollably. I grabbed the bedclothes with my fists to try to steady them, try to calm my heart. Try to keep myself from bursting into tears.

That had been the worst one, I decided. But only by a fraction. My dreams were so strange here, cryptic and frequently nonsensical. Sometimes they were vivid, like the one I'd just had—they'd linger with me for hours. But more often than not, they left me as soon as I awoke, and all that would remain was a feeling of unease. My dreams had been nothing like this when I was still connected to the System. They'd been calm, free of turmoil. The only odd dream I could remember having before was the one I'd had when I'd fallen asleep in my old classroom the night before we left for Elytherios. Had it just been my brain processing the message Gitrin had left in her apartment? Or had the System protocol that had initiated that day also caused the dream, as a way to give me the clues I needed to find her?

But if that were the case, what was the meaning of my dreams now? Or did they mean nothing at all? After a lifetime on the System, I didn't know which thoughts were my own, what was normal for my brain to do when it wasn't linked.

All I knew was that I was tired of nightmares.

Finally, when my heart stopped pounding, I managed to slide my legs over the side of the bed and stand. I couldn't bear to be in this room one more minute. I'd fallen into a routine by now—I'd creep downstairs quietly and find either Bryn or Delia waiting for me. They'd offer me a mug of the hot sokol-like drink and some warm bread to eat. Food and company would brush away the lingering memories of the night's dreams like cobwebs.

But when I opened the door to my room, I heard voices other than my hosts', and a strange sound echoing up the stairway. I froze in alarm for a moment, but then I recognized the voices and relaxed, making my way down the stairs and into one of the spacious rooms that opened onto the veranda overlooking the sea.

Tamara was sitting in front of a large black device, a table that opened. Its lid was propped up, exposing long wires. She ran her fingers over white and black keys, like a computer console, but I could not see a program. Instead, as she pressed each key, a different note rang out from the table. It was strange, but the sound it made was beautiful. I unconsciously took a step closer.

"Look, I know that's not what you're here to talk about. You're upset about something."

I started, looking around. Was she talking to me? But before I could speak, Henry appeared behind her; he had been obscured from my view by the lid of the black table. His brows knitted tightly over his dark eyes.

"I've been thinking," he said. "With Isaak back now... maybe this is all too much."

Tamara stopped pressing the keys and the sound trailed away, its last notes echoing off the room's high ceilings. She turned to face Henry. "What are you talking about?"

"I mean"—he scratched the back of his head uncomfortably, in a way I had seen Isaak do many times before—"us."

Tamara stared at him, her jaw slightly askew. She seemed unable to find words. She blinked rapidly a few times, and made a noise that was more of a squeak than anything intelligible.

He knelt before her, taking her hands into his. He whispered something I couldn't quite hear, and tucked a strand of hair behind her ear.

"But," Tamara finally said in a strained voice, "*why*?"

Henry looked down. "Well, because you and Isaak were..." I leaned forward curiously, my stomach twisting oddly, but Henry trailed off.

"Two annums ago. Things are different now. You *know* that."

"If things are different, why did he ask you out again?"

Silence. I listened as hard as I could, but I didn't hear a response.

"I just can't... Tam, he's my best friend," Henry said at last.

"He's my best friend, too!" Tamara's voice broke, and I winced. "But I love you, Henry. Isaak being back doesn't change that. Too much time has passed. You saw how it was yesterday. It was like we were strangers."

"How much of that was our fault, though?" asked Henry. "How much of it was our own guilt?"

She shook her head. "I don't know. I don't know, okay? About any of this. I don't want to hurt him, but..." She hunched forward, burying her face into her hands, trying to stifle the sob that followed. "He was gone so long. So long. I thought he was gone forever. I didn't think..."

"I know." Henry's eyes looked brighter than normal in the light, and his own shaking voice betrayed him. He got up off his knees, sitting on the black bench beside her, and pulled her into his chest. They said a few more things to each other, but I couldn't hear. I felt awkward, eavesdropping on a conversation like this. I was just wondering whether I should say something or leave when Henry took Tamara's face between his hands and pressed his lips against hers.

My stomach dropped at the memory of Ceilos doing the same to me, but Tamara did not seem to mind. She wrapped her arms around his neck and pulled him even closer. Like the *plivoi* I'd always mocked. But Tamara was certainly no *plivoin* here; her mothers were wealthy, and close to GSAF. On this world, she was as close to a *patroin* as they came.

Maybe Ceilos had been right. The problem wasn't everyone else. The problem was me.

I went back upstairs to my room until I saw Henry leaving through my window. A few moments later, I heard the sound of the black table again. It was still beautiful, but the pattern of notes sounded different this time. Something about them seemed mournful. It made me feel sad.

Downstairs, I found Tamara pressing the black and white keys again. I came to stand behind her.

"That's lovely," I said. "What is it?"

Tamara smiled. Her face looked strained, her eyes red and puffy. "It's a piano."

"A piano," I repeated. "Is it like a computer? What does it do?"

Her smile looked a bit less forced this time. "It doesn't *do* anything. It just makes music."

My brows furrowed. "This... this is music?"

Tamara stared at me for a long moment, as if she wasn't sure she'd heard me right. "Of course. Haven't you heard music before?"

My face burned under her scrutiny, and I turned away from her, unsure how to respond. Her incredulity made me feel both defensive and ashamed, and that made me angry. How could these otherworlders expect me to know everything about their ways and their customs, expect me to be the same as them when my world was so different?

Then I remembered that I had treated Isaak the exact same way.

Sighing, I looked back at Tamara. "Music is prohibited on Iamos."

Her jaw dropped. "But why?"

I crossed my arms, feeling the way the strange, soft fabric of these Martian clothes folded over them. "During the early part of the Progression, before the *gerotus* was established, the resistance was stronger. Not everyone agreed with the previous rulers' plans for preserving the planet, even though all the signs showed that if something didn't change, we would all die." I sounded defensive, falling back into my old habit of justifying the *geroi*. But the memory of everything I'd learned in Elytherios made the words die on my lips. The *geroi* had lied. There was no point in defending them. "During the Progression, music was used as a form of dissidence. So... the first *geroi* banned it."

I'd heard rumors that some *plivoi* still sang songs in their homes, but never in public. I never heard them. Once, Ceilos and I had tried to find some of the rebel songs in the System, but... that was before Ceilos had his cloaking program perfected. We'd gotten caught. The repercussions had been severe. We never tried that again.

Tamara was watching me, her eyes sympathetic. I didn't want her pity. I'd had enough of it from Isaak. Quickly, I changed the subject. "So what is its purpose?"

She lifted her fingers off the keys, considering. "To make people happy, I suppose."

Hesitantly, I said, "You don't look happy."

She shook her head. "Maybe not just happy. It's more like... it makes people feel emotions. Joy, sorrow. Even fear, if it's big enough." She smiled wistfully. "That's what I love about it."

It was quiet for a moment, Tamara staring down at the keys and me standing uncertainly behind her. I struggled to find a way to keep the conversation going, to ease her melancholy before it seeped into me, sending my thoughts back down the path they were treading when I awoke this morning. "Are there other instruments like this? To make music?" I asked.

She nodded, seeming pleased to change the subject. "Whole families of them. Strings, percussion, wind, brass. Some in between, like the piano—there's a bit of a debate about whether this is technically a percussion instrument or a string." She gestured toward the wires inside the open cabinet. "They all make different sounds, and when you bring them together, it's just mind-blowing. Some time I need to get you over to Herschel so you can hear the orchestra. Hundreds of different instruments all playing together, making music so full and loud that it's like you're cocooned inside it. Like you're floating on it."

"That would be wonderful," I said eagerly, trying to imagine what that would be like—floating on music like the waters we'd traversed yesterday in the small boat. Would it be just as beautiful? If Tamara's playing had been any indication, it must be. "There are instruments like this on the island?"

"Oh, yeah. Even nicer than this one, and this is a pretty good piano. It's been in Mama's family for years. I usually practice on campus these days, but—" She broke off abruptly, an odd look on her face. The melancholy was stealing over her again.

"But...?" I asked hesitantly.

"Nothing," she said quickly. When my eyebrows furrowed, she added, quietly, "When I'm meeting Henry I like for him to come here rather than taking the ferry over to Herschel. Especially if he's by himself. There are too many ways that could go wrong. Too easy for a sudden swell to 'knock someone off the boat'."

"You worry about him much?"

"All the time."

Silence hung between us, both our thoughts preoccupying us. Mine had come full circle. Tamara's worry for Henry felt too familiar, and now Ceilos' words from my dream were eating away at me like acid. I couldn't keep them in anymore. I needed to say it out loud.

"Tamara," I murmured finally, my voice barely audible to my own ears, "is it... normal for people who love each other to... press their mouths together?"

She blinked at me, at the abrupt change in topic. "You mean kiss?"

I looked down, my face hot. That was the word Isaak had used, too, that day in the plaza. "Yes."

"Um, yeah. Ordinarily."

"Oh." I twisted strands of coarse white hair around my fingers, pulling them back and away from my neck, though I had nothing to secure it with. "So it would be... *not* normal... for someone to not want to kiss the person they love."

Tamara turned around on the bench, leaning her back against the piano and looking up at me. "Nadin, is something wrong? Did your fiancé do something to you?"

"*Fiancé?*" I repeated in confusion.

"From what you've said this week, I got the impression that you're sort of... engaged to someone on your homeworld. Like a partner."

"Yes, Ceilos. But that's not... I mean..." I trailed off, unsure of what to say. Tamara patted the bench beside her, gesturing for me to sit with her. I sighed as I slumped down next to her. "It's very confusing. Ceilos and I are meant to be partnered. But just before Isaak and I left for Elytherios..."

She looked at me gravely. "Did Ceilos hurt you?" Her voice had an edge to it.

I studied my feet. "He didn't hurt me. But he kissed me, and I didn't like it. And..." It was difficult to find the words, and even worse to try to explain them in a language that wasn't my own. "I got the impression that he wanted to..." I froze, not having even the slightest idea what the word for this might be in English. My jaw worked soundlessly for a moment. Finally I gave up and said it in Iamoi.

Tamara's eyebrows furrowed. "You mean he wanted to have sex with you?"

I shrugged. "If that is the word."

"He can't make you do anything you don't want to do, Nadin," she said firmly.

"I know," I said. "I don't think he would try to force me. When I asked him to stop kissing me, he did. But it hurt him. Not physically, I mean, but his heart. And I feel like..." I squeezed my eyes shut and swallowed down the burning sensation in my throat. "Maybe I'm the one with the problem. If you say that"—I waved my hands—"*that* is normal."

Tamara turned back to the piano and ran her fingers across a few keys to the far right; they came out soft and high, dreamlike. "Is it just that you're not attracted to Ceilos specifically? Or do you think you'd feel this way about anybody?"

Involuntarily, I thought about Isaak that night in Elytherios. How he'd held me as I cried, but didn't try to push me farther. And yesterday, when he'd arrived at Tamara's house. The instinctual way I'd run to him. My cheeks grew hot. The thought of Isaak touching me was easier somehow than the thought of Ceilos, but I still felt sick to my stomach at the thought of... *having sex* with him. The thought of *having sex* in general.

"I don't know," I said. "But I think anybody."

"Maybe you're asexual, then."

"What's that?" I asked.

She reached into the pocket of her pants and pulled out the small tablet device I'd seen others use here—they called it a palmtop. In a moment, she began to read off a screen to me. "'An *asexual person is someone who does not experience sexual attraction. Unlike celibacy, which people choose, asexuality is an intrinsic part of who we are.'*"

I stared at her. "You mean there are other people like me?"

She nodded. "Think of it like my moms. Even though I'm attracted to men, they're only attracted to women, you know what I mean? The whole range of humanity has all these different spectrums we fall into. And then there's romantic attraction, which is different from sexual attraction. Like me and Henry, we're attracted to each other both romantically and—" She stopped short and squeezed her eyes shut.

"Tamara," I breathed. "I'm sorry. I know Henry was here, and you're probably..."

"No." She swallowed hard and smiled. "No. Anyway, that doesn't matter. The point is that even though I'm one way, someone else will be totally different. Some couples might love each other romantically, but not feel a sexual attraction. Other people have no romantic attraction at all. And sometimes there's a mix. Everybody's different, but it's all pretty normal."

She scooted closer and put her hand on my shoulder. "But no one can make you do anything you don't want to. If Ceilos loves you, he'll respect that. You can find a compromise."

I stared down at nothing, my mind struggling to process her words, trying to accept them as true. I was *normal*.

After a moment, Tamara stood. "I think we should talk to Scylla," she announced.

"Scylla? Why?" I asked.

"Because I think she can help you." She paused, then added, "And me."

"Do you need help?"

Tamara grimaced. "I guess there's no point hiding it. I need to figure out what to do about Isaak. He texted me last night—his mom gave him a reprieve. He's free to come and go as long as he's careful. So he wanted to get dinner with me tonight."

"Oh. That's nice," I said after a moment, once I'd found my voice.

"Yeah, we'll see," she said with a frown, but I barely registered it. There was a small sting in the back of my mind, the tiniest of hurts that he'd asked to see Tamara and not me. I refused to let it show, though, and Tamara didn't seem to notice anything amiss. Isaak was entitled to spend time with his friends. He'd had an entire lifetime before he'd met me, just as I had. He had actual friends, friends that he'd *chosen* rather than having an impossible set of circumstances thrust them together. Of course that would mean more to him. It would mean more to me, too, if I'd had any friends besides Ceilos. I wondered, for just the briefest instant, what it would have been like to grow up with friends. Surrounded by people who liked me because I was Nadin, rather than *pretending* to like me because I was *geroi*'s blood.

Then Tamara reached out her hand to me, smiling, and I took it. Her face was warm and open, without any of the reservation I'd seen for so many years on Iamos. When she took my hand, it almost felt like she was saying, "I *choose you.*"

"Come on, let's get you dressed," she said, pulling me up from the bench. "I think it's high time that we got you some clothes of your own, rather than making you wear my hand-me-downs all the time. And I have an idea for what we can do to keep you from being noticed when we go out."

"Really?" I said in surprise. "Do you think it will work?"

"Sure thing," she replied with a wink.

Everybody's different, but it's all pretty normal.

Heart lightening, I followed Tamara out of the room.

CHAPTER 9

- i s a a k -

I KNOCKED ON THE DORM ROOM DOOR, MY LEFT HAND BEHIND MY back, looking around awkwardly. Despite my mom's loudly-voiced fears—and my own subconscious ones—the evening thus far had been pretty uneventful. She'd been adamant that I not walk to the wharf by myself like I used to. I think if she'd had it her way, she would have driven me over to Tamara's moms' house and probably sat at the dinner table with us, but Erick had managed to talk some sense into her. He'd offered to drive me to the wharf himself, and to my own surprise, I eagerly took him up on the offer. I was grudgingly coming to realize that Erick was a good ally in the war to reclaim my independence now that I was home.

He'd told Mom that he'd walk me to the ferry docks and wait with me until the boat left, but when we got to the parking lot, he'd pulled into the stopping zone and given me a nod. "Looks like we made our escape unnoticed. I don't see any paparazzi around, do you?" When I shook my head, he nudged me. "I think you're in the clear. Have a good night."

I smiled in appreciation for just a second, then kicked the door to the truck open. Erick waved and drove away.

But I didn't go straight to the ferry like I'd said I would. Once I was sure he was gone, I wandered down the boardwalk, peeking into the storefronts. A lot had changed over the course of two annums—old stores had closed and new ones had opened—but I was relieved to see the one I was looking for was still there. It would just take a second. I quickly ducked inside.

No one had even glanced in my direction once I'd disembarked the ferry and entered Herschel's campus. Despite my notoriety, here I managed to blend in and look like any of the other university students—or close enough, anyway. It was freaky to me that all my friends had graduated from the Academy now, but I still had another annum left. I'd known a few kids in the lower grades, but not many. It would be like starting over for my senior year. I wondered how Mom would feel about homeschooling me. The way things were going now, she'd probably be delighted. On second thought, maybe one last year at the Academy wouldn't be so bad.

The red sunset had faded to purple as I approached Tamara's dorm building. It was three stories tall, with a stucco exterior that was painted an unfortunate orange-and-cream color scheme. The door to enter the building appeared to be accessible only with a keycard ordinarily, but someone had used a cinderblock to prop it open. I looked around to see if anyone was watching, but the few students milling around hadn't even glanced my way, so I'd shrugged and made my way to the second floor where Tamara said her room was.

A girl I'd never seen before wearing a navy blue hijab

answered the door at my knock. I blinked in surprise, worrying for just a moment that I'd come to the wrong room. "Is Tamara here?" I asked.

She looked at me appraisingly for a moment, and I was absolutely convinced that this was, indeed, the wrong room. Then she said, "I'm guessing you're Isaak."

"Oh, uh—Yeah. That's me."

"I'm Mariyah, Tamara's roommate. Come on in, she's finishing up getting ready." She moved away from the door enough for me to see that the dorm was L-shaped, with a small couch near the front with a mat spread out in front of it, and the corner of a desk visible around the corner. Laughter and girls' voices echoed off the wall, and I wondered just how many people lived here. "Tam, he's here," Mariyah called, turning to roll up the mat and tucking it under the couch.

"Oh, coming!" I heard Tamara call back, and then she came around the corner, accompanied by Scylla and a girl I didn't recognize.

No—I did recognize her. It was Nadin. She was wearing a wig, long and black and straight, with bangs that covered her eyebrows. I stared at her for a moment in surprise. She wasn't wearing Tamara's clothes today; now she had on a long-sleeved white t-shirt with a turquoise sweater over it, one of those crocheted ones with the holes around the flowers, and jeans that actually fit her, reaching the tops of her neon blue plaid sneakers. She looked completely Martian. She smiled at me quickly before looking down, fidgeting in place and picking at one of the flowers on her sweater with her fingers. There was a ring on her right hand—a black hematite one, on the middle finger. My eyes lingered on it for just an instant. Then Tamara stepped forward, and I quickly turned to her, blushing as I realized for the second time I'd found myself staring at Nadin when my attention should have been on Tamara.

"Hey," I said, my face growing redder as my eyes locked with hers. A sense of surreality washed over me as I realized this was really happening. I don't think I'd had a chance to process it before, with everything else that had happened in the time between. Everything had only just begun the day I disappeared. The day we...

"Here," I said quickly, before the memory of Tamara kissing me on the sky bridge—or the conflicting emotions it was causing me now—overwhelmed me. I held out my left hand, offering her the red rose I'd been trying to conceal behind my back.

She stared down at it for a second, blinking. "Oh," she said. Then, again, her voice shaking a little, "Oh." She took it from me gently. "Thank you. Is that from your mom's garden?"

"No. She only grows vegetables, remember?" I said sheepishly. "I stopped in at that gift shop on the boardwalk."

She looked up at me, her eyes shining. "That was so nice of you."

I frowned. Was she *crying*? "Hey... I'm sorry, should I have not?"

She shook her head and, still holding the rose, pulled me into a hug. The soft petals tickled the back of my neck. "Thank you," she said again. She turned to her roommate. "Could you...?"

Mariyah took the rose. "I'll put it on your desk."

"Thanks," said Tamara. She looked back up at me, blinking a couple times until the mistiness dissipated. "Ready?"

I nodded, and she paused by the couch, grabbing a wide-brimmed hat that had been sitting on the seat and placing it on her head. It seemed kind of an odd thing to be wearing out in the evening, but I remembered the paparazzi from yesterday and realized she must do this routinely to dodge them. Was this the life we all were destined for from now on? At least Tamara's fame had been chosen.

After adjusting the hat, she glanced back over her shoulder. "Scylla, can you get Nadin back to my moms' house okay?"

"Yeah. Have a nice night, guys," Scylla said, waving us out the door.

I hesitated for a second before reaching out my hand to take Tamara's. She paused, then accepted it. Hand in hand, we left the dorm. Just like a real couple, after all this time. Everything I'd ever wished for was coming true.

Right?

I didn't look back as the door swung closed.

CHAPTER 10

- n a d i n -

WHEN THE DOOR HAD CLOSED, SCYLLA TURNED TO MARIYAH. "Well," she said, her eyebrows disappearing beneath the choppy locks on her forehead.

"Well, indeed," Mariyah replied, setting the flower Isaak had given Tamara down on the desk beneath the window.

"What do you think the odds are that she's going to tell him?" asked Scylla.

"Knowing Tamara? Slim to none." Mariyah rolled her eyes. "She won't be able to stand hurting his feelings."

"Not that Henry's any better. God, after all the work we had to do to get those two together!" Scylla growled in frustration and kicked over a small wastebin. Crumpled bits of paper and plastic rolled out. Mariyah shook her head and knelt to scoop the items up. I bent to help her.

"Isaak doesn't know about Henry and Tamara?" I asked in confusion.

Scylla laughed humorlessly. "Nope."

"And they're not going to tell him?"

"They'll probably tell him in a good ten annums or so."

"Oh, come now," Mariyah interjected, straightening and folding her arms. "If we nag them enough, we might be able to get that down to eight."

"But I don't understand," I said, trying to resist the urge to scratch my scalp underneath the wig Tamara had given me earlier, before we'd gone to the marketplace to get my new clothes and my ring with Scylla and Mariyah. She'd said it was one she wore for shows—when she would sing and play her music for others. It had worked surprisingly well. Some people had recognized Tamara, but no one had appeared to recognize me. "Why are they keeping their relationship a secret from him? If they're his friends, shouldn't they want him to know the truth?"

"Don't ask me to explain the ways of the allos!" Scylla said, throwing her hands up in the air.

I frowned, staring at the door Isaak and Tamara had left through, thinking back on the day. Tamara's quiet introspection and the heated whispered conversations she'd had with Scylla. The way she'd said she needed help this morning. Scylla and Mariyah's repeated urgings of, "You've just got to tell him." What was going on here?

When I looked back, I saw Scylla was studying me. Her expression softened. "Hey. Sorry, I wasn't thinking. What about you? Are you okay?"

"Okay about what?"

She looked at Mariyah, then back at me. "About Isaak and Tamara going to dinner together."

"Of course," I said. "Why wouldn't I be?"

She shook her head, seeming almost exasperated—though I

couldn't fathom why she'd be exasperated with *me*. "Not just the allos."

Before I could ask her what that word meant, Mariyah interjected, "You know what? I think that this girls' day out isn't done yet. Shall we make a night of it and get some dinner? Anything is preferable to cafeteria food."

"I think that sounds lovely. Far better than studying for finals," Scylla said. "Nadin?"

"Um... all right..." My head was swimming from all these abrupt changes in subject.

"Lal Qila?" Scylla asked, slinging her handbag over her shoulder and looking at Mariyah.

"That sounds good. It's here on the island, so that will save us some time." Mariyah removed her palmtop from its stand on her bedside table and tapped on it, squinting at the screen. "It's seven. Are you going to be okay to get Nadin back home and still make the train before curfew?"

"I should be. We've got four hours," Scylla said, holding the door open for me. I followed her and Mariyah out of the insula-like building that Tamara had called their dorm. At the base of the stairs I paused, smoothing the hair from my wig as wisps of it snaked around my face in the breeze. The wind smelled crisp and briny from the sea. My gaze followed the lamps that were flickering to life now, lining the pathway down the gently sloping hill to the wharf where the ferry we'd taken this afternoon was moored. Another boat was just leaving the island, its silhouette a dark shape against the purple evening sky.

"Where are Isaak and Tamara going tonight? Back to Tierra Nueva?" I asked.

"I think so. Probably somewhere on the boardwalk," Scylla said, a note of false nonchalance in her voice. I frowned as she steered me away from the dorm, almost physically turning me away from the bay and the small boats bobbing along its surface, pulling me farther inland. Why was she acting so strange today? And not just her. Tamara, Henry—even Mariyah seemed to be wearing a forced smile now. What was going on here that everyone was so reluctant to speak about?

Then, abruptly, the pieces suddenly fell into place, like an optical illusion I'd been looking at all wrong. How could I have not seen it before?

"Isaak loves Tamara," I said slowly. "Doesn't he?"

"He did," Scylla replied, seeming to choose her words cautiously.

"Tamara and Henry don't want to hurt him."

"No. They don't." She watched me carefully, studying me. "Nadin, are you sure you're okay?"

"Of course I am," I replied automatically, though I felt a sudden, irrational desire to cry. This was why Tamara was lying to Isaak. Why *everyone* was. It was why Isaak had wanted to have dinner with Tamara alone tonight, rather than all of us. Why he'd brought her that flower. How could I have been so foolish as to have missed it? "I'm fine. It's none of my business, regardless. This is just... sad. I don't want Isaak to hurt. But I don't want Tamara to hurt, either. Or Henry. They're"—my voice cracked inexplicably—"they're my friends."

Scylla didn't say anything, but she put her arm around me, and I let her. She rubbed her hand along my bicep. "It's okay. They'll get through it. Don't worry about them tonight, okay? It's girls' night. Just you and me and Mariyah."

Mariyah nodded in agreement and joined the embrace, stretching her arms to fit around both me and Scylla. Instantly, my heart lightened. When they drew away, I smiled—a genuine smile—and swiped at my eyes with the back of my hand.

When my fit of sniffles had passed, Scylla and Mariyah led me down a concrete walkway that bisected green grass and cut between square buildings, not as tall as the ones on the mainland but much wider. Shortly, we passed a stela that seemed to mark the entrance of the school. Beyond this was the town. It was nowhere near the size of Tierra Nueva, but it bustled with the energy of the upper level of the citidome. Small cars drove down the narrow streets and groups of people clustered along the sidewalks, looking into the windows of brightly-colored buildings. One woman had a four-legged animal on a leash, covered with white-and-black fur and wearing a red jeweled collar around its neck. I stared at it as it walked past, and it wagged its tail at me, though the woman didn't seem to notice. Then the breeze picked up again, bringing with it the scent of cooking food, and my mouth watered, all thoughts of the strange animal vanishing from my mind.

We stopped in front of a large brick building with vaulted windows that reminded me of posterns, making a pang of homesickness bite into my chest. Brightly-colored lanterns adorned a courtyard outside, where people sat at tables eating and chattering. Scylla and Mariyah led me down a walkway lined with squat potted trees and through the front door of the building. Inside, more arches supported by elegant columns topped low abutments covered in blue tiles polished so brightly they seemed to glow in the lamplight. The smell of spices and the sound of laughter filled the air.

"Table for three?" asked a man who was standing just inside the door.

"Yes, please," Scylla said.

"Patio okay?" Scylla and Mariyah nodded, and the man escorted us across the large main room and through a door to an adjacent room. This room, though, was not completely enclosed—more columned arches supporting the roof opened up to the night air. The breeze cooled this room, mingling the slight tangy scent of the bay with the spicy aroma of the food.

The three of us sat at a table near one of the arches. I looked out at the darkening sky, then back as the man who'd led us to our table handed me a large, folded piece of paper and walked away. I unfolded the paper, but there was nothing inside but writing—dozens of foreign symbols that I didn't have the slightest hope of being able to decipher.

"Do you know what you want, Nadin?" Mariyah asked. "I mean, have you had desi food before?"

I shook my head. "I'm not sure. I've only had what Bryn and Delia have made for me. And lunch today, of course." We had stopped in a plaza at the marketplace this afternoon where various vendors were selling food from small carts. Tamara and I had wandered from cart to cart until I finally picked something at random, a plate full of brown noodles with green vegetables mixed in. I wasn't even sure what it was called, let alone if they would have something like that here. I'd learned this afternoon that different parts of Simos—of Earth, that is—had different traditional recipes. I wasn't sure if that had been the case on

Iamos before the Progression, but it certainly wasn't now. The *geroi*'s emphasis on unity had led to vigorously enforced conformity across citidomes, down to even the food we ate.

"She likes peanut butter and jelly sandwiches," Scylla said, and Mariyah laughed.

"Well, she's not going to find that here," she said.

I looked around the patio at the what the other patrons were eating. I started to say, "Honestly, you can pick something for—" but then I broke off, eyes wide, as a man walked past with a tray of sizzling meat and vegetables on a skewer. I pointed as he passed. "We have those on Iamos!"

"Kebabs?" Mariyah asked, watching the man set the platter down on a nearby table.

"Yes, I think that's what Isaak called them," I said eagerly. Finally, food that wasn't completely foreign!

Scylla made a face. "I wonder if you can get those vegetarian?"

Mariyah rolled her eyes. "Let her have the meat if she wants it, Scylla. Everything here is *halal*."

Scylla's frown just intensified, her nose scrunched. "I was thinking of the expense, too."

"I'll pay for her," Mariyah said. I smiled appreciatively at her, and she gave me a reassuring grin in return.

Soon our meals came, two skewers of *tikka kebab* for me and a plate of rice covered with a thick green sauce for Mariyah that she said was called *palak paneer*. Scylla had *daal karahi*, a dish of legumes and vegetables, and we each were given a plate of flatbread called *roti* as well—which Scylla informed me she liked because it was vegan, whatever that meant. Regardless, it was delicious. I relished every bite of the food here. The meat didn't quite taste like *kela* and the spices were unlike anything I'd had before, but apart from that, this was the closest I'd had to Iamoi food in the days I'd been here. I devoured it.

As we were finishing our meal, Mariyah sipping a hot drink called *chai* from a green earthenware mug, a man I didn't recognize approached our table. "Hello, ladies," he said. "Having a nice dinner?"

Scylla and Mariyah looked at each other with narrowed eyes. I didn't think this man worked for the restaurant; he was dressed differently than the man who had escorted us to our table, as well as the one who'd brought us our food. "Yes. Can we help you?" Scylla asked warily.

"I just was hoping to talk to your friend here." He looked directly at me. "You are Nadin, are you not?"

My eyes widened, panicked, and every word I knew of English completely fled my mind. How had he recognized me, even with Tamara's wig on?

"No, she's not," Mariyah said firmly.

"I'm sure she must be," countered the man in a pleasant voice.

"I'm sure you must be wrong," Scylla replied. "Now, if you don't mind, we're finishing our dinner. I'm sure you wouldn't want to make a scene." When he didn't move, she added, "I can promise you, I won't hesitate to call the manager."

"Of course. I must be mistaken." He looked at me. "After all, if you *were* Nadin, I'm sure you'd be interested in hearing how my people could help your people. So sorry for the inconvenience. I won't bother you a moment further."

He started to turn, but my mouth had caught up with me. I

spoke before I could think twice. "How could you help my people?"

My two dinner companions stared at me in shock, which quickly melted into frustration on Scylla's face. I avoided her gaze. If this man could help me, I couldn't afford to be cautious. I had to know.

He looked at me and smiled knowingly. "My name is Geoff Preston. I represent the GalaX Corporation."

"Wait—GalaX?" Scylla repeated, her brows furrowed. The word seemed to mean something to her. It sounded familiar to me, too. I'd heard Bryn and Delia say it a few times while I'd been staying with them, but I wasn't entirely sure what it was.

Geoff Preston nodded. His head was shaved, and the light from one of the wall sconces reflected orange off the top of it. "I understand your negotiations with GSAF have reached a standstill. That must be very frustrating to you. We at GalaX wanted to let you know you have our full support. We've borne the brunt of government red tape too many times, but never with such direct human costs."

"Thank you, Mister Preston," I said, taking care to use the English title I'd heard the people at GSAF say. After my slip-up with Joseph the other day, I didn't want to make the mistake of using Iamoi titles with these people again. "I appreciate your support. But I still don't understand what you want from me. How can you help my people?"

"GalaX was the true origin of the colonization of this world. Did you know that the first manned ship to reach Mars was a GalaX ship? Not a government ship."

I shook my head. I knew little of how the Simoi first came to this world.

He went on, "GSAF represents the official rule of law, but everyone knows that it was GalaX that got us here, not them. Our technology, our financing, our people doing the heavy lifting. There would be no Mars colony without us. They did more to hinder our progress than help it. But the upshot is that we have decades of experience dealing with GSAF when it comes to matters of colonization. I believe we could negotiate on your behalf."

My eyes widened. "That would be wonderful!" I exclaimed.

"Wait a minute," Scylla said quickly, her brows slanting sharply over her eyes. "What's the catch?"

"No catch. We believe that the presence of the Iamoi on Mars would be beneficial to all parties involved. From a cultural standpoint as well as a technological one."

"Ah-ha," Scylla said. "There you go. *Technological*. The magic word."

Then I understood, and my momentary relief dissolved. "You want the System," I said flatly.

He held up a finger. "I never said that. Nadin, you might not be aware, but the System has been a point of contention among our people for the last six months. We are very cognizant that our consumers will never accept a full-scale adoption of that technology. But your people have a whole knowledge base that no one on Earth or modern Mars has ever had exposure to. There's still so much that we can learn from each other, even without total System adoption."

"*Total*. But what about *partial*?" Scylla asked, her face drawn.

He spread his hands in a conciliatory manner. "I understand

why you may be apprehensive, Miss Hwang. I've seen you out there on the streets, fighting for our people. Many of us at GalaX support what the Free Mars movement stands for." Her demeanor seemed to shift at his words, some of her prickly distrust easing. "The last six months have been a strain on us all. Believe me, I know. But we believe that by working with the Iamoi, we can build a better Mars for all of us—your movement, too."

He turned back to me, smiling once more. "It's true, at our heart we're a tech company, Nadin. From AresTec to Rainier and even our space initiative, technology is our business. And your people have technology the world has never seen before. I want your people to work with us after they resettle here." He put his hand on our table, leaning against it casually. "Think about it: what are your people going to do once they arrive here? You want to form a new nation, but how is that nation going to become economically viable? How is it going to be competitive in the interplanetary marketplace? How are the Iamoi going to survive in a whole new era, a new time, a new world—none of which they're familiar with? You don't want to bring them to a life of abject poverty. You must want your people to succeed, to thrive, right?" He straightened, crossing his arms. "They'll need investment to help them build, to develop, to form a vibrant economy. And we'll need their technical expertise. It's a win-win situation."

"If you had access to the System," I said slowly, "what would you do with it?"

He shrugged. "So much of our technology is built on sharing culture—sharing our thoughts, our opinions, our beliefs. You know that. But we're still limited. There are still aspects of our lives that are not connected. The System could help us reach the ultimate in connectivity. Can you imagine it? A world with no misunderstanding. When everyone's thoughts are connected, there can be no conflict."

"That's what we were told on Iamos," I said quietly. "That's what the geroi insisted we had. But there was still conflict."

He pressed his lips together thoughtfully. "You would know best, of course. But we would still like to help you. We'd like to learn from you. And we'd like to invest in your future. I hope you'll give it some consideration." He handed me a small piece of paper and started to turn to leave.

"Wait," Mariyah said abruptly. He looked at her curiously. "If you're with GalaX, why seek Nadin out here? Why not just come over to the Randall-Torreses' house where you could talk more privately?"

Preston looked amused. "There's nothing I fear discussing in public, Miss Khan. I was here enjoying a meal, and so are you. We bumped into each other. Just a chance encounter, that's all." With that, he turned and strode back into the main part of the restaurant.

When he'd gone, Scylla let out a sigh that sounded more like a growl. She looked sidelong at Mariyah. "Did you buy that?"

"No," Mariyah said in a quiet, firm voice. "There's a reason he sought her out when Tamara and her moms weren't around. Whatever they're up to, they don't want them knowing about it."

"He knew who all of us were," Scylla pointed out. "That was a little creepy."

"Maybe he recognized us because of Tamara. If he really is

with GalaX, it wouldn't be completely out of the realm of possibility."

"Hmm."

I looked down at the small paper in my hand. It was covered in writing I couldn't read. "What is this?"

Mariyah took it, turning it over between her fingers. "His business card. So you can get in touch with him after you 'give it some consideration'." She made a gesture as she said this, two fingers of her free hand bending in the air.

"Do you think I should?"

Scylla let out a long breath. "I don't know. I didn't really trust that guy. But I trust GSAF even less."

"What about Henry's people?" I suggested.

She hesitated, twisting a red bracelet entwined around her left wrist. "I don't know what to say about that. Six months ago I would have told you to just go with Henry, but now I'm not sure. Things have been changing since Isaak's been back. The momentum just feels... lost." She sighed. "Maybe it's time to move on from Free Mars. Do what Preston said and start focusing on a more unified future. I wouldn't help GSAF, but GalaX might be all right. Tamara's moms work for them, after all. It wouldn't feel like a total surrender."

I frowned, chewing on the inside of my cheek. On the one hand, Preston was right—we would need help when we settled here. But I didn't like the fact that all these various factions seemed more concerned with the System than they were with the people behind it. The Elytherioi had denounced use of the System almost entirely. They constantly pointed out how easy it was to deceive a mind that was reliant on it. Had GalaX figured that out as well? Were they genuinely motivated by a desire to improve the lives of everyday people with this technology? Or, like the *geroi*, had it become about control?

The System had done so much for Iamos. It held our collective knowledge of the ages; it allowed us to communicate and even travel instantly. It detected anomalies in our bodies and regulated our body functions, kept us comfortable and healthy in a time when the ravages of our planet otherwise could have killed even more. But it also manipulated our minds in ways we never consciously realized—and even kept us from seeing things that were right in front of us, depending on who was controlling it. Though it had nearly killed me to be disconnected from it, now I wasn't sure I could go back to it.

The more I thought about it, the more I felt that Henry was right. Maybe the System did belong in the past. If I could keep it from coming to Mars, maybe that was what I should do.

"We're going to Elytherios in one week," I said. "If there is a working postern there and we're able to access it, we won't need GSAF. And we won't need GalaX, either."

"So that's your decision, then? We're sticking with Henry?" Scylla asked.

I nodded. "That's my decision."

Come what may.

CHAPTER 11

- i s a a k -

"SO, WHERE ARE WE GOING?" TAMARA ASKED AS WE STARTED UP the stairs from the ferry docks to the boardwalk. "Ivan's?"

"I was kind of thinking somewhere a little nicer than Ivan's," I said. She looked at me in surprise, and I rubbed the back of my neck. "Like Sur La Table?"

Tamara's eyebrows rose. "Are you sure?"

I shrugged. "Yeah. It's supposed to be good, right?"

"Yeah, but... it's really hard to get a seat there."

"That's okay. I made reservations." I grinned at her, hoping that would make her frown dissipate. I knew what she was thinking. It wasn't about whether we could get a seat or not—she was concerned about the expense. But I refused to let her worry about that. We were going to have one nice night out, and I wasn't going to let her split the bill with me, either. Now that I wasn't having to save for a palmtop, I could afford to splurge on one dinner.

She gave me a tight smile and pulled down the brim of her hat before taking my outstretched hand. A little thrill ran through me once more. *This is real. It's really happening.* I hoped my hand didn't feel too clammy. Just nerves, I told myself. I'd get used to it soon enough, I was sure. That made the thrill rush through me again.

We walked quietly down the boardwalk, and I found my eyes started lingering on all the different shops and restaurants we passed—more new than old, it seemed. I supposed it was hard to keep a business going, especially with rent as high as it must be here. Napoleon's ice cream parlor was still there, at least. And Ivan's must still be open, based on what Tamara had said earlier. The typical bustle of tourists seemed a bit more subdued than usual, but it was a Sunday night, after all.

It wasn't until we passed the fourth police officer standing on a corner or on the front stoop of a shop that I realized there were a hell of a lot of cops out tonight.

I leaned close to Tamara, murmuring, "Is there some kind of sting operation going on?"

She jumped at my voice in her ear, making me flush. I hadn't meant to startle her. "Huh?" she said.

I gestured with my right hand—which also happened to be the hand holding hers, so I kind of dragged her hand along with mine. "The cops," I whispered.

"Oh," she said. "No, that's pretty normal these days. Heightened security in heavy traffic areas. Just in case."

"Just in case," I repeated. "Like the curfew?"

She nodded, frowning. "Right. We'll need to make sure to get you home in time for that."

"Don't worry about it," I said in what I hoped was a cheerful voice. I didn't want this night to be overshadowed with worry about all this going on around us. "We've got plenty of time."

Sur La Table was located at the north end of the boardwalk, past the harbor and the more touristy sections, perched on pylons over the edge of the bay. Waves lapped picturesquely against the restaurant's side as Tamara and I approached, their white foam illuminated by the lights from the boardwalk.

I held open the door for Tamara, then followed her inside. The restaurant was dimly lit, with walls painted a burgundy color. The whole west wall was made of glass, which during the day probably made for a lovely view of the bay. By now it was dark enough that the windows effectively turned the wall into a floor-to-ceiling mirror.

"Do you have a reservation?" asked the maître d' as the door swung closed behind me.

"Yes, a table for two for Erick Gomez," I replied. Tamara looked at me in surprise, and I added under my breath, "Figured better safe than sorry."

"Ah, yes," the maître d' said. "The private table. Right this way."

I flushed as Tamara glanced inquisitively at me. "To avoid the paparazzi," I explained as we followed the maître d' to the back of the restaurant. On either side of the large windowed wall, a small nook jutted out over the water, boxed in on one side by an angled window and the other by a wall. There was one small table in each of these nooks, and the maître d' led us to the one on the left. From here we wouldn't be able to be seen by any of the other patrons unless they actually approached our table.

Tamara thanked the man before taking the chair in the rear of the nook. I sat across from her, my back to the rest of the dining room. The maître d' handed us each a menu before going on his way.

"That was so thoughtful, Isaak," Tamara said, removing her hat and shaking her hair out.

I beamed. "No problem. It'll be nice not to be stared at for once."

I flipped open the menu, glancing it over. Almost every option had meat, and a price tag to match.

"I can pay for mine," Tamara said, watching me with a frown.

"No."

"But we always used to split," she protested.

Yeah, but that was *before*. When we were just friends. I tried to say as much, but my tongue felt like lead. "Tonight is special," I finally managed. "To make up for missing the museum opening."

She sighed, twisting the braid of red yarn around her wrist. Desperate to change the subject, I said, "So what's the story about those bracelets? I saw Henry and Scylla wearing them, too."

"Oh, these?" She looked down at her hand, seeming wistful for a moment. "It's about you, actually."

"Me?"

"Yeah. Did your mom tell you what all went on when you were gone?"

"No. No one's told me anything. I've kind of guessed some of it, like you and Henry being famous all of a sudden. But he didn't seem to want to talk about it yesterday."

She colored. "Yeah. It's kind of a long story. We, uh... we thought GSAF had arrested you. And that they were holding you prisoner somewhere secret for all that time. We didn't know anything about... Iamos. Or any of that. So it was the only thing that made sense."

"Of course," I said quietly. "It's what I would have thought if the positions had been reversed."

"Right. So as time passed and no one from GSAF would give us any information about you, we thought they were covering something up. Well, I guess they were, in a way. But not what we thought. So Scylla came up with the idea for putting public pressure on them by having protests. And she made these little bracelets for us to wear as like..." She trailed off, picking at the yarn and shrugging. "Like a symbol, I guess. That's what it turned into, anyway."

"So all of this was Scylla's idea? How did Henry wind up as the leader, then?"

She grimaced. "Um... you know how Henry kind of... doesn't know how to back off when he needs to back off? Like about the government and conspiracy theories and stuff."

I rolled my eyes. I knew all too well. He practically lived in detention because of it back when we were at the Academy.

"He got on Joseph Condor's bad side. Like, he kept poking at him when they'd try to break up our protests. And then I guess he tried to hack GSAF—"

"What?" I hissed.

"He was desperate to find you, Isaak," Tamara said quickly, like she felt she needed to justify Henry's actions. "He was convinced they'd done something to you. We all were. Joseph Condor kept trying to get him to back off—he even pulled some strings to get him expelled from the Academy—"

I shook my head, squeezing my eyes shut. Dammit. We'd only had one year left. He'd only needed to hang in there one more year. Why did he have to push so much? How did he manage to get in so much trouble without me to rein him in?

No, this was my fault. It wasn't just that I wasn't there. I'd driven him to this desperation by going through that postern. Why hadn't I thought of any of this before I'd just gone charging in?

"—but Henry wouldn't give up. Then Joseph Condor blackmailed him—"

I looked up at her, trying to ignore the throbbing of my temples. "What did he blackmail him about?"

"Um." It looked like the color had drained out of her face, but it was hard to tell in this dimly lit restaurant. "I'm not sure. Anyway, I guess Condor figured that if he couldn't get him to back off GSAF, he'd get him to join them. So Henry worked for GSAF for a little while."

My mouth opened involuntarily. "Are you kidding me?"

She shook her head. "Nope. They had him working on the System."

The pieces clicked into place. "That's how he knew about it to blow the whistle."

"Right. He saw video of you on it. He thought it was proof that GSAF had you. We didn't know about the Iamoi then. GSAF didn't release any of that info until you came back." She sighed. "And I guess you know the rest from there."

I looked down blankly at the menu. "So basically Henry spent the last two annums getting in trouble."

Tamara chewed on her lip quietly. "Basically."

"I'm glad he had you to take care of him," I said. "I'm sure you held him back some. Who knows how much worse it would have been if you weren't there?"

She stared at me, her jaw slightly askew, the lines on her forehead getting progressively deeper. I don't know how she was planning to respond, though, because just then our waitress appeared, an older woman with brown hair graying at the temples, pulled back in a sleek bun.

"Oh, aren't you two adorable," she said in such a familial way that she seemed out of place in a restaurant like Sur La Table. Aside from her pressed clothes and her impeccable bun, everything about her seemed a better fit for Ivan's than a fancy French restaurant. "First date?"

My mouth went dry. I glanced at Tamara in a panic before mumbling, "Uh, yeah." Tamara laughed awkwardly, her face red, staring down at the table.

The waitress chuckled. "All right, all right, I won't embarrass you anymore. What can I get started for you?"

We ordered and then sat silently for several minutes. I stared into my reflection in the tall window, vaguely hoping that maybe a giant sneaker wave would suddenly break through the glass and sweep me out to sea. Why did I feel so self-conscious? I'd felt more awkward on this date than happy—like I was just going through the motions, playing a VR sim about being on a date than actually being on one. Was that normal? Were all first dates this uncomfortable? Maybe they were. I wasn't exactly drowning in dating experience as a comparison. I guess I'd just assumed this would be easier, since Tamara and I had been friends for so long. But maybe that had been a silly assumption.

I leaned back in my chair, glancing around the restaurant as much as I dared while still trying to keep my face hidden. The waitress hadn't seemed to recognize Tamara or me, but she looked older than my mom. Maybe she was like Erick and didn't "pay much attention to popular media." I wanted to play it safe, just in case.

Four people sat at the table closest to us. One of them, a black girl with long, straight dark hair glanced in my direction. My heart stopped for just a second as I thought it was Nadin— what was she doing here? Then she laughed, turning back to her friends, and I realized that it wasn't her. Of course it wasn't. Scylla wouldn't let her go off on her own, and there was no way Scylla would come to a restaurant like this, where the menu was mostly meat and/or cheese.

"I almost didn't recognize Nadin in that wig," I said to Tamara, sitting forward in my chair again.

"Yeah?" She grinned. "Good. No one seemed to recognize her when we went shopping this afternoon. Hopefully now she won't be stuck at my moms' house all the time."

"It was weird to see her in normal clothes. They looked good on her, though." I flushed as I realized what I was saying. *What the hell, Isaak?* I sounded like a perv.

Tamara just laughed, though. "It seems like you guys got really close."

Even my ears were hot. "Not really. I haven't known her that long."

"Oh," Tamara said, nodding.

"Do you think you're going to keep wearing those bracelets?" I said, blurting out the first thing that came to mind to steer the subject away from Nadin—which seemed extra ridiculous in retrospect, since I was the one who'd brought her up to begin with. "Since I'm back and everything?"

Tamara looked down at her wrist thoughtfully. "I think so. It... kind of turned into something more than how it started."

"Yeah," I said quietly, looking at my reflection in the window again. "I get that."

The waitress returned with our food then, sparing me from having to come up with any more conversation—and any more ways to put my foot in my mouth.

When we reached the stairs to the ferry docks, Tamara turned. "You don't have to come all the way back over to Herschel. I can get home from here," she said.

"Are you sure?" I asked, furrowing my brow.

"Yeah. You want to get back to your house before curfew. Besides, you already paid for one ticket tonight, no point paying for a second. I at least have an annual pass."

"Okay," I said.

We stood there staring at each other for a moment. Half a second too late, it occurred to me that I should probably kiss her good night. But I didn't and the moment passed. Tamara gave me an awkward half-wave.

"Well, I guess I'll see you this weekend, right?" she said with a smile.

"Yeah," I said, my face burning.

"I had fun tonight," said Tamara.

"We should do it again sometime."

"Yeah."

She waved again, turning and walking down the stairs. I watched her go before moving to pull my palmtop out of my pocket to text Erick to come pick me up. I was ready for this evening to be over.

As we drove up our street, I noticed a new car parked in front of our house, a Tesla SUV in an unnatural shade of neon blue. Even in the dark, it seemed to glow. Erick frowned as we pulled past it into the driveway.

"Company?" I asked, my stomach flopping nervously. The few photographers that had still been congregated outside our house when Erick and I left—they seemed to be losing interest as each day passed—had vanished by now, either of their own volition or chased off by the cops. I couldn't picture Joseph Condor or any of his goons driving a vehicle that color, but I couldn't think of who else it could be.

Erick just grunted as he opened the door to the garage.

I could hear voices from down the hall as I came into the kitchen, loud but not angry. I heard Celeste laugh, high and boisterous, and then a low, softer chuckle. A man's voice. I followed the sounds and found Mom standing in the doorway to Celeste's room, her arms folded, a thoughtful expression on her face. She turned as I approached, smiling tightly. "Did you have a good... dinner?" she asked, casually sidestepping the word *date*.

I shrugged, looking past her into Celeste's room. In the middle of the room, on the low table she sat at to draw or work on her homework, she'd spread out the new LEGO Disney set. It was pretty much put together now—it barely fit on the tabletop. She knelt in front of it, placing a figurine on the balcony of the castle. Across from her, Dad sat cross-legged, a plastic baggie in his hands. He pulled another figurine out, squinting at it. "And where does this bear go?"

"In the woods, obviously," Celeste said, taking it from him.

"Oh, of course. My mistake," Dad said with another chuckle. I smiled in spite of myself. Here was a sight I never thought I'd see again. Not in a million years. Dad here, with Celeste. Just... being our dad.

"It's getting late," Mom said, her voice soft. "Remember what I said, Celeste?"

Celeste looked up from her LEGOs with disappointment. "Aw, Mom."

"I said you could stay up until Isaak got home, remember? That was our promise."

"I need to get going, anyway," Dad said, getting to his feet, shaking his legs out with an audible *crack* of his knees. "Gotta make curfew and all." His voice was sarcastic, and he rolled his eyes like a kid whose mom had told him he needed to be home in time for dinner.

"Will you come back tomorrow?"

"We'll see," Mom said quickly, cutting off whatever Dad had been starting to say.

Mom escorted him to the door, but to my surprise, she didn't just open the door and shoo him out. She quietly followed him into the front garden.

I glanced down the hall back into the family room. I could just see the corner of the large armchair Erick had brought with him, replacing our old beat-up faux-leather one. Erick was sitting in it, staring off into the middle distance with a dark expression on his face.

Quietly I crept into my bedroom, not turning the light on in the hopes they wouldn't see me, not even bothering to close the door to the hall. I carefully snaked my hand under the closed blinds and cracked the window open. Cold night air seeped into my bedroom, and on it, my parents' voices. I sank down to the floor beside the window, listening.

"You can't keep coming here, Raymond," Mom was saying, her voice hushed and serious.

"Why not? I have every right to spend time with my children."

"Celeste is already getting attached to you. What am I going to do when you get bored with playing with her every day and she doesn't understand why her dad isn't coming around anymore?"

Dad let out an exasperated sigh. "Why do you just assume I'm going to get bored?"

"Because you always do," Mom said. "I know you, Raymond. In case you forgot, I was married to you for over fifteen years."

"Exactly. That's a lot of history to just throw away." His voice changed now, a pleading tone coloring the edges of his words. "Everything could be different now, Jess. Everything that's happened this last month, it's been so impossible. It seems like... anything could happen now, you know what I mean? Maybe even us."

Mom didn't say anything for a long minute. I quietly got up on my knees and lifted one slat of my blinds to peek out at them. Dad had put his hands on Mom's shoulders and was gazing down into her eyes. My heart stopped as for just one instant I thought they might kiss.

And for just one instant, my brain whispered, *But what about Erick?*

Then Mom stepped away from him, shaking her head. "It won't work."

"Maybe it will this time!"

She whirled on him, her voice breaking. "It *won't*. You always do this, Raymond. You get some money and everything is coming up roses. Then you spend it and everything goes to hell in a handbasket. I'm done with that. I decided I was done with that years ago. Too much time has passed to go back. I have a new life now, and I have a new husband. I love him." She paused, then added, slowly, deliberately, every word full of meaning, "And I *don't* love you. So please... It's time to move on."

Dad's face crumpled like it was a piece of paper she'd crushed with her fist. Mom came back into the house without another word. After a moment, Dad opened the door to the blue Tesla—I dimly registered that it must be his, but my mind was too overwhelmed to question how such an expensive car could be his—and disappeared as well.

I turned on the lamp on my nightstand, sitting at the foot of my bed and looking down at my hands. I could hear Mom and Erick talking after she came back in, their voices too low for me to pick out any words. Then there was the sound of crisp footsteps on the tile floor. I looked up as she passed my door. She noticed me staring at her and paused in the hallway.

"Isaak?" she asked in confusion. Then a second later my closed blinds clattered as a gust of wind whistled through the window, still open a crack. She sighed and came in, pushing the door closed behind her but not latching it. "Were you listening?"

I shrugged. "Mom, what if Dad has changed? What if things would be different this time?"

She sighed. "I know how hard this must be for you, *mijo*. I've seen you hurting over the years. Saw the way his... disappearance affected you. And then coming back here to find everything changed. I'm so proud of how you've been handling all this, even though I know it has to be killing you to try to get your life back when everyone else has moved on." She put her hand on my knee. "But I've given him too many chances already. So many. As long as you've been alive, I've been giving him chances. You're only just now getting to be old enough to see. People like Raymond don't change. He's being kind now, but this is just the upswing. When the fallout comes, you wouldn't want to be there."

I didn't respond, and finally she stood, leaving me alone in my room. She closed the door tightly behind her.

"*Too much time has passed to go back.*" Maybe she was right. And not just about herself and Dad.

Sighing, I unplugged my Speculus set and powered it on. I'd spent the afternoon getting the set charged and all the updates installed, linking up my old account and updating my figuscan, but I hadn't had a chance to check the messages that had piled up over the last two annums. The home menu loaded as I slipped the set over my eyes and I balked. Seven thousand, nine hundred and eighty-four messages, and that wasn't counting what was in the spam folder. I didn't want to face this tonight.

I flicked the messages bubble away and was about to turn the system off when I noticed a news bubble hovering to my right. *Long-missing Tierra Nueva man reveals all,* it said.

My stomach churned again. I had a terrible, terrible feeling that I knew what this vid clip was going to be. Gritting my teeth, I reached out and tapped it.

The chatspace around me melted into a generic living room-style set, with a couple chairs and couches placed around in a circle so the viewer would feel like they were part of a conversation—even though, since this was prerecorded, I couldn't interact with anyone. In one of the chairs, Nancy Ramirez's figuscan flickered into being. "Welcome back to *Downstream*. I'm excited to introduce you to tonight's special guest: a man who just a few years ago was an ordinary employee at the Victoriya shoe factory, but who now suddenly finds himself thrust into the limelight and a completely different world than the one he vanished from so mysteriously, along with his son. Please welcome Raymond Contreras."

I was going to be sick. Straight up. A figuscan of Dad appeared in the chair next to Nancy, dressed in the same clothes he was wearing last night when he brought the new Speculus sets and the new palmtop, and Celeste's LEGO playset. He smiled charmingly, looking straight at me as if we were on chat with each other, as if this wasn't a prerecorded interview. All around me comment notifications pinged, bubbles in the air around Nancy and my dad with remarks from other viewers. I swiped them away without looking. I just sat there, mute and numb, as my dad told all. All about the postern. All about the Iamoi.

All about Elytherios.

In a panic, I turned off the interview and pulled up a search window for any news about what may have happened since this video. It was like my worst nightmare come to life: *Interview with returned factory worker sparks treasure rush. A lost city in the Elysium Mountains. Experts call the revelation of Iamoan city the Troy of the twenty-first century.* I clenched my fist. Dammit, Dad! This interview had turned everyone's attention to Elytherios! How were we supposed to get there now and look for the postern?

We weren't. That was the bottom line. Just scanning the articles I'd found revealed that the governor of Elysium province had already closed off all access to the mountain range. No one was getting anywhere near those mountains apart from GSAF.

That was it. Nadin's last hope of getting to a postern and securing the link to her time without GSAF had been neatly crushed by my dad and his big mouth.

I sank down onto my bed, slowly removing my Speculus set from my head. A large part of me wanted to hurl it across my room, smash it to bits, but my more practical side won out. I finally had my lifeline back. I couldn't just throw it away. But what was the cost? Hadn't Dad even thought for a second what revealing this information to the public was going to mean? The people in Elytherios had gone out of their way to help him even though they hadn't known him from a load of hay. None of them could understand a word he said, but they still fed him and sheltered him and kept him safe from the *geroi*. And he repaid them by setting looters on their city. And the worst part was? I could already hear his justification ringing in my ears. *"They're not there anymore! It's just empty ruins now! This isn't hurting anyone!"* He couldn't have known that keeping those ruins intact might have been those people's only hope of survival.

No. He didn't think. That was all there was to it. He didn't think about anything apart from *Downstream* offering him money. That was *all* he ever thought about—what would benefit him here and now. I wondered how much they'd given him. Whatever it was, he'd burn through it in a week. Not worth the trade-off of potentially millions of lives.

Mom was right. Of course she was right. I should have listened to her from the beginning. Why was I so reluctant to believe her about him?

Because he's your dad, a small voice whispered glumly in my ear.

I shrugged the voice away and reached for my palmtop. Tamara hadn't known about this at dinner, obviously, or she would have said something. Henry and the others probably didn't know, either. Better for them to learn now than later. We were going to have to figure something out, some way to help Nadin get back to Iamos.

I just had no clue how.

CHAPTER 12

- n a d i n -

THE FIVE OF US SAT SILENTLY IN BRYN AND DELIA'S LIVING ROOM. I could feel everyone looking at me, but I couldn't bear to look back at them. Not yet. I needed to compose myself. I found myself staring at the coffee table between the two couches. It was made of white wood, but the center of the tabletop was glass, revealing a small cabinet underneath that was full of fine white sand. A variety of seashells were nestled on top of the sand. My eyes lingered on a small, round shell with a notch broken into it on one side. There was the delicate imprint of a feathery five-petaled flower in the center. I wondered what kind of creature left this shell. It must be from Simos... from Earth.

Scylla breathed out heavily. "All right, then. So we can't get to Elysium. What now?"

Henry shook his head. He sat slumped leaning forward on his elbows, looking down at his hands. "We look for another Iamoi site. One that GSAF doesn't know about, hopefully. And we try to beat them there."

"That could take months," I protested.

"Maybe not," Tamara said. "We have maps you could look at. We know where your citidome was compared to Tierra Nueva. And we know where Elytherios was, too. Could you use that to pinpoint where the other citidomes were?"

I frowned, folding my arms and resisting the urge to curl in on myself. "Possibly. But who knows what could be built over any of them now? If there were no visible signs of the citidomes from the surface when your people colonized here, then all remnants of our settlements must be deep underground. The underground portion of Hope Renewed is at least partially accessible, according to Isaak, but I can't guarantee that any of the others would be. Whatever natural forces caused the destruction of our cities"—I swallowed, trying to choke down the bile churning in my stomach—"may have also destroyed the underground areas as well."

"Or made them inaccessible without major excavation equipment," said Isaak.

"We don't have time to look for another postern. Especially when there's no guarantee that we will find one at all," I said glumly. "I'm just going to have to work with GSAF."

All four of them shouted over the top of each other, various protestations that made me wince.

"What else am I supposed to do?" I argued, raising my voice to be heard over them. "I have no other viable option!"

"We have GalaX," Scylla pointed out.

Tamara's face darkened. She and her mothers had had a long conversation about it this morning before Isaak and the others came to the house. Mariyah had told Tamara about our encounter with Geoff Preston at Lal Qila when she got back to her dorm last night, after Scylla and I had left the island. Neither Bryn nor Delia had ever heard of Geoff Preston. "*Granted, we haven't worked at GalaX itself for almost ten years now,*" Delia had said this morning. "*There's sure to be some new people there now, especially since Mister Kimbal passed on. But you'd think if he was high up enough to be in a position to offer you a deal, we'd know him.*"

Bryn had promised to do some digging to find out who he was and if his offer was legitimate or not. But in the meantime, their suspicion compounded my own. I had no intention of making a bargain with a shadow figure if there was no guarantee he could deliver what he'd promised.

"I don't trust Preston," I said finally. "I don't want to make any deals with him until we know who he really is."

"Tam's moms aside, I wouldn't necessarily trust GalaX anyway," Henry added. "There were GalaX contractors working with GSAF on the System when I was there. I don't know how entangled they are with them."

Scylla frowned but didn't argue.

After a moment, Henry said, almost reluctantly, "What about Wyatt? He's helped us before."

Isaak made a noise of disgust in the back of his throat. "Wyatt *Ponsford*? You've got to be kidding me, Henry."

Henry shrugged. "Things have changed."

Isaak looked away at Henry's words, like they affected him more than Henry had meant them to. I felt a twinge of sympathy—I didn't know how long it was going to take Isaak to get used to the changes that had occurred while he'd been gone, but he clearly wasn't there yet. I was grateful I wouldn't have to worry about that. The world I left behind wouldn't change while I was gone. There wouldn't be time for it to. It was *me* who would be changed when I returned.

If I returned.

"We can't ask Wyatt," Tamara said. "You're right, he has helped us before, but this is too much to ask. This could destroy his entire family."

"But—" Henry began, but Tamara cut him off.

"It's too dangerous. This is turning into 2073 all over again." Her words made Isaak flinch. "The government is bound to be watching us all again after Saturday. Am I right?"

Henry refused to meet her gaze. "There were some suits outside my apartment this morning. I think I gave them the slip before coming over here, though," he muttered.

"See? We're not going through that again. Condor's obsessed with you, and I'm not going to provoke him. Going to Elysium on our own time before GSAF knew about it would have been one thing. But if we ask Wyatt to sneak Nadin into a government-controlled area, that will be outright breaking the law. The only reason you're not in prison right now—or *worse*—is because his mom gave you amnesty. We're not throwing that all away, Henry."

I watched Isaak as Tamara spoke, her voice shaking with fervor. He looked miserable. It was obvious he blamed himself for GSAF's behavior toward Henry and the others. Everything that had happened to his friends since he'd found the postern to Iamos had been tied to that singular event, and the guilt from it was written across his face. A large part of me longed to reach across the coffee table and squeeze his hand, offer him some comfort. But I kept my hands in my lap. This wasn't my place.

"No," I said, shaking my head firmly. "We can't go to anyone else for help. It's too dangerous for everyone. I have to handle this. I'm just going to have to work with GSAF."

"But Nadin," Isaak said. His brown eyes met mine, holding them, making my insides churn. "You can't let them have the System."

"I'll try to find another way," I said, looking away from him. "But it may come down to that. I won't endanger anyone else."

"Nadin," he said imploringly. "Please."

I kept my eyes riveted on my feet. "There's nothing else I can do, Isaak. I'm sorry."

I didn't tell Bryn why I asked her to call Kate Ponsford for me. I'm sure she must have guessed, based on the things Tamara had said in front of her and Delia, but she said nothing, simply pulling out her palmtop, tapping a few things on the screen, and then handing it to me. I wasn't sure what to expect, but when Kate's voice came through the palmtop's speakers I realized it was not unlike using the System's voice comms.

I could still hear Isaak begging me to reconsider echoing through my mind as I asked her to meet with me—privately, without Joseph Condor present. It had been a gamble, I knew, but to my relief she'd agreed. There was no turning back now.

I was standing on the front step when the car pulled into the circular drive. A nondescript man in one of the black suits I'd come to recognize over the past week here opened the door to the vehicle for me, and I slipped into the backseat. I expected the car to take us down the hill toward the capitol building beside the river, but to my surprise it turned in a different direction. We rose higher into the hills as the street wound between more villas, larger and more opulent than Bryn and Delia's. We hadn't driven very far when the car turned again down a narrow drive closed off from the main street by a large metal gate that opened when the car approached. We continued down the drive a short distance before stopping in front of a grand brick villa.

My escort opened my door again and led me inside, up a wide spiral staircase and through a heavy wooden door. Kate was waiting for me inside. She nodded at the man who'd accompanied me. He nodded back and left, closing the door behind him.

"Hello, Nadin," Kate said once the man was gone. "How have you been finding Mars? Have you been enjoying your time in Tierra Nueva? I saw that you've been to Yellowknife Bay. I always enjoy boating on the Delta."

"It's lovely," I said automatically. "But that's not why I am here. Please pardon me for not lingering on pleasantries."

"Of course. Is there something you need?"

"Yes. I'm sure you must have gathered from what I said to you earlier that what I wanted to speak to you about requires... discretion." I hoped I was using that word correctly.

"Indeed," said Kate. "You said you needed help with something."

"Yes. Governor Ponsford, you have been kind to me since I've been here. You brought me to Bryn and Delia, who have been wonderful hosts. And you've treated me with respect. Can I be honest with you?"

"Of course, Nadin," she said, her brows furrowing.

I swallowed, squaring my shoulders. Be a *gerouin*. "I am concerned about your people's interest in the System. It's true that it has done much for my people to make our lives easier. But many of the parts of it that were beneficial to us your people already have, through your palmtops and your Speculus. Which makes me concerned that the reason your people want the System is for the *not* beneficial aspects."

Kate folded her hands on her desk. "I'm not sure what you mean."

"I'm afraid maybe you are," I said. "The System works by directly interfacing with our brains. In that way, a mind can be controlled. I believed that we had freedom on Iamos, at least as much as could be expected on a world on the cusp of destruction. But then I came to realize that a mind reliant on the System could also be tricked by it." I took a deep breath. "Your world is beautiful, Governor Ponsford. You have things here we could never dream of on Iamos. And I don't just mean the water and the thick atmosphere." I smiled wryly. "I mean music. Art. Individuality. Your people are free to be themselves, without expectations of rigid conformity. But the System is *designed* for conformity. With it, the *geroi* were able to shape the society they wanted. We were once more like you, I think... but in the course of just one hundred years, all of that was lost. I'm afraid that if I give you this technology, your people will end up the same way."

I sat back in my seat, hoping that I had expressed myself properly, that I'd used all the right words. That she would *understand*.

She sighed, looking down at her folded hands, her face drawn. "I understand your concern," she said slowly. My heart sank, knowing that there was a *but* to follow. There would be no deal without the System.

But then she shocked me by saying, "And I agree with you." Before I could react, though, she added, "But I'm just one person. There's only so much I can do." She held my eyes, her gaze intense. "But as long as I'm governor, I'll do what I can to stop the System from used in our time."

I gasped. "Truly? Governor Ponsford, I can't thank you enough."

She shrugged. "I don't know how much that will be, though. But it may help if you could offer us some of your other technology. My primary interest has been in postern travel. Is that reliant on the System?"

"Only to a small extent. The Elytherioi use a much more limited version of the System to program their posterns. Perhaps something like that could be implemented here?"

Kate nodded. "I think that would be an appealing alternative. Instantaneous travel between vast distances is far beyond anything our scientists have been able to accomplish. If you were to offer us that technology, we might be able to broker the deal on that."

I started to agree, but then I paused—the System was only half of the reason I'd come here today. "I'm prepared to make that offer, but I can't speak for the rest of my people. I need to consult with them. At least with my partner and the scholar who was intended to come along with me here. We were inadvertently separated as we were leaving Iamos, but if I had access to a postern, bringing them here would only be a matter of moments. I would feel more comfortable negotiating if I had them here to confer with. I know you understand the difficulty of working unilaterally." I closed my eyes for a heartbeat, hoping that I'd used that word correctly.

She drummed her fingers on her desk, silently considering. After a long moment, she said, "If I were to give you access, you would only use the postern to bring those two people forward?"

"And one of your citizens, an old man named Emil. He was also supposed to return with us."

"That would be good for optics," she said in a low voice, seemingly more to herself than me. She met my eyes. "All right. I'll make the arrangements. I should be able to get you to the postern in the foothills in a few days. Does that work for you?"

I leapt to my feet, trying to resist the urge to throw my arms around her. "Yes! Thank you so much."

She smiled. "You're welcome. I'm hoping this will be the start of a productive negotiation session between our people."

I straightened my shoulders again, forcing myself to regain my composure. "I believe it will be," I said as coolly as I could manage.

"One last thing, Nadin," she went on softly. "Don't tell anyone about this."

I came up short. "No one?" I'd been eager to tell Isaak, at the very least. He'd argued with me so much about working with GSAF, but I'd been right after all. I'd managed to negotiate a concession out of GSAF that even he would be sure to be satisfied with. Having to keep my victory to myself seemed unbearable.

"Not until it's over," Kate urged me. "I don't want any... complications." I realized then that she meant Joseph Condor. I suspected he would not be pleased with the deal she'd made with me—clearly, the governor shared my concerns. Her gamble was that he wouldn't find out until it was too late.

I nodded my assent, and she shook my hand. I could wait. I could keep it secret for just a few days. And then this would all be over. Ceilos and Gitrin would be here, and everything would work out.

I tried to ignore the way my stomach wrenched at the thought of seeing Ceilos again. Everything would work out. I was sure of it.

Two days later, the doorbell rang when Bryn and Delia were at work. The first day I'd been here they had shown me how to use the small tablet in the entryway to check who was at the door before answering it, and to my surprise, I saw Wyatt standing there. I opened the door.

"Hey," he said with a smile. "You ready?"

"Ready for what?" I asked.

"To go get your friends."

I stared at him in confusion for a moment, thinking he meant Isaak and the others and wondering why we needed to go *get* them—they usually came here. Then I realized what he meant and my face grew hot. I'd been here ten days and was already thinking of these Martians as my friends before Ceilos and Gitrin. Ceilos' words from my dream echoed in my brain, and I struggled to keep them out. *That was just a dream,* I scolded myself. *He would never say anything so cruel to you. He is your partner.*

I nodded at Wyatt. "Yes. Just a moment."

I hurried upstairs to retrieve the posternkey from the drawer in my bedside table, and I tucked it into the satchel Tamara had bought for me the day we'd gone shopping for my clothing. As I passed the bathroom door, I caught my reflection in the mirror, looking pale and haggard. I ran my fingers through my hair, smoothing it, and took a deep breath to compose myself. I reached for my medallion around my neck, squeezing it for just an instant. Then I tucked it under my shirt and hurried back downstairs.

I followed him to his car, the white vehicle we'd taken the day he brought me here. When he'd climbed into the car beside me and his door was safely closed, I asked, "What are you doing here? Your mother told me not to tell anyone what we were planning... I assumed she would handle this herself."

"She's trying to keep a low profile," he said, his voice as low as mine had been, as though he were afraid that we might be overheard. "She's at the office as usual today. I'm her designated special agent. If everything goes smoothly, no one will know we were there except you, me, and the guard at the site. Well, I guess they'll figure it out when we get back. But it will be too late for them to do anything then." He grinned and held up his right hand, fingers crossed. I'd seen the others do this as well—I'd guessed it must be some Martian good luck gesture, so I crossed my own fingers as well. We needed all the luck we could get.

Wyatt programmed the coordinates into the vehicle's control panel and it began to pull out of the driveway. I watched as the trees and villas of these hills gave way to wider streets and concrete bustle of the city center. We drove in the same way that I'd taken to the capitol before, but this time we steered away from the tall building with its two towers and instead crossed the river on a large bridge. The car accelerated to match the pace of the other vehicles on the road, and soon we were leaving the city behind us, following the road into another set of hills. There were a few buildings scattered here and there, but no luxurious villas like there were along the coastal cliffs of Tierra Nueva. As we drove through this barren area, completely devoid of plant life save for a few scattered *fraouloi* here and there, I could see for the first time, now, how this was Iamos. The mountains around us were red, completely oxidized, finishing what had been started in my time. It was like a wasteland. The only difference was that blue, blue sky overhead, that atmosphere so thick that it completely obstructed Hamos from view.

I frowned, looking into that sky now. Through the upper part of the windshield, I could see an object in the sky. Much smaller than Hamos, and much less bright. Not quite round, more of an oblong shape. "Wyatt, what is that?" I asked, pointing.

He looked in confusion for a moment, not seeming to understand what I was gesturing to. "What, the moon?" he finally said.

"Maybe. That thing in the sky."

"Yeah, that's one of our moons. Phobos. Don't you recognize it?"

"No." I shook my head. "That was not there in my time. Did it come from your terraformation efforts? Like your space mirrors?"

"No, Phobos and Deimos have been there longer than we have. If they weren't there in your time, they must have shown up in between. Maybe they were drawn in from the asteroid belt."

"Maybe." I twisted the black ring on my right hand. It was strange that an asteroid would be visible in the sky, but not Hamos. "Everything is so different here."

"There's a long time in between your era and now. It's

incredible, honestly. I can't believe you guys invented time travel. I bet you've seen it all. How many time periods have you visited?"

"Only this one. And my own, of course. The time postern was only a theory until Isaak proved its concept."

Wyatt looked surprised. "I didn't realize that," he said. "So what do you think is going to happen now? Are the Iamoi going to become Time Lords?"

"I'm not sure," I admitted, shifting awkwardly in my seat. I hadn't thought about anything beyond the immediate goal of getting my people to Mars. But what if the *geroi* weren't satisfied to come here and leave it at that? What if they wanted to conquer other eras?

"There would have to be some kind of protocol, I suppose. To prevent people from using the technology in ways that could cause problems. Altering history would be extremely dangerous."

Wyatt nodded. "Right. We don't need to be opening rips in the time-space continuum. But by the same token, what if you're *supposed* to go to another time? Obviously Isaak was, or else we wouldn't all be sitting here now. You'd have to know when you *need* to use it and when you shouldn't."

My head was starting to hurt. Why hadn't I considered any of these implications when Gitrin and I were working on the time postern together? All I'd thought about was what would be beneficial to us, not the consequences it might have not only for our world, but for Simos and Hamos as well.

Wyatt was talking about the different eras of Earth's history that he would like to visit if he could, but I was only half listening—partly because I had absolutely no clue what he was talking about, and partly because my own worry was occupying the larger portion of my mind now.

Soon we turned off the main highway and onto a smaller, narrower road. I drew in my breath as the car passed into an open space between two hills and I could see the whole of Tierra Nueva, and beyond it the bay. If I'd thought the view was beautiful from Bryn and Delia's home, I could never have been prepared for this. I could see Herschel Island, a crescent-shaped land formation in the water, and beyond it a smaller, similarly-shaped formation Tamara had told me was called Knobel Island. The sea stretched into the horizon, fading out into a blue-green blur where it touched the sky. *So much water.* In the foreground, Tierra Nueva filled the valley, bisected by shining silver rivers. The tops of the tall towers of GSAF and the building where Tamara's mothers worked—AresTec—soared high above the rest of the city. On the side of the valley the car was approaching from above, structures with smokestacks atop them loomed, a hazy gray cloud hovering in the air above them. I suspected this was the source of the acrid smell I'd sometimes caught in the air while in the city.

Then it all disappeared from view, obscured by the massive red rocks around me.

We drove in silence for some time. Finally, the car began to slow, exiting the road and moving down a rough gravel path. The car shook and vibrated as we approached a sheer cliff face. I could see a door cut into the rock. Small mechanical devices—*drones*, Wyatt called them—buzzed around the opening. Wyatt withdrew his palmtop from his pocket and swiped his fingers across it a few times. The propellers on the drones began to stall, and they landed neatly around the doorway.

As the car came to a stop, a man in a black suit emerged from the door. "Good afternoon, Mister Ponsford," the man said when Wyatt got out of the car. He didn't acknowledge me, but the meaningful look he gave Wyatt almost made me think that perhaps that was arranged. I wasn't here, as it were.

"Do you have everything?" Wyatt asked me as I closed the car door behind me. I nodded, shrugging the straps of my bag over my shoulder and feeling the weight of the posternkey inside. My medallion was around my neck as always—I had everything I needed.

I followed Wyatt and the man in the suit through the door in the mountain. It was much dimmer in the cave than it had been outside, and I blinked as my eyes adjusted to the change in lighting. After a moment, my surroundings became clearer. We were in a tunnel that must have been part of the esotoi's dwelling level, based on its proximity to the surface. Artificial lighting had been added to the walls by the Martians, but I could see the dimly glowing remnants of our old phosphorescent designs on the walls. They would have once formed elaborate spiraled patterns, but most of the stones in the mosaics were gone now, leaving just a random jumble of blues and greens on the wall. I ran my finger sadly over one of the still-glowing stones. Suddenly I wasn't sure this was such a good idea. My stomach was starting to churn with dread of what I might find here under the mountain.

"This way, Nadin. We need to move quickly," Wyatt said, looking over his shoulder at me. He stopped walking when he saw my expression. "Are you okay?"

I opened my mouth to say that I was, but my voice wouldn't come.

He came over to where I was standing. "What's wrong?"

"Do you know what the rest of this tunnel looks like?" I finally managed to ask.

"I'm sorry, I don't. I've never been down here before." His eyes widened with comprehension. "Do you know this place?"

I tried to swallow, but my mouth was dry. "I believe this is part of the underground portion of my city."

"Oh," he said, not seeming to know how to respond.

"I didn't see any remnant of the citidome in the hills above this area," I said.

"There's not any. Um, that is... we haven't found anything. There are a lot of craters up there, so I'm assuming something might have hit it."

My eyes were burning. "Oh," I said, trying to sound nonchalant.

"Maybe not everything, though," he added quickly. "It's been thousands of years, and Mars has always been windy and dusty. Some of it might just be buried in the sand."

Destroyed by a falling meteor or buried in the sand. Did it really matter, the method of our cities' destruction? They were gone. So far gone that the modern inhabitants of this world hadn't even known we'd been there to begin with.

"Let's just get this over with," I said softly.

We followed the tunnel deeper into the mountain, past toppled columns and smashed glass doorways. Parts of the tunnel were flooded, and we had to step carefully through pools and puddles where the natural cave had reclaimed the *vi'in*, and any evidence of our past presence was barely visible. The canvas shoes I wore were waterproof, but one particularly deep puddle made water seep in over the top, soaking my socks and the hem of my pants.

Soon we had come to a large open chamber I recognized. It was a plaza, at the intersection of several *vi'i*. Water dripped from the ceiling of the cavern, and it had formed stalagmites all over the floor, uprooting our old mosaics and leaving them in broken pieces scattered throughout the area. In the center was the remnant of a fountain, a postern rising from it that would have once delivered water here.

This was the postern Isaak and I used the day we left Hope Renewed.

"Will this work?" Wyatt asked.

"Yes," I said. I knew all too well that it would.

I started to slip my satchel off my shoulder when the suited man escorting us said, "Afraid not."

I looked up at him in confusion. But before I could say anything, I heard footsteps on the stone floor of the cavern. *Many* footsteps.

An instant later, we were surrounded by men in black armor, brandishing weapons. They surrounded Wyatt and me. And then a familiar figure pushed through the crowd, approaching me.

I squeezed my eyes closed. Kate's plan had failed.

"Mister Condor, what are you doing here?" Wyatt said, his voice remarkably even.

"I think the question is, what are *you* doing here?" Joseph Condor responded, his arms folded.

"We have permission to be here. From the governor," I said, my grip on my satchel tightening.

"I'm afraid not," Joseph replied, leveling his blue eyes on me.

"Kate Ponsford has been relieved of her duties. She is no longer governor of Aeolis Province, effective immediately."

"What? Why?" Wyatt burst out.

"She's being indicted on suspicion of corruption, conspiracy and treason," Joseph said. "And I suggest you cooperate before you're charged with the same."

Wyatt's face blanched.

Joseph turned to me. "I'm going to need you to come with me now, *kyrin*."

I squared my shoulders stubbornly and raised my chin. "Not until I'm allowed to activate this postern."

He scoffed. "You're not in a position to be making demands on me, *kyrin*. I am in control of this province now. GSAF has appointed me acting governor of this province. I'm afraid things are going to be different from now on. I'm not going to stand for a foreign envoy colluding with known enemies of the state. That could be considered an act of war. If you want a treaty between your people and ours, you're going to need to cooperate with GSAF from now on."

The cavern suddenly seemed very cold, the chill from my wet socks overpowering. It seemed to be turning me numb.

"Now let's go," Joseph said.

Wyatt and I followed him out of the broken remnants of my former home without a word.

CHAPTER 13

- i s a a k -

I GOT TO TAMARA'S HOUSE AS QUICKLY AS I COULD. MOM HAD gone back to work this week, so I was alone at the house when the text came in. In a panic, I'd found myself doing something I never would have expected: messaging Erick to ask him what I should do. He'd told me to take his truck, since he and Mom had carpooled over to Curiosity Bay in her sedan. I'd grabbed his fob off the hook in the kitchen and raced out, grateful for once to have that deathtrap of a vehicle in our driveway. To my relief, the throng of paparazzi had dissipated from outside the house—with news of Governor Ponsford's arrest, they had more important things to focus on. But I was still glad to not have to worry about taking the train and possibly being recognized.

Tamara opened the door just seconds after I rang the doorbell. "Thank God you're here," she cried, throwing her arms around me. I froze for a moment, arms rigidly at my side, uncertain how to react. The awkwardness of Saturday night's date played over and over again in my mind, paralyzing me.

"I'm sorry," she said, releasing me, her face red as a beet. Her eyes were almost as red. She'd clearly been crying for a while.

"Don't apologize," I said hollowly, trying to ignore the discomfort I was feeling. Why did this have to be so weird? Was it her or me? Or both of us?

"I shouldn't have—I just—I'm so glad you're safe. I didn't say everything in my text, just in case. It's not just Wyatt's mom. Henry's been arrested."

Her words shook all the other thoughts out of my mind. "What? Why?"

"Now that Wyatt's mom isn't governor anymore, Joseph Condor nullified his amnesty. They're prosecuting him for treason."

My knees wobbled, and I grabbed the door jamb for support. This was all my fault. Everything Henry had done—blowing the whistle about GSAF and the System, starting the Free Mars movement and crossing Condor repeatedly—it had been because of me. I had caused this, and now Henry could go to jail for the rest of his life because of it.

"There's got to be something we can do..." I started, but broke off when Scylla appeared in the entryway behind Tamara.

"You guys shouldn't stand there talking. They're going to be here any minute."

"Oh, right," Tamara said, swiping at her eyes with the ends of her long-sleeved t-shirt and ushering me inside.

"Who's going to be here?" I asked as she closed the door behind me.

"Condor is bringing Nadin back here to get her things. She's not allowed to stay here anymore."

"Wait a minute, she's not here?" I asked, panic filling my voice.

Tamara shook her head.

"Wyatt managed to get a text through to Tam before they confiscated his phone," Scylla explained. "Apparently she met with Kate Ponsford privately earlier this week to try to figure out a way to get to the time postern. None of us knew about it. They made some kind of deal where she could bring Ceilos and Gitrin here without having to divulge everything about the System. Someone at GSAF got wind of the deal and that's why Kate Ponsford's been ousted."

"And now Joseph Condor is governor," I said numbly. The way colonial government worked here, they might as well have named him king. The governor didn't answer to anyone apart from the GSAF Council back on Earth, who took their orders—at least nominally—from the UN. But considering the corruption I'd witnessed from the appointed government officials here on Mars, all the way down to when Condor had just been the Director of Land Use, I didn't think they were being overseen too carefully. As long as they kept the colonies in order, they seemed to have *carte blanche*.

"So what's going to happen to Nadin?" I asked.

"I don't know," said Tamara. "All I know is that she's being moved somewhere else."

"We can't just leave her alone with them," I protested.

"What are we supposed to do to prevent it, though?" Scylla said. "It would take an army to stop Joseph Condor at this point.

And I don't know where we're supposed to find one."

"What about your Free Mars people?"

"We're not an army," Scylla said, sounding utterly defeated. "We're just a bunch of college kids and socially awkward libertarians. We don't even have any weapons. Well, maybe the libertarians do, but the college kids don't. And Henry was the closest thing we had to a leader. I don't think I could get them to follow me."

"There's no time, anyway," Tamara said, looking out the patio door onto the veranda. "They're going to be here any minute."

As she spoke, a door opened somewhere else in the house. I jolted alert, expecting to see Joseph Condor and his army of suits, but instead, Bryn and Mama D rushed in.

"We got here as soon as we could, baby," Mama D said, hurrying over to Tamara and sweeping her into a hug.

"Are the rest of you all right?" Bryn asked.

"We're fine," Scylla said. "It's just Henry..."

"We're going to get him the best defense money can buy, don't you worry," Delia said emphatically, tufts of curly red hair falling out of her ponytail.

"But what about Nadin?" I asked, frustrated that no one seemed to be thinking of her. "Henry's not the only one in danger right now. We've got to get her away from Joseph Condor." As if on cue, I heard the slamming of a car door outside.

"Don't worry. I'll handle that," Bryn said, striding out of the living room. I trailed after her curiously, trying to stay out of sight of the front door. She'd flung the door open before I'd made it halfway across the living room.

"Step aside, Mrs. Torres," I heard Joseph Condor say.

Bryn didn't even flinch. "Randall-Torres. Do you have a warrant?"

"I don't need a warrant. I'm in charge of this province."

"I don't care if you're Alexander the Great. You're not coming into my house without a warrant," Bryn replied.

"Mrs. Torres—"

She raised her voice to talk over the top of him. "You may think you're above the law, Mr. Condor. And that might work for ordinary citizens. But I don't think you remember who I am. Who my family is. The connections we have. Your little power games aren't going to work with me the way they do with everyone else. You're. Not. Coming. Into. My. House."

I cringed, expecting Condor to arrest her next, and then what would we do? But to my surprise, after a short silence, I heard, "She has ten minutes. And if she's not back outside in those ten minutes, I will rip this door off its hinges."

There was no reply. A moment later, the door closed.

Delia brushed past me out of the living room and into the entryway, Scylla and Tamara on her heels. I hurried after them. Bryn was leaning against the closed front door, her eyes squeezed shut.

"You are a titan," Delia said, pulling her wife away from the door and into her arms. "An absolute madwoman. That was brilliant."

Bryn nodded. "I think I need to sit down." She looked up at Nadin, standing silently in the entryway, looking as shell-shocked as Bryn. "Are you all right?"

Nadin opened her mouth, but didn't seem to know how to respond. She glanced around at all of us. "I suppose I had better go get my things," she finally whispered.

"Let me help you," Tamara said, moving to her side.

Nadin shook her head. "It's all right. I need... a moment alone, I think."

"Where are they going to take you?" Scylla asked, her voice laden with worry.

"Joseph Condor said there is a place called the Plaza where I will be staying until further notice."

"What about Ceilos and the others?" I asked.

She avoided my gaze and shrugged, then turned to head up the stairs.

"Nadin, wait—" I started, but Mama D reached out to me.

"Give her some time, love."

How much time was I supposed to give her, though, when Joseph Condor was going to be ripping the door off its hinges in less than ten minutes? I wanted to argue, but I knew arguing with Mama D was about as effective as trying to argue with my own mom.

Delia and Bryn went to sit in the living room. Tamara hovered behind them, not seeming to know what to do with herself. "You don't look good, Mom. Let me get you some water," she said at last, going into the kitchen. Scylla sighed, opening the French door to the veranda and stepping outside. I looked back and forth between the open door and Tamara's moms sitting on the couch—Bryn with her head back, resting against the scalloped back of the couch, eyes squeezed shut; Delia slouched forward, staring resolutely at the coffee table—before following Scylla outside.

She was leaning against the balustrade, staring past the backyard, out to the sea beyond. The sun was low on the horizon, the sky so dark red it looked bloody. Black clouds in the distance seemed to warn of a storm. I wondered if it was finally going to rain. We could do with some rain, if nothing else.

"You know," she said softly as I joined her at the railing, "even when you were missing, I never really felt like there was no hope. There always felt like something more we could do. There were periods where Tamara or Henry would get really pessimistic, but I never felt that way. I was positive that everything was going to work out, you know? Like it was going to be okay." The wind out there was strong, whipping the spiky fronds of the narrow palm trees in the backyard around, but it was sheltered on the veranda. Just breezy enough to make Scylla's bangs dance gently on her forehead. "I don't know if I believe it anymore," she said, her voice barely audible.

I wanted to tell her it was going to be okay. That everything would work out. But I wasn't sure if I believed it, either. So we just stood there, staring quietly out at the sunset-streaked horizon.

After a moment, Scylla turned, shuffling back into the house, leaving me alone with my thoughts. When the door opened again a minute or so later, I thought maybe she was returning, but to my surprise, Nadin came out onto the deck. My heart jumped. "Hey," I said in surprise.

"Hi," she responded. She came to join me at the balustrade.

Neither of us spoke as she looked out at the darkening sky.

"It looks like a storm is coming," she finally murmured.

"No *gamadas*, at least," I said wryly.

A taut smile pulled at the corners of her mouth. "I suppose not." She twisted the hematite ring on her finger absently.

"I was going to ask you about that," I said.

She looked at me in confusion. "About what?"

"Your ring." I gestured.

"Oh," she said, looking down at her hand. "Scylla got it for me. The day we went shopping for my clothes. It..." She trailed off, seeming unsure of whether to go on, but then she squared her shoulders. "It means I'm asexual. Do you know what that is?"

I smiled involuntarily. She sounded so defiant when she said it, like she was expecting me to argue with her about it. I felt like I was looking at a reflection of myself. "I do. It kind of makes sense, actually. Now that you mention it. Back in Hope Renewed..."

I stopped when I saw the flash in her eyes. That was clearly a touchy subject, so I decided let it drop.

"Tamara says it's normal," she said, a challenge in her tone.

"It is normal," I said firmly. "I'm not that different, you know. You don't have to explain to me."

Her eyebrow quirked. "You're not?"

"No. I'm not. Did Tamara tell you about demis?"

She shook her head.

"We're on the ace spectrum. We don't *never* feel sexual attraction, but we don't feel it often. At least I don't. So... I'm kind of like you."

Her jaw dropped. For a moment, she almost seemed angry at

me. "Then why didn't you—" she started, but then she squeezed her eyes closed. She let out a long breath. "Only with the right person," she said, barely audible.

"Yeah," I murmured. "Only then."

She took another deep breath and opened her eyes. "It doesn't matter. I'm just glad I figured it out."

I smiled, turning to look back out at the bay. "Me, too."

The wind was picking up. The waves crashing far below sounded louder, angrier.

"I have to go soon," Nadin whispered. "Joseph Condor is waiting for me."

"Yeah."

"Do you think I'll see you again?" she asked.

I swallowed. I wanted to tell her, *Yeah, of course,* but I couldn't get my mouth to form the words. They felt too much like a lie.

"I hope so," I finally managed.

She squeezed her eyes closed again, struggling to keep her composure. It was hard to keep my arms at my side, to keep from drawing her into a hug, but I managed to stay rooted firmly in place.

"It isn't over," I said, trying to sound confident. "This is just... a passing storm." I gestured to the sky. "Like that. It looks dark and horrible, but there will be a break in the clouds." As I spoke, as if on command, a patchy smear of purple-red sky opened up between the dark clouds, revealing a bright yellow light. "See, look. There's a promise. And Venus looks gorgeous tonight." It was the brightest I'd seen it in years, in fact. Brighter than the few pinpricks of stars around it.

It was only as I turned to smile at Nadin that I realized what I'd done.

"Venus?" She stared at me in horror. "*That's* Venus?"

"Nadin, wait," I stammered, trying to think of a way to cover my blunder, but in my panic my mind went completely blank. There would be no excuses this time. That much was clear on her face.

"That tiny little light is Hamos?" she asked, reverting to Iamoi, her voice rising over the howl of wind that ripped past us, whistling through the veranda, making her hair fly wildly about her face.

"Nadin—"

"What happened to it? Why is it so far, so small?"

"Nadin, please, listen," I said desperately. "Honestly, I don't know. I don't know how any of this is possible. All I know is— Venus isn't the third world anymore. It's the second."

"*What?*" she shrieked.

"It's true. Its... its orbit must have been disrupted. But we don't know how. I'd heard that something catastrophic happened to it in order for its rotation to be the way it is, but that was supposed to be eons ago—at the beginning of the universe—" I don't know how I'd thought that would help. I was just babbling incoherently at this point. But when I said the word catastrophic, Nadin backed away from me, looking like I'd punched her hard in the stomach. "Nadin, wait," I said, reaching a hand out to touch her shoulder.

"*Get away from me!*" she screamed, shrinking back even

further. "You lied to me, Isaak! What else have you lied to me about? Did you know the truth about what happened to my people all along? Bringing me here, promising my people help, was that a lie as well?"

"No, of course not!"

"I don't believe you!" She lurched away from me, running down the covered deck. She didn't go back into the house—instead, she raced to the veranda's end and down the steps into the backyard, into the roaring wind.

I vaulted after her, ducking as a small branch from one of the palm trees went flying past my head. A narrow path skirted the backs of the yards on this street, giving the residents a private walking place with views of the bay, and Nadin ran down this now, away from me, away from the house, away from Joseph Condor. For a terrifying moment I had a vision of her losing her balance and toppling over the steep edge down the cliff to the rocks below, but she hugged the inner edge of the path as it went down toward a rocky beach.

The wind was howling in my ears, compounded by the deafening crash of the waves. The beach was usually calm, but with the weather this wild, who knew how high the waves would get, or if a sneaker wave would cover the beach. "Nadin, come back! It's too dangerous!" I shouted, but the wind ripped my voice away.

What stopped her was the roar behind us. She skidded to a stop at the sound, whirling around. My heart stopped dead in my chest.

I knew that sound.

"Get down!" she called, running back to me, colliding with me and pulling me against the rocky outcropping beside us. I looked up just in time to see the wall of dust bearing down on us from the north. It was like an amorphous blob of darkness, devouring the houses and trees that it passed. I remembered how Tuupa and Thork had shielded us with their bodies, and I pulled Nadin into my chest, trying to do the same for her.

"Isaak," she shouted. Her voice was muffled by the roar of the wind, so I felt it reverberate through me more than I heard it.

I pulled the collar of my shirt up over my nose and mouth and squeezed my eyes tightly closed just as it hit us.

It was no *gamada* storm. Within twenty seconds, the wall of dust had passed, leaving us coughing and gasping for air but ultimately unharmed. I stood shakily, my hand still on Nadin's arm, looking around us at the thin layer of red silt that had covered everything. The crashing waves were already washing away the dusting on the craggy rocks along the beach. My eyes burned where small bits of grit had gotten into them, but I didn't dare wipe at them Every part of me was covered in dust—my hands, my clothes; I could feel it falling out of my hair.

"Are you okay?" I asked Nadin. She didn't respond; she merely shook her hair off her shoulders, clouds of red dust flying off her and disappearing on the wind.

"Isaak! Nadin!" I heard voices shouting our names. Tamara and Scylla were racing down the path toward us, Bryn and Delia at their heels.

"Rinse your eyes," Scylla said urgently, handing me a water bottle. Mama D came up beside me as I did so, brushing me off with a towel. Tamara and Bryn did the same for Nadin. When I'd poured half the bottle over my eyes, I started to drink the rest, desperate to get the scratchy grit out of my throat.

"What was that?" asked Tamara. "I've never seen anything like it."

"It's the beginning," Nadin said. I looked at her in surprise. Her voice was firm and dark, and the expression on her face matched it. "The beginning of the end."

PART TWO
BETWEEN

Chapter 14

- i s a a k -

TWO WEEKS LATER, I STOOD IN THE B TERMINAL AT JOHANN
Kimbal Interplanetary Airport, staring at the spacejet through the
window and wondering if this was really a dream. And, if it was,
when I was ever going to wake up.

Everything had changed after that sandstorm. I'd known it
from the hard expression on Nadin's face. The knowledge that
Hamos had been destroyed had made her frantic, but that storm
had seemed to freeze her over. All the wild panic that had driven
her down the cliffside seemed to fossilize, like magma solidifying
after a volcanic eruption.

"It's *the beginning of the end*," she'd said. And she'd been right,
in more ways than one.

She'd made her way back up to Tamara's house, her shoulders
back, determination in her stride. I'd hurried to keep up with her,
Tamara and Scylla trailing behind. With the chaos created by the
storm, the GSAF suits didn't seem to notice that she was a little
late on those ten minutes Condor had allotted her. Their vehicles,
like the driveway they were parked on, were coated in red dust

five centimeters thick. Branches from trees lay scattered on the ground around them, stripped of their leaves. Half of them were on voice calls on their palmtops, barking out orders in voices rough with grit.

"Mister Condor," Nadin said, raising her voice to be heard over the commotion. He was standing beside a black SUV. When he turned to face her, for a moment I thought I could see the aftermath of fear on his face. The storm had shaken him. Just for an instant, he almost looked human. Then he straightened, the mask coming back into place.

"Are you ready, *kyrin*?" He looked her up and down, taking in her disheveled appearance.

Nadin didn't react. "Almost. My items are packed and ready inside. But before I come with you, I want an agreement."

He cocked his eyebrow. "You're in no position to make demands, Nadin."

"You are wrong, Mister Condor. I am in every position to make demands. It is you who need me, not the other way around."

He let out a bark of laughter. "I'm interested to know how you arrived at that conclusion, Nadin. If you don't cooperate with GSAF, your people will never reach our time."

She shook her head, her expression not changing in the slightest. "No. I am supposed to return three minutes after we left. If I am never permitted to return, those minutes will pass. And then my people will want to know what happened to me. There is nothing to prevent them from coming to this time at some future date."

My jaw dropped slightly at her words. She had him. I could

see it on his face. He tried to keep his composure, but I could see, now, the way his blue eyes changed. He looked shaken—almost as shaken as he had when we'd come out here after the storm.

Quickly, I put in, "And you don't know what kind of reaction they'll have. Remember, Nadin is basically a princess to them." I didn't add that she was an *exiled* princess, or that the Elytherioi—the only people who knew where she went—weren't exactly keen on her or her parents. "How do you know that six months from now we won't get an army of Iamoi beaming in with who knows what kind of weapons?"

"And you with no knowledge of the System to protect yourselves," Nadin added. "Because I promise you now—I will never tell your people a single thing about the System unless I get what I'm asking for."

"You are a guest here, and you're here on my sufferance only," Condor said through gritted teeth.

Behind me, Scylla snorted. "What are you going to do, deport her? Might be kind of difficult when you can't work the System, right?"

Condor's eyes flashed as he looked at her, but he didn't respond. After a long minute of silence, he turned to Nadin. "What is this agreement you propose?"

"I have three conditions," Nadin said. "First, you must arrange a meeting for me with your leaders at GSAF on Earth. I will not deal directly with you. I want to speak to them as Kate Ponsford promised."

"Done," said Condor, so quickly that I wondered, frowning, if that had been his plan to begin with.

"Secondly, I want Isaak to accompany me as my interpreter.

Not Stephen Moyer or anyone else."

I looked at her in surprise. She refused to meet my gaze. I knew she must be furious with me—she had every right to be—so I was shocked that she still wanted me to be a part of this.

"Do you really need an interpreter? I think you've made it clear at this point that you know more than enough English to get by," Condor said drily.

"Not always. Sometimes I need help. If I'm to negotiate with your people, I want to be certain that we understand each other completely."

Condor's eyes moved over me for a moment, considering. Weighing the odds of whether I would be a hindrance to his cause. Finally, slowly, he said, "Done. And your last condition?"

Nadin swallowed, the first sign of hesitancy she'd shown since the storm had passed. Whatever she was asking for, it was big. Maybe too big.

"I want you to pardon Henry."

"Absolutely not," Condor said, folding his arms.

"Do you want my help or not?" Nadin said.

"Not enough for that. Henry Sandhu is a traitor. He has proven this time and time again. Kate Ponsford was far too lenient with him, but I will not be making that mistake. Every time we've shown lenience with him, he has sown discord across the province. That ends now. He *will* be taken back to Earth and tried for his crimes."

"Then at least let me bring his case before GSAF," Nadin said. "Henry has done much to advance the cause of the Iamoi in your time. In just the short weeks I've been here, that much has been apparent. Perhaps GSAF will see his value where you may not."

"Nadin—"

"Do you want the System or not?" she interrupted. "These are my conditions."

Another long silence; then, grudgingly, he said, "All right. Henry Sandhu will remain as part of your company... for now. But he'll be under guard. And when we reach Earth, he will stand trial. Are we clear?"

"Clear as glass, Mister Condor," Nadin said in a cool voice. She looked at me then—her eyes distant, detached. She was still angry with me. Of course she was. What I'd done was inexcusable. But even if she no longer considered me her friend, we were still allies, for now at least. We were in this together for the foreseeable future.

Which meant that the next two weeks were a scramble of getting ready for an unexpected trip to Earth. I think the only thing that kept Mom from absolutely forbidding me from going was the fact that Joseph Condor specifically requested my presence on this "diplomatic mission." It was amazing how he managed to spin it as having been his idea all along rather than a desperate attempt on Nadin's part to maintain some control over these negotiations with GSAF. No one was really happy for me to go, but they acknowledged that it was for the *good of the colony*.

But Mom was adamantly opposed to letting me make the trip on my own. There was a week's worth of heated arguments about whether Mom or Erick could get off work—Mom had used up most of her vacation time the week I'd come home, and there was also the issue of Celeste. Even though the universities would be out for term break by the time we left, Celeste's elementary school still had almost another month left.

The ultimate solution was one none of us had anticipated.

Over the intercom, a cheerful voice said, "*Flight thirty-seven, now boarding from terminal B. Flight thirty-seven, now boarding from terminal B.*" Behind me, the small handful of people who'd been sitting on the black plastic chairs in the waiting area stood, gathering their luggage and loose coats and other belongings to line up for boarding. The airport was quiet today, not the usual madhouse of travelers and tourists it had been before the regime change. All travel in and out of Aeolis was being monitored more closely now, and the other provinces as well, if the news was to be believed. Fewer tourists were being allowed in as the government implemented a stricter screening process, which meant less people on the streets and far less in the airports. GSAF was cracking down on its wayward colony. There'd been a surge of new protests after Governor Ponsford's and Henry's arrests, followed swiftly by the implementation of more strict curfews and stronger police presence on the street. GSAF seemed to have realized that they'd given us too long of a leash, and they were reining us in now.

This was what I'd missed while I'd been gone. What I'd indirectly caused.

In the reflected glass of the window, I saw Dad grinning as he approached me. He didn't seem to have noticed the dark cloud hanging over everyone else's heads these days.

"Ready to go?" he asked.

"Ready as I'll ever be," I said, picking up my carry-on duffel bag and slinging the strap over my shoulder.

It had been the obvious solution, of course. Dad didn't have a job on Mars. What he *did* have was a number of interview requests back on Earth, each offering a hefty compensation plan. More money to add to his rapidly-diminishing pile. He could have done these by Speculus, of course, but he wasn't about to turn down the offer of travel and hotel costs one of the larger shows had offered him. And it just so happened that he would be traveling to Earth at the same time I needed to go along with Nadin. Wasn't that convenient?

I tried not to let my own bitterness eat away at me. I was still furious with him for profiting off Nadin's people this way, but there wasn't really anything I could say to stop him. The damage had already been done now.

I pulled my palmtop out of my pocket and opened a new message to Tamara. *Boarding now. See u tonight?* She and Scylla were catching the last flight out to the IPS *Athena*, the large passenger ship that we were taking to Earth. Of course they weren't about to let Nadin, Henry and I go to Earth without them. They'd spent the weekend getting Scylla's stuff moved out of her dorm and back to her parents', and now Scylla was over at Herschel helping Tamara pack—Mariyah had already gone home, so they just needed to get the last of Tamara's things cleared out.

Just as a cheerful attendant in a GalaX Air uniform started to scan my palmtop, I heard a commotion behind me. I turned to see Nadin and Henry approaching, flanked by GSAF suits. They were dressed casually, both wearing jeans and t-shirts. The hem of Henry's jeans was bunched up on his right leg around an ankle monitor. I frowned at the sight of it. GSAF wasn't letting him out of their sights for even a minute. I was surprised Joseph Condor wasn't here, too, personally supervising.

"Have a nice flight," the attendant said, turning my attention away from Henry and Nadin. I followed my dad through the door and down the ramp onto the spacejet. It looked just like a regular airplane in just about every regard, but this one had an engine strong enough to take us through the atmosphere, and a fuselage designed to not burn up once we made it there.

Dad and I were seated near the rear of the plane, Dad in a window seat and me in the middle. I shoved my duffel bag and Dad's small suitcase into the storage bin over the seats. Other passengers trickled in after us, only taking up about half the jet when it was all said and done. The aisle seat next to me was empty. I considered moving over for a minute, but decided that would probably too obviously look like I was trying to avoid my dad.

Finally, Nadin, Henry and their escorts boarded. I watched as one of the suits led Henry down the central aisle to the back of the plane. He caught my eye as he passed, a wry smirk on his face. I couldn't bring myself to smile back. It was the first time I'd seen him since the day after Dad's interview with Nancy Ramirez, when we'd all been at Tamara's house. The calm before the storm, though I hadn't known it at the time.

I *did this.*

I tried not to let my thoughts be consumed with worry about what was going to happen to him—and the rest of us—when we got to Earth. We had a ten-day journey through space in front of us. It might be the last time we were all together. All we could do was enjoy that time as best we could.

I found my eyes wandering over to Nadin in the front of the plane. They'd seated her in first class. I supposed it was fitting for a diplomatic guest. As much as she and Joseph Condor were clashing, I think even he realized that he still needed to show the Martian princess, as I'd called her, a modicum of respect.

She glanced down the aisle of the plane, watching Henry. Then her head turned and her eyes met mine and held them, for just an instant.

She looked away, taking her seat next to the window, her back to me once more. I sighed, slumping in my seat.

I wondered what she was thinking right now.

CHAPTER 15

- n a d i n -

I SANK DOWN INTO MY SEAT BESIDE MY GSAF BODYGUARD, TRYING to ignore the irregular beating of my heart. I hadn't seen Isaak in two Martian weeks—I'd essentially been a prisoner in the grand luxury suite that Condor had insisted upon moving me too, so I hadn't seen much of anyone—and a small part of me cried out now, longing to jump up and run down the aisle to sit beside him. But I shoved that urge aside. It wasn't just that my bodyguard would stop me if I tried to move. Isaak had lied to me. He'd lied to me multiple times since I'd known him. He'd pretended to know nothing of my people's fate, but it was clear that he knew more than he'd been willing to admit. Maybe he was sincere that the things he omitted were things he didn't understand, and that he'd done it all to spare my feelings, but a lie was still a lie. I wasn't ready to forgive him for that yet.

At the front of the craft, a man began speaking into a microphone, giving us instructions on what to expect for this flight. The cold chill of nerves crept over me as he spoke, as I followed his instructions, pulling on and securing a vest not unlike the one I'd worn on the boat weeks ago and then strapping myself into my chair with a belt that looped through hooks on the vest. I'd never been in space before. I'd never stepped foot off this planet before—though we had a few small stations in space between Iamos and Hamos that had served as research outposts during the construction of our interplanetary posterns, I had never been to them, or to our citidome on Hamos. That had been Antos and Melusin's province as *geroi*; I was still just a student during that time. I'd needed to stay in the citidome with Gitrin. And even in making the journey from my time to Isaak's, I still hadn't left Iamos—Mars.

I was leaving my homeworld for the first time.

The man with the microphone finished speaking, taking his own seat and strapping himself in, and we began to move. I'd watched a few of these crafts taking off as we'd arrived at this place my bodyguard had called the *airport*. Though they flew through the air, they looked more like *psaras* with long pectoral fins than they did *gamadas*. There was no flapping of these wings; they merely glided through the air like they were cutting through water.

The craft began to move faster and faster down one of the long runways I'd seen through the airport windows, making my stomach feel as though it was climbing into my throat. Then we tilted back, my body pressed into its seat, and somehow, we were in the sky.

For a long moment I stared straight in front of me, one hot tear leaking from the corner of my eye. I blinked it away. *Look,* my mind whispered to me. But I was afraid. I was afraid to see my planet falling away from me as we climbed higher and higher.

But finally I couldn't resist anymore. My curiosity won out. I looked out the window.

Below us, Tierra Nueva was already turning into an indistinct gray splotch on the red earth, broken into sections by the gleaming silver stripes of the rivers. From the sky, I could see how the thin lines of water disappeared into the bay, absorbed by the massive blue-green of the sea. It went on seemingly forever, beyond the horizon. Two tiny crescents of land, Herschel and Knobel Islands, were the only thing that broke up that infinite blue.

We climbed higher and higher, the white-capped peak of the mountain Isaak had called Sharp turning into a speck, the basket-weave network of rivers that formed the delta morphing into a green blob. Then we passed through a cloud, and my view of the ground was obscured.

Everything grew brighter and brighter and brighter.

And then we were in darkness, weightless, held in place only by our safety belts, and surrounded by nothing but stars.

The flight was short, probably less than an hour. The longest part of it seemed to be the docking of the spacejet to the ship, the IPS *Athena*. It was a massive metal behemoth, a tubular body with engines on its back, connected to an utterly enormous round disc. The disc was so covered with windows that it almost appeared to be made entirely of glass, and it slowly rotated. As it turned, I could see the reflection of the approaching spacejet, and behind it, the red, green and blue orb of Mars.

Our craft seemed to approach the *Athena* at a crawl. The vest was chafing my neck as it held me in my seat. I was grateful I'd worn my hair in a braid today, because looking around at the other passengers, I could see their hair floating around them as if we were underwater.

After what felt like an eternity, I felt the *thud* of the spacejet as it docked against the tubular segment of the giant ship. A few minutes later, the man who'd spoken to us at the beginning of the flight unfastened the belt from his vest, his body drifting upward as the straps fell away. "Please remain seated with your seatbelts secured," he said, speaking into the microphone on the wall. "A flight attendant will come around to help you off the plane." He turned in midair, grasping the metal handrail that went down the central aisle between our seats. Then he nimbly floated over to me, hand over hand on the railing.

"Do you have any carry-on luggage, miss?" he asked.

"No," I replied. I hadn't even brought my satchel with me. The efficient brown-haired woman who'd been Kate's assistant—and now seemed to be Joseph's—had come this morning to pack my few possessions in a suitcase that I was told would be brought to my stateroom on board the *Athena*. The only thing I had with me now was the posternkey, which I'd been careful not to let Joseph or anyone else from GSAF see. It was currently zipped inside a pocket on the inside of my jacket, and that's where it would remain until we reached Earth.

"Then let's get you out of here," the man said with a smile. I unfastened the seatbelt, feeling with a lurch of my stomach the way my body immediately drifted upward when the straps holding it down gave way. The man guided me over to the handrail, pulling a retractable strap from my vest and attaching it to a hook on the handrail. "Ready?" he asked. I nodded, and he said, "Then hold on." He pressed a button on an electronic device clipped to his collar, and the hook on the handrail began to move, pulling me along. My stomach lurched once more, and I took a sharp breath through my nose.

At the door we'd entered the craft through, another flight attendant waited, floating easily with just a light hand on the ceiling to keep herself in place. Moving in zero gravity was clearly second nature to her. She smiled as the mechanized hook pulled me over to her. "Is this your first time flying?" she asked me pleasantly. It was such a casual thing to say that I almost wondered if she even knew who I was. Maybe she didn't, though that seemed impossible. Everyone on Mars seemed to recognize me when I wasn't wearing the wig Tamara had given me. Or maybe she just wanted to make conversation with me—maybe she didn't know that we did most of our travel by postern on Iamos.

I forced a nauseous smile back. "Yes."

"Well, you're doing great," she said, reaching up to guide the hook that was pulling my vest over the slightly misaligned place where the handrail from the spacejet connected with the one on the *Athena*'s boarding jetty. "Have a nice trip to Earth."

"Thank you," I said, looking around myself as the hook pulled me along, onto the ship. Kate's former assistant had given me an idea of what to expect about the ship this morning as she'd helped me pack. The rotating disc was the main body of the ship where the passengers spent most of their time. The spinning created gravity, which meant that we only had to endure this floating when we boarded and disembarked. But there were people down here working now, the crew of this ship. They glided here and there as casually as the flight attendants, used to the feeling of weightlessness. "Hi there," one of them said to me as I drifted past.

At the end of the hallway, another attendant waited next to a tube with round platforms rotating through every ten seconds or so. It reminded me of the moving stairs in the shopping mall I'd gone to with Tamara, Scylla, and Mariyah. The ones they'd called *escalators*. This must be what brought us into the part of the ship with gravity. I glanced behind me—my GSAF bodyguard was just a few arms' lengths away. I sighed. Not letting me out of his sight for even a minute.

"Hey there," the attendant said as the mechanized hook pulling me reached the end of the handrail and scraped to a stop. "Do you have any health restrictions or any need for personal assistance entering the gravity area?"

"I don't think so," I said.

He laughed. "All right then." He unhooked my strap from the handrail and guided me into the opening of the tube. "Hold on to the support rail, your legs might be a little shaky." One of the moving platforms swept up under my feet and I was inside.

A few seconds later, my weight returned in a sudden rush, and I gripped the railing as my knees wobbled. It was hard to keep my balance, but I managed to remain upright. If I could handle travel by postern, I could handle this.

Then I was out of the tube, the platform moving across the floor toward yet another attendant. She helped me off the platform just before it disappeared into a slot in the floor, just like the top step of the escalator back on Mars had done.

Shakily I made my way over to a seating area and gratefully

sat down, waiting for my body to readjust to the feeling of weight again. For having been in zero gravity for less than an hour, readjusting was surprisingly harder than I would have expected it to be. As I sat, I unfastened my vest, tossing it into a collection bin a short distance from my feet. I slumped forward, breathing in deeply through my nose, waiting for the dizziness and disorientation to subside.

"Ready to go, *kyrin*?" a man's voice asked much too soon. I looked up to see my bodyguard standing disinterestedly, as if this strange shifting from gravity to none and back again was normal to him.

I wouldn't let him see that I was struggling. "Of course," I said, getting steadily to my feet.

CHAPTER 16

- i s a a k -

ONCE WE'D DISEMBARKED FROM THE SPACEJET ONTO THE ATHENA and picked up our checked luggage, Dad and I headed to our small shared cabin. I winced when Dad opened the door and it just barely cleared the double bed. Apparently the talk show on Earth that had paid for his board was working on a more limited budget than he'd indicated.

Just one bed. Stellar. I would definitely need to plan to spend as little time in this room as possible, then.

As dad set his unnecessarily-large suitcase on the bed beside his carry-on, I took a peek into the bathroom. It was one of those ones where the whole bathroom was also the shower stall, the toilet just out of range of the overhead spout, a giant drain hole in the middle of the tile floor.

"You better call your mom before she starts nagging us," Dad called as I frowned at my reflection in the tiny, square mirror over the toilet. I came back into the bedroom and perched on the far edge of the bed. There was about half a meter between the bed and the wall. I pulled my palmtop out of my pocket and tapped the video chat icon.

Mom answered on the first ring. "Oh, good," she said as her face filled my screen. Behind her I could see the white walls of her office at the university. The fluorescent lighting made her complexion look washed out. "You made it. How was your flight?"

"It was fine. You guys doing okay?" My stomach twisted uncomfortably as I remembered saying goodbye this morning. Dad came to pick me up just as Mom and Erick were about to leave to take Celeste to school and then head over to Curiosity Bay. Celeste had done a good job of not crying—better than Mom had—but the look she'd given me had said it all.

"Are you going to go away again?"

"Yeah, we're fine," Mom replied. "We'll be glad when you're back home, though."

"Me too," I said hollowly. "Hopefully just a few weeks." The plan was that after Nadin's meeting with GSAF, I would take a flight to California to stay with Abuelo. Mom and Celeste would be joining us and we'd have our annual visit—just a week this time, since Mom had used up most of her time off when I'd gotten back from Iamos. Then we'd all head back to Mars.

But that was if everything worked out according to plan. And for some reason, I just couldn't shake this unpleasant feeling that things *weren't* going to work out according to plan. When had they ever over the last two annums?

"Keep me posted, okay?" Mom said. "Call me every day. And let me know when you're getting ready for your flight down. And when you land in Canaveral. All right?"

"I will," I said.

After I got off chat with Mom, I made a quick excuse to my dad and got the hell out of that tiny cabin. If the Athena was anything like the other interplanetary ships I'd traveled on, there would be plenty of other places to be. I had every intention of only being in our cabin when it was time to sleep.

I glanced at my palmtop to check the time. Tamara and Scylla wouldn't be arriving for a few more hours. I had some time to kill.

My first inclination was to try to meet up with Henry or Nadin, but I didn't know how to find them. I assumed Nadin was probably in first class, but I wasn't sure which cabin was hers— or, frankly, if her GSAF bodyguard would even let me near her. I was supposed to be her "interpreter" when she met with GSAF, but I wasn't sure if that meant I was allowed to talk with her outside that meeting. And I didn't know about Henry, either. He had that ankle monitor on, which I'd think would mean they would give him some degree of freedom on board the ship, but maybe not. Maybe they were just that afraid of him getting away from them. I did know that he didn't have his palmtop anymore, not since he'd been arrested two weeks ago, so I couldn't get in touch with him that way.

I wandered the main recreation deck, wondering if I should try to track them down or just wait for Tamara and Scylla to get here. The good news was that no one seemed to be staring at me. Everyone seemed to have lost interest in me by now—there were more interesting things going on. I was just a minor player now. Nadin, the governor, Henry... they were center-stage these days. I was just the idiot who put all of this in motion.

I paused as I started to pass a glass-fronted room marked

Arcade.

Where would Henry go if they let him go off on his own on this trip?

Inside, the arcade was dark, with neon lights in blues and pinks overhead. In the front there were a number of retro game machines, but these were mostly unoccupied. Beyond this was a second room, and I could see people inside with Speculus headsets. A VR party.

I wandered toward the back. A cursory glance told me that Henry wasn't here, but that didn't mean he wouldn't come here later if he got the chance. This seemed like a good place to wait.

An attendant in a GalaX Air uniform stopped me as I went by. "Interested in renting a set?" he asked.

I hesitated a moment. "How much?"

"Ten an hour. Cash, e-pay, or we can bill it to your cabin."

"Do that," I said, half wondering if my dad would be torqued about it but mostly not caring.

"Sure thing. Are you nano compatible?"

I stared at him. I knew he was asking if I had nanobots, but the way he phrased it was so creepy. Am I compatible?

"No. Does it matter?" I asked, and he shrugged.

"They say it gives you an edge in-game, but I haven't upgraded yet so I couldn't tell you. Have fun."

I slipped on the headset he handed me and looked around the room. There were two different games going on at once, mostly breaking the room down the middle. The left side was playing *Sherwood Forest*, a sword-and-sorcery MMORPG, and the right side was playing *Enigma*, an FPS set during the Greek Civil War. I decided to join the *Sherwood Forest* party. I'd started this game a couple years ago, though as my figuscan began syncing I noticed that my character was a pitifully low level compared to the others. I'd been close to the level cap the last time I'd played, but they'd obviously increased the cap since then. I sighed.

There was a flicker, and the environment loaded. I was standing in a forest clearing, the dirt beneath my feet compacted by thousands of feet and horse hooves going over it for years. Or at least that was the impression it was supposed to give. Birds chirped in my ears, but beyond that, I could hear voices—more than just those of the people in the real room around me—and the sound of thunder. There was a battle happening nearby.

Text blinked in my periphery. *Seasonal quest: Hungry, Hungry Hippogryphs. Defeat twelve hippogryphs for a prize.*

All right, then. Easy enough.

I drew my sword and followed the sound of the voices down a dirt trail edged with tall coniferous trees. I hadn't made it far when I encountered a group of people battling a massive creature with an eagle's head and sharp talons to match, rearing up on the hind legs of a horse. It roared, a sound like thunder that shook the forest around us, and to my left, a mage retaliated with a blast of lightning.

"Hey, are you joining the quest?" a guy to my right yelled over his shoulder. "We need a tank!"

"I can tank," I said quickly. Usually Henry was the tank when we gamed together, but I'd filled in enough before that hopefully my low level wouldn't be too much of a detriment to the party.

"Hurry and pull," the guy who'd called to me—he was playing an archer—said, dodging an AOE that appeared on the ground. He shot an arrow at the beast's side.

I took a deep breath, trying to remember my knight's rotation. "On it!" Taking a stance behind the monster, I began hurling damage. The hippogryph pivoted my way, its red eyes flashing as it tried to gore me with its talons. I got in a couple of hits first. Good. Its attention was on me, and the other players could focus on dealing as much damage as possible. I hacked and slashed, slowly whittling away at its HP.

"What are you doing?" the archer demanded after a few moments. "Use your buffs!"

"I was just about to do that," I retorted, activating my Valor ability, decreasing the damage I took while increasing the damage I dealt.

"Incoming—it's summoning friends!" the mage called to me.

I turned my attention to the two hippogryphs that were now running toward us, but as I glanced in their direction, the one I was already fighting dealt a hard blow to my back that made my camera shake. The HP bar in my periphery began to drop.

"Guiding Light!" the healer called out, her companion fairy casting a restorative spell on my character.

· "Thanks," I replied, chagrined. I switched tactics, focusing my aggro on the new hippogryphs to draw them to the middle of the forest where I stood. I dealt the damage, but they diverted from me, running toward the other party members.

"Use Dragon Slash!" the archer shouted, aiming a Blazing Arrow arrow at the main hippogryph.

I grimaced. Dragon Slash must be an ability they'd added in a recent patch—one I hadn't unlocked yet. "No can do," I muttered, parrying with my sword and activating Lion's Rage, my attack that dealt the most damage. My stomach clenched when it did no good. I must not be a high enough level to get their attention off of the other players. "No, stop!" I yelled, trying desperately to draw the mob away from the mage and the healer. But the first hippogryph cast an AOE on the ground, and I didn't make it out in time. My sensors flashed red as my HP fell dangerously low. "Come on," I muttered, unleashing all I had on the hippogryphs that now surrounded us.

It didn't matter. They hit me again, and my screen went dark.

And then the girl beside me—the one playing the healer—screamed. Not in-game, in real life. And not the normal kind of scream you'd expect from wiping in a video game. Not an angry, curse-filled yell of frustration, an actual scream of pain. *Real* pain.

In a panic, I ripped off my Speculus set, my eyes squinting as they adjusted to the dim neon lights of the arcade. "What's wrong?" I yelled. "What happened?"

No one responded. Everyone around me was still wrapped up in the worlds of their games, thrusting and parrying, running in place. Beside me, the girl was on her knees, holding her side. Her headset still covered her eyes, but her mouth was drawn into a grimace. She whimpered quietly.

"Hey," I cried, running over to her and crouching beside her. "Are you okay?" She didn't respond until I touched her shoulder; then she jumped, ripping off her headset.

"What the hell?" she snapped, shrinking away from me. "What's your problem?"

I blinked in confusion. "I'm sorry... you sounded like you were in pain."

Her teeth were clenched. She was still holding her side—the spot where the hippogryph had slashed her before her avatar

K.O.ed. "It's just the nanos," she hissed. "I'll be fine in a second. What the hell were you doing? You were supposed to be drawing aggro *away* from me!"

"I'm sorry," I repeated, getting back to my feet and backing away as she glared at me. From the doorway, the attendant was watching me. The girl put her headset back on, straightening. As soon as her gaze was off me, I whirled around, handing my headset to the attendant. I hadn't used my full hour, but I was done.

"Why would someone voluntarily put that shit in their body if that's what it does to them?" I asked in a harsh whisper.

He shrugged. "Beats me. Part of me thinks it's stupid, but... it's supposed to be really fun, too. Makes the games more real. So I'll probably still upgrade when I get the money." When I gawked, he shrugged again. "Can't stop the wave of the future, dude," he said.

CHAPTER 17

- n a d i n -

MY STATEROOM ABOARD THE ATHENA WAS LARGE, JUST AS BIG AS the suite in the Plaza back on Mars. A bed easily big enough for three people stood in the center of the room. Against one wall, a stone-topped bar framed a glass cabinet filled with multi-colored bottles of strong drink. When you entered the room, to the left there was a door leading to an immense bathroom, far larger than the one at Delia and Bryn's house, with a jetted bathtub and a sauna inside. Across from that door was a door to the connecting suite, where my bodyguard was staying. I'd locked it as soon as he left me, but I had no delusions that that would stop him if he wanted to enter.

Between these doors, giant windows filled the back wall of the room with the black void of space. The stars spun as the disc of the ship rotated, and every so often the round orb of Mars came into view. From here, I could see the two moons, Phobos and Deimos, no bigger than asteroids, circling the planet. And orbiting at the northern end of the planet, close to the pole, a gleaming satellite that must have been the space mirror the others had spoken about, which had melted the ice cap and directed extra warmth to the cold planet.

And extra ultraviolet light, I thought with a shudder. But unlike Iamos, Mars had a thick enough atmosphere to counteract that. Or so they said. But it was clear that their efforts to counteract nature weren't as successful as I'd previously thought. With all the water they had, it seemed preposterous to me to think that the Martian colony was in danger. But that dust storm had made me see otherwise. This was how it started on Iamos. Drought. Dust storms. It was how the end had begun. These people needed the Elytherioi and their knowledge of climate restoration just as much as the whole of Iamos needed Mars. GSAF would have to understand that. They must.

The disc turned again, and Mars disappeared from my view. I tried to put it out of my mind, along with any thoughts I'd had about what was missing from that view—Hamos.

"Its orbit must have been disrupted. But we don't know how."

There was a knock at my door. The main door, not the one leading to my bodyguard's room. I looked up in surprise. For a fleeting instant, my heart leapt with the thought that it might be Isaak.

No. I wasn't ready to forgive him just yet.

The knock came again. Reluctantly I went over to the door and opened it.

Geoff Preston stood on the other side.

"Hello, Nadin. I happened to be traveling to Earth on business and just wanted to see how you were enjoying the accommodations. This ship is owned by GalaX, you see. Just another example of our many enterprises," he explained cheerfully. "May I come in?"

I hesitated, but he pushed his way into the suite anyway. I sighed, closing the door behind him. As soon as it was closed, Preston's pleasant expression dissipated, replaced by a sense of urgency. "Have you considered my offer?" he asked without any form of prelude.

"Yes," I said, straightening my back and hoping my posture exuded the confidence I didn't feel. "I appreciate your company's concern for my people's welfare after relocation, but right now I think that our most important focus needs to be on negotiating with GSAF to ensure that we are able to relocate at all. Maybe we can revisit this in the future, but in the meantime I think we're going to have to"—I paused, desperately trying to think of how I'd heard people phrase this on Mars, Kate and Joseph and Bryn and—"table this discussion."

Preston took a step closer to me. I resisted the urge to shrink back. I met his gaze with my own. "I wish you'd reconsider, Nadin. If you work with GSAF, we'll have no choice but to work with GSAF as well."

I blinked in surprise. What was that supposed to mean? Warning alarms chimed in the back of my head, almost as if I was reconnected to the System. A subtle blip in my subconscious. Bryn and Delia worked for GalaX, but they hadn't known who this man was. Bryn had been going to investigate further, but we'd been separated before she had a chance to get any information to me, and I'd had no contact with her since then. What if Preston didn't work for GalaX at all? What if he had some kind of malicious intent toward my people, and was trying to trick me into cooperating with him?

"Mister Preston, who are you?" I asked tersely.

"I am exactly who I told you I was. A representative of GalaX."

"But in what capacity? Bryn Randall-Torres had never heard of you."

"I don't expect she would have. GalaX is a massive company, Nadin. Technology, travel, space exploration, deep sea initiatives, automotives, you name it. If GalaX were a sovereign nation instead of a corporation, we'd be the third largest economy on Earth. AresTec is just one small part of what comprises GalaX. My position and hers are two that would probably never cross paths." He folded his arms. "I'm going to be frank with you, Nadin. We have a working partnership with GSAF, but as with all relationships between government entities and private enterprise, it's tense. GalaX wants to work with the Iamoi. We would rather work with you directly rather than having to go through GSAF. But if you refuse to deal with us, we won't have a choice."

I shook my head, taking a step away from him and looking out the windows. The stars wheeled, and Mars came into view again. Blue and green... and red. Too red. Still too red.

"I'm sorry, Mister Preston. Perhaps we can make a bargain at some point in the future. But for now my hands are tied." I turned back to meet his eyes. "This isn't just about me or what I think is the best decision. I have six million lives on my hands. And that's just the people back in my time. Here..." I glanced down at my palms, at the black ring on my middle finger. "I have to do what I can to help my friends. Henry and Tamara and Scylla and... and Isaak. All of them. For now, I have to work with GSAF."

I looked up at him. He was frowning, but his expression

wasn't angry. It was more resigned.

"All right, then. I'm sorry, Nadin. And I'm sorry for everything that's to come." I raised my brows in surprise, but he walked past me before I could respond. The door closed quietly behind him.

I turned, exhaling shakily. Mars had disappeared from my window. All I could see was blackness and stars. I was alone with the darkness.

And the overwhelming feeling that I'd just made a huge mistake.

Chapter 18

- i s a a k -

Tamara and Scylla's flight was supposed to come in at 5:20. With all the time disembarking would take, I was sure they wouldn't be on the *Athena* with their luggage until close to six, but by five o'clock I'd about lost my mind with boredom, so I went back down to the waiting area just outside the boarding zone and sat in one of the black plastic chairs that matched the ones in the airport back in Tierra Nueva.

Just like on the rest of the ship, the walls here were covered with windows, allowing a gorgeous view of the void of space. Potted artificial plants about a meter and a half tall were dotted around the area, cheerful green shrubs to add some color to the otherwise dull gray of the ship. As I stared out the window, Mars came into view. Smaller already than it was when we arrived this morning. Almost out of reach. Scylla and Tamara's flight was the last connection before the *Athena* was out of range.

We were moving out of Mars' orbit now. There was no going back.

"Hey." I looked up in surprise to see Henry approaching me—

without his GSAF bodyguard.

"Where's your babysitter?" I asked.

He sank into the chair beside me. "I gave him the afternoon off."

I quirked an eyebrow. "He let you?"

"Yeah. He's actually not that bad. You know, for working for GSAF. I think he's not super enthused about his new boss. Can't say I blame him." Henry shrugged. "Besides, it's not like I can go anywhere on this ship. And they're keeping tabs on me regardless." He gestured to his ankle monitor.

I frowned. "I guess you're right." It wasn't like he could sneak away in a lifeboat or something. We weren't at escape pod technology, after all. If something went wrong on this ship, we were all dead.

"Nadin's the one they're really watching, if you ask me," he added in a low voice. "She's the one they're going to want to keep away from us. I think Condor thinks he can manipulate her if he keeps her isolated."

"He's underestimating her, then," I said. "Nadin's not so easy to control. The *geroi* learned that the hard way."

"Good."

I just wish I knew what she was planning for this trip. She'd wanted me along, but I didn't know how much help to her I was going to be if I didn't know what was going on in her head.

Through the window, I caught the corner of a blue wing, the tip of a vertical tail. The last connection was here. Henry and I waited quietly as a subdued voice over the intercom announced that Flight 89 from Tierra Nueva was arriving now. Long minutes passed before finally the sound of voices from the boarding zone began to trickle out to the waiting area where we sat.

At the end of the last group of stragglers to emerge from the boarding area were Scylla and Tamara. I got to my feet, waving them over. Scylla grinned as she hurried over. Tamara followed but drew up short when she saw Henry stand up beside me. She adjusted her hat to try to cover her reaction, but I still caught it.

"Hey, guys," I said as they reached us.

"Hey," Scylla said, looking at Henry with an arched brow. "This is a surprise. They're letting you talk to us?"

"Apparently. For now." He was watching Tamara, who was making a point out of not looking at him. "You okay, Tam?"

She nodded. "I'm fine. But are you?" She looked up at him. "There's not been anything like"—she hesitated, seeming to struggle to find a way to phrase it—"New Year's going on?"

Henry grinned. "No. I'm fine." He laughed at her unconvinced expression. "I swear, I'm fine! No hidden bruises. Do I need to take off my shirt to show you?"

Her face turned beet red. "Oh my God! No!"

Scylla and Henry laughed. I tried to laugh with them, but my insides were squirming too much. What had happened on New Year's? The fact that Henry had said *hidden bruises* made me afraid to ask and find out. I decided I was probably better off not knowing.

"Did you guys eat before your flight?" Henry asked.

"No. We just barely managed to get her R.A. to sign off on the room before we had to be at the airport," Scylla said.

"Let's get dinner, then," said Henry. "Anywhere you want. I've got an all-expenses-paid trip thanks to GSAF."

"Too soon, Henry." I laughed, but Tamara's dour expression

didn't change.

"Well, I'm not going to stop, so she's just going to have to learn to smile again," he replied, nudging her with his elbow.

"Is there anywhere on this ship that serves breakfast all day?" Scylla asked loudly, as if volume would lighten the mood. "I want pancakes. Fluffy vegan pancakes with strawberries on top. And loads of maple syrup."

"That sounds good to me. There's a bunch of restaurants on the dining level, I'm sure one of them will have something," I said. I glanced over my shoulder at Tamara. She was still frowning, her hand on her upper arm where Henry had nudged her.

"Relax, Tam," I murmured, falling into step beside her. "He said the guy GSAF has with him on the trip is okay. He's letting him go around unsupervised. It's probably not that bad. And we've got ten whole days together, right?"

"Right," she said, still looking down at the floor.

Dinner was okay. I hadn't eaten at Ivan's at all since I'd been back, and the diner on board the *Athena* made me regret that. Their food was all right, but it couldn't really compare to that little wannabe-log-cabin on the boardwalk in Tierra Nueva. Scylla and Henry were in good spirits, and eventually Tamara brightened up enough to smile a little, but the more I watched her, the worse I felt for her. She'd been a bundle of nerves the last two weeks, and I think now that we were on our way to Earth it was catching up with her. Her face was pale and there were dark circles under her eyes that her makeup couldn't quite cover.

I frowned, shoving my last ketchup-dunked French fry into my mouth and chewing without tasting it. Tamara had been dealing with anxiety and the effects stress had on that since around the time we'd started high school. Judging by her expression over dinner, I worried now that all of this might be too much.

"So, where's Nadin at?" Scylla asked cheerfully after we'd paid and left the diner. Her arm was looped through Tamara's.

"I'm not sure. I'm guessing they've got her somewhere in first class, based on our connecting flight, but I'm not sure where," I said.

"We could probably check the ship's log. They list the passenger's rooms unless the passenger requests they be private. Most people don't bother," said Tamara.

"The question is whether they'll let us near her, even if we figure out which room she's in," Henry pointed out. "I said to Isaak earlier, I feel like GSAF security is more here to be watching her than me."

Scylla scoffed. "That seems backwards. You're the criminal, after all."

"I think they realize that Nadin might be more of a danger to them in the long run," I said quickly, before Scylla had a chance to make any more tactless jokes. Not just for Tamara's sake, either—every time one of them reminded me of Henry's current status with the law, a wave of guilt ran through me.

"Okay. So where would we check the ship's log at?" Scylla asked.

"There's usually consoles in random places around the ship," said Tamara. "Let's try near the elevator."

We made our way through the mall-like recreation level, where restaurants were interspersed with activity rooms. I gave a sideways glance at the arcade as we passed it.

"You been in there yet?" Henry asked, following my gaze.

"Yeah. It sucked," I said darkly.

"Lame."

Kitty-corner from the arcade was a karaoke bar. The familiar bars of a pop song drifted out of the wide-open doors to reach us. A teenage girl was singing along with it, slightly out of key.

"Oh, now that's just sad," Henry said, his nose wrinkled.

"Henry!" Tamara gasped. "Seriously? You're so rude."

He shrugged. "I call 'em like I see 'em."

"That reminds me," I said with a frown. "How do you think the paparazzi are going to be? I haven't seen any aboard ship." Tamara was still wearing the hat she'd had on when she boarded, but she seemed a little bit less guarded.

"I'm not worried about it where we're going," she said. "It's more of an issue on Mars than on Earth. Especially in the US. I get a little radio time there, but they go through pop stars like candy there. I'm doing a little better in Britain and Europe, but I'm not some kind of megastar or anything. The only reason it's so bad here is because I'm the first Martian singer to chart on Earth. I'm hoping it will calm down a little the more traction Martian singers start getting. We have a lot of really promising people at Herschel—"

"You still doing your summer tour?" Henry interrupted.

Tamara faltered. "Uh, no. I canceled it."

Henry let out a little grunt of exasperation. "You shouldn't have done that."

"I have more important things going on right now."

"Your career is important."

"Not as important as—" She broke off, seeming unsure of how to put it. She gestured around at the four of us. "This."

Henry sighed. Before he could say anything else, I intervened. "This is stressful for her, Henry. She shouldn't push herself any more than she already is."

He didn't respond. He just chewed on the inside of his cheek.

"Look, there's one of those consoles," Scylla said, pointing. Sure enough, at the end of the row of shops, a silver podium that looked kind of like an ATM machine stood by itself. The lit sign over it read *Information & Ship's Log*.

We went over to it, Tamara tapping an icon on the main screen, then another. She tapped a few times, typing periodically into the touchpad's on-screen keyboard. "Nothing," she finally said. "It figures. They requested a private listing."

"Maybe it's not reserved under her name. Let me try," Scylla said.

"I tried Condor and a few other names. I even tried just GSAF." Tamara shrugged, watching as Scylla tried a few other search results to no avail. "We figured they didn't want Nadin talking to us. That just confirms it."

I sighed, rubbing my temples. "Can you hack it, Henry?"

Tamara's eyes bulged. "Isaak! Are you crazy?" She whirled on Henry, who'd been opening his mouth—whether to tell me he could or not, though, I had no idea. "Absolutely not! He's in enough trouble as it is."

I flushed. "It was just a joke," I said. But the truth was that I'd been about ninety percent sincere in my request. I didn't like how isolated they were keeping Nadin. The thought of not being able to talk to her again until we reached Earth made me a little queasy. But Tamara was right, of course. I couldn't ask Henry to do something that would draw more fire to him.

Scylla squeezed her eyes shut. "Okay, all right. I think we've all had enough for one day. Everyone's stressed. We're all going to be at each other's throats if we don't cool it." She opened her eyes, looking us over. "Why don't we call it a night? We can figure out what to do about Nadin in the morning."

I looked glumly back at the console, the ship's log mocking us. I supposed it didn't matter. Even if we could figure out what room she was in, if GSAF really wanted to keep her away from us, the guard would just turn us away at the door. "Fine," I said. "Let's just go."

When I got back to our tiny cabin, Dad was already there. I wasn't sure he'd ever left the room, to be honest. He was lying on the bed with a bag of pistachios from the little minibar wedged between the foot of the bed and the wall. There was a pile of shells spilled across his chest and on the coverlet. I perched awkwardly at the foot of the bed, pulling out my palmtop to distract me from the sound of the cracking shells and his noisy chewing.

"Did you have a nice dinner?" he asked around a mouthful of pistachio.

"Yeah. We ate at that diner down on the rec level. Have you eaten yet?" I kind of hoped he hadn't yet, that he might be leaving soon to do so and I could have the minuscule room to myself for a little bit.

"Yup. Couple hours ago."

"Oh." I tried not to sigh and looked down at my palmtop. The browser had opened to top news stories for the day. *Earth prepares for visit from native Martian princess.* My stomach flipped at the words.

"How do you think they decide what time it is on this ship?" Dad asked. He pulled another nut out of the bag, examining it. The shell hadn't split completely—it had been harvested too early. He was going for it anyway, though. He wedged his thumbnail into the small split in the shell. "Like, the clock on the wall says eleven thirty, but my watch says it's only nine thirty. People who are traveling are coming from all over Mars and Earth. They're all from different time zones. So how do they pick which one to have the ship set on?"

"I think it's set to UTC," I said, tapping on the headline. A picture of Nadin taken at the press conference last month appeared. Her hair braided, the black blazer over her turtleneck making her look at least ten years older.

"Oh, yeah?" He let out a hiss suddenly, flinching and shaking his hand out. The pistachio shell had bent his thumbnail back. "Which UTC? Ours or Earth's?"

"They're the same. That's why it's *universal* coordinated time."

Dad narrowed his eyes, mouthing the words to himself. "Why's the acronym UTC instead of UCT?"

Was he going to keep this up all night? "I don't know," I replied.

I scrolled through the news story, not really reading it until my eyes caught on this sentence: *Incoming Aeolis Province governor Joseph Condor will be participating in negotiations between the Iamoi and GSAF. The governor arrived in New Canaveral earlier this week as part of his transition —*

Dad cursed under his breath, still wrangling with the stubborn pistachio shell. I couldn't take any more of this.

"You know what," I announced, "you're right. It's too early to go to bed. I'm going to go look around some more, see if there's anything else going on on the rec level."

Dad nodded, still concentrating on his nut. I tried to keep from clenching my teeth and left the cabin.

Tamara's room was on level 5. I headed down the hall to the elevator. The lighting had dimmed, switching from the warm white LEDs that were on during the day to a blueish hue to mimic night. Since there was no natural lighting for the duration of the voyage, the ship tried to simulate it to keep our bodies' circadian rhythms relatively normal. The hall was quiet; several doors had Do Not Disturb signs hanging from the knobs already. Probably people from other parts of Mars, in later time zones, were actually ready for sleep. But not me. With my dad in the same torquing bed as me, I probably wouldn't be sleeping at all the entire trip.

The elevator dinged as it deposited me on level 5. I stepped through the doors and almost collided with someone passing. "Oh, sorry," I started to say, but I realized a moment later it was Henry. "Hey. You on this level, too?"

He shook his head. He looked tired, much more tired than I felt. I wondered if he'd gotten much sleep over the last couple weeks, or if he'd be getting any tonight. "No, I'm just sightseeing," he said. I quirked my head at him, but he didn't elaborate. Instead, he asked, "You looking for Tamara?"

I opened my mouth, uncertain how to respond. My first inclination was to say *no*, but then I realized how ridiculous that would be. It's not like it was a secret. Like I wanted to have some kind of clandestine meeting with her or something. "Yeah," I finally said.

He gestured over his shoulder. "She's not in her room. She's down at the end of the hall. On the observation deck thing."

"Thanks. You want the elevator?" The doors were still open, since I was standing in the sensor zone still.

"Nah, I'll take the stairs. You never know who's going to show up on an elevator."

I furrowed my brows. "I mean, if that's what you're thinking, you never know who's going to show up in a dark stairwell, either."

"Yeah, but it's easier to fight in the stairs. You can push your assailant down them if need be. What are you going to do in an elevator?"

Well, that got grim in a hurry. I tried to smile at him, but I think it turned out more like a grimace. "Well. Good luck, then."

"Thanks," he said blandly, shuffling away at his usual leisurely pace. "Night."

"Night," I murmured, watching him for a moment before turning and heading down the dim hallway in the direction he'd indicated. This level was just as quiet as the one I'd left behind. People were obviously sleeping or still out having fun on the rec level.

The hall came around a corner that opened up to a large, windowed area with a few chairs and potted plants sprinkled around it. Standing beside the window, her hand against the glass, was a slim, short figure with long hair. Tamara. She was looking out at the stars as they slowly spun around her. The distant, blinding orb of the sun. The shrinking dot of Mars, Phobos and Deimos already invisible to our eyes. The small striped blob of Jupiter. The even tinier blue speck that was our destination, Earth. They all danced in and out of view as the ship silently turned.

"Hey," I said, coming up beside her.

She jumped, startled. "Oh, Isaak," she said, jerking her hand away from the glass. In the shadows and starlight I couldn't quite see her face, but her voice was watery. She'd been crying.

"You okay?" I asked softly.

She swiped at her eyes with the back of her hand. Her head turned enough that I could see her a little better now, in the bluish lighting from the sconces on the wall behind us. "As okay as I'm going to be."

I frowned at her dark expression and even darker words.

She shook her head. "I'm sorry. I'm just stressed. You know me. I have trouble coping with stress anyway. And I'm just... worried. About everyone." She squeezed her eyes shut, struggling to keep more tears from slipping out. "I'm so worried, Isaak. I can't shake this horrible, horrible feeling that one of us isn't going to make it out of this. I've tried so hard to keep it together. All these years." A shining tear slid down her cheek. She wiped it away in annoyance. I felt like I should do something—take her hand, put my arms around her, *any* kind of reassuring gesture— but I was rooted in place. Just as I'd been that night on the boardwalk.

"You know," she said, "when you were gone, I tried so hard to keep us all together without you. It felt like you were the glue that held us together, and without you it was like trying to get broken pieces of pottery together just by balancing them. Or something." She shrugged. "I know that's a terrible metaphor."

"No, I get it," I said softly. I felt miserable. I could see the aftermath of it every day, but no one had seemed really willing to talk about it. How hard it is to maintain a friendship when your world is falling apart.

"We got through it," she murmured. "And I thought we were stronger for it. And now that you're home, I wanted everything to go back... back to how it was. All of us together. Easy friends, like it always used to be. But maybe we're too broken for that now." She swallowed stickily. "I'm sorry. I think it's just the stress talking," she said, running a hand through her long, long hair. "I just wanted us to all be together. I want to keep us all together. But GSAF wants to rip us all apart. And I feel like someone's going to get lost in the shuffle. Or... or worse."

She was talking about Henry, I realized. She thought GSAF was going to do something to him. She'd been alluding to it all evening. Even Henry had, with his black joke about the stairwell. They didn't believe Nadin was going to be able to save him.

I couldn't bring myself to say it aloud, but I was starting to fear the same thing. But would it just be prison? Or worse?

Faced with a lifetime of prison, maybe worse wouldn't be the worst.

The thought horrified me. It snaked into my mind unbidden, making nausea overwhelm me.

"Listen, Tamara." I was speaking before I'd even realized the words had formed in my mind. "Maybe this is too much."

"What is?"

I hesitated, unsure of how to say it. "Us."

She stared at me, her expression guarded.

"What I mean is, if you're so stressed out, maybe now isn't a good time for a relationship. Maybe it would be easier if we could just go back to being friends. If, um, if that sounds good to you."

"If that's what you want," she said. Her voice was as unreadable to me as her face. I couldn't tell what she was feeling. Had I hurt her, or was she relieved? I was shocked to find that I was relieved. The words had felt like a lead weight on my tongue, but once I said them, I suddenly felt a hundred kilos lighter.

"Yeah. I think that would be best. For both of us," I said.

"Okay," she said quietly, turning back to look out the window, resting her forehead against the glass.

I started to open my mouth to say something, even just "Sorry." But I couldn't get the words to come. I couldn't get any words to come at all. Anything I could think to say just seemed insufficient right now.

We stood quietly, looking out at the unending stars.

Chapter 19

- n a d i n -

MY BODYGUARD HADN'T LEFT MY SIDE FOR MOST OF THE EVENING. He was so conspicuously present—periodically opening the door to look up and down the hall, and even screening the waiters who'd brought lunch and dinner to my room—that I was growing ever more convinced that Geoff Preston's visit to me hadn't just been a chance encounter. GSAF wasn't letting me speak with anyone. So why had they allowed Preston into my room unsupervised?

The guard had turned on a box against the wall hours ago that played video. I'd had one of these as well in the hotel GSAF had moved me to after taking me from Bryn and Delia's home. It was called a *television*, they said. Not very commonly used these days, I was told, since most people preferred virtual reality like Speculus, or else to stream videos on their palmtops or deskpads. The implication had been that they didn't trust me enough to give me any of those devices—something I found amusing, since, not being able to read English, I likely wouldn't have been able to get far with it. A television, on the other hand, was acceptable. All you could do on it was turn the channels to different videos, and I'd gathered a while ago that I was only receiving pre-approved channels—ones that played videos of fictionalized stories rather than anything that had news or real-world content.

Weeks of television watching had had one advantage, at least. A lot of times there would be text on the screen that seemed to match something the characters were saying. I'd slowly managed to determine that the English alphabet used letters rather than syllable glyphs. The problem was figuring out which symbol made which sound. If I was still allowed to talk to Isaak, I would have asked him to show me how to read. It would have saved me weeks of boredom. But if I'd been allowed to talk to Isaak, I wouldn't have had the weeks of boredom to begin with. And Stephen Moyer, who'd been at my hotel every day during my exile, had clearly been instructed not to teach me anything at all. I was there to instruct him, not the other way around. I was grateful he hadn't come along on this voyage, at least.

The bodyguard yawned as the video he'd been watching ended, a moving wall of text scrolling across a dark screen as music played. "Well, princess, ready for bed?"

This was the moment I'd been waiting for. "Yes," I said, miming a yawn of my own. "Are you going to sleep in here with me? I have trouble falling asleep with others in the room."

"I'll be next door. But don't worry, I'll check on you throughout the night. You'll be safe."

Safe from whom? I wondered irritably. There were only a few people on Mars I'd felt threatened by, and I was firmly in their grip now. Would this bodyguard protect me from himself?

My pajamas had been unpacked and neatly folded on shelves

in the large closet attached to the luxurious bathroom. I changed into these quickly, not wasting any time on ablutions. The sooner I "went to sleep," the sooner I could try my plan.

The bodyguard watched from the doorway of his adjoining room as I pulled back the covers and slipped into bed. I rolled onto my side, my back to the door, and then pulled up the sheets so that they covered almost all of my head.

I heard the man in the doorway laugh. "Can you breathe that way?"

"Yes. This is how I'm used to sleeping," I lied. It was uncomfortably stifling under these covers, but I'd thought about it all evening and this was the best strategy I could come up with.

"All right, then. Suit yourself. Good night."

Against the far wall, the rectangle of light from his room disappeared, and I heard the door latch.

I lay there quietly, waiting.

Ten minutes later, I heard the latch again. No light came this time, but I knew the door had opened.

I closed my eyes, breathing slowly and evenly.

Soft footsteps moved across the floor of my room, barely audible. My heart raced a little, but I forced myself to keep my breathing regular.

The footsteps crept slowly around my bed, coming up on my right side. Then I heard his breathing, close to me. Felt his shadow fall over my bed, across my face. I didn't move. Soft, shallow breath. In... out.

He stood over me for a long moment, watching the square of my face that was exposed. Checking to make sure I was really asleep. Finally, I heard him move away. I didn't react. I just kept breathing. In... out. In... out.

The door closed behind me.

I didn't move. Not just yet. I waited another ten minutes, and sure enough, there was the sound of the latch turning again. This time he didn't approach me, though. He watched me for a moment from the door, making sure I was still there. I could hear the sound of the television in his room, now. His companion for this overnight vigil. Would he sleep at all tonight? Or would another guard replace him in the morning?

The door closed.

I waited another minute, then sprang out of bed. Quickly I gathered the spare pillows I'd found in the closet, the rolled-up blankets, and shoved them up under my covers. I fussed with them in the dark, arranging them in what I could only hope was a close enough approximation to my body that the guard wouldn't be suspicious the next time he opened the door. When I was finally satisfied that the pile of pillows looked enough like me to fool him, I hurried over to the bar that took up the wall across from the door to his room. I crouched behind it, waiting.

A few minutes later, the door opened again. Through the glass cabinet of the bar, I could see his blurry silhouette.

He stared at the blanket pile. I held my breath.

The door closed. He was gone. He'd fallen for it.

I let out the breath I was holding, shakily sinking back against the wall, my heart beating erratically. I only gave myself a moment to steady myself. Then I jumped to my feet and hurried to the door.

I needed to figure out a way to keep it from locking, which it seemed to do automatically. I hadn't been given a key, so I had no way to let myself back in. To my relief, though, when I opened the door I saw that there was a placard of some kind hanging from the doorknob. It had three words written on it in English, two short ones and a longer one. I didn't puzzle over its meaning—quickly, I slipped out the door, shoving the placard in between the jamb and the latch. The latch held. I pushed it once to test, and the door slipped silently open. I breathed out in relief, replacing the placard against the jamb and scurrying silently down the hall.

This was the part I hadn't thought through. Once I was out, what would I do next? I needed to try to find someone I knew—Isaak, Tamara, Scylla or Henry—somewhere on this massive ship, without running into anyone else who might recognize me. A tall task, considering I'd be instantly recognizable to just about everyone aboard this ship, apart from maybe the friendly GalaX employee who'd welcomed me aboard.

It was late enough, at least, that the floor was deserted. Most of the doors had the same placard as the one I'd used to prop my door open hanging from their handles. The lights were dim, and everything was quiet.

I couldn't take the elevator—someone might see me—but I knew there must be a flight of stairs around here somewhere. Back on Mars, that day we had all gone shopping, Mariyah had said in the parking garage that she didn't like to take the elevator because it made her nauseous. Scylla had commented that all buildings were required to have stairs in addition to an elevator for safety reasons, in case of fire or in case the elevator broke down. I assumed this ship was likely built the same way.

I crept quietly down the hallway, trying to keep to the

shadowed area along the wall. Before long, I spotted a door that had a diagram over it, a zigzagging line that sort of resembled steps. There had been one of these over the stairway in the parking structure as well. I opened the door and, to my relief, found a staircase inside.

Now, which way to go? Down, or up?

I decided to go down, since I knew my room was in the upper levels of the disc. Probably Isaak and the others were on a lower level. But where? As I descended the steps, my senses seemed to catch up with me and I realized how utterly ridiculous this idea was. Isaak would most likely be in his room now. How was I supposed to find him? I couldn't just knock on every door, hoping that he would open up before someone who'd report me to GSAF. And what if he *wasn't* in his room? If he was in one of the public areas, there'd be dozens of other people around him, all staring at my undisguisable hair.

As my thoughts swirled, a door opened to my right. I gasped, shrinking away in horror. This was it. I was caught. I'd only made it two flights down and I was already caught. Of all the stupid—

"Nadin?"

I blinked. Henry was standing in the doorway, staring at me.

"Henry!" I cried. "Thank goodness! I need to talk to you. Or to someone, anyone—"

"How did you get away from GSAF?" he asked, looking me over. I flushed as I realized I was in my pajamas.

"It's a long story. And I have to hurry and get back before my guard notices that I'm gone."

"Do you want me to find Isaak for you?" Henry asked.

"No," I said, even though it was a lie. I *did* want to talk to

Isaak. But there was no time. "But can I talk with you? Somewhere private?"

He nodded. "Come on. I know a good place."

He led me down a couple more flights of stairs, then stopped in front of a door, cautiously opening it a crack and peeking inside. Then he opened it wide. "It's clear. Come on."

The floor the door opened up onto wasn't like the others. There were exposed pipes, bits of machinery, cleaning supplies, and piles of boxes. The windows on this level were smaller, sporadic squares only a few hands' widths across.

"What is this place?" I asked, looking around myself.

"It's a maintenance floor. Hopefully nobody will come through here while we're talking. But we probably ought to make it quick. What's up?"

My mind felt like a sudden blur. I had a million and one things to say, the foremost of which seemed to be a hysterical sob of, "*Please don't make me go back to that room.*" I couldn't bear being alone with no one but GSAF guards for another ten days. But there was nothing Henry could do, and an emotional outburst like that would just waste precious time. So I swallowed it down and focused on the most important thing.

"Geoff Preston is aboard this ship. He came to my room earlier."

"The GalaX guy who talked to you on Herschel?"

"Yes. He seemed impatient. He spoke urgently. He asked me if I'd considered his offer."

"What did you say?" Henry asked, watching me curiously.

"I told him I had to decline. It seemed to make him angry."

Henry made a thoughtful noise, but didn't say anything.

I took a deep breath, trying to articulate what about this was bothering me most. The reason why my guard had disappeared long enough for Preston to talk to me. Almost like he'd *let* him in. "Henry," I said, "did I understand you correctly when you said that GalaX was working with GSAF on the System?"

"Yeah. They were independent contractors. But they were from GalaX."

"Didn't that bother Bryn and Delia? To know that their company was involved with GSAF that way?"

"I think so. I didn't go into it a lot with them. But I think there's more going on at GalaX than they have any idea about," he admitted. "Delia's kind of touchy about it because she was close with GalaX's founder, Johann Kimbal. He gave her a job when she was really young. But he's gone now. He died at least fifteen annums ago. I don't necessarily know that the company's in good hands anymore. I'm not so sure about their higher-ups."

"Like Geoff Preston?"

"Yeah. I have no clue who he is, but I'm taking it you don't trust him."

"No. I don't." I kept thinking about what he said before he'd left my suite earlier. "*I'm sorry.*" Sorry for what? "But I can't help but feel like maybe I'm making a mistake. Maybe I shouldn't have been so quick to work with GSAF. But they're the leaders. They're the *geroi* of this time. I don't know how to help my people without them."

Henry studied me for a moment. Finally, he said, "You just have to go with your gut, Nadin."

"What does that mean?"

"It means trust your instinct."

"But that's the problem, Henry," I said, turning away from him, looking out one of the small, square windows. "I *don't* trust my instinct. I was never meant to come here on my own. Ceilos and Gitrin should have been here with me. I can't do anything without them."

He watched me quietly. "If that's what you believe," he said solemnly, "then it's probably true."

His words deflated me. They were like a blow, pummeling my spirit. A confirmation of everything I'd been telling myself these last several weeks. Of the words from my nightmares.

Then, softly, he added, "But it's only true because you believe it." I looked over at him in surprise as he went on, "You need to have faith in yourself. You. Nadin. You've got to rely on yourself. You've got to trust that you can handle what life's throwing at you. If you don't have that trust, you'll never make it. But if you do, you'll be surprised by what you can accomplish."

"I want to," I protested. "I just... don't know how. It's hard for me to look at the world the way you all do. Everyone on Mars seems to place so much value on being yourself, believing in yourself." I twisted my ace ring. It was a symbol of my being different, but here that was something to celebrate, not something to be ashamed of. It was a symbol of pride. But on Iamos, the only such symbol that was worth acquiring was the medallion around my neck. The symbol of being part of the highest caste. That was the only thing that distinguished me from the hive, the oneness of our lives on Iamos. Everyone with the same skin color, the same eye color, the same hair color. The same facial traits. The same clothing every day. A new standardized language to replace the different dialects the world had had before. No music. No laughter. No love.

"You know what I think your problem is?" Henry said after a moment. "Your problem is that you're looking at the world as a collectivist rather than an individualist."

"I don't know what that means," I said with a sigh.

"It means... Look, you're Iamoan. Iamoi?" He stumbled over the word. "So you're different from us Martians. But that doesn't mean you're the same as every other Iamoi. Or every other... what's that word for your caste?"

"*Patroin*."

"Yeah, that. You're *not* the same as every other *patroin*. You're you. You have your own set of life experiences that have made you what you are. And you're not the only one who's different. Every single *patroin*, every single person on Iamos, every person on Mars, every person on Earth... They're all different. No two people's experiences will ever be the same, no matter how similar they are. And that's why you need to believe in yourself, Nadin. Because those experiences that are unique to you are what make you strong."

I looked at my reflection in the window, semi-transparent, and beyond it the dark spiral of stars. Henry's words made my mind hurt. But... I wanted them to be true. I wanted to believe that I was strong. Strong enough to trust my instincts. Strong enough to face GSAF. Strong *because* I was different, not in spite of it.

"On Iamos they told us that individualism is what led us to the cataclysm in the first place. That the collective only exists because we had no other choice."

Henry's reflection beside me smirked. "That's always what

they want you to believe."

I smiled back, a little spark growing in my chest. Maybe Henry was right. Maybe I was here for a reason—because I was the right person to do this.

"Thank you, Henry. Any other words of wisdom?" I asked teasingly.

"Yeah. Taxation is theft."

I laughed aloud. "I'll keep that in mind," I said. Then I sighed. "I suppose I should get back now. Hopefully I've timed this all right and my guard won't have noticed my absence." Or what I'd done to the door to keep it from locking. "Could you give Isaak a message for me?"

"Sure."

I inhaled through my nose, looking down. "Let him know I'm all right, but GSAF is watching me. Watching everything I do. Tell him not to worry. I have a backup plan for dealing with GSAF."

Henry smirked with approval. "Good. He'll be glad to hear that. I'm glad to hear it, too."

I smiled, my face hot. "And one more thing, Henry..." I hesitated, the sentence frozen on my tongue. I'd wanted to say it, but now that it came time to form the words, I couldn't quite bring myself to it. Not just yet.

I still wasn't ready to forgive him.

"Nadin?" Henry asked.

I shook my head. "Never mind. That's all."

Henry nodded. "Okay. Good luck, Nadin. Hang in there."

I gave him a taut smile. "You too."

I crept silently back up the stairs and down the darkened hallway toward my room, hoping I'd remembered the way correctly—and that I'd remember which room was mine.

"It's okay," I whispered to myself. It would all be okay. I had to have faith in myself. I had to be strong. Because when I faced GSAF next week, I was going to need that strength.

Not just for me. For everyone.

PART THREE
EARTH

New Canaveral, Florida
United States of America
2075 C.E.

CHAPTER 20

- i s a a k -

I CLENCHED MY TEETH, BRACING MYSELF FOR THE TURBULENCE of entering Earth's atmosphere, and the transition from weightlessness to the strong, uncomfortable pressure of Earth's gravity. The artificial gravity on the *Athena* created by the rotating habitable area was designed to ease us between planets over the ten-day travel period. Each day as we'd approached Earth, the *Athena*'s disc had rotated a bit more quickly. Not enough to be noticeable to us, but enough for our bodies to gradually adjust from the lighter weight of Mars to the heavier one of Earth. At least, in theory. I knew very few people who didn't feel disoriented in their first few days on one planet or another, particularly if they spent most of their life on one. I suspected that the brief period of weightlessness on the spacejet coming and going exacerbated things. Maybe it wouldn't be so bad if we went straight from the ship's artificial gravity to Earth, but there was always that flight in between that made my body secretly hope I was going to be back on Mars in a minute, and not on Earth where it would discover I'd suddenly almost doubled my weight in a very short amount of time.

I hoped Nadin would be okay with it. I'd been here several times, so I knew what to expect. But this was her first time—as far as I knew, she'd never left Mars. I wished I could be with her when she took her first steps on Earth, but this time we weren't even on the same connecting flight. I was on this flight alone with my dad. A GSAF agent had come to our door yesterday to give me instructions on what to expect for our meeting with the Council on Monday, but it was clear that they weren't going to let Nadin and I see each other before then. They didn't want to give us time to come up with any kind of scheme against them. I was there to be Nadin's interpreter, and that was it.

She'd told Henry she had a "backup plan," whatever that meant. I wish I knew what she was thinking. At this point it had been close to a month since the last time I'd spoken to her, and it was driving me crazy. Especially because our last words to each other hadn't exactly been cordial. I kept replaying that moment in my mind, over and over and over again. "*Venus looks gorgeous tonight.*" How could I have been so stupid?

She deserved to know the truth. She should have been told the truth from the beginning. But not like that. I wished I could do it over, but I still had no clue how I could have handled it better.

My thoughts were disrupted by a rough wave of shaking from the spacejet, and my body landing firmly in its seat. We'd entered Earth's atmosphere. The flight attendant said something cheerful over the intercom about remaining in our seats with our safety belts attached, and where the air sickness bags could be located. My stomach roiled, and beside me, Dad was turning green, but neither of us moved to grab a bag. We'd traveled by postern. Nothing was worse than that.

We passed through a seemingly endless bank of clouds, and then the sky opened up below us, clear and blue. The narrow strip of land that was the Florida peninsula bisected the pure blue waters of the Atlantic ocean and the Gulf of Mexico. In my periphery, I could see blots of green and tan clustered to the south and east of the peninsula: Cuba, the Bahamas, and the multitude of islands, both natural and artificial, that filled the waters between. The sweeping archipelago of the Keysteads, and to the east, the UFS. There'd been more islands, once, but the rising sea levels had swallowed many of them, along with much of the Florida coastline. Coastal cities all over Earth had been affected over the last few decades—some like San Francisco, near where Abuelo lived, had built sea walls to hold back the water; but most had simply shifted, gradually moving inland as their coastal edges crumbled, unless some sort of natural disaster like a hurricane came along to speed up the process. Like it had in Florida.

New Canaveral was one of the major spaceports in the United States, and this was our destination now. Rather than meet with her at the GSAF headquarters in New York City, the Council had opted for the more private location of Lago Verde. I'd looked this place up online when one of Condor's flunkies had brought the travel information to my mom before we left. It was a barrier island, part of the broken chain of islands that had once been one land mass, Palm Beach. A resort that had belonged to a former US president had been there at the turn of the century, but it had been destroyed in the same hurricane in the 2040s that also destroyed most of the original city. The US government had acquired Lago Verde along with several of the other decimated islands, and they eventually transferred its ownership to GSAF to provide a base of operations closer to the spaceport.

I was a little nervous, frankly, about GSAF wanting to meet with Nadin here rather than at their more public headquarters up north. It added to the sense that they were up to something they didn't want getting out. Before, I would have said that was Henry's paranoia talking. But now I knew better.

When the spacejet landed, I dutifully sent a text to Mom and another to Abuelo, letting them know we'd landed safely. Dad and I grabbed our carry-ons and wobbled our way into the airport. I sat in the recovery area much longer than I'd needed to when we'd boarded the *Athena*. More than Earth's gravity was weighing on me. Now that we were here, we were reaching the end of the road. Everything would be over in a few days. And what would be the result? What would become of Nadin and the Iamoi? Would I see her again after this? And what about Henry?

Eventually Dad stood, bracing himself on the handrail that ran around the perimeter of the recovery area. "My suitcase has probably come out by now. You ready to go?"

I swallowed and struggled to my own feet. "Yeah."

It was as we stood by the baggage claim, watching suitcases circle around on the conveyor belt, that I saw him. I'd known the last ten days had been too good to be true.

"Contreras and son," Joseph Condor said pleasantly as he approached us. "I hope you had a nice flight."

"As good as expected," Dad said. I silently nodded.

"Good, good. Well, Isaak, I'm here to collect you. We've

arranged for your accommodations on Lago Verde."

I looked back and forth between him and my dad in alarm. To my relief, Dad spoke up. "We've already got a hotel booked in Cocoa Beach. I was going to send Isaak down in a rental car tomorrow."

Condor smiled. "We'll save you the expense, then. Isaak will be coming with me now. We'll bring him back to join you on Tuesday."

On Tuesday? GSAF was anticipating that the negotiations with Nadin were only going to last one day? Or was that the maximum amount of time they were going to let me be part of them?

"Hey, man," my dad said—I felt a little swell of pride at the irreverence with which he was treating our esteemed governor— "I'm his guardian. You can't just take the kid."

Condor raised his brows. "Mr. Contreras. I'm not just *taking the kid.* That would be unthinkable. You, as his guardian, are permitting him to accompany me. Correct?"

Dad scowled at him, but he seemed unsure of how to respond. "Just leave it, Dad," I said with a sigh. "Mom will understand. Since she has so much *faith* in Mr. Condor here." I followed this up with a glare, but Condor merely smirked. He was getting his way. Of course he was. He always did. Why had we ever thought we could stand up to the juggernaut of government?

I grabbed my bags and followed him out of the airport. A black sedan with exempt plates on it was waiting for us in the curbside pickup lane. As I followed Condor into the backseat of the car, I realized that Tamara and Scylla would have to be alerted to the change in plans. They were on a later connecting flight, since they'd booked their tickets together a few days after I'd booked mine. They weren't officially part of this whole GSAF debacle—they'd come on their own for moral support. They wouldn't be able to enter Lago Verde, but I at least wanted to keep them in the loop.

As the car pulled away from the curb, Condor pulled his palmtop out and began tapping on it, just as he had the day he'd brought me back from Erick's dig site. The day I'd returned from Iamos and everything had gone to hell. He didn't seem to be paying much attention to him. Maybe I could just—

I slipped my palmtop out of my pocket as surreptitiously as possible. Just one quick text...

"You know, you're not under arrest, Isaak," Condor said from beside me, not looking up from his palmtop. When I gawked at him, he laughed. "You can text your friends if you wish. Let your mother know where you're going. She'll be worried about you."

I stared at him, suspicious. But there wasn't much I could do about it. If he said I could keep my palmtop, I wasn't going to argue. Quickly I group messaged Scylla and Tamara: *Change of plans. They're bringing me down to Lago Verde tonight.*

While I waited for their response, I sent another text to my mom informing her of what had happened. She, of course, replied nearly instantly, demanding to know if I was okay and that I keep her posted every hour until we got there.

After satisfying Mom's paranoia, another five minutes passed before my palmtop buzzed in my pocket again. It was a message from Tamara.

We'll meet u there. There's a coffee shop in West Palm Beach, the Purple Parrot Cafe. It's near the bridge. We'll wait for u there.

I kept my face neutral and put my palmtop back in my pocket.

The drive down to Lago Verde took about three hours. We drove along I-95 through cities with scenic white beaches dotted with palm trees, and through rural, swampy areas teeming with mangrove trees and hurricane debris. A storm had passed through here in the not-so-distant past. I wondered if there would be another while I was here. It was smack in the middle of hurricane season.

Finally, just as my butt had gone from *numb* to *get me out of this torquing car* and I was considering breaking the car's silence to request a pit stop, we passed a sign indicating we were entering West Palm Beach. There wasn't really a divide between this city or any of the others we'd passed through since entering Palm Beach County, but I knew this city was the one with the bridge to Lago Verde. We were close.

The city was dense, both sides of the freeway lined with strip malls and restaurants and hotels. To the west, the city seemed to go on forever. But eastward, past the various beach houses with their red-tile roofs and walls of climbing bougainvillea, beyond the clusters of docks and the tall masts of sailboats, I could make out the blue-green strip of Lake Worth Lagoon, separated from the Atlantic Ocean only by the broken chain of barrier islands that had once been a resort town.

We exited the freeway onto a street called Southern Boulevard. As the car turned, a bridge came into view a few blocks ahead, and beyond it on the far side of the lagoon, Lago Verde. It was larger than most of the other remnant islands we'd passed on the freeway, but I couldn't see much on it. The island appeared to have been completely reclaimed by nature—a thick green wall of trees and bushes seemed to surround it, blocking whatever lay within from the eyes of the rest of the city. The spiky fronds of tall sabal palms jutted out above the green canopy, and mangrove trees wandered out beyond the shore, but otherwise it was an indistinct green mound in the water, notable only for the narrow bridge crossing the lagoon into the city—blocked off from outsider access by a guard station.

When the car stopped at the guard station and the man inside the booth began examining Condor's credentials, I peered out the window down the bridge's length. About halfway across, I could see now that there was another narrow island south of the bridge. It was too small to be seen from the freeway, barely wider than a sandbar, but it was possibly even more densely forested than Lago Verde. Chunks of dead wood and the green tops of mangrove trees that were still holding on somehow spread out into the lagoon far beyond the island's shoreline, indicating how much wider this island used to be not that long ago. They crawled along up to the bridge, making me think that this bridge's feet were probably anchored in soil that was once above the waterline, and that the road had at one time crossed the island rather than passing north of it. The sign next to the guard station informed me that this was the remnant of Bingham Island, and that it was an Audubon preserve. *Home to the Ancient Gumbo Limbo Tree*, the sign read. *Access by permission only.* I couldn't see any birds from here, and I had no clue what a gumbo limbo tree looked like, but I wouldn't be surprised if some of the trees on that little strip of land had been there since Ponce de León first arrived. Anything could be hiding in there.

The guard bar blocking access to the bridge began to smoothly rise, and the car rolled forward once more, toward Lago Verde and GSAF and everything that was to come after.

As we crossed the lagoon, I stared into the thick tangle of trees on Bingham Island. From one of the contorted limbs of a massive red-barked tree that grew along the shore, at the edge of the woods—was this a gumbo limbo?—a vulture peeked out at me, reminding me uncomfortably of the *gamadas* on Iamos.

Beyond, something moved in the shadows. I only caught a glimpse of it for an instant. It might have been nothing. It might have been a bird or some other kind of wild animal, gliding between the branches and over the creeping vines that climbed up the red tree, over the bushes and shrubs, around the trunks of the palms and mangroves and other trees I had no name for.

But for some reason, it made me more uneasy than the vulture's piercing gaze had.

Chapter 21

- n a d i n -

THEY BROUGHT ME TO A PALACE IN A JUNGLE.

That was the only way I could describe this place, this island that GSAF called *Lago Verde*. It was nothing like the city that surrounded it, or the other islands I'd been able to see from the windows of the car. This island was densely covered with trees and plantlife, in a way that shielded it perfectly from the outside. No one could see in. And, standing on the balcony of my opulent second-floor suite, I could not see out.

I couldn't help but think this was intentional. This jungle had been deliberately cultivated.

I gripped the balustrade tightly, taking an uncomfortable breath. The gravity of Earth was nearly unbearable. My joints ached, my legs strained to keep my body upright, and my lungs struggled to take a breath almost as much as they had when I'd been standing outside the citidome on Iamos with no breathing apparatus. But while the atmosphere back home had thinned to almost nothing, this air was thick—much too thick—heavy with heat and humidity that made sweat bead on my forehead and my hair cling stickily to my scalp. Even now that the sun had long since disappeared behind the trees and the sky was darkening, the heat was oppressive. I could go back inside, I supposed, to the cooler air-conditioned suite they'd brought me to this morning, but after so many weeks trapped inside, first in the hotel and then in the stateroom on the *Athena*, a GSAF guard constantly at my side, I was eager to have even the small amount of freedom standing on this balcony afforded me.

I'd thought perhaps now that I was here, my confinement period would be nearing an end, but that hope had been dashed when lunch and then dinner were brought to my room on a tray. I supposed I'd earned their distrust by using Kate Ponsford to try to covertly sneak back to Iamos, but it still grated on me. They weren't taking any risks with me now. My guard hadn't appeared to have noticed my disappearance the first night on the *Athena*, but I didn't dare take that risk again. Especially not now, on the eve of my audience with the GSAF Council. I couldn't do anything to endanger my cause now.

In the trees, there was the sound of animals, a chorus of trilling sounds. The creatures had been much noisier during the daytime, but even now when I would expect they should be sleeping, I still heard small chirrups here and there. Earlier I'd seen one of the creatures making the noise, peering at me from the branches of a nearby tree. It was small, with a beak like a *kela* and beady black eyes. It trilled at me a couple times and then flew away on feather-covered wings. I'd watched it for a moment, awestruck. It was so simple for that creature to just fly away, never even looking back.

Right now, I'd give just about anything for some wings of my own. They'd finally dismissed my ever-present GSAF escorts, but that was simply because this place was so well-guarded that there was no need for them. There seemed to be cameras mounted in every corner of every room, and drones quietly buzzed around the perimeter outside.

I sighed with difficulty and looked around at the opulent courtyard beneath me. A pool of clear blue water stood in the middle, surrounded by mosaic tiles that reminded me of the *geroi*'s villa. Soft lights beneath the water made it glow supernaturally. A small waterfall gurgled on one side of the pool, the trickling sound of its waters soothing to my fraught nerves. Beyond the pool, across a neatly trimmed lawn, stood a squat outbuilding, detached from the rest of the villa. Sconce lights glowed on either side of its door, but the windows along its side were dark. Past this outbuilding, a stone wall topped with iron spikes surrounded the property. It looked ornate, decorative, like it was there for purely ornamental purposes and not to keep people out—or in.

There was nowhere I could go. I couldn't even get out of this suite of rooms, let alone across the courtyard and over the wall. A trellis with beautiful red flowers climbing up it was mounted to the wall right beside my balcony, taunting me, because I knew I could never climb it. Even now, a drone was buzzing by, watching me. I'd never even make it over the balustrade before an alarm sounded.

I was trapped in a palace in a jungle.

Dealing with GSAF was your idea, I thought glumly to myself. I was the one who'd turned down Geoff Preston twice. I had no choice but to remain in this gilded prison and hope that my meeting with the Council tomorrow went well. I had to trust my instincts—that this was the best choice, that declining GalaX's mysterious offer had been the right thing to do.

Outside the walls, I heard the sound of tires on pavement. Another car was coming. I couldn't see it from the balcony; this suite appeared to be on the rear of the villa, facing away from the gated drive we'd entered via. It was hard to tell, though. When we'd arrived, I'd been taken aback by the size of this building. It was only two stories tall, but there were wings tacked onto it in all directions, like it had been built one way and then added onto time and time again. Most of the building appeared to be made out of mud brick, but it was hard to tell for sure because the trellises with the climbing flowers covered much of the structure, stretching all the way to the red tile roof. Inside it had been like a maze of gold. Even the villas of the *patroi* were not so lavishly decorated. A woman wearing a suit not unlike the one I'd worn to the press conference on Mars had led me through a confusing patchwork of hallways, past rooms with dark, heavy-looking wooden doors. Finally she'd stopped in front of the door to this suite, unlocking it and ushering me inside. By that time, I was so turned around I wasn't really sure what part of the villa I was in.

All I knew was that I couldn't see the drive from here, but I'd been hearing cars coming and going all day. Was it the GSAF Council arriving, or were they already here? I'd been told that Joseph Condor would be waiting for me, but I hadn't seen him yet. I dreaded having to face those ice blue eyes again.

Pinpricks of stars were starting to form in the darkening sky. They seemed pale and distant compared to the perfect view I'd had aboard the *Athena*. The light pollution from the city across the lagoon probably didn't help matters. Here, on this densely wooded island, it felt like we were far removed from civilization. It was hard to believe a massive city sat just across the bridge.

One of the stars was brighter than the others, more yellow. Was this Venus? My chest clenched painfully. I leaned against the balustrade again, cursing this awful gravity.

There was movement in the courtyard below me. Shadows across the tile. I watched, curiously, and as they passed into the light thrown by one of the lamps along the walkway, I recognized one of the figures. It was Henry with a GSAF guard.

I gasped, followed by another painful chest clench. Henry paused, looking up at the sound. He noticed me standing on the balcony and met my eyes for just an instant. He waved, and I started to wave back, but then the GSAF guard muttered something at him and gave him a shove down the path that made me wince.

I lowered my hand, frowning. Where was that man taking him?

They kept walking, past the pool and across the lawn to the darkened outbuilding. The guard fumbled with the lock for a moment; then the door opened. Light poured out from within, but the windows of the building were still dark. They'd been blackened, so no one could see in, or even tell that the building was occupied.

What were they up to?

I looked around me, from the flower-colored trellis to my left to the thick branches of the tree to my right. Either of these would be a perfect escape route, but—

A drone buzzed past, the blinking red light on its camera fixed directly on me.

I slouched against the balustrade again, glowering. They were watching me too closely. And I didn't trust my body to be able to handle a climb down a tree or a trellis when I could barely take a full breath.

The sky faded from blue to purple. More stars began to peek through the darkness. The yellow orb of Venus rose slightly higher above the tree line.

I heard the sound of a door closing and footsteps on tile, and I straightened. Sure enough, another shadow was moving across the courtyard toward the outbuilding Henry had been brought to. I watched him, a tall man's figure. I expected it to be Joseph Condor, but to my shock, when he passed into the lamplight I saw it was Geoff Preston. My jaw fell open involuntarily. What was he doing here?

I gripped the railing until my knuckles ached, watching him cross the lawn and approach the door of the outbuilding. He knocked, and a moment later the door opened and he disappeared inside just as Henry had.

I stood there until my calves trembled and pain was shooting through my knees and hips. Until I was so exhausted I almost couldn't bear it. Until Venus was a hand's width above the trees, and Earth's moon had appeared in the sky like a pale slice of tokíl fruit, and I knew it was late, and I just could not stand there any longer.

No one emerged from the building.

The next morning I awoke in pain. A dull, throbbing ache across my body, centralized in each of my joints, and the distinct feeling that I'd slept with a heavy weight across my chest. I groaned, rolling over and slowly managing to push myself into a sitting position from my side. The only part of me that didn't hurt was my head, for once. Good. I needed it to be as clear as possible for this audience. Everything came down to this moment. Everything came down to me.

I took a deep breath, trying to summon the confidence that Henry had spoken about on the *Athena*. I'd never imagined that I would be doing this on my own. In all my preconceived notions, whether of being a *gerouin* or of facing GSAF, Ceilos had always been there. Ceilos with his mastery of persuasion. His ability to win people over that I'd never shared. We'd needed each other, I'd told myself, but I realized now it was that I had needed *him*. Because I didn't believe I could do it on my own.

I'd been thinking like a collectivist, Henry said, but I realized now with a jolt that Ceilos never had. And that was where that strength I'd so envied him came from. Ceilos valued himself as an individual, and he had confidence in himself because of it. Not because he was a *patros*, not because he was *geroi*'s blood, not because he was destined to become a *geros*. Because he was Ceilos. He had confidence in *himself*.

And I realized, distantly, that that was what Gitrin had asked of me during our evaluation. To think for myself. To have confidence in myself and my own individual morality. To make a decision for myself that didn't involve relying on Ceilos or the *geroi* or the hive mind.

That was why I'd failed. That was what she'd tried to explain to me when I reached Elytherios. But I still hadn't quite understood. She'd thought my choosing to come to Elytherios had been enough, but it wasn't. I'd needed that one extra step.

I'd needed to come here alone.

I got out of bed slowly and went into the opulent gold bathroom. I ran a bath, letting the warm water soak into my aching joints and muscles. When I emerged, I felt a bit better. I dressed, braiding my hair as I'd always done on Iamos and tucking my medallion under the collar of the blue turtleneck sweater I'd worn my second day on Mars. It was much too hot to wear the black jacket over the sweater. It was much too hot for the sweater, honestly, but I wanted to ensure I was dressed appropriately.

As I came out of the bathroom, my muscles starting to stretch out the more I moved, there was a knock at the door. Probably my breakfast. I opened the door. Isaak stood there.

"Hey," he said with an awkward smile. "Can I come in?"

I stared dumbfounded as he came through the door, followed by a woman in a suit, and a second woman holding a tray that must be my breakfast.

"Eat up," the woman in the suit said, without so much as a word of introduction. "You've got twenty minutes. The meeting is in the Blue Room. I'll escort you and your interpreter over when it's time."

"Thank you," I said quietly, taking the lid off my breakfast tray and staring down at the assortment of meat and eggs I'd grown accustomed to them serving me at the Plaza and aboard the *Athena*. I didn't have much of an appetite today. I took a piece of fruit and bit into it numbly, looking over at Isaak.

"Why are they letting you talk to me now?" I asked Isaak in Iamoi.

"I don't know," he responded. "As a courtesy? Maybe they figure it's too late now for us to try anything fishy."

I glanced over at the woman in the suit. She was watching us. I wasn't sure if she could understand Iamoi or not, but it was probably better to not push our luck. I ate a few more bites in silence.

"You ready?" Isaak asked, still speaking Iamoi.

"As I'll ever be." I hesitated, then decided to tell him about the thing that had been bothering me all night. I chose my words carefully, so that if the woman watching us didn't speak Iamoi she wouldn't hear any familiar names. "Last night I saw the man I told you about before. He was in the courtyard. Our hosts brought your friend to meet with him."

Isaak blinked at me. "What man?" He seemed to understand I mean Henry by *friend*, at least. I hoped.

"The man I told you about." I struggled to think of how to describe him without giving too much away. "The one who came up to me during dinner."

"The one who made you that offer?" Isaak asked, realization dawning in his eyes.

"Yes, him."

"The brought He—my friend to him?"

"Yes."

Isaak frowned. "Why?"

"I have no idea."

He looked at my tray of meats and eggs. "You going to eat your bacon?" he asked in English. I shook my head, and he reached over, taking the two strips of salted meat off my plate. "So he's here," he mused in Iamoi.

I wasn't sure which *he* he meant. I'd been surprised to see both of them here. I hadn't been sure what they'd been planning to do with Henry. And as for Geoff Preston... he seemed to turn up everywhere I went. I remembered his words just before he left me: "*We would rather work with you directly rather than having to go through GSAF. But if you refuse to deal with us, we won't have a choice.*"

And then, "*I'm sorry.*"

The woman in the suit got to her feet. "It's time," she said.

I looked at Isaak, trying to ignore the way my stomach was roiling within me. No going back.

"I'm ready," I said.

The woman led us down a set of stairs and through the confusing labyrinth of hallways before finally stopping in front of a wooden door that looked just like all the others here. She rapped twice, and the door opened. Isaak and I stepped inside, and she closed the door behind us.

The Blue Room was as blue as its name suggested. The large room was papered with a blue textured print, a stylized pattern that I'd seen in a few places in this time but had no name for. Huge framed paintings of the sea hung on the walls to my left and right, a small light built into the golden frame illuminating the paintings even in the semi-darkness of this room. The back wall had two windows, both of which were covered with heavy, deep blue velvet drapes, drawn closed.

A long table made of the same dark wood as the door took up the middle of the room. In the center of the table was a device in the shape of a pyramid, but with the top point squared off, making each of its four sides a trapezoid shape rather than a triangle. The GSAF emblem I'd seen many times on Mars lit up each of the sides. It was some sort of viewing device, though it didn't appear to be in use just now. Seated around the table were eleven people. Nine—three women and six men—I didn't recognize. These, I assumed, were the members of the GSAF council.

And two others I did know: Joseph Condor, and Geoff Preston.

I found myself staring at Preston. He stared back, his expression guarded. When I looked away, I saw everyone in the room was staring at me, in fact.

"Please, have a seat," the woman situated in the back center of the table said. She gestured at the two empty chairs opposite her. As Isaak and I sank into these, the woman said, "Mister Contreras, would you be so kind as to make the introductions?"

"Oh. Of course," Isaak said, his face coloring. He had no more idea of what he was doing than I did—what sort of protocol was expected for this situation. "Um. I'm Isaak, and this is Nadin." The Council members stared at him. Across the table, Joseph Condor let out a snicker. Isaak flushed more. "I guess you knew that." Switching to Iamoi, he said to me, "The Council's made up of representatives of the different continental unions. The idea is that they represent the interests of each of those groups' unified space programs. So there's four from the NAEU, the North American-European Union, including the president of the Council, Jeanette Gamberetti"—he gestured to two men and a woman in the back-left part of the room, plus the woman in the back-center who had done the speaking so far—"three from the Pan-Asian Alliance"—two men and a woman on the right side of the table, beside Joseph Condor and Geoff Preston—"one from the UASE, Unified African Space Exploration, and one from AESA, the South American Space Agency."

The man from the UASE was the only one of the nine whose skin was as dark as mine. The man from AESA had a complexion somewhere between mine and Isaak's, but the rest were much fairer. It didn't mesh with what I'd seen in Tierra Nueva, where everyone looked different but most were somewhere around Isaak or Henry's skin tone. There were also only three women here. This surprised me—the *gerotus* was comprised of equal numbers of men and women. A partnership from each of the citidomes.

"Well, now that the formalities have been taken care of, let's get started," President Gamberetti said. "Mister Preston, if you would?"

My eyes shot over to Preston. He stood up and began circling the table, handing something to each person seated. It wasn't until he reached me that I saw what it was: a System earpiece. I stared down at the small piece of metal in my hand in horror. When I looked up, he'd already moved on, avoiding my gaze.

"What's the meaning of this?" I demanded.

President Gamberetti glanced up from the deskpad in front of her. I realized that as Preston had been passing out the earpieces, the screens on the pyramidal display had lit up. Now they showed a large white room lined with multicolored flags. Fifteen people sat around a table not unlike the one in this room.

"Mister Preston is our System specialist," Gamberetti said as if it were the most uninteresting fact in the world.

"I thought he worked for GalaX," I said, watching with narrowed eyes as Preston sat back down beside Joseph Condor.

Gamberetti's eyes flicked back and forth between us for a moment. "Yes. We contracted with GalaX for this job. They reconstructed these earpieces for us using scans of archaeological artifacts found in the cave network east of Tierra Nueva."

Isaak put a quick hand on my knee under the table, silencing the boiling invective that was about to burst out of my mouth. His touch grounded me. There was more to this than met the eye. Had Preston's meetings with me been a warning? He knew GSAF was planning something with the System, and he wanted to give me an out? If so, I'd completely squandered my opportunity. Suddenly the meaning of his words hit home—"*If you refuse to deal with us, we won't have a choice.*"

I'd gone to GSAF in an attempt to *prevent* the System from being used in this time. But by not dealing with GalaX, I'd all but guaranteed the opposite.

Henry had told me to trust my instincts. And look where it brought me.

"What's with the livestream?" Isaak asked then, gesturing to the pyramidal display on the table.

"The UN Security Council," Gamberetti said, turning her scrutiny off me. "This is a matter of utmost importance not just to GSAF, but to the entirety of the United Nations. Now, let's get started." The others around the table raised the earpieces, fitting them into their ears with familiarity that showed they had done this before.

Isaak and I looked at each other in confusion. After a moment, Isaak said, "I'm sorry, am I misunderstanding something? Aren't you going to let Nadin have the floor? I thought this meeting was supposed to be about negotiating a settlement for her people."

"This meeting is about the System," Gamberetti said.

"That's not what we agreed on," I protested.

The president of the GSAF council glanced up at me, a light brown eyebrow arched over her hazel eyes. "We never made an agreement with you."

I looked at Joseph Condor, aghast. "But he said—"

"You have to let her talk," Isaak interrupted. "You can't just dismiss her without even listening to what she has to say. Her people need help!" He suddenly focused on the pyramidal display. "I thought the UN was all about human rights! And yet you're planning on just standing by while an entire race of people is wiped out?"

One of the men from the Pan-Asian Alliance scoffed loudly. "Human rights? You come here with *her* to talk to *us* about human rights?" He pointed an accusatory finger at me. "The Iamoi have a poor track record in regards to human rights. How would letting them come here be in our best interests?"

"What are they talking about?" I hissed to Isaak in a panic.

"I don't know! How do they know anything about you guys? Unless—" He broke off, looking down at the earpiece on the table in front of him, and suddenly I remembered the video recordings. The ones Henry had seen Isaak on. The ones Stephen Moyer had used to learn to speak Iamoi.

What else had they seen?

I picked up my own earpiece, staring at it in horror. I was almost afraid to find out.

"Let's be frank here. There's no need for pretense behind

281

closed doors," said President Gamberetti. "We know what your people really want from us. And we aren't prepared to bow to them so easily."

I squeezed my eyes closed, taking a deep breath in through my nose. And I slipped in the earpiece.

A wave of dizziness rolled over me, like it had the first time I'd stepped onto the boat back at Yellowknife Bay. The sound of static and the indistinct babble of voices in my mind as my brain reconnected to the System. After so many weeks without it, I found that putting the earpiece back on was almost as disorienting as taking it off had been.

It was only then, as the dizziness began to subside, that I realized:

The System works on Earth.

They'd said it didn't. The *geroi* said the System didn't work on Earth because of its magnetic field. The magnetic field disrupted the System's functions. That was the reason we'd lost contact with the groups of colonists who left Iamos hoping to settle Simos. Why they all disappeared.

But it was working now.

I opened my eyes to look at President Gamberetti.

"Mister Preston, if you please," she said.

Preston opened a System panel as effortlessly as if he were an Iamoi himself. "Play audio file: *gerotus* session," he said. He gave the command in English, but the System still responded. It had decoded English. Whether this was because of the scans we'd done on Isaak's brainwaves, or from these Earth people's apparent use of it, I wasn't sure. But the System had evolved in the time since I'd disconnected from it. If it recognized English commands now, that meant the auto-translator was working, too. The Council would understand everything they heard.

Voices were speaking in my ear now. I recognized them. This was the *gerotus* session that the Liberator had patched Isaak and me in on the day we left Hope Renewed.

"Medic Heros *oversaw the genetic testing conducted on the subject his first evening in Hope Renewed,*" said the voice of my father, Geros Antos. "*Neurological behavior, blood type, genetic composition and other factors were analyzed thoroughly by the System. Medic, if you would please report your findings to the gerotus?*"

"Yes, Geros," replied the medic. "*Preliminary findings indicate that though this boy demonstrates differences in physical traits — particularly in regards to skin tone, hair color, facial features and so on —anatomically and genetically, there is no significant difference between him and the Iamoi. The primary differentiation is neurological. His brainwave patterns are unfamiliar, and they show little responsiveness to the System. But while the subject was unconscious, I did some testing with an electroencephalogram. I would need to conduct further studies to be sure, but his brain seems to be attuned to the electromagnetic wavelength that the System calculates as approximate Simoi levels.*"

An unfamiliar woman's voice said, "*So the boy is from Simos.*"

"*It appears so, Gerouin.*"

"*But apart from the neurological patterns, you're saying there is no genetic difference between the Iamoi and the Simoi?*" asked the voice of Tibros, Ceilos' father.

"*No, Geros.*"

"*What does this mean, then? That the Simoi are actually*

Iamoi?"

"That seems the most logical conclusion, Geros. The Simoi are descended from an ancient colonization effort, and their brains have evolved to tolerate Simos' electromagnetic field."

"If this is the case, then it is possible we can use this boy's sudden appearance to our advantage. Simos is the most hospitable of the other planets, far more suitable than Hamos. The magnetic field has been our only barrier so far—that, and the hostility of its current inhabitants. Having one of them here on Iamos where we can study him may prove to be the key for colonization on Simos. Conquering the field, subduing the natives—this may now be in our grasp."

"How soon can more tests be conducted on the subject?"

"As soon as the gerotus approves the procedure. He is still in the hospital level in Hope Renewed. I have assigned Nadin to guard him." My mother, Gerouin Melusin, spoke those words. My stomach twisted at her voice and the memory of what was to come next.

The sound of Geros Tibros clearing his throat grated in my ears. "Are you sure that's wise, Melusin? Considering her... record?"

"I'm quite sure, Tibros. Nadin may be a simpleton, but she is absolutely loyal to the geroi. And she's desperate to prove herself— enough that she wouldn't think to question a direct order from the gerotus. At a time like this, that's exactly what we need."

I flinched, hearing the words again. A simpleton. Had my actions since that day proved them right?

"If there are no further remarks," Antos said, "a motion to approve further study on the subject from Simos —"

There was the sound of the members of the gerotus voting

their approval. This was where the Liberator had ended the transmission. I hadn't heard anything beyond this. As far as I'd known, that was the end. But the Council didn't move now. The recording wasn't over. I sat still, every muscle clenched, as Antos began to speak again.

"*Heros, begin the study immediately.*" There was a pause as the man left, and then I heard Tibros speaking again, in a subdued voice.

"*This couldn't have come at a better time. Now the development of the neurotoxin can resume.*"

"*Yes, this was quite a boon. The only thing holding us back was the physiological analysis. With a Simoi here, we should finally have the key. A toxin that attacks Simoi neural pathways without damaging Iamoi —an unstoppable weapon.*"

In a soft, even voice, Melusin interjected, "*It may be difficult, if the Simoi are as genetically similar to us as Heros' preliminary tests show. Maybe even impossible. There may not be enough of a difference for it to be safely used without the risk of contaminating our own people.*"

"*We are out of options,*" Tibros said, his voice hard. "*Our planet is dying. Our people are dying. Clodin —*" He broke off roughly, seeming to need a moment to compose himself. When he spoke again, his words were smooth. "*If we are to survive, we must find another world. Simos is our only option left now. And the only way to ensure that the current inhabitants of that world do not try to oppose us is with a weapon they can't fight against.*"

I felt sick. This was worse, far worse, than the portion of the session I'd heard before. I saw, now, why GSAF was so opposed to negotiating with us. Why they didn't want us to come here. How could they? Why would they ever trust us now?

"Stop audio file," Geoff Preston said.

Across the table, eleven pairs of eyes stared at me. Next to me, Isaak did, too. I couldn't look at any of them. I felt furious and disgusted and ashamed.

"You see, *kyrin*, why we could not possibly entertain discussion of bringing the Iamoi to this time," President Gamberetti said. "To do so could spell genocide for our people."

"But that's not fair!" Isaak cried, ripping his earpiece from his ear. "It's no secret that the *geroi* are shady. But what about the people subjugated by them? There are six million other innocent people on Iamos right now. They have no say over their government. The *gerotus* is a totalitarian dictatorship. The Iamoi have a torquing caste system, for God's sake. What about the poor people on the bottom caste who are trapped there under that dictatorship. Isn't turning a blind eye while they all die just as genocidal as what the *geroi* had planned?"

"Isaak is right," I added quickly. "Only the *gerotus* and the few scientists working with them would be aware of this plan. Most of my people would not agree to this. They would adamantly oppose it."

"Why should we trust what you have to say?" asked the man from the Pan-Asian Alliance who'd spoken before. "It says right there on the recording that you are loyal to the *geroi*."

"They also called her a simpleton," Isaak snapped. "They were too blind to see what was going on under their noses. Nadin's no pawn. She's the one who got me away from them—before they were able to conduct any more tests on me, I might add. She's no more loyal to the *geroi* than any of the rest of us."

I smiled at his words. I felt oddly conflicted at hearing it said aloud that I was disloyal to the *geroi*—it went against the grain of a lifetime of believing I was part of that world—but the fierce way he'd said I was no pawn made my chest swell with pride.

"So you say Isaak escaped the citidome before these tests the *gerotus* authorized here were conducted?" Joseph Condor asked, looking down at the deskpad in front of him thoughtfully, as if he was taking notes.

"Yes. The only scans they took from him were the ones Heros mentioned in this recording."

"To your knowledge."

I hesitated. "Yes. To my knowledge."

"But if they come here, they'll have unfettered access to our people. They could try again."

"They could try again anyway. Emil Hassan was separated from us when we left Elytherios. If we don't go back for him, there's a chance the *geroi* will find him and use his DNA to make the neurotoxin," Isaak pointed out.

The president turned to Condor. "Is this true?"

"There's a man by that name listed as a missing person in my province," he replied. "Both Isaak and his father testified that he had used the time postern to travel back to Iamos. That's the extent of my knowledge."

"He's there," I said firmly. I was sure he had to be. I was sure that he and the others hadn't entered the postern yet when Ceilos let go of my hand. They couldn't be... lost.

"And there's an entire rebel faction trying to overthrow the *geroi*," Isaak added. "Why not help them, at least?"

The members of the Council began to murmur to each other.

I tried to listen to what they were saying, but I realized that not all of them were speaking English. On the pyramidal display, the UN representatives were also discussing.

A tinny voice over the display's speakers asked, "If we were to help the Iamoi rebels, what would be the trade-off?" The camera switched to show a man with tanned skin and gray hair. He wore a wide patterned scarf around his neck, tucked under the lapels of his jacket. He looked directly at me. "What can you offer us in return?"

I took a breath, my lungs struggling against the gravity and my own nerves. "We can offer much. Our advanced knowledge of terraformation, our familiarity with Mars' geological history, the reintroduction of species native to Mars' ecosystem, our use of postern travel."

"That's not what we want. We want the System."

Beside me, Isaak scoffed. "What do you need her for? It's obvious now that your people have full access to the System already. Or at least way more than you'd claimed to."

"Access to view, but not to edit," Joseph Condor said before the man from the UN could respond. "Our linguists were able to translate the Iamoi spoken language, but its writing system, its numerical system, its programming language—they're too complex. They would take years to decode on our own. But Nadin could show us."

All eyes in the room turned back to me. I wanted to shrink under their scrutiny, but I sat tall instead. I'd come prepared for this question. I already knew my answer.

"I can't agree to that. The System is too dangerous. It's been used as a means of oppression on my world for too long," I said.

"So you want us to allow your people to come here, with their knowledge of System functions, and leave us with no means of defending ourselves? Even without the neurotoxin, there are myriad ways the System could be used as a weapon against us."

"The System must be destroyed," I said. "The aspects that interface with human brains, at least. That part of the System is not needed for postern travel. I could help you. We could ensure that the System is unable to be used again."

"Your people invented the System," President Gamberetti said. "They know how it functions. They could reactivate it. They could build it again. Our only defense is to have complete access to it now." I opened my mouth to argue, but she folded her arms, silencing me. "Those are our conditions, Nadin. We will *consider* aiding your rebel group. But only if you give us what we want. We want complete, unrestricted access to the System. Only then will we negotiate."

Cold fury was coursing through my veins like blood. They didn't want peace. They wanted control. They wanted me to give them complete access to the System now, and then *maybe* they'd consider helping the Elytherioi. Years could go by. I might grow old in the time Ceilos, Gitrin and Emil waited for those three minutes to pass. And the day of our return may still never come. I remembered Isaak's bluff back on Mars—that the Elytherioi might come after us if we never returned. But what would be waiting for them if they did? A hostile world with the same System that had been used to manipulate and control the entire populace of Iamos since the time of the Progression? They'd be walking into a trap, a second *gerotus* waiting to ensnare them.

And what of the *plivoi* who remained in the citidomes? Even if

I could persuade GSAF to help the Elytherioi, would they be willing to extend their mercy to the millions of others who were still trapped under the *geroi*? Or would only the few hundred people in Elytherios be saved?

The *geroi* were *gamadas*. But GSAF was no better. But did that matter? They had me cornered nonetheless. There was nothing I could do to oppose them.

"You just have to go with your gut, Nadin."

I took a deep breath and said, "Very well. I will give you what you want."

Beside me, Isaak hissed, "What?"

A ripple of surprise went through the group. President Gamberetti sat up straighter. "Excellent."

I touched my earpiece, opening a System panel. "The System has already decoded English, as I'm sure you've realized by Geoff Preston's ability to access the recordings he wished without speaking Iamoi."

Through the transparent screen of the System panel, Preston was watching me. The light from one of the triangular wall sconces was reflecting off his bald scalp, making the top of his head look blue.

"So it's simply a matter of instructing the System to use English as an administrative language." I swiped across the panel a few times. In my ear, a soft voice said, *"Biological patterns recognized. Geroi DNA detected."*

Next to me, Isaak slumped in his seat, glowering as he twisted his earpiece between his fingers.

"It's as easy as that?" Joseph Condor asked, his eyes narrowed.

"You just needed someone with override access." I held up my medallion, the symbol of my status as *geroi*'s blood. "Someone like me." I swiped across the panel one more time. "And it's as easy as that."

President Gamberetti smiled, clearly pleased that she was getting her way. Around the table, eleven faces watched me with approval. Eleven humans, connected to the System through their earpieces. Eleven bodies highlighted in blue by the program I'd just initiated.

In Iamoi, I said, "Adherence protocol activate."

An instant later, the room exploded into pandemonium. Around the table, the members of the Council screamed, crumpling forward in their seats, clutching their heads between their hands. On the pyramidal display, the representatives of the UN jumped to their feet, shouting, trying to figure out what was going on at the other end of their screens. But there was nothing they could do. They were too far away. By the time they were able to act, we'd be gone.

I hoped.

Isaak was already on his feet, flinging the door open and tearing out into the hallway. The sound of screams from the Blue Room followed us. I yanked out my earpiece, hurling it onto the floor as we ran. The sound of screaming was sure to attract the attention of guards. We needed to be as far away as possible before they arrived.

"What do we do now?" Isaak asked as we rounded a corner.

"We have to get out of here," I replied.

"Easier said than done. And what about Henry? We can't just leave him here! You didn't even get a chance to talk to GSAF on his behalf. And I don't think they'll be too inclined to listen to you now."

"We can't leave him. We have to get him out, too."

"But we don't even know where he is!" Isaak protested.

"I do. Remember? I saw him last night." I just had to hope that he was still there—and that his GSAF bodyguard wasn't. It was an impossible hope. There was no way we were going to make it out of here alive. There was no way—

There was an explosion in my ears, and the building shook, knocking artwork to the ground and shattering glassware. I barely heard my own scream as I fell to the floor.

CHAPTER 22

- i s a a k -

I STRUGGLED TO MY KNEES, LOOKING AROUND. THE HALLWAY WAS suddenly dark. Whatever that blast had been, the power had gone out with it.

"What the hell was that?" I asked.

"It doesn't matter," Nadin said. She was already on her feet, and she grabbed my hand, yanking me to mine. "We have to find Henry. Come on!"

We raced down the darkened hallway. At the end, I could see natural light. A window.

"Come on," I said, running to the window. There was a tall bronze vase on the ground next to it. I hefted it up and hurled it as hard as I could.

The window shattered.

I jumped the half meter through the window to the ground, Nadin right behind me. "Where's Henry?" I asked when her feet hit the grass. It was loud out here. Not far off I could hear the sound of footfalls, yelling, crashes and bangs and other noises that I didn't like at all, but the trees muffled it all. I wasn't quite sure how close they were, and I didn't want to wait around and find out.

"In one of the outbuildings by the big pool with the waterfall," she replied, seeming to struggle to catch her breath. I couldn't blame her. Earth's gravity was doing a number on me, too. You weren't supposed to physically exert yourself like this so soon after landing. I didn't know how much longer we could keep this up.

We came around the side of the mansion and skidded to a stop. We'd somehow turned the corner and entered a war zone. Security drones lay scattered across the lawn, powerless. Smoke was pouring from the door of what looked like a poolhouse, and small fires were consuming the bushes surrounding the building, licking up a wooden bougainvillea trellis toward the canopy of trees above. I hoped that wasn't where Nadin had seen Henry— but a quick glance in her direction and the stricken look on her face told me that it was.

"We have to get him out of there," she cried, racing forward.

I tore after her, but we were only halfway across the grass when three people in black burst from the smoking door. Their faces were covered by black bandanas, pulled up to just under their eyes. The black hoodies they wore, zipped up and with the hood covering their heads, combined with the kerchiefs made them look almost like ninjas. As they emerged from the door, a fourth figure followed: Henry. His ankle monitor was gone— whether removed officially or severed by the three figures in black, I had no idea.

The four of them raced across the grass and over to the wall, where a narrow section of the wrought-iron spikes that surrounded the perimeter had been removed. In a panic, Nadin and I raced after them.

Henry heard us coming, stopping to look over his shoulder. "Isaak! Nadin!" He turned back to the masked figures. "Wait! My friends—"

The shortest of the three figures turned to eye us. "Hurry up! If you're coming, you need to make it fast!" It was a girl's voice, and it was impatient.

Nadin drew up short beside the wall. "Who are these people?" she asked.

"Who cares? They're getting us out of here! Come on!" Henry bellowed. The first masked figure was already scrambling over the wall. The other two were wearing backpacks, but this one wasn't, and with his back turned to me, I could see a blue emblem screen printed on the back of the black hoodie: a seven-pointed star.

Then he was over the wall. "Henry first!" he shouted from the other side.

"Wait—" Henry said, but one of the other masked figures shoved him forward, and without another word he hefted himself over the wall.

Another masked figure vaulted the wall, and called, "The boy!"

I hesitated, looking back and forth between Nadin and the last remaining masked figure, the girl who'd spoken before. "No, I can't—"

"No offense, but you're more important to us than the Martian princess. So get your ass over the wall *now*," snapped the girl.

Behind us, I heard shouting. "Over here! Stop!"

"Goddammit," the girl spat under her breath. "Go!" she shouted to me. I looked to Nadin, but Nadin just shoved me forward.

"Go," Nadin whispered.

I scrambled up to the top of the wall, but instead of dropping to the other side, I looked back. The masked girl had pulled a glass bottle from her black backpack and was holding it in her left hand. With her right, she pulled a lighter out of her pocket, and in a quick, practiced motion, she ignited the contents of the bottle and hurled it at the approaching GSAF security. It exploded as it hit the ground, lighting up the grass with flame.

"Nadin!" I called, reaching my hand down to her.

She grabbed it and I pulled, dropping down to the ground as she pulled herself up onto the top of the wall. Her medallion was still hanging loose around her neck—she hadn't tucked it back under her turtleneck—and as I watched, it swung to her right, catching on the iron spike next to her. She dropped to the ground, but the medallion was caught. The chain snapped, Nadin letting out a cry as it pinched her skin. The medallion dropped to the ground—inside the wall.

"No!" she shouted, turning to scramble back up the wall.

"Leave it!" I yelled, grabbing her and pulling her away, after Henry and the other two figures in black. The masked girl was coming over the wall now. She jumped to the ground and kept right on running.

I followed the others blindly through the thick tangle of jungle around us. The ground was covered with gnarled roots and thorny vines that tripped me repeatedly, scratching at my ankles and cutting my palms bloody when I fell on them. Behind us, the sound of shouting was growing louder, and I heard barking dogs. They were tracking us through the wilderness.

We burst through the bushes and found ourselves at the shore almost without warning. Mangrove trees crawled out into the water beside us, effectively obstructing the edge of the waterline, but a narrow strip of sand had been cleared and a small motorboat was beached on it. The masked figure who'd led us over the wall charged into the shallows, pulling the boat backward off the sand even as the rest of us dove into the boat. The girl pulled on the engine's chain with a sharp motion, and the engine caught. We sped into the lagoon.

Behind us, I saw two other boats pull away from Lago Verde at the same time. I drew in a sharp breath, thinking they were GSAF, that we were already caught, but then I saw the black hoodies, the blue stars on the back.

"Decoys," the girl growled beside me. "We're going to mix them up. You three, get under this." She reached under the seat and yanked out a black tarp, hurling it at me. Henry, Nadin and I huddled together, throwing the canvas over ourselves. A small corner of the tarp didn't quite cover us, and through this I could see the branches of trees, the blue-green stripe of water, and the blur of another boat full of black-clad figures speeding past.

Beside me, Nadin was breathing heavily.

"Are you okay?" I asked.

"Yes. But my medallion—"

"It's okay. You don't need it."

"Get ready to run," the masked girl commanded, and my muscles tensed. A moment later, I felt the impact of the boat hitting another shore, and then the tarp was ripped off us.

"Come on."

We followed them into another thick clump of woods. I looked around as I ran, straining to get my bearings. Then I saw a mangled red tree and realized—gumbo limbo. We were on Bingham Island.

"Where's GSAF?" Henry asked, craning his neck. "Are they still following us?"

"We may have shaken them for now, but we need to keep moving. Come on." The small girl herded us through the thick underbrush, birds crying out as she disturbed their roosts, fluttering and flying in our faces as we crashed past them. A snake slithered between the vines on the ground and I blanched. But the others kept running, so I did too.

At the north edge of the island, a filthy white delivery van was parked just out of sight from the bridge. How had they managed to get it onto this island?

One of the masked figures flung open the back hatch, ushering us in. "Come on, come on, let's go," he barked. I raced after him, my eyes lingering on the dirt-encrusted license plate for just an instant. Two oranges, a small orange blossom, and the green numbers 762—

Henry, Nadin, the masked girl, and I jumped into the back, and he slammed the hatch closed. The other masked man was already waiting in the driver's seat, and when the one who'd shut the hatch on us hopped into the passenger seat, he turned the ignition. No automatic steering for these people. He slammed his foot down on the gas and the van lurched forward.

I crouched behind the driver's seat, trying to see through the windshield without much luck. There were no windows back here—no other way to see. The driver barreled forward across what seemed to be a trail that had been cut into the native growth and then carefully disguised from the road, based on the lack of opposition the van was facing. After a few seconds, we emerged from the trees and my mouth fell open at the sight before us.

The eastern half of the bridge had collapsed. Smoke still hovered in the air over the lagoon, a telltale sign that it had not been a natural disaster that caused this. The western portion of the bridge slumped into the water at an angle, like a broken bone.

"Did you guys do this?" I asked, my voice barely audible above the ringing in my ears.

"Yup," the girl said. I glanced at her—she'd pulled off her hood and her bandana was hanging loosely around her neck. Her hair was black on top, but it faded into blue at the edges, and it was cut shorter on one side than it was on the other. She looked Latina, but I wasn't a hundred percent sure. She smirked at me, the small mole next to her mouth disappearing into her smile line.

"Fresh," Henry said, seeming to catch his breath. "Great job. A-plus collateral damage."

"Who are you people?" I asked, not sharing Henry's enthusiasm. "And what do you want with us?"

She waited a moment to answer, watching the driver as he drove forward. When I realized what he was doing, I gasped—but it caught in my throat as the van entered the water but didn't sink. The water rose only as high as the van's tires. The tide was out, I realized with a jolt. The moons on Mars weren't big enough to cause any tidal action on our waters. But here, the tides shifted enough that things that were underwater some of the time could brush the surface at others.

The van sloshed through the water and up the ramp the broken west half of the bridge formed as it sagged into the lagoon. I held my breath for an instant, but the driver just pressed his foot down and we surged forward onto the bridge.

As the van sped along, the girl turned back to me. "We are the Stateless," she said, as if that were explanation enough. "And we didn't want all of you, exactly. We wanted Henry. But you were there, so..." She shrugged.

"But what do you want with me?" Henry asked.

"Our group has a vested interest in bringing down the current world order. I understand that this is a personal interest of yours as well."

Henry twitched an eyebrow. "My reputation precedes me."

"We've been keeping tabs on you," the girl said. "There's been a media blackout, of course, keeping almost any news about the Free Mars movement from reaching the people here on Earth. And I assume there's been a similar blackout on stories about us reaching Mars."

"Yeah, can't say I've heard of you guys before," Henry said. "Granted, I've been a little isolated recently."

We were approaching the guard station. I expected there to be trouble here—even a shootout, I thought with dread—but the bar was raised and the station was empty. Had they taken out the guard ahead of time? Or had he been in on it with these people? Maybe they had people on the inside helping them out, whoever they were. It would explain how they'd gotten that van onto Bingham Island unnoticed.

"That was intentional," the girl was saying, paying no attention to the road or the guard house. The van turned off Southern Boulevard onto a street that ran parallel with the lagoon. "The globalist powers are doing everything they can to squash dissent, and top on that list is suppressing information from the public." As she spoke, I saw another white delivery van merge in front of us. It looked almost identical to this one. The license plate read 762-GLE. This van's license plate had started with a 762 as well, hadn't it?

"You blowing the whistle on GSAF had a major impact," Lizeth said, "even if hardly anyone on Earth was allowed to know about it. GSAF is the weakest link, now. If we're going to break the globalists' power, we need to take them out before they get a chance to recover. And if they'd succeeded in making you disappear, we'd have lost our best chance at dismantling their power structure on Mars. We couldn't let that happen."

"Hang on," I said, glancing over at Nadin. She looked even more confused than I felt. "Would you mind explaining some of this? I've been out of the loop for a couple annums, and"—I gestured to Nadin with my thumb—"she's new to it altogether."

The girl sighed. "Fine. What do you want to know?"

"Your name would be nice."

"Lizeth," she said, sounding bored. "And those two in the front are Dante and Brandon." As she spoke, a third white van passed us on the right and merged in front of us. Another almost identical, nondescript delivery van. With the license plate 762-GLE.

Decoys.

"All right. Lizeth," I said, taking a shaky breath. "And your group is called the Stateless...?"

"Yes. We fight for the individuals and communities that have been betrayed by our governments. Disenfranchised by them. Left powerless." She sighed, looking out the windshield. "That's most everyone these days. Ever since passive citizenry became the law of the lands."

"*Passive citizenry?*" Nadin repeated. "What's that?"

"It used to be in most countries, this one included, that every citizen had a vote. The system was flawed, of course, and there were all sorts of avenues for abuse, but the general idea was that everyone had a voice. But economic times got tough. People were having trouble making ends meet, getting by on the wages they were being paid. So some brilliant politician came up with the idea that everyone would get a universal basic income—but only if they forfeited their voting rights."

"Meaning that only the rich would be able to vote," Henry added.

"Right. I can't believe the tradeoff would be worth it to anyone, but apparently it was to a lot of people. *Enough* people. Some folks didn't care about their vote—they didn't use it, anyway. Other people cared, but they needed the money in order to survive. And it did so well in one country, it started spreading everywhere."

"That's what the Greek Civil War was fought over," I said.

"Exactly. And that's how you wind up with what we've got today: only about thirty percent of people living in the NAEU have the right to vote. Everyone else is left without a say. And without that voice, the government just started sapping up more and more power. The North American Union joined with the

European Union to form the NAEU. The entire Asian continent and Russia formed the PAA. Both of those unions adopted mandatory passive citizenship for all their member nations. The whole thing is supposedly overseen by the UN, but that organization's a joke. Unelected bureaucrats who answer only to themselves. The continental unions can do whatever they want, and whatever they want is all in the interest of consolidating their own power."

"Just like GSAF," Nadin murmured.

"Right. GSAF is a part of this, too. These positions are all unelected, and they have complete, unchecked power over three-quarters of the world, and all of Mars. Even the so-called nations are run by leaders that were elected by only a tiny fraction of their citizens. The whole thing is a farce. The UN and the councils of the continental unions are the ones who control everything on this planet—in this *solar system*. Everyone else is voiceless. Stateless."

"So you're thinking if you can bring down GSAF, it would weaken the continental unions?"

Lizeth nodded. "Can you imagine if Mars were independent? If it was controlled by its own government, rather than the globalist cabal here on Earth? Free to form nations of its own, develop its own systems of government. It would be a beacon of freedom to this world. If they can break away, so can we. We can take back our votes, our voices. Our nations."

Henry folded his arms, leaning against the back of the passenger seat in front of him. "All right. But what made you so sure I'd be willing to help you out?"

Lizeth rolled her eyes. "Please. Anyone who uses the screen

name *PunjabiAnarchist* and posts the sort of manifestos you used to on the agorist chatspace is worth taking a risk on."

He sat up again. "Wait, what? How did you know about that? My account was encrypted."

"We've met before," she replied. "I've spoken with you on Speculus."

Henry gaped at her. "What? I've never talked to you before."

Lizeth grinned, revealing a crooked eye tooth that made her look like she had a fang. "Oh, but you have. I'm the one who wanted to talk to you about that coin you found."

"No way!" Henry exclaimed. "I talked to that guy! I saw him! He was—that was—" He broke off, looking her up and down, seeming to be trying to figure out how to phrase this without being an asshole. "Not you."

Lizeth laughed. "That was one of my burner figuscans. Complete with voice modulator. We keep tabs on those chatspaces, looking for new recruits for our organization. I can't exactly go on there as myself, can I? If I don't want to be arrested, anyway. I'm what you call a frontman. And frontmen like me have to be good at blending in. At adapting, changing—not being married to one identity. Most of us have adopted several, which we enhance in VR chatspaces with modified figuscans. If the feds are looking for a tall, middle-aged white man, they're not going to waste their time going after, you know, me."

I glanced over at Nadin, wondering if she was following this. If she was making the same connections I was. For some reason, Lizeth's words reminded me of Iamos. Maybe because the sound of that explosion earlier put it to the forefront of my mind, reminded me that we still didn't know what had caused that sound when we passed through the postern. Shared identities and burner figuscans—it made me think about Elytherios, and how the Liberator was a pseudonym they used when running Ferre into the citidomes and refugees out. The Liberator was a frontman.

But someone else had been using that identity, too. Whoever had recorded that session of the *gerotus* and kidnapped Ceilos had used that name. Like a burner account.

I can't exactly go out there as myself, can I?

Something about it set an uncomfortable niggle in the back of my brain. Like my subconscious was putting pieces of a puzzle together, but my waking mind couldn't figure out what the picture was showing me.

Henry was arguing, "But Joseph Condor said the man I'd been talking to about the coin had been detained by the FBI!" He broke off, cursing under his breath. "Of course he did. It was a setup. He was hoping I'd give something away about you, wasn't he?"

Lizeth nodded. "I'm not surprised. Everyone's been trying to shut us down. We're just lucky we haven't been traced to the UFS yet."

"You guys are based out of the UFS?" I asked.

"Yup. Last free nation on Earth," Lizeth said proudly. "The NAEU's been threatening to sanction the hell out of the UFS because they suspect they're aiding us somehow, but there's no proof. And the UFS operates on a different wavelength than other nations. There's no centralized government there, it's just a confederation of private entities. *Very* wealthy private entities. International finger wags mean nothing to them. If it gets too hot in one area, they can just pack up their steads and go somewhere else. Hopefully it will stay that way for a long, long time."

"What's the UFS?" Nadin whispered to me.

"Oh, the United Federation of Seasteads," I explained. "Artificial islands. You might have seen them on the flight down. Actually, that's where Tamara's moms met—" I broke off. *Tamara. Cristo,* what was wrong with me?!

I turned to Lizeth. "Two of our friends came to Earth, too, but they weren't on Lago Verde with us. Tamara Randall-Torres and Scylla Hwang. They're waiting for us at the Purple Parrot Cafe in West Palm Beach. What do we do?"

Across from me, Henry suddenly looked like I'd punched him hard. "Tamara's here?"

"Yeah, they were waiting just over the bridge."

"She's supposed to be in New Canaveral!" he roared.

I blinked, startled by his reaction. "I texted them when Joseph Condor was at the airport. They said they'd come down here and meet me when we were done."

Henry looked absolutely murderous. I'd never seen such a wild look in his eyes. It made me want to shrink away from him.

"Relax, we'll get them," Lizeth said.

"If you don't, you might as well turn this van right back around. I'm not letting Condor have her."

Lizeth rolled her eyes. "We got you out of a maximum security government facility, we can get two girls out of a coffee shop."

Henry didn't look convinced. His clenched fist alarmed me.

"We've got more important things to worry about right now," the driver, Dante, called over his shoulder. He rolled down his window slightly, letting in the sound of approaching sirens.

"GSAF's caught up."

"Right. Just in time for our switch. Glad to know that the cops still can't think their way out of a paper bag," Lizeth said cheerfully, grabbing onto a strap hanging from the van's ceiling.

Ahead of us, the second 762-GLE slammed its brakes and swerved into the right lane. Dante pressed his foot down on the gas, lurching forward. Around us, the self-driving cars on the street began to stall, unsure of what to make of the erratic behavior of the other vehicles on their sensors.

The first van that had passed us hit its signal, turning off the lagoon frontage road onto a street heading west. Dante continued to go straight, weaving between the slowed or stopped cars on the road. A passenger in a convertible actually stood up in her seat as we passed, lifting her sunglasses in surprise as she watched us go tearing by. The sirens were getting louder. I wasn't sure if it made me more or less nervous that I couldn't see them.

Suddenly, another 762-GLE turned onto the road ahead of us from a side street. I didn't know whether it was one of the ones we'd already passed, or a fourth van with the same license plate. Dante accelerated, coming up alongside the newcomer. From the passenger seat, Brandon waved at the driver of the other Stateless van as we tore by.

Two more blocks, and then Dante made an abrupt right without signaling and then turned into a parking garage on our left so quickly I was surprised the van didn't spin out of control or roll us over. I gripped the back of Dante's seat so hard my knuckles cried out in pain.

Out of the corner of my eye, I caught a glimpse of another 762-GLE speeding past us through Brandon's window, continuing straight down the street beyond the parking garage. Our van careened up the driveway into the garage, and Dante pulled smoothly into a parking spot and shut off the van just as three police cars, sirens blaring and lights flashing, screeched past the entrance, following the other van.

"Right, switcheroo time," Lizeth said, kicking open the back hatch. "Come on, guys, move it." My legs were numb, but I somehow managed to squeeze out after Henry and Nadin.

"You guys good from here?" Lizeth asked as Dante turned the van back on.

"Yup. We got it. We'll lead them on a wild goose chase they'll tell their grandkids about. Stay safe, Lizeth."

She gave him a sloppy imitation of a salute. "You too, Dante."

As the van backed out of the parking spot and screeched out of the garage, Lizeth quickly unlocked the beat-up sedan that was parked in the spot next to where the van had pulled in. "Let's roll. But first"—she yanked off her hoodie, tossing it to Nadin—"put that on and pull the hood over your hair. My windows are dark, but I don't want to risk anyone seeing you."

We piled into the sedan, Lizeth in front and Henry, Nadin and I in the back where the windows were tinted.

"Stay as low as you can," she said, hitting the ignition. "And whatever you do, don't look out the window."

She put the car in reverse.

CHAPTER 23

- n a d i n -

LIZETH DROVE US AROUND THE CITY IN A CONVOLUTED PATTERN that seemed to double back on itself several times. I was unsure whether this was meant to confuse GSAF or us. Not that I could see much of our surroundings, sandwiched between Henry and Isaak as I was and with the hood of Lizeth's sweatshirt pulled up so far that it blocked my peripheral vision. It was sweltering with that hood up, even with the air conditioner blasting lukewarm air into my face—she'd apologetically explained that the vehicle's air conditioner only worked around half the time.

"Nobody has any electronics on them, right?" she asked after we'd been driving for a few moments. "We checked Henry but we didn't get a chance when you two showed up."

Beside me, Isaak shook his head. "They made me leave my palmtop in my room on Lago Verde. I figured they didn't want me to be able to record the meeting."

"I don't have anything, either," I said quietly. It wasn't entirely true, but I was pretty sure the item I had was not something GSAF could trace, and I wasn't about to let Lizeth or her group take it away from me. It was the posternkey to open the link to Elytherios, tucked firmly in my pocket. Not that I'd ever be able to use it at this point. Not only did I now have next to no chance of ever getting close enough to a postern to use it, I also no longer had my medallion—which meant the key could not be opened. It was useless.

I was trapped here forever. I probably wouldn't even be able to get back to Mars now, let alone my own time. My lungs constricted at the thought, squeezed by the cold fist of Earth's gravity.

"Hey," Isaak murmured, watching me. "You doing okay?"

"I'm fine," I lied, turning my face slightly so he couldn't see it past the black hood of Lizeth's sweatshirt.

We circled back and forth until the sun was getting low in the sky. By this point, we'd left the shopping areas behind and were driving through neighborhoods now. Small, nondescript houses of mud brick were sandwiched together in rows, most not looking any different from their neighbors apart from a few different plants in the yard, perhaps a different window configuration.

At last, Lizeth pulled into a driveway, pressing a button that made a large door on the front of the house roll open. The car slid forward into a garage just large enough to hold two vehicles. An unfamiliar car was already parked in the spot beside Lizeth, small and dirty and painted a green so dark it almost looked black.

As we entered the house, a cry rang out, and then Tamara collided with us. Scylla was right behind her.

"Thank God you're safe. Thank God. Thank God," Tamara said over and over, her arms tightly around Henry. I glanced at Isaak, but he didn't seem to react.

"Relax, Tam," Henry said, pulling away from her after a moment. His fingers had tangled around her long hair, and he dropped his hand self-consciously. "I told you it would be fine."

Scylla scoffed. "Right. Try believing that when we're watching the bridge blowing up from the window of a coffee shop."

"What happened on your side?" Isaak asked fretfully. "Did it go nuts?"

"Oh, son," Scylla said, shaking her head. "That is an understatement. Purple Parrot went on lockdown. We were all hiding under the tables until someone threw a Molotov cocktail through the front window. Then this guy grabbed us." She gestured over her shoulder with her thumb.

It was only then that I noticed the young man who'd followed Tamara and Scylla into the room. He looked older than us, but not by much. Heavy-set, with curly dark hair and thick eyebrows to match. "Bruno," Lizeth said. "Good job."

"Thanks, Sis," the young man replied.

"Yeah, we thought we were being kidnapped by terrorists, or GSAF, or possibly terrorists on GSAF's payroll," Scylla said, crossing her arms and scowling.

"Well, you figured it out, right?" Lizeth said with a shrug, leading us out of the small, soapy-smelling room adjacent to the garage and into the kitchen.

"Eventually," Tamara said with a sigh, absently running a hand through her hair as we followed her.

"But what do we do now?" Scylla demanded as Lizeth flopped into a chair that was upholstered with what I assumed was once a bright floral pattern, but which now appeared faded and dusty.

"Where are we, anyway?"

"This is a safe house," Lizeth said.

"My house, actually," Bruno supplied. He leaned against the back of her chair. He'd called her *Sis*—an abbreviation of sister? He looked enough like her, though where she was lithe he was broad. They were close enough in age as well. If this was her brother's home, it would explain why Lizeth considered it so safe. Though she'd seemed as close as family with the two men who'd helped us escape, men who'd looked too different from her to be related. The tight-knitted feel of this rebel group reminded me of the Elytherioi. Isaak's face in the van earlier had told me it reminded him of them, too.

I wondered what Lizeth and Bruno's roles were in this organization. Runners, like the smugglers who'd brought Ferre in and people out of the citidomes?

"But we can't stay here," Isaak said, interrupting my thoughts. He sank into the couch across from the siblings. Henry sat next to him, and Scylla perched on the arm next to him. Out of seats, Tamara and I remained standing.

"No. You can't," Lizeth agreed. "We're going to have to get you out of here. And that's going to be a job. We'd only been planning on one of you. Now we've got five. Five are harder to transport—and to disguise."

"Transport where?" Scylla asked.

"The UFS, right?" said Henry.

Lizeth nodded. "Right. The UFS is going to be the only safe place for you guys until things cool off. The government's going to be looking for you all."

"Getting them out of Florida's going to be a pain in the ass, though," Bruno murmured.

"I know. And we've only got a short time to do it. We'll figure it out, though. I've got some calls to make." She looked up. "But in the meantime, we're going to need to figure out what to do to make you stick out less. Especially her." She nodded in my direction.

"Her name's Nadin," Isaak said.

"Right. Nadin. Her hair is like a beacon."

"When we were on Mars, I used to wear a wig Tamara gave me," I suggested.

"That won't work," Lizeth said with a shake of her head. "We're going to have to dye it."

"Dye it?" I repeated, putting a hand to my head. Coarse chunks of hair had fallen from my braid, spiraling messily around my head. I dreaded to think how it must look after an escape through the jungle and across the lagoon.

"We can't risk what might happen if a wig were to slip," Lizeth said, sinking back into her chair and crossing her legs at the knee. "Or if she takes it off for a little bit and someone sees her or something. At least her eyes won't be noticeable from a distance, but her hair is like a red flag. There are tourists everywhere down here. Thousands of people with cameras, with drones—what happens if someone's got a drone out for some aerial footage of the island and he catches a shot of her?"

"You can't dye her hair!" Isaak protested, jumping to his feet. I glanced at him in surprise. "Her hair has cultural significance to her."

"We could use wash-out dye," Scylla suggested.

"That'll still stain, though," murmured Tamara.

"It's Nadin's hair," Isaak said fiercely. "It should be her choice."

"She's a liability to our entire organization," Lizeth snapped, standing as well. "I'm not going to risk getting the Stateless shut down or any of our people hurt or killed because of some Martian princess's hair."

"It's all right!" I said quickly, stepping between them. "It's all right." I met Isaak's eyes. He looked down at me so intensely that I felt my face begin to flush, but I didn't turn away. "Thank you," I said softly. His gaze was still burning into me as I turned back to Lizeth. "I'll dye it. We really don't have a choice. I can't risk giving us all away."

"Good. We'll have to do something about the rest of you, too. Especially you," she said to Tamara. "Out of the group, you're the second most likely to be recognized."

Tamara nodded.

"Right." Lizeth turned to Bruno. "Call Zero. Tell them to bring the works. And I"—she took a shuddering breath—"will call Mom."

Lizeth disappeared down a hallway to make her call. Bruno stayed in the living room with us, flopping down in the chair Lizeth had just vacated. He swiped across his palmtop a few times before holding it to his ear the way Bryn had had me do when she'd voice-called Kate Ponsford for me. After a moment, he spoke. "Sup, Zero. My sister needs a haircut. You got an appointment open tonight?" A pause as the person on the other end spoke. "Yeah, dye job too. Oh, and can you bring by those clothes you borrowed? Thanks. See you soon."

As he put his palmtop back in his pocket, Henry said, "I assume you've got those things encrypted six ways from Sunday so that the government can't trace them." As he spoke, he got up off the couch, gesturing for Tamara to sit down. Isaak scooted over, making room for both her and me if we squeezed. Tamara took the end, leaving me to wedge myself between her and Isaak. I tried not to feel self-conscious about the way Isaak's knee brushed against mine when I sat down. Henry, meanwhile, sat on the floor in front of us, cross-legged, facing Bruno.

"For the secure stuff," Bruno said. "If we were completely off the grid, that might attract more attention. So we drop breadcrumbs when it's safe to do so. This one wasn't anything unusual—just a regular old hair appointment." His thick lips drew up into a smile. "That one, though..." He jerked his thumb in the direction Lizeth had disappeared. "That'll be invisible."

A short time later, the doorbell rang. The five of us tensed, instinctively shrinking away from the sound, but Bruno got up from his chair and shuffled over to the door at a slow, relaxed pace. He looked through the peekhole, then straightened and opened the door.

Standing just outside was a short person with purple hair, holding a large cardboard box that took up most of the doorway. "Got your shit," the newcomer announced cheerfully. The person spoke with an accent I didn't recognize, with a bit of a low drawl to it.

"Finally. You've had it long enough. C'mon in," Bruno said, shutting the door behind them.

As soon as the door was closed and locked, the purple-haired person's demeanor changed. "Wow. Okay. What have we got here?"

"Operation: Mars netted us a few bonus catches," Bruno

replied.

"I can see that. Well, nice to meet y'all." The person set the box down and straightened, revealing a loose-fitting black shirt with colorful writing on the front of it, and a denim vest covered with round metal buttons that had more writing on them. I wondered for a frustrated moment what all that writing said. "I'm Zero. I take it one of you needs a—oh." The newcomer trailed off at the sight of me. "The Martian princess? Seriously, Bruno?"

Bruno shrugged. "Lizeth said she wanted to come along. Can you make her a bit less conspicuous?"

"Of course. I *am* the master, aren't I?" Zero sighed. "I'll hate to cover that up, though. Hair like that is like a blank canvas. Once you get paint on it, it'll never be the same."

I frowned, fingers reaching involuntarily for one of the loose tendrils of my hair.

Beside me, Isaak watched my reaction. "Nadin, you don't have to do this," he whispered.

"No," I said firmly. "I do."

"Right. Well," Zero said, "let's get you in the bathroom. Pop princess, I'll need you, too. And everyone else, the stuff in the box is for you."

Zero led Tamara and me down the hallway, chatting cheerfully as we went. Bruno followed behind us with a wooden kitchen chair slung under each muscled arm. He placed these in front of the small counter in the bathroom. A sink was in the direct center of the chipped tile counter, while a large mirror took up the wall behind. Tamara and I each took a seat as Zero announced, "Okay, y'all sit tight, I'll be right back with my beauty kit."

"Let me get the door for you," Bruno said, following Zero back down the hallway.

As soon as the two of them were gone, I whispered to Tamara, "Is Zero a man or a woman?"

"Oh, they're enby," Tamara replied. "Did you see the pronoun pin on their shirt?"

I shrugged helplessly. "I *saw* the pins, but I didn't *understand* any of them."

Tamara flushed. "Oh, sorry. I forgot. You speak English so well, it's easy to forget that you haven't learned to read it yet. Um, so Zero is non-binary. They aren't a man or a woman. They're kind of... a little bit of both. And at the same time, neither. It's different for every person, of course. You'd have to ask Zero what it means for them personally. But that's the beginner version. Does that make sense?"

"I think so," I said. "So I say *they* instead of *he* or *she*?"

"Right." Tamara smiled as I filed this information away mentally.

A moment later, Zero reappeared, pulling a bright pink suitcase behind them. "Let's get down to business, ladies," they sang. They propped the suitcase against the toilet and turned to look at Tamara and me appraisingly. "Right, so what color were you thinking for Princess Number One?" they asked, making a circular gesture in my direction, as if framing my face with their fingers.

"Black," Bruno said from the bathroom door.

Zero looked aghast. "Boring!" they cried.

"Boring is what we're going for with her," Bruno replied.

"Can I put some blue highlights in?"

Bruno rolled his eyes. "As long as they're *subtle*."

"Of course, of course." There was a piercing through Zero's upper lip, and they chewed on the backing of it thoughtfully as they looked me over. I tried not to wince at the crunching sound. "Subtlety is my middle name."

Bruno snorted, leaving the bathroom. "Riiiight."

Zero opened the pink suitcase. Inside were dozens of pouches containing various bottles and jars. They hummed to themself for a moment before pulling out a bottle of clear liquid, which they set on the closed toilet lid, and a pair of rubber gloves which they pulled on. They paused a moment, thinking, and then reached back into the suitcase, withdrawing a tablet which they handed to Tamara.

"Okay, I'm going to get started on..." They trailed off, looking at me. "What was your name again, hon?"

"Nadin."

"Right, Nadin." They smiled warmly at me. "I'll start on Nadin's dye job if you wanna look through that, T-RT—"

"Tamara," she interrupted with a laugh. "Dear God, please don't call me that awful nickname."

Zero laughed as well. "Okay, *Tamara*. Pick out a shorter hairstyle from the ones on that tablet. Preferably one you haven't done before. I know you wear those wigs sometimes."

Tamara nodded. "Right."

As Tamara swiped across the tablet, Zero took the bottle from the toilet lid and removed the cap. They poured a little of the liquid inside onto their fingertips and began to rub it onto my face around my hairline and around my ears. It didn't have much of a scent at all, but what I could smell was sweet. "Grapeseed oil," Zero said by means of explanation. "To keep any dye that touches your skin from staining."

Next, they began to gently loosen my hair from its braid. "When's the last time you washed your hair, darlin'?"

"This morning."

"Good enough for government work," they decreed, turning back to the suitcase and pulling out a couple of jars, then a bowl, and a plastic comb.

Soon the dye was being worked into my scalp. Unlike the grapeseed oil, the dye did smell—strong enough to make my eyes water. I told myself that it was just the sharp odor of the dye that made the tear leak from the corner of my eye. Not the fact that in a few hours, I'd be looking in the mirror and seeing a stranger looking back.

It didn't matter, I told myself. Without my medallion, I was trapped here. Possibly forever. If I was going to have to stay on Earth, I needed to look like I was from here. Letting go of my Iamoi hair was just closing the door on my old life.

It's just the fumes from the dye. That's all, I thought as another tear slid down my face.

When Zero was done applying the dye, they covered my hair with a plastic cap and then wrapped a scarf around that to hold it in place. "Now we gotta let it set," they said. "Probably not real long, since we're going light to dark rather than vice versa. I'll come track you down in an hour." They turned to Tamara. "As for you..."

Tamara swallowed, holding up the tablet to show Zero the style she'd chosen. Zero nodded. "Probably oughta shampoo you first. Wet hair is easier to cut."

I stood as Zero began to run the water in the sink. I went to the door of the bathroom, then paused, turning back for a moment to watch them. Their purple hair was cut short on the sides, longer and spiked on top. Piercings went down the side of their left ear, hoops and bars and sparkling stones. Everything about them was a fashion statement.

"Zero," I said after a moment. "Lizeth also has hair that's dyed an unnatural color. Aren't you worried about attracting attention like that? If the Stateless is supposed to be undercover..."

Zero laughed. "This is Florida. If you want to blend in, you need to stand out."

"But then why...?" I reached a hand up to touch the scarf wrapped around my head.

"Ah," they said, chewing on the stud in their lip again. "There's a fine line. I'm afraid you stand out a little *too* much, darlin'."

I nodded, breathing out and leaving the bathroom.

Across the hall, the door was open to a drab bedroom. Bruno stood just outside this door, looking in at someone. I came up behind him, glancing over his shoulder to see Isaak rummaging through the box Zero had brought. There were clothes in it. The box was tipped now, shirts and pants and dresses and skirts spilling out across the dull brown bedspread.

"Take something you wouldn't ordinarily wear," Bruno said.

"Well, I'm not taking a dress," Isaak replied.

Bruno snorted. "Just a different color, or a different style. If you usually wear grays and browns, grab something bright. If you usually wear t-shirts, take a polo or something."

Through the closed door at the end of the hall, I heard Lizeth yell, "I know that, *Mother*. I'm not completely stupid, despite what you may think."

I glanced in the direction of the voice, my eyebrows raised.

"What's that about?" Isaak asked. "Is she really talking to your mom?"

"She is indeed," Bruno said, shaking his head.

"Your mother is involved with the Stateless?" I asked.

"Yeah. She's one of the head financiers of the organization. She owns a lot of the properties we use for meetings and safe houses. Not this one, though," he added almost defensively. "I bought this house on my own." I quirked my head at him, and he shrugged, running a hand through his hair. "Sorry. Mom brings it out in me. Anyway, she thinks because of her money, she can call all the shots. Lizeth, though, she thinks that we should be more of a grassroots organization."

"Well, that makes sense," Isaak said. "Considering the whole point is the fact that passive citizenship put the voice of the people entirely in the hands of those with money."

Bruno made a noise in the back of his throat. "That's the whole point in Lizeth's eyes, anyway. Mom's interests are a little different. But they both want to see the continental unions broken up. That's the common goal. Regardless, you can see how they might butt heads."

I nodded quietly.

"I'm going to try these on," Isaak said after a minute, holding up a green-and-white striped collared shirt and a pair of denim shorts.

"'Kay," Bruno said, pulling the door closed.

I wandered down the hallway into the living room, where Scylla and Henry were awaiting their turns with the clothes box.

As I reached the end of the hall, I could hear them speaking to each other in hushed voices.

"I know Tamara told you what he said," Scylla muttered. "He said he doesn't want a relationship with her."

"Right now," Henry said flatly.

"I think he means *ever*, Henry. He said he just wanted to go back to being friends."

My heart sped up a little, involuntarily. Were they talking about Isaak? He didn't want to be with Tamara anymore? Did that mean—

"Okay. But there's a difference between not wanting to date her himself and being okay with *me* dating her."

Scylla groaned, running a frustrated hand through her hair. "Henry, you two are grown-ass adults. You don't need Isaak's permission—"

"I didn't say we needed his *permission*," Henry hissed. "But do you really think now is a good time to be worrying about this? We're on the run. We need to all stick together. The last thing we need is something that could make everyone pissed off at each other. That's how mistakes are made. And besides. I would like to *stay* friends with him, you know?"

"Do you really believe that this would end your friendship with him?" Scylla asked quietly.

Henry sighed. "I don't know."

Scylla didn't say anything for a long moment. Finally, in a low voice, she murmured, "If Isaak is your friend—if he's friend to either of you—he'll want you two to be happy."

He turned, smirking at her. "I wish I could live in your fairytale world, Scylla."

She rolled her eyes. "Fine. Be a goddamn martyr, Henry. If that's how you want it to be, I'm not going to say anything else." She got up off the couch, storming over to the hallway where I stood awkwardly. I knew she had to know I'd been listening, but she didn't acknowledge it. She just said, "Hey, Nadin," before pushing past me and down the hall to the bathroom, where the sound of water running in the sink had been replaced with that of a blow dryer.

I stood there long after she was gone, my heart pounding. I distantly wondered at that, how fast it was racing. At how this conversation affected me—or how it didn't, really. It didn't affect me at all.

Ceilos, Nadin. You have a partner already. You love him.

Of course I loved him. I'd always loved him. Even though he'd driven me crazy when we first met, those feelings had quickly evolved as we'd become friends.

Friends. I hadn't had any friends before, apart from him. Gitrin didn't really count. She was more like family. Like the mother that Melusin couldn't be. The mother to only me. Now I had several friends. Tamara, Scylla, Henry, Mariyah, Wyatt. Possibly Lizeth, if she could be trusted, and Zero and Bruno.

And Isaak.

Now I had enough friends that I was starting to be able to tell the difference between loving someone as a friend and... maybe something else. Something *more*.

"So Isaak can comfort you when your partner cannot?"

I didn't want to think about this anymore. I shoved the thoughts out of my mind, locked them away in a little box buried deep inside of me. I'd carry it until I was ready to face it.

"So, what do you think?" a voice behind me said loudly. I jumped, just managing to not let out a startled squeak. I turned to see Isaak wearing the clothes he'd picked out. They were very different than anything I'd ever seen him in before, that was for sure.

"You look like a tool," Henry said with a laugh, getting to his feet and coming over to where we stood. "You look like torquing Wyatt Ponsford."

"I will pay you to never repeat that to another soul," Isaak replied.

"You look like you're going to go play golf," Henry cackled. "You look like you're trying out for the tennis team."

"You just wait!" Isaak said, trying not to double over with laughter. "You just wait and see what they've got in that box for you!"

"I want to see Henry in something other than black," I said with a grin.

"Hey, I've worn other colors!" he protested.

"Not that I've seen."

"Back me up, Isaak. Remember that green shirt I used to have?"

"The one you wrote on with Sharpie? Oh, I remember."

They laughed, and I laughed with them, enjoying this moment. In spite of the situation, this was the most relaxed I'd seen them with one another since we'd arrived on Mars all those weeks ago. It was almost enough to make me forget about the way Earth's gravity dragged me down.

Everything had changed almost impossibly since this morning. Twelve hours ago, I never would have believed that all five of us would be here now, away from GSAF. Laughing together. *Safe.* For a wild moment, I felt like if this much could change, anything could happen. That maybe this situation wasn't hopeless after all.

I reached for the posternkey, still tucked in my pocket, and squeezed it. *I'll find a way, Ceilos. I promise.*

For everyone.

CHAPTER 24

- i s a a k -

WE LEFT THE NEXT MORNING. LIZETH SAID WE COULDN'T AFFORD to wait any longer. She'd gotten clearance for the five of us to come to the UFS, but we needed to leave now.

When we staggered out of the house into the early morning light, there was an RV parked in front of Bruno's house. Dante, the guy who'd been driving the van yesterday when we escaped Lago Verde, was at the wheel of the vehicle. He hopped out to help Lizeth with one of her two suitcases. In these she'd managed to cram extra clothes for all six of us. Just two suitcases, so it would look like it was just luggage for herself and Dante.

She led us into the kitchenette of the RV and crouched in front of the table, which was bolted to the floor to keep it from moving while the vehicle was in motion. "I'm really sorry, guys, but this is where you're going to have to stay until we get past the checkpoints." She crouched, reaching up under one of the bench seats behind the table where there must have been a latch on the floor. There was a click, and part of the floor popped up, just a couple centimeters, revealing a hatch that had been invisible just a moment ago. She straightened and grabbed onto the edge of the table, pulling. The floor swung up like the door to a root cellar—and that's approximately the size of the cubby we were expected to cram ourselves into.

"Well. Now we'll know how sardines feel when they're crammed into those ethically heinous cans, won't we?" Scylla said, looking down into the small space. Zero had styled her hair so that her bangs no longer lay across her forehead, but were swooped back with hairspray in a smooth side part. Now when she pursed her lips and exhaled, her hair stayed firmly in place.

We'd all been given a makeover, though none as drastic as Nadin and Tamara. It had taken all night, with none of us getting much sleep as a result—least of all poor Zero. Since Henry, Scylla and I all had short hair, they'd just cut it into styles different enough to trick the eye into thinking our faces looked a little bit different. Henry and I were told to grow our beards out as much as possible, though I suspected Henry would have better luck with his than I would—he had a head start on me, and the most I'd ever been able to manage was a pathetic little mustache. I'd always kept my face clean-shaven, per Academy regulations. Even when I was on Iamos, I'd kept shaving, since Eliin had included a razor in with our supply kit before we left for Elytherios. Iamoi men didn't appear to do facial hair. The only reason Dad had gotten so stubbly was because he wouldn't let anyone near him before I'd arrived in Elytherios. Shaving hadn't been the only hygiene he'd neglected in those weeks.

I frowned at the thought of my dad. Lizeth had approached me last night after she got off the phone with her mom, at almost two o'clock in the morning.

"I need to talk to you about your dad," she'd told me, swiping at her red-rimmed eyes—more from exhaustion than emotion, it seemed—with the back of her hand.

"What about him?" The tone in her voice had made me dread what was to come next. It never seemed to end well when someone said "I need to talk to you."

"We sent people to check on him. GSAF had already brought him in for questioning by the time we caught up with him. It was obvious that he doesn't know anything, so they let him go. They're going to be watching him, though. And the rest of your family. I know it's hard, but you're going to have to stay under the radar for now."

"How long is 'for now'?"

She just shrugged and wandered off. I hadn't been surprised, really. I think I'd known, subconsciously, that I wasn't going to be able to contact my family. None of us could. GSAF would be monitoring all their conversations. And I knew too well that my mom would be perfectly willing to cooperate with GSAF, whatever they asked of her. She couldn't know where we were. None of them could. Guilt gnawed at me as I remembered the way Celeste had said, "*If you have to go again, you'll tell us this time, right?*" I'd promised her that I would. And now I'd broken that promise. And who knew when the next time I'd see her would be? What if another two annums passed before I saw my sister again?

"We're going to misdirect GSAF west while we go south," Lizeth was saying now, dragging me back to the present. I would have to worry about my family later. The more immediate worry of getting out of Palm Beach needed to be my focus now. "We dumped Tamara and Scylla's palmtops in a location off Interstate Ten. We've got decoys leading them toward Texas. Meanwhile, I'll get you guys out through the Keysteads."

"The Keysteads?" Nadin asked. I glanced in her direction, trying to keep myself from reacting to her hair. It was disorienting, seeing her wild curls tinted black instead of white. It was going to take a lot of getting used to. It didn't show in the dim shadows of the kitchenette, but last night under the full lighting I'd seen that the dye Zero had used had blue undertones to it that brought out the vibrancy of her eyes. Lizeth had warned her that she'd need to wear sunglasses whenever we were anywhere people could see us, to hide those eyes. She'd probably need them, anyway, considering where we were going.

"Mm-hmm," Lizeth answered. "There used to be a chain of natural islands not far from here. They were called the Florida Keys. Most of them are gone now, but artificial islands went up in their place. Seasteads. So, Keysteads. They're owned by the United States, though. They're not part of the UFS, so we'll need to be careful."

Behind us, a tired-sounding voice with an American Southern accent said, "Well, I'm gonna get rolling now. Have a nice trip."

We turned to see Zero leaning in the door of the RV. "Thanks, Ze," Lizeth said with a tired smile. "Go get some sleep."

"You can bet on it. You try to get some sleep when you can, too, Ze."

They gave a droopy half-wave as I grinned to myself about the shared nickname. Then Zero disappeared. Through the open door, I could see that the light was getting brighter outside. We'd have to leave soon to avoid running into neighbors.

Dante shut the door, then came around the front and got into the driver's seat. "If we're going to go, we'd better go," he said, pressing the ignition.

"Right. Well, get cramming, sardines," Lizeth said.

Henry and I squeezed next to each other on the left side of the cubby, Scylla in the middle and Tamara—looking almost as odd as Nadin with a short, feathered hairstyle bleached as blond as Bryn's—on the right end next to Nadin.

"I'll get you out of here once we're past the city. You should get a couple hours' freedom before the next checkpoint," Lizeth said, peering down at us from above. She gave us a tight smile that was probably meant to be reassuring, but just made me feel more nervous. Then the hatch swung shut, and we were in darkness.

An hour later, we were on the outskirts of Miami. We'd been stopped at the checkpoint leaving West Palm Beach, but the officer had merely stuck his head in the door of the RV and looked around. "They'll do a more thorough check when we reach the border," Lizeth said when she came back to let us out of our hiding place. "They figured we'd already gotten you out of the city last night, when they were still scrambling to deal with the mess we made of Lago Verde. So the heightened security is at all the exits out of Florida itself."

"I bet there's a media frenzy going on down by the bridge," Scylla said with a chuckle as she sank into the bench seat beside the table.

"There is, but the government's already working on covering it up." Lizeth rolled her eyes. "Can't let the public know there's a resistance group organized enough to pull that heist off. They're saying that a lone wolf terrorist bombed the bridge. There hasn't been any official announcement given about the five of you being missing yet. They don't want anyone to know that their high-security island was breached so easily."

"They can't keep it covered up forever, though!" Scylla exclaimed. Then, after a moment's consideration, she added, "Or can they?"

"They're going to have to say something," said Lizeth. "But what, I don't know. And what it will mean for the Stateless... that's another question."

Most of the drive was quiet. Lizeth sat in the front with Dante while the rest of us stayed in the kitchenette, squeezed in around the table, barely managing to stay awake after the long day and night before. All the curtains in the RV were pulled closed, but we stayed away from the windows just in case. Despite Lizeth's assurance that no one—apart from our families, I assumed, based on their questioning of my dad—knew about our disappearance, I didn't trust her words or my new disguise enough to take the risk of being seen. The others seemed to share my trepidation.

Nadin was perched next to me on the edge of the bench, absently twisting the ring around her finger. Lizeth had made Henry, Tamara and Scylla take off their red yarn bracelets for fear those would be too identifying for anyone who knew about the Free Mars movement—or anyone, like Zero, familiar enough with so-called "B-list" pop star T-RT to recognize the red braid she always wore around her wrist. They'd let Nadin keep her ace ring, though. Those were common enough everywhere to not mean anything, especially since the "Martian princess" hadn't made any public appearances since she started wearing it.

After a long silence, she said, barely loud enough for me to hear over the steady rattling of the RV on the freeway, "Isaak..."

I glanced over at her, head tilted curiously. She kept her gaze on her fingers.

"I wanted to tell you... Thank you for yesterday," she murmured, speaking Iamoi.

"Yesterday?"

"At Bruno's house. When you fought for me to keep my hair its natural color. I really appreciated it."

I smiled at her. "I know it was important to you. To everyone in your citidome."

"Yes." She stopped twisting her ring and let out a sigh. "I've always been different from them. Now, if I ever go back, everyone will be able to see that."

"Maybe when this is all over, if you bleach it enough..." I trailed off lamely. I wasn't sure there would ever be enough bleach to get her hair back to its old color.

She shook her head. "That's all right. My strength is in my differences."

I raised my eyebrows in surprise. I'd never thought I'd hear Nadin say something like that before. I nudged her with my elbow. "Well, good. I agree."

Silence fell over us again. Part of me wanted to apologize to her about the Venus thing, but I held back. She was speaking to me again. I didn't want to remind her and risk her going back to giving me the cold shoulder.

"Henry," Nadin said after a moment. "What did Geoff Preston want with you? On Lago Verde?"

Henry let out a long breath. Scylla and Tamara looked at him in surprise, and I realized they must not have known what Nadin saw. "He made me the same offer he made you. He knew that I'd done a lot of work on the System last annum, and he knew that I was friends with you, at least tangentially. I guess he thought I could persuade you."

Nadin narrowed her eyes. "GSAF knew of this?"

"I don't think they did. My bodyguard did, but I think he'd been bought."

"So GalaX is working against GSAF behind the scenes, while pretending to work with them?" Tamara asked, shaking her long blond bangs out of her eyes.

"Sneaky," Scylla said. "So what'd you tell him, Henry?"

"I told him no. Said I trusted Nadin's judgment."

Nadin sighed. "And look how that turned out. If they're working against GSAF, they might have been a good ally," she said glumly.

"No." I shifted in my seat to face her. "You were right, Nadin. Regardless of whether they oppose GSAF, they still want the System. Frankly," I said, remembering the incident in the arcade aboard the *Athena*, "they might be in a position to do even more damage with it than the government. You did the right thing."

She nodded thoughtfully, tucking a strand of hair behind her ear. New look, same mannerisms. I smiled before I even realized it.

"We've got a checkpoint coming up," Dante called over his shoulder. We jumped to our feet as Lizeth scrambled back to the kitchenette, quickly popping the hatch open again and ushering us all back into the storage compartment. There was no time to arrange our positions this time—Scylla dove in first, followed by Tamara and Henry. I pushed Nadin ahead of me before jumping in myself. Lizeth slammed the hatch after us. I could hear the thud of her feet loudly above us as the RV began to slow. Then it was quiet. Lizeth must be back in her seat.

A few minutes later, the RV came to a halt. Then I heard the sound of voices.

"Destination?" a man's voice asked, sounding muffled and distant.

Dante started to say something, but then I heard Lizeth say loudly over the top of him, "Hey, Ricky! How are you? We're just heading back to Conch."

"Oh, hi, Miss Senghas," the first man's voice replied, losing some of its sternness. "Visiting your brother again?"

"Yeah, Bruno had the week off so we planned a road trip."

"I got roped into being the chauffeur," Dante said with a tone of light put-uponedness.

"Babe, you know I can't handle anything bigger than a minivan!"

"That's what the self-steer is for."

Lizeth groaned. "Self-steer on cars is one thing, but I don't trust it on something as big as an RV."

The officer laughed. "You sound just like my wife. Listen, we're supposed to check every vehicle that comes through. Mind if I take a look in the back?"

"Go for it," Dante said easily.

It was quiet for a moment, and then I heard the sound of the door opening. Beside me, I felt Nadin stiffen, could hear her holding her breath. I reached for her hand in the dark. She took it, squeezing my fingers tightly.

Footsteps above us. He didn't just peek in the way they had when we left Palm Beach: he was actually investigating the RV's interior. Would he notice the seam on the floor? I hadn't noticed it before Lizeth opened it earlier, but I wasn't a trained professional. And what if he had a dog with him? A dog would smell us for sure.

Thud. Thud. His footsteps crossed through the kitchenette and on to the bathroom in the back of the RV.

A breathless minute passed, and then the footsteps returned, walking at a more normal pace. The slam of the door, and then a moment later, the officer's voice again. "You're all set. Sorry for the inconvenience."

"No problem, man," Dante said cheerfully.

"Miss Senghas, you tell your father I said hi, okay?"

"Sure thing, Ricky! Have fun snooping through the next two hundred cars."

The officer groaned. "Don't remind me. Have a good day."

The RV rolled forward once more, but Lizeth didn't come back to collect us until the sounds of the road had been steady for at least five minutes.

At last, the hatch finally opened and Lizeth grinned down at us. "All clear," she announced. "We're on Key Largo now."

I sat up, my muscles shaking from a combination of nerves and the cramped quarters we'd been in. "Senghas, huh?" I said as I climbed out of the cubby and reached down to help Nadin out. "You're German?"

"Half. My mom's Cuban."

"And it sounds like you've got some connections. Now I see how the Stateless has gotten this far," said Henry.

Lizeth shrugged modestly. "My dad's mayor of Conch. There's actually a surprising amount of officials on the local levels that aren't as enthused about passive citizenry as Congress is. So we have several connections, in fact. It's worked out pretty well."

"What's Conch?" Nadin asked, brushing the grit from the storage cubby off her bare knees. Like the rest of us, the Stateless had her decked out in *haute touriste*—neon floral shorts and a pink tank top, in her case.

"One of the islands that used to be here was called Key West," Lizeth explained. "When the residents relocated to a keystead, they decided to name it that rather than 'New Key West' or something. There's a whole long story about it, it goes back almost a hundred years at this point."

Nadin nodded as Lizeth shoved the hatch closed again and left us for the front seat beside Dante. That reminded me that she'd called him *babe* when the officer was talking to them. I wondered if they were really a couple, or if it was just part of the act.

When I turned back to Nadin, I saw she was still watching Lizeth, a frown on her face. "What's up?" I asked.

"Oh, nothing," she said, wrapping her arms around herself almost like she was cold—though how she could be in this weather, especially in this stuffy RV, I had no idea. "I was just thinking about what Lizeth said. Having connections will only get you so far if you're not careful."

"You mean like Governor Ponsford?"

"Yes. What do you think will happen to her? And to Wyatt?"

I scratched the back of my head. "I don't know," I said truthfully. Especially not now that we'd escaped from GSAF and their key to completely unlocking the System had been lost.

She nodded, turning away from the front seat. "I just hope the Stateless know how to be more careful than I did."

CHAPTER 25

- n a d i n -

IT TOOK TWO DAYS FOR US TO REACH SEA-STAR ISLAND. WE DROVE down along a road that crossed the ocean and linked the artificial islands with one another, but we didn't go as far as Conch. About twenty-five minutes after Lizeth freed us from our hiding place the second time, Dante parked the RV on a place Lizeth said was called Islamorada. Lizeth disappeared for a while, and when she came back, she ushered us quickly down a quiet, seemingly abandoned dock to where a boat was moored. This was larger than the *Merrow's Jewel*, with an enclosed cabin and space under the deck where we would be concealed.

"Stay below until we're out to sea. I'll come get you when we're clear," Lizeth instructed us.

We spent the next two days on the boat. Every time we drew near another vessel or a small island, Lizeth would order us back below deck, but apart from that, it was just the seven of us, the bright sun, and the endless blue, blue sea.

"We're lucky," Lizeth said as I leaned over the railing, looking down into the clear water where I could see *psara* darting to and fro between colorful undersea growth Isaak said was called coral. "The weather's supposed to hold until we reach the UFS. This trip isn't nearly so fun when the weather's bad. Or so fast."

The trip was too short, in a way. I was finding that the more time I spent on a boat, the more I enjoyed it. I'd marveled at the water on Isaak's Mars, but it was nothing compared to what they had here on Earth. This sea was not only endless, but it teemed with life. I hadn't seen a wild animal anywhere on Mars, but here there were more creatures than I could name, both swimming below the waves and soaring through the sky above them.

"I don't suppose you know how to swim," Isaak said the second afternoon, when we were nearing our destination of Sea-Star Island, which Lizeth informed us was the largest and most established of the artificial islands in the United Federation of Seasteads. He laughed at the expression I gave him. "I figured as much. You couldn't play *ulama* either," he teased.

I tucked a dark lock of hair behind my ears. It still was disconcerting to catch it in my periphery, this strange blue-black hair. "I don't think anyone on the whole of Iamos knows how to swim. There isn't enough water. Even in Elytherios, I don't think there's enough to do more than bathe in."

Isaak watched as a white creature he'd told me was called a *seagull*, a type of bird, circled overhead. "Well, if you're stuck here anyway, maybe one of us could teach you how. I think you'd like it. Especially here. You'd probably love snorkeling. There's not as much as there used to be, because of the warm water die-off, but the coral reefs are still gorgeous. And there are all sorts of animals. Fish, turtles, dolphins..." He trailed off, then said, almost conspiratorially, "Plus, the gravity isn't so bad when you're in the water."

I looked down into the blue ocean, sunlight glinting off the waves. The corners of my lips turned up wryly. I was more used to the gravity now, but I still woke up with pains in my joints and a weight on my chest. "I'd like that."

Soon we were drawing close to Sea-Star Island, and Lizeth ushered us back below deck. As we plunked down the steps, Tamara said over her shoulder to no one in particular, "It feels weird to be coming here like this. I've been here so many times before with my moms. They met here, you know. So we've vacationed here probably a dozen times. And now we're sneaking in like pirates or something."

A short time later, Lizeth came to collect us. She was carrying a tote bag, from which she withdrew hats and sunglasses for all of us. "Come help Dante and me with the luggage and stuff," she said as I adjusted a large floppy had over my curls. "This is the one place where a big group of people will look less conspicuous than if I brought you out one at a time."

As I emerged onto the deck, I saw what she meant. This island was clearly a vacationers' destination. It was edged with sandy beaches filled with people wearing very little clothing. The sea behind us was dotted with colorful sails, and as I watched, two people riding a small, fast-moving craft zipped by. Lizeth's boat was moored at a private dock behind a house that looked like a much smaller—but not necessarily less elaborate—version of Lago Verde. Similar docks attached to similar homes were just a stone's throw from us on either side. She'd concealed us from the prying eyes of the people on those boats I could see on the open water behind us, but we were close enough to her neighbors that if one should happen out onto his deck now, he'd be sure to see us. Better to look like a party of vacationers like the rest of the people on the beaches.

"A private residence on Sea-Star Island?" Tamara said, lifting her sunglasses to get a better look. "How rich is your mom, exactly?"

Dante barked out a laugh. "Pretty damn rich."

Lizeth grumbled in annoyance but didn't contradict him. I suspected she disliked her mother's wealth on principle, despite its obvious helpfulness to her cause.

Her mother, we came to learn, was not here. She was in a place called Brunei on business.

"And we're going to need to figure out what to do with you guys before she gets back," Lizeth said after we'd finished moving our few possessions into the allotted guest rooms—despite the apparent expense of a home on Sea-Star Island, it wasn't as large even as Bryn and Delia's small villa on Mars, so we were sharing rooms: Henry and Isaak together, and me with Scylla and Tamara. Dante had departed by then, citing his need to get back to work. He'd taken "vacation" time for the planned Stateless evacuation of Henry from Lago Verde, but he needed to return before his absence looked suspicious. He was flying back to Florida this evening.

"Didn't she have something in mind?" Henry asked. He watched as Lizeth poured herself a drink from a glass cabinet similar to the one that had been in my stateroom aboard the Athena. "I thought that was the whole point of us coming here."

"Um," Lizeth said, sitting on a stool next to the bar. "Not quite." She looked around at us. "Do you want something to drink?"

"Based on the direction this conversation sounds like it's headed, I'm going to say yes," Scylla said. She began rooting through the glass cabinet.

Lizeth stirred her drink with her fourth finger, ice cubes clinking together in the glass. "So, coming here was the plan originally, when it was just Henry we were busting out. When she found out we'd brought the rest of you, my mom had a minor meltdown. But we needed to get you out of West Palm Beach before GSAF figured out we were still in the city, so I made an executive decision."

My stomach sank. "She didn't want the rest of us to come here?"

Lizeth took a sip of her drink, stalling for time while she considered her answer. "I'm sure that she *would* if we could get her to see your value to the Stateless. I just... don't quite know what that is, yet." She winced at my horrified expression. "I'm sure I can get her to see reason. I mean, she's not the most reasonable person—just ask my dad, there's a reason she's here and he's back on Conch—that is—" She broke off, taking another swig of her drink. Whatever it was smelled sharp and unpleasant, and for some reason just then I had an overwhelming sensation that maybe I should drink some myself.

"Nadin does have value to the Stateless," Isaak said then. "The Iamoi would be an asset to you the same way they'd be an asset to the Free Mars movement: they're the only ones with a legitimate claim to the planet. You want to overthrow GSAF, bring native Martians into the mix."

I sighed, running a hand through my hair. "That's a nice

thought, Isaak, but how are we supposed to do that? We don't have access to a postern. And even if we did, the key is useless without my medallion. We wouldn't be able to open it."

"You said there were arches like that on Earth, Lizeth," Henry said. "Back when you were masking on the agorist chatspace. Does that mean the Stateless were researching Iamoi tech?"

My eyes widened in alarm—yet *another* faction after the System?—but Lizeth shook her head. "No. I was there to watch for recruits for the Stateless, but when I saw your post about the coin... that was me going a little rogue. I have a bit of a personal interest in the Atlantis connection." She glanced at me with her round, dark eyes. "Or what I thought was Atlantis, anyway. Iamoi. My uncle's the curator at the Museo de Antropología in Xalapa."

"Wait a minute," Isaak interrupted. "In Veracruz?"

"Yeah."

"*That's* why your last name sounded familiar," he went on eagerly. "Karl Senghas. Abuelo's worked with him for years."

"Who's your grandfather?" Lizeth asked.

"Hector Garcia."

She raised her eyebrows in surprise. "Holy shit," was all she said.

"So when you messaged Henry asking about the coin..." said Tamara.

"I told him it was because I'd seen one like it turn up in private auction. Didn't want to reveal any personally identifying information in case it got back to the government." She slid off the barstool, moving back to the glass cabinet to replenish her drink. "But I actually saw it at the museum. I kind of had this theory going for a while about those arches that seemed to be turning up all over the world. A lot of times those coins were found near them, along with other weird things. Unexplainable stuff, like the Antikythera mechanism. When I was younger I thought for sure that those artifacts turning up at the same sites where arches existed meant that there was an Atlantean Stargate or something, and that the government was covering it up." She shrugged. "I guess I wasn't that wrong, was I?"

"Wait," I said. "You saw a *coin* at the museum?" When she nodded, I turned to Isaak and asked in Iamoi, "Isn't that what you were calling my medallion?"

"Yeah. When we found the one I used to unlock the key in the first place, Henry posted about it on Speculus looking for someone who might have information. That's how Lizeth found him, apparently."

I jumped to my feet, suddenly finding I could barely catch my breath. "But don't you see what that means? If there's another medallion here on Earth, we'll be able to use it to unlock the time posternkey."

"And if there's a postern in Veracruz..." Scylla said, her eyes gleaming with a mischief I hadn't seen in weeks.

"Then we can get back to Elytherios," I breathed.

"And that deal you offered GSAF—that they turned their noses up at—you can offer it to the Stateless instead," said Isaak.

"Rebels on both worlds working together. I like it," Henry said. "What do you think, Lizeth? Do you think that might convince your mom?"

She looked down into the amber liquid in her glass quietly for a moment. "I don't know." She put the glass down on the bar and grinned. "But it would convince me. I say we do it. Or at least try.

And if it works, I'll go over her head. She might think she's in charge of this organization, but on the grassroots level, most of the operatives would listen to me over her."

Scylla jumped to her feet and threw her arms around me. "It's happening!" she squealed.

"What do you say, Nadin?" Isaak asked, his eyes locking with mine. "Do you want to go to Veracruz?"

"Yes," I replied without hesitation.

Lizeth got to her feet as well, dusting off her hands. "All right, then," she said. "Let's make it happen."

CHAPTER 26

- i s a a k -

THAT NIGHT, LIZETH CALLED HER UNCLE TO WORK OUT THE arrangements. It was too risky for us to come to the museum while it was open, in case any tourists visiting should happen to spot us. It was decided we'd come on Sunday, when the museum would be closed. Lizeth would arrange for us to fly in on Saturday night and stay somewhere unobtrusive. In the meantime, the safest place for us was the UFS, so we'd spend Thursday and Friday at Lizeth's mother's house on Sea-Star Island.

That was the plan, anyway. But when I woke up the next morning and staggered out to the kitchen, leaving a snoring Henry behind in our shared guest room, I found Lizeth scrambling around, throwing things we'd unpacked yesterday back into their suitcases.

"Oh, no," I groaned. "Now what?"

"Change of plans. Mom's coming home. Today. I think she suspected I'm up to something. So you guys have gotta go."

"Where are we supposed to go? You said you needed a couple days to get our fake passports and stuff to get into Mexico."

"Right. You need to stay in the UFS until then. But don't worry, I've got a backup plan. We should have done this to begin with, honestly. One of Mom's vacation rentals is empty right now, so I'm going to move you all there."

"Is it here on Sea-Star?" I asked.

"No, it's a private island. It's actually got about five hundred meters of private waters around it, too, so boats won't get close. You won't have to be holed up the way you would be here."

I could feel my expression brightening at that. "Really? Fresh. I think we could all go for a mini-vacation."

"As long as you remember to play it safe, all right?" Lizeth stopped throwing random food items from the refrigerator into the ice chest on the kitchen counter long enough to hurl a severe expression at me. "If you see any boats around, get off the beach. Five hundred meters is nothing to a decent camera lens. And keep an eye out for drones, too, okay?"

"All right, all right," I said, holding my hands up. "Geez, we're not torquing idiots."

"I'm holding you to that," she said, turning back to the refrigerator and pulling out more food for the ice chest.

Within an hour, we were all up, dressed, and carrying all the items we'd just removed yesterday back onto Lizeth's boat. The island she brought us to wasn't far from Sea-Star—only about twenty minutes later, we were approaching the small stead. It was just big enough to hold the house, a few beach areas covered in picturesque sand dunes, and a backyard-sized green patch where tall palm trees emerged between bushes.

"Does it have a pool?" Henry asked as our boat passed the buoy indicating the island's private waters.

Lizeth gave him a look. "It's got the ocean."

"What kind of tacky hovel has no swimming pool?" He shook his head, making a soft tutting noise under his breath.

I had to struggle not to laugh. Lizeth clearly hadn't been prepared for Henry's brand of sarcasm. She started spluttering defensively before Tamara broke in, "It's really nice, Lizeth. Thank you."

We got the boat unloaded quickly and Lizeth opened the house up for us. It was a small, two-bedroom condo, so, as we had at her mom's house, Henry and I took one room and the girls took the other.

"Okay, I have to get back to Sea-Star before Mom gets home and make sure I didn't leave any sign of you guys lying around," Lizeth said. "Try not to burn the house down. And for God's sake, don't let anyone see you. I'll try to sneak back over here later, but if I can't get away from Mom, I'll be back on Saturday morning."

After Lizeth left, Scylla and I unloaded the groceries that Lizeth had hastily packed for us into the refrigerator. My mouth dropped open at all the perishables she'd given us—real milk, eggs, cheese, fish and meat. There were even frozen pre-formed hamburger patties for us to grill. This refrigerator's contents would cost a fortune on Mars. A small, selfish part of me thought sadly for just a moment how it was too bad that GSAF hadn't been willing to deal just for postern technology. Instant travel would mean regular people on Mars like my family could eat meat whenever we wanted and not be limited to our "flexitarian" diet, as many of us jokingly referred to it.

After lunch, everyone drifted to their own corners. No one seemed like they wanted to say it, but we were all tired, and we were all getting a little sick of each other after a week in fraught, close quarters. There was a hammock on the deck outside our bedroom, and Henry called dibs on this. Before long, snores were drifting in through the screen door.

I thought about sleeping, but I felt simultaneously exhausted and wired. What I needed, I decided, was some peace, quiet, and sunshine. After all, we were in the UFS, the vacation capital of the worlds. The last three months had been insane. I needed some relaxation, dammit.

I started rummaging through the suitcase of tacky hand-me-down clothes in search of something that seemed likely to survive a soak in the ocean. To my delight, I discovered someone—Bruno, or maybe Zero?—had thrown in a pair of swim trunks in my size among the other items of clothing. I changed in the bathroom, grabbed a pair of sunglasses, and left the condo, wandering down a rocky path to one of the island's private beaches.

Like many of the other seasteads, this island had a shelf extending off its sides to create a shallow swimming area before dropping off to deeper water about a hundred meters offshore. Bright aquamarine waves lapped gently over the white sands of the beach. Apart from a few pieces of driftwood and a clump of seaweed, the beach was absolutely pristine. I kicked off my sandals, enjoying the feel of the sand beneath my toes. I loved the sea, no matter what planet I was on. In Tierra Nueva, Escalante Bay was the most calming place around for me, but I had to admit, the warmth made this beach even more appealing. Walking barefoot without cold nipping at my toes, feeling warm sunlight on my bare arms instead of having to bundle in thermals all the time... I was proud to be a Martian, but Earth did hold its charms.

I waded into the water, so crystal clear that I could see my feet sinking into the wet sand beneath them. When the water was up to my waist, I surged forward, my feet kicking up off the sand, and began to swim. I started paddling toward the deeper water near where the seastead's shelf dropped off, then thought better of it—needed to stay close to shore, away from any prying eyes. I turned, planning to swim parallel to the line of the beach instead, when I saw a figure standing at the edge of the waves, holding a striped towel and looking lost.

I swam back to her. Nadin was wearing a sapphire blue bathing suit that matched the highlights her dyed hair now shone with under the bright sunlight. Her hair was pulled back in a ponytail, and large round sunglasses covered most of her face.

"Hey," I said once I was close enough to stand and wade out of the waves. She stood just outside the line of damp sand at the edge of the beach. "What's up?"

"Scylla said you were down here swimming, and I thought..."

I grinned. "That's right! I promised I'd teach you."

She looked at the water with a frown, like the sight of it was giving her second thoughts.

"Don't worry," I said reassuringly. "The water is shallow. You won't drown. If you feel uncomfortable at all, you can just stand up."

For a second I thought she was going to say no, that she'd changed her mind. But this was Nadin. Of course she wasn't going to back down from a challenge. After a moment she squared her shoulders like she always did, and tossed the striped towel down on the dry sand, setting her sunglasses on top of it. She kicked off her sandals and turned to face the ocean almost defiantly. Then she waded into the water beside me.

"It's warm," she said with a smile as the waves licked at her ankles, then her knees.

"Yeah, and it's as clear as a swimming pool. Can't get a better place to learn how to swim," I said cheerfully.

She waded in until the water was lapping around her stomach. "Now what?" she asked.

"Do you know how to float at all?"

"A bit. I used to float in the baths in the *geroi*'s villa when I was small. They were more shallow than this, though."

"But you're taller now." I grinned. "Do you want to try it now?"

She frowned again, and I laughed, holding out my hand. "Here. Brace yourself on me."

She hesitated a moment before taking my hand, gently. Then she breathed deeply, filling her lungs with air, and leaned back, kicking her legs away from the sea floor.

"There," I said, her fingers still between mine. "You know more than you let on. I don't know what you were so worried about."

"The baths were small, though," she said defensively, turning upright and planting her feet back in the sand. "You can't get swept out to sea in a bath."

I smirked. Her idea of a small bathtub differed from mine, I suspected. The baths in Elytherios were similar to Roman baths—basically public pools. I was sure the private ones in the *geroi*'s villa were the same.

"Okay, so, to swim, the general idea is the same. Make sure

you breathe. Air in your lungs keeps you buoyant. There are ways you can breathe while swimming, but for today we'll just do a basic dog paddle, keep your head above water so you don't have to worry about any of that. Recreational swimming, if you will."

I showed her how to turn around while floating, from her back to her side to her stomach. She kept her fingers laced through mine while I stood, to balance herself. "Now just kick," I said.

She thrashed her legs so hard that water sprayed up, hitting me in the face. "Wow," I said when I'd finally caught my breath, splurting water out of my mouth. "Okay, don't need to kick that hard."

"Sorry," she said, standing upright again.

"No, no, it's okay! You're learning. Let's try it again."

I towed her around the shallows while she practiced her kicks, practiced keeping herself buoyant and her head above water. Soon her kicks became smoother, less erratic, and she was getting the hang of keeping her body long rather than curling up into herself. First I was walking, but soon my feet couldn't quite reach the sandy bed without my head going underwater, and I began to tread water beside her, holding her with only one arm while I paddled with the other.

As I pulled her away from the beach, toward the end of the underwater shelf, facing out to the sea, she looked beyond my shoulder. "Isaak, what's that?" she asked.

In a panic, I turned, expecting to see a boat or a drone or some other spy from GSAF, catching us out here alone and unguarded, without a boat to leave with and without Lizeth and the Stateless to defend us. My heart pounded, but when I saw what Nadin was gesturing to, I relaxed, grinning.

"It's a dolphin!" I exclaimed, watching as the creature breached the surface, swimming up close enough that we could see its form through the clear waters.

Beside me, Nadin stared as the animal swam by, her eyes wide. I watched her, bobbing above the surface like a mermaid.

It was only then I realized that she'd let go of my hand.

Nadin and I swam for a good couple hours, until I was pretty sure I was going to have a sunburn and I could hear Nadin's stomach growling over the sound of the waves. Worn out but grinning, we walked back to the condo.

It was still inside. Scylla had fallen asleep on the leather sectional in the living room. Nadin and I quietly rummaged through the kitchen for snacks, and then Nadin went to change out of her bathing suit and rinse the salt water out of her skin and hair.

I took a bite out of a sweet peach I found in the fridge and went over to the patio door. The ocean spread as far as the eye could see, an unending blanket of blue. I pushed the patio door open, taking another bite of peach and walking out on the deck. Henry's hammock was abandoned now. I hadn't seen him from the beach Nadin and I had been swimming at, so maybe he'd gone through the backyard or down to the beach on the island's other end.

I went down the steps from the deck and through the garden. At the edge of the backyard, the brick patio met wooden steps and a small wooden walkway down to another beach. A tall sand dune covered with beachgrass obscured the wooden walkway's end from view. A private cove, maybe? I could hear voices from there. Henry must be there, and Tamara with him. I tossed the pit of my peach into the bushes and started down the walkway.

Beyond the narrow strip of beach, a small dock—not big enough to moor a boat at but probably ideal for fishing—jutted out a short distance into the water. At the end of the dock, the two of them sat shoulder to shoulder. The bright sunlight glinted off of Tamara's blond hair, as odd on her as Nadin's new dark color was.

Henry said something I couldn't hear, but Tamara laughed, her voice echoing across the water. I grinned, starting toward them, but as I stepped off the wooden steps onto the soft sand, Tamara turned and leaned into Henry, resting her forehead on his shoulder with her eyes closed. It only lasted a moment, this small gesture of affection, before she straightened and looked back out at the waves. But in that moment, everything seemed to click into place. Everything that had been happening right in front of my face that I hadn't been paying attention to suddenly came into laser focus.

And I realized what a complete idiot I'd been. And more than that—what a torquing jerk. I'd been so self-absorbed, so preoccupied with my own experiences, my own feelings and the way they were changing, it hadn't even occurred to me that maybe her feelings could have changed, too. Had I always been this selfish? Maybe I had, and I was only just now realizing it.

I'd never even *asked* her how she felt.

There was a small noise behind me. I turned, startled, to see Scylla standing there at the foot of the stairs. She was breathing heavily, just ever so slightly, like she'd hurried to catch up with me and stopped short when she saw what was happening. Now she was watching me carefully, waiting to see how I would react.

"Hey," I said, as nonchalantly as I could manage.

"Isaak," she began.

I shook my head. "You don't need to explain anything. I was blind, wasn't I?"

"No. You weren't. None of this started before you left."

"I know," I said. And I did. Despite the fact that I'd been completely encased in my own little bubble the past couple of weeks and had missed every single sign they'd given, I knew my best friends. I knew *Henry*. And Henry had known my feelings for Tamara. If he'd had feelings for her as well—the thought made my chest ache a little—he would never, ever have acted on them. But what were they supposed to do when I was gone for two annums? Had I really thought that Tamara was just going to sit there waiting for me like a video game on pause until I got back? When neither of them had any idea whether I was ever going to come back at all? When the whole world thought I was dead?

"It was my fault," Scylla blurted, and I looked at her in surprise. "I saw it happening, and I... encouraged them. Especially when I realized that Tamara liked him back. Henry's been in love with her for years, but... Your friendship is just as important to him. To both of them. They'd rather be apart than hurt you. That's why they broke up when you came back. I told them they should tell you, but everything's been so crazy since you got back, there was just never a good time." She said it all in a rush, her face red and her eyes shining. "I'm sorry, Isaak. I'm so sorry."

I stepped forward, putting a hand on Scylla's shoulder. "Don't be sorry, Scylla. Honestly. Tamara and I—we never really were a couple. I had a crush on her, but it never went beyond that." Even the kiss on the sky bridge had been only that: one kiss. I'd been trying to hold on to that singular moment ever since I'd been back, but it had felt like trying to keep water from draining out of a cupped hand. Our date had been miserable, and every time we'd been alone together since then had been almost as bad. The lightness I'd felt on the *Athena* when I'd told Tamara that now wasn't a good time for a relationship suddenly seemed to come full circle and fill me entirely, like a giant weight had been removed from my shoulders. Saying the words out loud was like a release of some sort. Maybe Tamara and I could have had something once. But that time was gone. And honestly? I felt more relieved than anything.

Scylla smiled in a pained sort of way. "So what are you going to do about it?"

"I'll talk to them, but"—I glanced over my shoulder—"not right now. Let's just leave them alone for now. Tamara's been stressed out for weeks about all of this. Let them have some quiet time alone."

Nadin appeared at the top of the dune, the sea breeze pulling tendrils of dark hair out of her ponytail. She shielded her eyes, looking down at us. I smiled and waved back at her, starting back up the wooden steps to join her.

Scylla followed, glancing from me to Nadin. "Yeah," she said. "I think that sounds like a good idea."

We went back to the condo together.

CHAPTER 27

- n a d i n -

LIZETH RETURNED FOR US ON SATURDAY MORNING, DANTE WITH her again—it was the weekend, he explained, so he'd been able to take a flight over the night before when he'd gotten off work. Lizeth apologized profusely that she hadn't been able to come back sooner. Her mother had been watching her, she said, "like a hawk," suspicious that she was up to something that probably involved us. This subterfuge and the dissonance among the rebels made me uncomfortable, but there wasn't anything I could do about it, I supposed. It didn't involve me. All that mattered was getting to Mexico, retrieving the medallion and getting to the postern. Trying to have faith that the medallion truly was an Iamoi one, and that the postern would work here on Earth.

Believing in the nearly impossible. Because there wasn't anything left to do.

We set out from the private island in Lizeth's boat. She was taking us to a location far from the other seasteads and natural islands, where it would be less likely for tourists and other prying eyes to see us. When we were far out to sea, with no sight of land on the horizon in any direction, Dante dropped anchor and Lizeth did something with her palmtop. "A beacon," she said by way of explanation.

Before long, a small airplane came into view in the sky. It circled us a few times. I shrank back nervously, wondering if it was a GSAF spy, but Lizeth said, "Don't worry. That's our ride."

The plane circled a couple more times before beginning to descend. I looked around in confusion—there was no land anywhere in sight, no runway, nothing for the plane to touch down on. But to my surprise, the plane landed in the water some distance away from our boat. In place of wheels on its bottom, pontoons extended out from underneath it like feet, allowing it to bob on the water like a boat.

"A seaplane," Isaak said to me in a low voice.

To transport us from the boat to the seaplane, Dante and Lizeth loaded us and our luggage into a small rubber watercraft called a *dinghy*. Dante informed us that he would take Lizeth's boat back to the Keysteads where we'd originally picked it up at, while Lizeth took us on to Veracruz. To her uncle, and to whatever would happen next.

The flight took several hours. By the time land came into view, it was evening. We soared over a rounded peninsula Isaak informed me was called the Yucatán, and then over more water. Finally, the seaplane went down, this time not out in the open ocean, but at a small, quiet harbor.

"We're about an hour outside Xalapa now," Lizeth informed us.

"The capital of Veracruz," Isaak explained in a low voice.

"That's where the museum is."

Lizeth said something to the pilot of the seaplane in a language I couldn't understand. She'd been speaking to him this way all afternoon. Spanish, Isaak had said. When he'd been teaching me English on our journey to Elytherios, he'd also told me a few words of this language, though I couldn't remember them now for the life of me. This was the language they spoke in Mexico. Henry and Scylla couldn't speak it, either, and Tamara knew only a few words, but Lizeth and Isaak were both fluent in it and would be able to translate for us on the journey... providing we didn't get separated. I tried not to dwell on this. We'd managed to evade GSAF so far. We just had to hope our luck would hold out.

Lizeth led us down the dock and into the small town we were to stay in tonight. Lizeth had made a reservation for us in a dingy motel near the docks. She went inside with Isaak to check us in, while the rest of us waited out of sight. They returned with a key card and led us around the back. The rooms in this place all opened to the outside rather than having an interior entrance— ideal for staying out of sight of the proprietors. Lizeth had told them only she and Isaak were staying in the room. As long as we were quiet, hopefully they'd never know more than that.

I slept fitfully that night. The room was small and cramped, with most of us sleeping on the floor on piles of sheets or towels. The room was hot and smelled stale, and the walls were thin, letting in the voices of our neighbors on both sides. Nerves overwhelmed me; when I wasn't preoccupied with fear that we were dangerously close to being caught, I felt anxious about the day ahead of me tomorrow. Meeting Lizeth's uncle at the museum, and finding out whether the artifacts his archaeologists had found were truly a remnant of my people's failed attempt to colonize this world, or if our last well of hope had run dry.

The next morning before dawn, Lizeth woke us up. She'd rented a car with an app on her palmtop, and it would be arriving soon. We needed to be ready to go.

I was sitting on the foot of the bed blearily when the vehicle rolled up. We hurried from the motel room to the car, stowing our luggage in its cramped trunk. Lizeth went to check us out, and we departed just as the sun was climbing into the sky.

The hot mugginess of the air outside had never dissipated in the night. Even in the early morning, it was so humid that my hair clung to my scalp and my clothes felt soggy and uncomfortable. But soon the car was climbing into hills, leaving the humidity of the coast behind us. Lizeth opened one of the windows of the car, letting cool air in, and I breathed out in relief. Still hotter than I was used to on Iamos, but closer to how it had been on Mars.

Soon we were entering a bustling city in the hills, similar to the size of Tierra Nueva, but with the more colorful architecture I'd seen on Herschel Island.

"We're getting close," Lizeth said over her shoulder. "Hang in there, guys."

Before long, car pulled into an empty parking lot and Isaak nudged me. "We're here," he murmured. I craned my neck to look out the window at the building we'd arrived at. The museum itself was a large, boxy concrete structure, its rectangular face covered with square windows. It was almost ugly compared to the colorful architecture we'd seen traveling through the other parts of the city. The building was nestled among trees, and a plain circular fountain created a burbling geyser of water into the air in front of it.

After we'd parked, Lizeth led us past the fountain and up a short set of steps where the glass entrance to the museum stood. Beside this, a flag hung—green, white, and red, with the depiction of a creature that resembled a *gamada* clutching another creature that resembled an *anguis* between its talons. I stared at the flag until movement behind the glass caught my eye. An instant later, the doors slid open. A man with thinning fair hair and a matching beard stood just inside. "Lizeth," he said cheerfully. "Come in, come in. And your friends, so nice to meet you." This must be Lizeth's uncle, Professor Karl Senghas. He smiled at everyone as they went by, but his eyes lingered on me. I managed to avoid squirming under his scrutiny, returning his gaze steadily.

The doors slid closed once we were inside, and Senghas locked them again. Then he turned back, looking at Isaak now. "Of course, I've met you before," he added. "Though you may not remember me. You were quite small at the time. We were having an exhibit of your grandfather's work, and he brought you here with your mother. You were here on vacation, he said." He spoke with an accent, though not the same as Delia's or Zero's.

Isaak scratched the back of his neck. "I remember a little. Especially the inside of the museum. I remember the plants growing inside, next to the colossal heads."

Senghas laughed. "Yes, you were quite interested in the colossi. Well, it's only to be expected that a small boy would remember something like that more than a boring old professor. No matter, it's good to see you again. I hope you'll pass my greetings on to your grandfather... whenever you might be able to see him again."

"Yeah," Isaak said quietly, his eyes darkening for a moment. I watched him, frowning, but Professor Senghas began speaking again before I could react.

"So, I understand you're here about one of the artifacts from the Los Tuxtlas site," he said.

"Right," Lizeth said. "The coin."

Professor Senghas nodded. "That site always was of particular interest to you as a young girl," he said with a smile. Lizeth flushed, shifting uncomfortably on the balls of her feet, and Senghas turned back to the rest of us. "An Olmec site, discovered relatively recently, in the 2040s. It's been a bit of an anomaly since its discovery. Though clearly an Olmec settlement, there are a number of indicators that it was in use prior to the classical Olmec period. And there have been other odd things about it, too. Artifacts that have been unearthed that don't quite fit the stylistic mold we typically associate with the Olmec. That coin, for example. Metallurgy was common throughout the Olmec empire, but coinage isn't known to have been used in the pre-Columbian period. Typically, older coins found in Mesoamerican sites tend to have originated from the so-called 'Old World,' brought here by European invaders. But the glyphs on the coin have been difficult to decipher, which is what led us to believe this coin did not originate from any known European civilization, or Asiatic or African for that matter. The glyphs are similar in nature to classical Olmec writing, which seemed to indicate an American origin. There were theories that perhaps it might not be a coin, but a medallion of some sort. This seems to be reinforced by the presence of a hole near the top of the coin. While it could be for use on a coin belt, it's just as likely to indicate a pendant on a piece of jewelry."

My mind had begun to drift as he spoke, confused by his meaning and overwhelmed by the flood of unfamiliar English words. But the word *medallion* snapped me back to attention. *Coin. Medallion.* It was too much of a coincidence. It had to be a relic from one of our lost colonization parties. They must have been here. But what had happened to them? And why had we lost contact with them?

"But that still leaves us with the glyph conundrum," Senghas went on. "Classical Olmec, I assume you know"—he glanced at Isaak as he said this—"is quite different from other Mesoamerican languages as it is. But these symbols are different than the ones decoded by the Cascajal block. They appear to be an earlier form of that same writing system."

"So what are you saying?" Henry asked. "If this site was an Iamoi settlement site, the Iamoi are, like... precursors to the Olmec?"

"Possibly. Or, more likely, that they had a cultural influence on the population that was already established here, those precursors to the Olmec. If this new theory is correct, and people from"—he paused, his eyes locking with mine again—"*your* world established a colony here, it's possible that they attempted to integrate with the people who already lived here. The exchange of knowledge could have led to the development of a written language more closely related to... to Iamoi." He said the word slowly, like he was experimenting with the feel of it on his tongue. "This could explain why written Olmec differs so drastically from the languages of other cultures that emerged in other areas at later periods."

"Can you show us the artifacts from the site?" Scylla asked. "Maybe if she sees them, Nadin will be able to tell if they came from her people or not."

"Yes, please," I said eagerly. I couldn't bear standing in this lobby anymore, not when my answers could be right here in this building.

"Of course," replied Professor Senghas. "Right this way."

He led us through a door and into a large, brightly-lit room. The square windows that had looked so drab on the exterior of the concrete building made the room glow in the early morning sunlight. Huge glass skylights in the ceiling added to the effect. Small trees grew inside here—not artificial ones like those aboard the *Athena*, but real, living trees. Nestled between these were massive stone heads, twice as large as I was tall. My jaw dropped at the sight of them, and not just at their size. The features of the man depicted on this head...

He looked Iamoi.

I looked around the room in wonder. More stone heads peeked between the branches of the trees. Our footsteps echoed off the glistening concrete floor. I quickened my pace, coming up alongside Isaak and touching his elbow. "Isaak, where did these statues come from?"

"Various Olmec sites here in Veracruz and Tabasco, I think," he replied.

"They are ancient?" I whispered.

"Yeah. You think your people maybe had something to do with it?"

"Maybe. I don't know." I glanced at another head as we passed. "They just look so familiar."

Senghas walked briskly past a square pool cut into the floor between two colossal heads, but I paused here to look at it. There was a stone carving floating on top of the water. No... it was an optical illusion. The more I stared at it, I realized that the carving was at the bottom of the pool, inside the water. But the way it was carved and positioned in the water, and the way the light reflected off the pool, gave the impression that it was floating there, suspended in space. Appropriate, considering what it appeared to be.

A model of the solar system.

"What is this?" I asked, staying Isaak before he could walk past with the others.

He looked at it more carefully. "Oh, fresh! I've heard of this before. It's a map of the universe. Well, the universe that they knew about, anyway. It's Aztec, not Olmec, though. This is a replica of a much bigger carving that was found near Mexico City, that depicts their mythology about the creation of the universe. It says here on the plaque that the monster Cipatli split heaven and Earth—"

"Venus is the second world from the sun on this map," I said softly, interrupting him.

"Huh? Oh." He looked down, frowning. "Oh. Yeah. Listen, Nadin, I'm so—"

I shook my head, turning away from him. I didn't want to talk about it. "It's all right," I murmured.

Whenever the people here created this map, Hamos' orbit had already been disrupted. What had the repercussions been?

Surely enough to destroy all of Hamos and Iamos. But what about here? Earth—Simos. Had they been affected by the cataclysm as well? If only we knew *when* it had happened. And whether my people had escaped in time.

Senghas led us through a door out of the large, atrium-like room and into a plainer room, dimly lit, as if to direct the eye to the illuminated glass display cases that were the primary source of light in the room. "Here is our section about the Los Tuxtlas finds," he said. "And I believe the item you're looking for is in this case."

I followed him to a display case that held a number of small objects within it. In the center of the case was a sculpture of a seated man, carved out of some kind of red stone. The man appeared to be wearing a hat or helmet that fit close to his scalp. His ears peeked out behind ear flaps, revealing elongated lobes with large holes in them, as if he typically wore heavy jewelry in his ears that had stretched the holes to be large enough for a finger to fit through. His arms were folded across his middle; above them, a jewel was set at his throat. Like a medallion.

Around this small sculpture in the case were various items carved of green stone or forged of gold and copper. Jewelry for the ears and fingers, and to be worn around the neck. We didn't wear jewelry on Iamos, apart from the medallions that the *patroi* used. But before the Progression, items like these had been common. Gitrin had a small collection of them in our classroom, for historical purposes.

I glanced around the cabinet, then froze as my eyes landed on an object in the lower right-hand corner of the case. A small sound escaped from my throat. Worn with age, corroded almost beyond recognition, even despite the restoration work the museum must have done to it. But I recognized it anyway. This wasn't just any *patroi* medallion. It belonged to a *geros*.

"You recognize it, then?" Senghas said, watching me.

"I think so. Please, could you...?"

Senghas withdrew a set of keys from his pocket and unlocked the display case, handing the medallion to me. I ran my fingers over it gingerly, flipping it over and reading the writing on the back, the three glyph symbols over the delicately carved postern that identified the medallion's owner.

"Achillios," I breathed.

"You can read it, then?" Lizeth asked eagerly. "What does it say?"

"This medallion belonged to *Geros* Achillios. He was about five years older than me, from Radiant Tomorrow citidome. He and his partner Eristin led the final colonization party to attempt to reach Simos before we abandoned it. They disappeared about half a year before my *enilikin*." I glanced over at Isaak. "When you arrived on Iamos."

"So your people did make it here," Professor Senghas said in wonder. "They made contact with the ancient Olmec."

"How many other parties did your people send here?" asked Tamara. "If Achillios and Eristin were the last."

"There were four total. The first we remained in contact with for a few days, but their connection to the System was erratic. They sent us a few reports about the native population of Simoi they encountered, and some information about the flora and the fauna. But their signal was disrupted soon afterward, and we were never able to get it back. The other three parties we sent lost contact with us immediately after passing through the postern. Achillios' party was the final one we sent. There was a System expert with him who believed he had solved the issues with Simos' magnetic field causing System interference. But we lost contact with them immediately, just like we had with the others."

"They came here, obviously," Scylla said, "based on his medallion being here."

"But what I don't understand is how you lost contact with them," Isaak said. "The System does work here. GSAF showed us that much last week. So that should mean that the System expert guy's tweaks worked, right? That he was able to get it to work around the magnetic field. So why did you lose contact with them?"

"I don't know," I said, rubbing the medallion between my fingers. If only I could speak to its former bearer. Surely he would have answers for me. But he was long, long dead.

"You may find more answers if you were to actually visit the Los Tuxtlas site," Senghas suggested. "Excavation is still in progress there. It's the middle of the season right now. I've heard reports that more odd artifacts have been discovered this season, but they obviously have to be cataloged and studied before any announcements can be made."

"Do you think you could get us out there, Uncle Karl? This whole thing with the Iamoi—it's not just important for our cause. This is, like... the biggest archaeological discovery of all time."

"Absolutely. I can make the arrangements for you," Senghas said. Out of the corner of my eye, I saw him watching me. I was still staring down at the medallion in my hand. A thought was beginning to form in my mind. One I didn't like at all.

"Is something wrong, Miss Nadin?" Senghas asked me.

I looked up at him, frowning. "Professor, when did you say this site you've been excavated was settled?"

"The Olmec period is generally agreed by scientists to have begun sometime around 1200 B.C.E. It's entirely possible that this site was settled sometime before that, but I would estimate no earlier than around 1500 B.C.E. or so. Roughly three thousand years ago."

Gooseflesh began to ripple up the back of my neck. "Three thousand Earth years?"

"Yes, of course. Why?"

Isaak looked at me, his brows narrowed over his dark eyes. "Did you think of something, Nadin?"

"Yes. When Gitrin and I did the calculations for your posternkey, we calculated that you'd traveled back approximately six thousand, nine hundred and fifteen years. Iamoi years," I clarified.

Senghas stared at me, understanding making his green eyes flash. "A Martian orbit is, what, six hundred some days?"

"Six hundred and eighty-seven," Scylla said. "So that's..." She closed her eyes, her lips moving as she did the math in her head. "That's about thirteen thousand Earth years. Ish."

"Wait a minute," Henry said, confusion written on his face. "You're telling me that this Achillios guy left Mars thirteen thousand years ago, and wound up here ten thousand years later?"

My knees felt weak. I had to grab the side of the glass cabinet to support myself. "The time postern," I breathed.

"You mean... they traveled through time? And that's why your people lost contact with them?" Tamara asked.

"But how is that possible?" Isaak asked, his raised voice echoing off the ceiling. "You said that before I came, the time postern was just a theory!"

"I thought it was," I cried. I felt sick. This was sabotage. It had to have been. Just like the early warning protocols on Hamos being disabled before the earthquake. All those injuries it had caused, including *Gerouin* Clodin...

Someone was manipulating the System. With the singular purpose of destroying Iamos. Destroying all our hopes at evacuation. Ensuring the utter decimation of our entire population.

"The Liberator," I said. "The man who kidnapped Ceilos. It's the only possibility. We know he has access to all parts of the System. He's the mastermind behind all this. He's—he's a psychopath. He won't be satisfied until every single Iamoi is dead. That's the only possible explanation."

"Oh my God," said Scylla. Her face was pale in the dim lighting. "That's insane."

"I have to go back," I said. "I have to warn them."

"But you've got to be careful," Tamara said. "You could be walking into a trap. If this man was able to do all this, who knows what else he's capable of?"

"The last thing we need is you bringing someone like that into our time," Lizeth said, a hard edge to her voice.

"We're going to have to find a way to stop him," Isaak said. "So far his advantage has been in going undetected. But now we're onto him."

"We'll figure it out," Henry said. "We can come up with a plan of some sort. But I think first of all we need to get out to Los Tuxtlas to see if there's anything else out there from your people. Maybe there's more to this that we're just not aware of yet."

"I can make arrangements for you to visit the site tomorrow," Professor Senghas said. "It's about a day's trip south of here along the coast. Be aware, though, it's a bit of rough going. The road doesn't go all the way to the site. You'll have to walk through the jungle for part of it."

"We'll be fine," Lizeth said firmly, her tone leaving no room for argument. While my body had adjusted somewhat to Earth's gravity at this point, I wasn't overly enthused about having to hike my way through an overgrown jungle. But it was clear that Lizeth wasn't going to take no for an answer. And Henry was right—I needed to get out there. If Achillios' party had left any kind of record behind, it may contain clues about what we were up against. There was no getting out of this.

"Can I bring this?" I asked Professor Senghas, holding up the medallion.

"N-now, I don't know about that," he stammered. "That's a valuable part of the museum's collection."

"But if there was anything left behind at the site, I might need a medallion to access it. I don't have my own anymore. I lost it back on Lago Verde."

"Come on, Uncle Karl," Lizeth said. "Think of the scientific breakthroughs this could lead to! If this coin is the key to unlocking the mysteries of Los Tuxtlas, isn't that worth a temporary loan of one small little artifact?"

He pulled a round metal object out of his breast pocket,

twisting it between his fingers before opening the face of it. Inside, a timepiece ticked quietly. He stared at it for a moment before snapping it shut and putting it back in his pocket. "All right. I will loan it to you, temporarily."

Lizeth grinned and gave him a hug. "You won't regret it."

"Yes, yes. Now the group of you had better get going before our cleaning staff comes by and happens across you. And I need to make the arrangements to get you out to that site."

He led us back out through the atrium with its colossal heads. But as we passed the pool with the map of the solar system on it, Isaak paused. "Excuse me, Professor Senghas?" he said. "I had a question. We're assuming that the time of Iamos' destruction was around 11,000 B.C.E. Was there... any particular celestial event that we know of at that time?"

Senghas frowned. "That's a very difficult question, Isaak. That pre-dates all known writing here on Earth. Even the earliest known artistic depiction of the stars only dates back about four thousand, five hundred years. Any sort of celestial event such as an eclipse would have only been passed down through oral histories, and anything like that would be lost by now."

"I didn't necessarily mean something that we'd have a written record about." Isaak was looking into the water. I followed his eyes. They were fixed on Venus. "I meant maybe something that might have had a physical effect on our planet. Like maybe an asteroid collision."

"Ah." Senghas nodded. "Yes. Now that you mention it, that does fit. The Clovis impact."

"What was that?" I asked, holding my breath, my heartbeat seeming to freeze along with it.

371

"An incredibly massive piece of space debris struck Earth at that time. Possibly a comet, or an asteroid. Whatever it was, it was so enormous that the impact was devastating to our planet. It led to what is known as the Younger Dryas cooling period. Temperatures on this planet cooled to their lowest point since the end of the last Ice Age. It's believed that this impact even led to the extinction of species like the woolly mammoth. But scientists are unsure about the origin of the space debris. Whatever it was, it was surely catastrophic."

Surely catastrophic. I stared at the small round orb seeming to hover there in the waters of the pool.

Thirteen thousand Earth years. Six thousand, nine hundred Iamoi years.

Whatever it was, it was coming. And it was coming soon. Something devastating enough to destroy two worlds and nearly wipe out a third. Something powerful enough to disrupt the orbit of an entire planet and obliterate any sign that life had ever existed upon it or its twin. A cataclysm so great that Iamos' failing atmosphere paled in comparison.

And it seemed that there was truly nothing I could do to stop it.

Chapter 28

- i s a a k -

THAT EVENING WE STAYED IN ANOTHER SEEDY MOTEL, THIS ONE with two stories instead of one. We were on the second floor, so this one at least had a balcony, such as it was—a narrow strip of metal, a meter wide or less, bolted to the outside of the building. Just barely large enough to hold a plastic lawn chair and little else. Lizeth grudgingly allowed us to take turns standing on it, staring at the scenic view of the parking lot, as long as we were sure to come in if we saw any sign of movement outside. I didn't see anyone from where I was standing, though the telltale smell of cigarette smoke meant someone must be nearby. I wasn't about to let Lizeth know that, though, and have her make me come inside and bar us all access to the balcony for the rest of the night. Despite the lack of view, I was taking advantage of every five-minute allotment I was given. Anything was preferable to being crammed in that motel room again, especially after the relaxing freedom our two days on the private island had given us.

Those two days would have been the best time to clear the air, I thought as I stared up at the stars above my head. The clouds from earlier had dissipated, leaving an unobstructed view of the night sky. But I'd found that every time I thought about attempting to talk to Nadin about Venus or Tamara and Henry about... them, I got tongue-tied. I was bone tired, and afraid of putting my foot in my mouth with either conversation. But I couldn't put it off forever. It wasn't right, to any of them.

I wished it was easier to find words.

My turn was just about up when the vertical blinds to the room clacked as someone opened the sliding door and stepped through them—we were keeping them pulled to prevent anyone from seeing inside. A second later, Nadin joined me at the railing, sandwiched between the plastic lawn chair and the wall.

"Hi," she said quietly, looking at the sky.

"Hi," I murmured back. When she didn't speak again, I sighed. It was time to find my words.

"Nadin, I need to talk to you," I said in Iamoi. I expected her to argue or evade like she'd done repeatedly over the last month, but to my surprise, she just nodded. I took a deep breath. "I want to apologize for not telling you about Hamos. I know it was wrong. I knew it all along. I just didn't know how to tell you. I kept thinking some answer would present itself, but it... just never did. It was inexcusable for me to keep you in the dark that long."

"It's all right," she said quietly, speaking Iamoi as well. "I forgive you. I... I forgave you a while ago, to be honest. I know you, Isaak. You wouldn't have lied to me deliberately. When you said you didn't understand... I knew you were telling the truth. I was just angry. Not even at you, specifically. At the universe. We've been through so much. I went through so much to get here, just for one desperate chance to try to save my people. And now I find that it may be too late anyway. Maybe destiny always intended that the Liberator should win. That the Iamoi should die."

Her voice was numb, but I looked at her in surprise when she said those words. Her eyes were glistening in the starlight. A shining tear ran down her cheek.

"But you're here," I said softly. "And Achillios and Eristin made it here. Not all your people died out."

"We may as well have."

I turned, leaning my elbows against the railing of the balcony. "So what are you going to do? Do you want to just give up? Throw in the towel and stay here? Make a life for yourself?" Maybe it wouldn't be the worst idea, honestly. All of us to start over here on Earth. We'd have to take new identities, but maybe it wouldn't be too bad.

But even as I thought it, I knew it was impossible. I could never do that to my family. To Celeste, and to Mom and Dad and Abuelo and... and Erick. I wanted to go home. I wanted to see them again. And the only way that would ever be possible would be to stop GSAF. Even if it felt impossible.

Beside me, Nadin was shaking her head, and I knew she was thinking the same thing. "I can't do that," she whispered. "I can't leave them to die. Not even with the *geroi* planning what... what they were planning. That's not a reflection of the millions of innocent lives on Iamos. But I don't know how to stop the Liberator. I don't know how to face this enemy."

"You're not going to face him alone," I said, straightening and putting a hand on her shoulder. "Whatever you decide to do, I'm with you."

"Even if it means returning to Iamos?" she asked, not meeting my gaze.

I swallowed. I'd gone through so much to get away from that world. To get back to my own time. The thought of returning to Iamos, where the *geroi* and the mysterious Liberator waited, made me sick to my stomach. But things weren't much better here, either. Not just because of GSAF and the globalists, as Lizeth called them, oppressing everybody, threatening to turn the modern worlds into a repeat of Iamos. Mars was falling apart, too. The drought and that sandstorm made it perfectly obvious: we didn't know what we were doing with terraformation. We needed the Elytherioi's help. The only solution I could see to everyone's problems—mine, Nadin's, the Stateless', and all of Mars'—was to bring the Iamoi here. And if it meant we had to face the shadow figure of the Liberator, then so be it.

"If it means we have to return to Iamos, then I will return to Iamos with you," I said.

Nadin looked up at me for a moment, her eyes shining. Then slowly, tentatively, she stepped closer, wrapping her arms around my torso, her face in my chest. My heart jolted at the touch.

"Thank you, Isaak," she murmured.

I swallowed and returned her embrace, giving her a reassuring squeeze. Above our heads, the yellow star of Venus twinkled.

The next morning, the sound of a knock at the door jolted me out of my fitful sleep. My pulse shot up wildly. They'd found us. They knew we were here. The Stateless' subterfuge hadn't worked. GSAF was always one step ahead—

Lizeth looked out the peekhole and then opened the door. I breathed out loudly in relief when Karl Senghas came cheerfully in. "Hullo," he said. I'd been struggling to place his accent yesterday. I'd thought maybe Australian, but it was possible it was a British accent that had started to evolve into something else. I wondered if it would have been easier to tell if I'd been able to hear his brother, Lizeth's dad. "Everything's all set. I've got clearance to visit the site, er, on 'museum business'. So we're all ready to go as soon as we can get your things loaded into my Jeep."

"You're coming with us, Professor?" I asked, clearing my throat to get the croakiness of sleep out of it.

"Yes, it's all arranged. I've told the site managers that I'm bringing some interns from the museum out. There's another expert supposed to be meeting us on the way, so it should look quite convincing. Don't worry, he's been thoroughly vetted. You can trust him."

I stared at Senghas as he spoke. I wouldn't have been able to picture the reedy scholar we'd met yesterday surviving a trek into the jungle. Tall and narrow, with pointy limbs, he'd been dressed so much like a caricature it was hard to believe he was real. He'd worn a long-sleeved white shirt with a waistcoat over it, pants with cuffs on them, and glasses with round lenses. When he'd pulled that pocket watch out near the end I'd about lost it. I'd never seen anyone dress that way apart from "professor" characters in flix. But today he looked a little bit hardier, in his khaki shorts and matching khaki sports shirt. Granted, he did look a little like a cartoon character decked out for a safari—all he needed was a pith helmet—but at least now I didn't think he'd end up a meal for the first boa constrictor that crossed his path. Probably.

"You guys stay in here and pack," Lizeth said, looking from Scylla to Nadin to Tamara to Henry. "Isaak can help me and Uncle Karl carry stuff down. He'll be the least conspicuous."

I nodded, getting slowly to my aching feet, my joints cracking. We hadn't done much unpacking at either place, so there wasn't a whole lot to do before I was able to start carrying our bags down. I grabbed the two suitcases first, one under each arm, following Lizeth as she carried the ice chest.

I'd been a little worried when Senghas said "Jeep" that his car was going to be one of those topless numbers that you saw in flix out in the desert or on a safari in Africa, since he definitely seemed to have acquired his fashion sense from fictional characters. But to my relief, it was a practical Jeep SUV, albeit a bit beat up. Large enough to hold us all, with three rows of seats, it was the perfect vehicle to get us out of town discreetly and as far into the jungle as we could manage before the road ended and we had to trek the rest of the way on foot. The thought of the last leg of the journey gave me a little thrill of excitement. It reminded me of the days I used to go out to Abuelo's dig site with him, cutting our way through the overgrowth with machetes. His site wasn't too far from Los Tuxtlas, actually. It was in the general Sierra de los Tuxtlas area, but farther away from the mountains, right at the edge of the coastline. As water levels had grown higher, excavating any sites close to the water's edge was critical. He'd tried to retrieve as much information as he could before erosion finally made the site too dangerous to excavate any further. But of course, it never really was enough, was it? There was always more we could have learned before the site was lost.

I shoved the suitcases into the open hatch and turned back around, tromping back up the outdoor staircase and following Lizeth along the open-air hallway into the room. When I came in the door, I could see Nadin and Scylla standing in the bathroom, Scylla brushing her teeth and Nadin finger-combing her hair. In the main room, Tamara sat on the foot of the bed, deep circles under her eyes. Her short blond hair was standing up in the back. Henry stood in front of her, laughing as she tried to smooth it down and it kept popping back up.

"It's like a jack-in-the-box," he teased, reaching out to try to hold it down himself and laughing as it sprang back every time he let go.

"It looks awful," Tamara moaned. "My hair does not like this cut."

"Nah, you look fine," Henry said, holding her hair down once more, and then laughing when it flew up again when he let go.

I smiled, watching them. Then I took a deep breath. "Hey, guys," I said, "can I talk to you?" I glanced at Lizeth, who was reaching for another bag. "Um, in private?"

Lizeth rolled her eyes and dropped the suitcase, going into the bathroom with Scylla and Nadin and pulling the door shut.

"Something wrong?" Henry asked.

"No, no. I just wanted to tell you guys... I'm sorry."

"Sorry?" Tamara asked, her brows furrowed. "Sorry for what?"

"For not noticing"—I struggled with the words; this was the most awkward conversation I'd ever had, far worse than apologizing to Nadin last night—"how you guys feel."

They looked at each other. Quickly, Henry started to protest, but I held up a hand to cut him off. "No, really. You don't have to pretend. And I'm sorry you guys had to pretend to begin with. I'm sorry that I made you guys have to be apart for so long."

Tamara got to her feet. "Isaak, you didn't *make* us do anything."

"No, but I did. I came back out of nowhere, and I tried to act like nothing had changed in the time I'd been gone. Even though reality kept showing me time and time again that everything was different now, I just kept pretending that it wasn't." I sighed, rubbing the back of my neck. "I didn't even *ask* you, Tam. I didn't ask you how you felt. And I didn't think about your feelings either, Henry. All those years you ignored your own feelings to spare mine."

"Isaak, this was our fault," Tamara said. Her face was pale, making the circles under her eyes seem to stand out even more. "We should have told you to begin with. We just... we didn't know how. The last thing in the world we wanted was to hurt you, especially after everything you've been through. So we both felt it would be better to just... stop for now, rather than risk your friendship. That seemed like the more important thing." She looked down glumly. "But that was wrong. I'm sorry, Isaak."

"No, seriously. Please don't," I said, feeling miserable. "It's honestly okay. Because you guys... you're not the only ones whose feelings have changed. Mine did, too." In a lot of ways. Some ways that I wasn't quite ready to name, yet. "Everything has changed. The only thing that hasn't is... you guys are still my best friends. And I want it to stay that way."

"That's what we want, too," Henry said, his voice unusually quiet. "That's all we wanted."

I smiled awkwardly. "Good. Me too. So no more pretending, okay? Just be yourselves."

Tamara opened her mouth to respond, but before she could speak, Lizeth yelled through the closed bathroom door, "This doesn't mean you're allowed to make out with each other in front of everybody!"

Tamara's face reddened, her expression turning to one of horror. "We never did that, anyway! God!"

The door opened and Lizeth strolled out, followed by a grinning Scylla. "Good," she said. "As long as we're clear about that. Ain't nobody here want to see that."

Everyone laughed, and I breathed out a sigh of relief, grateful that the air had been cleared. I felt lightweight, buoyant. This felt like the last step I'd needed to take to get everything back to normal. Not back to how it had been before. That time was never going to come again. But *normal*. Just now, that honestly felt even better.

Ten minutes later, the suitcases were loaded into the Jeep, the pillows and blankets we'd strewn all over the floor had been tidied up and folded, and the room looked like what you'd expect from just two people sleeping in it. If we were lucky, the motel staff wouldn't be any the wiser.

Outside, the sun was up, but the clouds had come back at some point in the night, making the sky gray. The noise of traffic on the street was starting to pick up, audible beneath the sound of early morning birdsong. The motel was quiet. As long as we left now, no one would see us go.

The five of us crept down to the parking lot while Lizeth went to turn in the key and check out. Professor Senghas folded down the middle row of seats in the Jeep and Scylla, Tamara and Nadin were just starting to climb over these and into the back when the sound of a car pulling into the parking lot caught my attention. I watched the vehicle nervously, praying for its occupant to not notice us, to just pass us and pull into a parking spot. But to my horror, the car drove directly toward us, the sensor lights on it flashing off, indicating the person sitting in the driver's seat had switched the car into manual steer.

The car pulled into the parking spot next to the Jeep. I kept my head ducked, heart pounding, and urged Nadin to jump into the back. I yanked the seat up, hoping to leap into the Jeep before the driver of the new car could get out and speak to us. As if that would help. We couldn't just go tearing out of here without Lizeth. And besides, Senghas didn't seem like he was in any kind of hurry to get moving. He just stood there, smiling stupidly over the hood of the Jeep as the car beside us shut off and the driver's door opened. Henry and I shot each other anxious looks. We were screwed. GSAF had us now, I was sure of it.

"There you are," Senghas said cheerfully. "I was starting to think you weren't coming."

I froze, rooted in place, as a man with a deep, rich voice responded, "I almost didn't. This was very short notice. I only just got into town."

Senghas turned to me with a grin. "Isaak, say hello to our other expert."

Slowly, I managed to get my feet to move. To come around the side of the Jeep and see the man emerge from the car next to us, slamming the door shut behind him. He turned to look at me, his flannel shirt rolled halfway up his arms, revealing deeply tanned forearms that he folded over his chest. He'd gotten thin, but not as frail as he'd looked over Mom's deskpad webcam. Older, but still sturdy and strong-looking. Strong enough to easily manage a trek through the jungle, gripping a machete to cut away the undergrowth.

"Abuelo," I said when I finally found my voice. He grinned, opening his arms, and I collided with him. It had been so long since I'd seen him in person, I could hardly believe he was standing here in front of me.

"What are you doing here?" I asked when we separated. "How could you—Lizeth said GSAF was watching my whole family."

"They are," Abuelo admitted. "It was difficult to sneak away from them."

"Then how did you manage to get to Mexico?"

"Ah." He looked chagrined, not meeting my eyes. "I've made a few connections over the years. You'll find most archaeologists do, especially by the time they get to my age. Though I certainly never imagined I'd be smuggling myself."

My jaw dropped at his insinuation that he'd dealt with smugglers over his career. But I wasn't able to respond, because Senghas was saying, "I've never been much for working in the trenches, so I reckoned it would look much more believable if a well-known excavator were to accompany us. It needed to be someone I could trust—who better than the foremost authority on Olmec archaeology?"

I nodded, grinning. "Glad to have you aboard, Professor Garcia," I said.

Abuelo laughed. "Glad to be with you. It sounds like we've got a lot of catching up to do."

"You don't know the half of it."

Lizeth appeared then, looking from Abuelo and me to her uncle in confusion.

"I'll explain on the way," Senghas said to her, and then to us, "and you can catch up as well. We've got a long drive ahead of us. About three and a half hours by car, and then a good few hours' walking once the road ends."

We locked the middle row of seats into place, and Henry, Lizeth and I climbed in. Abuelo hopped into the front with Professor Senghas. The Jeep powered on and began to back out of its parking spot, and we turned onto the road, leaving Xalapa behind.

Chapter 29

- n a d i n -

THE DRIVE FROM XALAPA WAS LONG, AS PROFESSOR SENGHAS
had said it would be. The scenery was beautiful and very different
than anything I'd encountered on Mars or in Florida, with rocky
mountains and taller trees than I'd ever seen in my life. But soon I
found I couldn't keep my eyes open any longer. I hadn't slept well
since we'd left the UFS, and it was catching up with me. As Isaak
chatted with his grandfather from the seat in front of me, I began
to doze, and the next thing I knew, I was waking up with my face
pressed against the glass of the back window and my neck stiff
from staying in the same position so long.

"Wake up, Nadin," Tamara said softly beside me, and I
realized her hand was on my shoulder. "Sorry," she murmured as
I turned groggily to face her. "We're here. Well, we've gone as far
as we can before we need to start walking."

The hatch to the Jeep's storage area lifted as I rubbed the
sleep from my eyes. "These suitcases are quite impractical,"
Professor Senghas said from behind me. "Backpacks would have
been a better choice."

"Hey, we were in a hurry," Lizeth said. "And I didn't know where we were going when we left Florida. I didn't even know we were coming out here until yesterday."

"Let's try to consolidate," Isaak's grandfather said. "You won't need all these things on the dig site. Everyone grab a change of clothes or two and your toiletries and we can try to get them into my bags."

Henry folded down the row of seats in front of us and Scylla, Tamara and I crawled clumsily out. I found my legs had gone numb from sitting for so long, and I had to brace myself against the Jeep and shake one foot then the other to get my circulation to return. Behind the Jeep, Isaak's grandfather was helping the others select their most practical clothing and showing them how to roll it tightly to make it all fit into his backpack. With his help, we managed to consolidate all our effects into his and Professor Senghas' backpacks and one duffel bag, which Isaak carried. The rest of us weren't empty-handed, though. Senghas had packed food and medical supplies, plus an extra tent and cots, since we were bringing more bodies to the dig site than the coordinators had originally intended. Each of us carried a box or a bag and had a rolled-up tarp or metal tent pole strapped to our backs. Senghas locked the remaining suitcases in his Jeep, and—after applying a liberal coating of insect repellent spray to every part of our bodies where skin was exposed—we set off.

The trail was mostly clear due to the excavators arriving at the site for the season just a few weeks before, but nature had already begun to reclaim it in just this short amount of time. Isaak's grandfather led the way, holding a long, sharp blade he called a *machete*, to cut away any overgrowth that blocked our path. "And," he said with a chuckle, "to fight off any critters that might try to get in our way."

Isaak grinned at my alarmed expression. "There probably won't be," he said reassuringly. "Every once in a while you'll get a snake, but most animals know to stay clear of humans."

"Right," I said, wondering what a snake was and trying not to let my imagination run away with me. Senghas and Isaak's grandfather didn't look worried. They did this sort of thing all the time, after all. They knew what they were doing.

"That's the trouble with excavating out here," Isaak's grandfather said conversationally. "That's why so many sites have gone undiscovered, even with our advanced satellite technology. It doesn't take long before the jungle reclaims its land. Every year you have to cut your trail anew. Every season you have to spend a few days taking back what you excavated last year. Whenever a city was abandoned, Olmec or Maya or any other civilization that lived in the rainforest, whether because of war or famine, the jungle swallowed it up in mere years. There are centuries' worth of undiscovered settlements buried underneath all this greenery. Anything could be hidden out here."

Including the last remaining artifacts of my people, I thought. Some things had been found, like Achillios' medallion. But how much was still lost? We wouldn't know until we reached the site.

We walked for what felt like hours, though it was hard to say for sure—the afternoon sun was obscured by the thick green canopy of the trees above us, so I couldn't see its position. I had no idea what time it was when we finally heard the sound of voices and Professor Senghas announced that we were close. All I knew was that my feet were sore, my shoulders ached from the weight of the provisions strapped to my back, and every part of me felt as heavy as it had the day we'd arrived on Earth.

We broke through the trees and found ourselves in a clearing, unnaturally square, cut into the forest by the excavators. The foreground was sectioned off into grids, and various workers crouched within these, digging quietly with small trowels and brushes. Beyond this, a huge mound filled most of the clearing. It was so large that were it not for the massive trees covering it with their canopy, it would surely be visible from a great distance. I stared at it, my eyes narrowed. It was overgrown, but remnants of stone facing here and there showed that this was no natural hill. This structure was man-made. The remnants of a pyramid.

Like our capitol buildings on Iamos.

And, like our pyramids on Iamos, there was a vaulted stone arch on the top, further proof of its man-made status. Unlike much of the rest of the stone façade on this pyramid, the vault appeared to be entirely intact. Arches like these were found atop many of our official buildings on Iamos, a representation of the postern, one of the symbols of our civilization. But the ones on Iamos tended to be decorative. Was this one also decorative? Or had it been built to be functional? And even if it had been built to work, *did* it work? Was Earth's magnetic field enough to disrupt it? Or, like we'd been told about the System not working here, was that also a lie?

"The Olmecs were the first great builders in this region, but most of their cities and monuments were deliberately destroyed around the time their civilization collapsed, some thirteen hundred years after its initial rise," Isaak's grandfather said as we entered the clearing. "We're not really sure what led to its collapse—warfare, class strife, famine, some environmental factor. All we know is that the deliberate vandalization of their cities has made it even easier for nature to reclaim their sites and make them almost impossible to detect. You can see that even after a thorough excavation, this pyramid is difficult to discern from a natural mound or hill, apart from that arch at the top. That feature is unusual. It doesn't occur in later pyramids—at least, to our knowledge. It's possible, however, that later arches were simply destroyed."

As he finished speaking, a shout rang out from one of the trenches. "Hector! Over here!" A man with dark hair and tan skin who appeared closer to Senghas' age than Isaak's grandfather's waved to us.

"José, it's good to see you," Isaak's grandfather said. "Thanks for meeting with us on such short notice."

"Of course. Anything to help the museum. Karl said your interns were working on a project for an upcoming exhibit." He glanced past Isaak's grandfather and the group of us hovering nervously at the entrance to the clearing.

"Yes, indeed. Everyone, I'd like you to meet Professor Espinoza."

The professor nodded at us before turning back to Isaak's grandfather. "Is there anything specific I can help you with?"

"There is, actually," Senghas said, stepping forward. "Is there somewhere private we could speak?"

"Sure. My tent is back this way. It's a bit small for the whole group, though," he said, giving us another look.

"That's fine. Our, er, interns can wait here," replied Senghas.

Professor Espinoza nodded and, brushing his dirt-encrusted

hands off on his pants, led Isaak's grandfather and Professor Senghas between the trenches and around the side of the pyramid.

Isaak drifted over to one of the gridded-off sections, his eyes betraying his eagerness. He watched the people kneeling inside, patiently digging out their squares. "I always wanted to be an archaeologist," he told me quietly as I came up beside him. "Abuelo used to work at a different site like this, not far from here. This was always my dream. But I hadn't thought it was possible on Mars, since, you know. We'd always been told that we were the first humans to live there." He looked up at me, his head quirked at an angle. "This is how we found the posternkey, actually. How I managed to find my way to Iamos. We were digging out in the craters. We never expected to find anything like what we found, though."

"Digging like this?" I asked, watching the excavators. It looked very tedious to me. All that time, crouched so uncomfortably for hours on end, in the hopes of finding some minute item in the dirt. But I supposed sometimes it had a big payoff. If there hadn't been an excavation like this on Mars, and if Isaak hadn't been on it, he would never have come to Iamos. And I would not be here now.

"Isaak?" We looked over at the sound of his grandfather calling. He caught our eyes and waved. "Can you and... your friend come back here?"

I followed Isaak down the dirt path and around the pyramid to a group of tents clustered together in the mound's shade. Isaak's grandfather led us through the flap of one of the larger structures in the middle. Inside, a small table stood holding several plastic bins, each containing a number of dirt-encrusted artifacts. Many were in pieces. All of them had paper tags tied around them, marked with writing.

"Your grandfather says you have insight on some of the stranger objects that we've encountered on this dig," said Professor Espinoza. "I didn't want to believe it, but both he and Professor Senghas are quite adamant."

"What kind of objects?" Isaak asked, his voice sounding wary. The man beckoned him over to the table, gesturing to an object in one of the boxes. Isaak took one look at it and gasped.

"What is it?" I said, coming up behind him. My own breath hitched in my throat at the sight of what they'd found.

A System earpiece. It was worn, ancient-looking, but it was unmistakable.

"Do you think it still works?" Isaak asked quietly in Iamoi.

"I don't know. It's possible."

"So you do know?" Espinoza asked, but his voice sounded flat. Like he didn't quite believe us.

"I do..." Isaak glanced at his grandfather. "What does he know?" he whispered.

"I know enough," said Espinoza. "I know that the government has been withholding information about the archaeological findings on Mars. I know that they've been restricting funding and access to sites here as well as there if they believe there's something that they can profit from. I know that they are perfectly willing to stifle scientific study if it runs the risk of impeding one of their political goals. And I know that if the government knew what we've found out here, they'd shut us down in a heartbeat. The coin in the Museo has somehow managed to slip under their radar. But if things like that"—he gestured to the earpiece—"went public, I can guarantee you this site would be shut down in an instant and my life's work would be lost." He folded his arms. "I'm a scientist. I'm not interested in their politics. I want the truth. I want to know what really went on at this site. So tell me: do you know?"

Isaak hesitated.

"I know," I said before he could answer. "I know what this artifact is. And I suspect that if you showed me, I'd recognize others as well."

Professor Espinoza stared hard at me, his eyes locked with mine. I hadn't been wearing sunglasses since we'd entered the canopy of this rainforest. My blue eyes were like a beacon. I knew this man must know what they meant. But if Lizeth's uncle trusted him, then I would, too.

He smiled. "Then come with me."

He led us out of the tents and around to the far side of the pyramid. The structure's original steps had been worn beyond repair, but a makeshift set of wooden steps had been installed over the top of them, allowing us access to the building's entrance near the top of the mound. My heart beat erratically. Whatever it was he wanted to show me, I wasn't quite sure I was ready to see it.

The light in the clearing, filtered through the trees soaring high into the sky above us, was by no means bright, but I still had to blink several times before my eyes adjusted to the dimness of the inside of the pyramid. Professor Espinoza walked ahead of me, over to the wall. He fumbled in the dark for a moment, and then an artificial lantern flickered to life, offering a bit of illumination to the small chamber we were now standing in. Prickles ran down my neck as I looked around.

"What is this place?" I asked, afraid of the answer.

"It's a tomb," Espinoza said.

I swallowed. I'd feared as much. And if he brought me here, expecting answers, then I had a horrible feeling that I knew whose.

He turned, the light from his lantern flashing over the wall, revealing writing carved into the stone.

Writing I could read.

"Do you recognize this?" he asked.

I swallowed again, struggling to find words. I squeezed my eyes closed, my voice unwilling to come.

"It looks like Olmec," Isaak's grandfather said. "But it's not. The symbols are similar, but the syntax is not the same as what was used at the time of the Cascajal block. A precursor to classical Olmec, perhaps?"

"It's Iamoi," I said. "It's the old writing."

"Like what was in Gitrin's apartment?" Isaak asked.

"Yes." I twisted the ring around my finger. "It says *N'atlatoi nou akoúste. Hear our words.* And below that, their names. *Geros Achillios.* And *Gerouin* Eristin." It was as I'd feared. This was their final resting place. They had never returned to Iamos. They'd died here, along with the others.

"*Hear my words?*" Isaak's grandfather repeated, looking at the glyphs on the wall, as if trying to decode them, to see in his mind how they spelled out the words.

"An epitaph?" asked Espinoza.

"No," said Isaak. "I think it's a message. Nadin, do you think something like this might initiate a System protocol like the writing in Gitrin's apartment did?"

My skin tingled at the thought. Could it be possible? We had every reason to believe the System might have worked here. It would only make sense for the *geroi* who lived here to leave a message, in case future travelers from Iamos were to arrive here.

"We'd need the earpiece to know for sure," I said.

"The artifact from your tent," Isaak said to Espinoza, and he hurried to retrieve it. As we waited, I wandered the perimeter of the small, dark room.

"Are they buried beneath this chamber?" I asked. My voice was barely a whisper, but it echoed off the walls, the floor, the ceiling.

"It's possible," Isaak's grandfather said, "but... it's more likely that they're gone. It's very rare to find an intact tomb when you're dealing with archaeology."

I flinched, trying not to let my mind imagine what had happened to their bodies in the thousands of years after their death. It didn't matter, after all. Once you were dead, that was it. Preserving the body was nothing more than clinging to a false hope of immortality.

Espinoza returned, breathing heavily from running back up the staircase. "Thank you," I said, taking the earpiece from him. I slipped it into my ear. The soft rubber that made it fit comfortably had crumbled away long ago, and the metal end scratched at my ear. I pressed the small button on the device and felt it hum to life, the antenna transmitting my brainwaves to the System and vice versa. There was static in my ear, noisy and irritating—the earpiece was damaged, barely functional. But it did function. I recognized that immediately, when the wave of dizziness rolled over me as my brain readjusted to its connection.

When my vision steadied, I took a step forward and placed my fingers against the engraved glyphs on the wall.

System protocol initiated. Geroi DNA detected. Begin transmission.

There was a flicker of light behind me, and I turned. Standing in the center of the room, invisible to everyone here but me, was *Geros* Achillios. He was much older than he'd been the last time I'd seen him. At least ten Iamoi years must have passed by the time this recording was taken.

"Is it working?" Isaak asked.

"Shh," I hissed at him. "Yes." I subconsciously noticed him staring at me as I stared at the recording, and I felt heat begin to creep across my face. But I didn't have time to be distracted. I needed to pay attention.

"*Degiim*," the recorded Achillios said, looking directly at me, as if he could see me. "If any Iamoi finds this recording, I hope against hope that you and our people are well. This log is the final account of the fourth expedition to Simos... and possibly the ultimate fate of the people of the fourth world, Iamos.

"This year marks the twentieth rotation this planet has made around the sun. The twentieth Simoi year since we lost contact with our people. Upon our arrival, we immediately lost contact with Iamos, but contrary to our expectations, we did not lose contact with the System. We were able to connect but received only a blank signal in response. Upon further study, we concluded that the System had been shut down at some point after we left Iamos. We have not been able to restore enough connectivity to determine when this shutdown occurred, but we believe the System may be on a timed sleep mode and will reactivate at a future date. We are not able to calculate when this may be, however.

"What we do know is that we did not arrive on Simos on the date we were expected to. The date we left Iamos—which should have been the exact date we arrived on this world as well—was the eleventh day of the fourteenth month of S.C.D. 8377. However, we quickly realized from astronomical data that we did not arrive here when we should have. Calculations run by *Gerouin* Eristin and our chief mathematician lead us now to believe that we arrived on Simos in what would have been the third month of S.C.D. 13,424—five thousand forty-seven of our years in the future."

Achillios' image sighed heavily, though his features were resigned, as if this were a wound that had healed long ago, but the scars from it still caused pain.

"Some time before we left Iamos, the *gerotus* was presented with a theoretical design. A simple System program which, if implemented, could convert our existing postern technology from transportation in three dimensions to four—adding a time component. I was there when we voted to reject the proposal. We told the designer that it wasn't viable, but the truth is that we knew it was. The designers intended to use the postern to rewrite history, to undo the decisions of our past that led to Iamos' climate disaster to begin with. But if the climate disaster were undone, the Progression would be as well. In spite of everything, the social progress we as a people had made since the Progression was too great to lose."

I frowned, arching a brow. *You mean the power the* geroi *stood to lose was too great,* I thought acidly. *Without the Progression, there would be no* geroi *at all.*

"Not that it mattered in the end," Achillios was saying. "Everything we achieved has been lost. Iamos is gone.

"After we determined that we had traveled forward in time, we began to formulate a plan to try to return to Iamos in an attempt to determine what had happened there, if the System could be restarted, and if we could access the knowledge base to program a new posternkey and attempt to return to our own time. Our System specialist, Tirios, volunteered for this job. He believed that if he were able to return to one of our citidomes, even if abandoned, by manually accessing a System terminal he could override the sleep mode. Construction began immediately on a new postern, which we were able to complete in about one Simoi year. We outfitted him with food, water, and oxygen, programmed coordinates that would take him to Hope Renewed citidome, and, with great trepidation, sent him on his way."

Hope Renewed. He'd gone to my citidome. To the place where Tierra Nueva now stood.

"To our astonishment, the postern worked flawlessly. This confirmed our suspicions that our previous posternkey had been tampered with. We believe that the other colonization parties' keys were tampered with as well. All but the first party, the one we were originally in contact with for some days before they disappeared, we believe were sent to other times as well— though certainly not to this same time, or else we would be able to contact each other with our earpieces. As for the first party, we are still unsure whether communication with them was truly lost due to interference from Simos' magnetic field, or if they were sabotaged as well. Whoever this saboteur is—or was—he must have had a very thorough understanding of the System's workings and manipulated it in such a way that we were only able to see what he wanted us to see until it was too late."

I blanched, remembering what I'd heard the Elytherioi often say to one another—"It's *so easy to manipulate a mind that's reliant on the System.*" I'd seen firsthand the illusions they were able to produce in order to keep themselves hidden from any System user, such as the wall of rock that wasn't there, the one that hid Eliin and her outpost outside Bright Horizon. They surely had this capability. And Gitrin had been allied with them long before I ever knew about it—that's how she was able to escape so quickly after my failed evaluation, when she knew the *geroi* had begun to suspect her connection to the rebels. Had they lied to me? They claimed to have not been involved with Ceilos' kidnapping. They swore they didn't know who the man who'd contacted me was. But their runners shared the identity of Liberator among them, crafting a shadow figure together to deceive the *geroi* and inspire the *plivoi*. What if they'd lied to me? What if they—or one of them, at least—knew more than they'd let on? Were they so desperate to overthrow the *geroi* that they'd be willing to sabotage our evacuation colonies to Simos, and to Hamos as well? After all, someone must have tampered with the early warning protocols at Ascendant Dawn as well.

I had the sudden, discomfiting memory of my nightmare all those weeks ago, the night after we went to Yellowknife Bay. Of *Gerouin* Clodin, Ceilos' mother, screaming, "*This is your fault— you knew —*"

Did I know? Had I met the saboteur before and not recognized it? Could I have prevented any of this?

The recording of Achillios was still speaking. I jerked back to attention. "When Tirios arrived on our homeworld, it was unrecognizable. He'd expected to find our citidomes abandoned, empty, possibly crumbling; but what he found instead was far worse. All signs of the city had disappeared altogether. All that remained in its place was a massive impact crater, filled with red sand. There was no sign of life on the planet, or of water. Even the *frauoloi* had vanished. Oxidation had turned the entire surface of the planet, from the sand to the stones, red as rust. Atmospheric degradation was complete—there was no atmosphere left to speak of at all. Even in his bodysuit, with his oxygen canisters, there was little to separate him from the cosmic radiation. And without a sign of the citidome, there was no sign of a postern he could use to return with, either." Achillios swallowed, looking down. "He searched for some hours for any kind of entrance to Hope Renewed's underground. Any kind of escape. But there was nothing. If any remnant of our civilization remained, it was lost. Buried far underground, inaccessible to one man carrying nothing but his own hands.

"We'd given him enough supplies to last a week. He only made it a day. We lost contact with him the following afternoon. He was delirious with radiation poisoning. In the end, we're not sure if that's what killed him, or if he removed his oxygen tank to end the suffering. Regardless, he was gone. We'd lost one of our people... and our sole System expert."

My legs felt unsteady. I stared at the recording, horrified, my mind unable to stop envisioning the gruesome end Tirios must have faced.

Isaak stepped forward. "Nadin, are you okay?"

"I'm fine," I said, holding up a hand to hush him. There was more.

"The complete annihilation of all trace of our civilization, the presence of the impact craters... it all seemed to add up to one thing. Something we had seen our first day here but hadn't dared to try to comprehend. A disaster beyond anything we could have imagined. We do not know how—we are unable to run major calculations on the System—but we believe a massive celestial body impacted Hamos. Eristin's speculation is that it was one of Pemos' outer moons. She believes it may have escaped Pemos' gravity and been drawn into our worlds' dual orbit. The System's early warning protocol should have alerted us to it long before it was close enough to endanger us, but..." He squeezed his eyes closed. "It is my hope that our people were already gone, and not that this saboteur prevented the protocol from warning us until it was too late. Regardless, the impact was powerful enough to disrupt Hamos' orbit. Hamos has been drawn far closer to the sun. Eristin has been unable to run the calculations to determine how this could have been possible, what kind of force would be required to disrupt it so much, but the end result is clear to the naked eye. Simos and Hamos have exchanged places. Simos is now the third world, not the second. Eristin estimates this must have occurred soon after we left Iamos, though how soon we cannot say. Such an impact would not only have caused the annihilation we saw on Iamos, but would also surely have led to impacts on this planet. However, the stability of this climate indicates that enough time must have passed in order for this world to have recovered.

"Regardless of what happened, we know now that there can be no going back. We must move on, and try to find a life for ourselves on this planet.

"We arrived on the coast, but were soon driven back by hostile Simoi. We could not hope to subjugate them as originally planned, not on our own like this. Our weaponry relies too greatly on the System, which is inaccessible to us. They outnumber us and their weapons, though primitive, are still much better than anything we could hope to muster on our own. Our only choice was to treat with them. We have established a small city at this location, about halfway between the coast and the mountains, in a place no Simoi held claim to. We've made trade with some of the neighboring tribes, bartering primarily with knowledge. The tools we brought with us are far superior to those the people here have developed, and our knowledge of architecture and advanced construction methods helped us much in our early days here. Our structures are stronger than their weapons, strong enough to endure any onslaught as long as we have enough food. And we have this in plenty now.

"We've been here long enough now to have allies. More than that—our numbers have grown, though we must deign to count Simoi among us. Several dissidents from neighboring tribes have broken away from their kinsmen and joined with us, helping to fortify our city. Primitive as these Simoi are, their knowledge of this region's ecology and agriculture has been invaluable. I wonder what the other *geroi* would think of this fellowship we've created. I hope you will understand that it was done out of need. At this point, without any assurance that our people escaped the cataclysm safely, the only hope I can find for our species to continue is through partnership with Simoi, as detestable as this may seem—or may have seemed—to our Iamoi kin. Our bloodline will go on, diluted though it may be.

"We have built this city here, which we are calling New Home. The Simoi call it *Ipilchan*, which they say means something similar. We've gradually learned to speak one another's languages, or some approximation of it. A new language, cobbled together of the two. And we are teaching them writing. The city we've built here is far greater than any seen on Simos before. The central pyramid serves as our capitol, as it would have on Iamos. The postern we built for Tirios' failed return to Iamos was placed on top, as a beacon. A symbol. A... memorial. And if any Iamoi come here in the future, we leave it to you with our blessing. From this pyramid, we hope to form a new civilization, as strong as the one we left behind."

My skin crawled. Achillios' and Eristin's capitol building had become their tomb. Was this what they'd wanted? Had they asked for it? One last, eternal monument to the glory of the *geroi*?

Isaak had told me that the Olmec were the first great empire of Mesoamerica. My people had begun it, but I'd seen the artifacts in the museum. It had evolved into something distinctly different. More Simoi than Iamoi. But their influence still remained, from the origins of the writing system to the faces on the colossal heads in the museum. The pyramids that dotted the landscape all over this continent had been inspired by my people. Was it possible, even now, that some people who lived on Earth had a drop of Iamoi blood running through their veins?

"My only hope," the recording of Achillios said now, "lies in the knowledge that the System appears to have been deliberately shut down, with a future restart date programmed into it. We were sent forward in time. Does that mean that others have traveled forward as well? The System's early warning protocol would surely have alerted our people to the impending danger from whatever cataclysm led to the disruption of Hamos' orbit. Perhaps our people have evacuated not only to another world, but to another time. Farther in the future than even we have traveled. If that is the case—if our people come here some time in the future—I want them to know the truth. What happened to their lost expeditions.

"I am growing older. I have begun to feel, down to my core, that I will not see another Iamoi again, save those who came with us on this mission. But I must believe that this is not the end of our people. That one day you will find this, and that our people will live on."

He inclined his head, placing three fingers on his brow. "*Gamoak*," he said, and the recording disappeared.

I leaned back against the stone wall his words had been carved into, sinking shakily to the floor.

Isaak hurried over to my side, crouching beside me. "What happened, Nadin?" he asked. "What did you see?"

So much. Too much. It made my head spin. He'd have to be told all of it, soon, but for now I wanted him to know the most important thing.

"They were here," I said raggedly. "They built this. And... they built that arch out there, too. The one on top of the pyramid. It's a postern. And it works. The only thing that kept them trapped here is that they didn't have the right key."

"So you're saying we can use it? We can open the door to Elytherios from here?"

I closed my eyes, leaning my face against the cool stone of the wall. My head swam. I yanked out the ancient earpiece, tossing it away from me. The static ringing in my ears from the System quieted.

"Yes," I whispered. "We can open the door from here."

My journey was almost at its end. The reunion I'd been longing for since the moment I arrived here was just an arm's length away. If I wanted to, I could take the posternkey and Achillios' medallion, run up those stairs and activate the postern right now. Ceilos and Gitrin would be waiting on just the other side—they had to be. I should have been elated, ecstatic.

But all I felt was anxious. Because I had an unshakable feeling that something was waiting for me on the other side of that door, something I didn't want to face. But I didn't have any other choice.

Whatever it was, I *had* to face it.

CHAPTER 30

- n a d i n -

WHILE THE FOUR OF US HAD BEEN IN THE PYRAMID, PROFESSOR Espinoza's assistants had set the others to the task of assembling our tent at the end of camp. This was where Tamara, Scylla, Lizeth, Henry, Isaak and I were to sleep. The tent only had room for six, so Isaak's grandfather and Professor Senghas were staying with Professor Espinoza while we were here.

"But no funny business," Senghas said before he left us. "Tents are not known to be good sound buffers. Try any hanky panky and the entire camp will know about it."

"Yes, okay, whatever, Uncle Karl," Lizeth said between clenched teeth as she ushered him out the flap of the tent and rolled it down behind him. "All right, Nadin," she said then, turning back to face us. "What did you find out?"

I told them a condensed version of what Achillios had said, but I found I couldn't bring myself to tell them everything. Especially not about the saboteur. My mind was going around in circles about that, thinking about the Elytherioi and their knowledge of the System. And others. Other people I knew who had more than enough knowledge of the System to be able to manipulate it in the same way. A pattern was emerging in my mind, one that made me go numb and cold inside. But I didn't dare voice it aloud, especially not to Lizeth. If I gave her any reason to suspect that someone dangerous may be in Elytherios, she might shut down our plan right now. And it was too late for me to go back. I had to stop the Liberator's plan. I had to save my people, no matter what.

So in the end I simply told them that our suspicions had been confirmed: that the Iamoi had been here. That they had built this city, as we'd suspected since arriving at the museum.

"I knew it," Lizeth breathed, grinning widely and revealing her crooked eye tooth. "The Atlantean link was there all along. An ancient civilization that connected dozens across this world before its ultimate destruction. But who would have believed that Atlantis was never on Earth to begin with? That it was another world entirely."

"The ultimate in freshness," Scylla said, her grin matching Lizeth's. She turned to me. "So now you can open the postern, right? And we can start working with the Elytherioi to take down the evil governments of all our worlds. We're one step closer to independence."

"Yes," I said, rubbing my temples. "But if it's all right with all of you, I'd like to wait until morning. I'm too exhausted to deal with this tonight."

"She's right," Isaak said. "It was early morning when we left Elytherios. We'll have another long day ahead of us if we go now. Better to face it all on a good night's sleep."

I smiled appreciatively at him.

We ate dinner together with the other workers at the dig. Lizeth was worried about this, but Professor Senghas pointed out to her that this excavation had already been ongoing when we'd escaped from Lago Verde. The only means of communication in or out was through the radio Senghas had used to contact Professor Espinoza. There had been no news from the outside world, no internet, no palmtop usage. No one here knew anything about what had happened in Florida, so they had no reason to suspect us. It would look more suspicious if we stayed away from the others than if we came out to sit with them. Regardless, though, I kept my eyes down on my plate as much as I could. Even with my hair blending in now, I knew my eyes never would.

After dinner, everyone went their separate ways. Scylla and Lizeth joined some of the student excavators who were playing a card game. Isaak stayed by the campfire with his grandfather, chatting animatedly. Tamara and Henry drifted quietly away from the group, following a trail into the jungle that the other excavators said led to another clearing and a small stream.

That left me alone with my thoughts.

I returned to our shared tent, lying back on my cot and staring out the open tent flap at the pyramid outside. Earth's moon had risen, casting silvery light over it, illuminating the stacked stones of the postern on the top. I couldn't take my eyes away from it. I could see it in my mind's eye: the way the grooves between the stones would begin to glow, brighter and brighter. A doorway of light. To another world. Another time.

The Liberator would be waiting for me. A faceless enemy, an anarchist whose sole purpose seemed to be the genocide of our entire world. He knew me. He knew how to hurt me. But would I know him if I saw him?

Something had been bothering me since the day I met with GSAF. When I'd had my epiphany—that maybe I was meant to come here alone. Maybe that's what I'd needed in order to pass Gitrin's test. Since that day, a thought had been germinating stubbornly in my mind, and it had been growing stronger since this afternoon, since I'd seen Achillios' final message:

What if it wasn't an accident when Ceilos let go of my hand?

I rolled onto my side, looking away from the pyramid.

Finally, I couldn't stand it anymore. I stood, winding my way between the other tents back to the campfire. Isaak's grandfather sat there, but now José Espinoza sat beside him, and Isaak was nowhere to be seen.

"You looking for my grandson?" he asked.

"Yes, I am."

He nodded toward the path into the woods. "He went to the stream, to go wash his face and brush his teeth before bed. You should probably do the same, and turn in early. You've got a big day tomorrow."

I exhaled, nodding, and headed down the trail into the jungle.

Not far ahead of me, I could hear the burbling sound of running water. A short distance into the trees, the trail forked into two paths. I hesitated, unsure of which direction to go. Isaak's grandfather hadn't told me there was more than one path. I paused, listening for which direction the water seemed to be coming from. But before I could decide, the sound of footsteps through the underbrush stayed me.

A moment later, Isaak appeared around the trunk of a tree on the path to my right. "Hey, Nadin," Isaak said, approaching me through the trees. He was holding a long-stemmed blue flower with large pointed petals, twirling it absently between his fingers. "Looking for the watering hole?"

I shook my head. "Maybe later. I'm just kind of... I thought I'd walk around a bit. Get a look at the place my people lived in after they came here." The place they *died* in.

I started to turn toward the fork to my left, to see where it led, but Isaak said, "Don't go that way." When I looked at him in surprise, he added in a low voice, "I was just down that way. Henry and Tamara are down there. I thought I'd give them some privacy."

"Oh." I'd been so preoccupied with my own worries, I'd almost forgotten about the conversation this morning in the motel. When Isaak had told Tamara and Henry the truth. It felt like a lifetime ago. Like Xalapa was eons behind us. "Are you all right about that?" I asked.

"You know, I really am. I'm kind of surprised by how little it bothers me." He sighed, gazing up at the canopy of trees above us. There was a gap in the foliage directly overhead, and through it, stars twinkled. "Have you ever felt like... maybe if you feel a way about someone for a long time, you just kind of assume that those feelings will stay the same forever? You stop paying attention, and you don't even notice until much later that they're gone. That maybe they've been gone for a while." He looked at me, twisting the flower between his fingers. "Probably not, huh?"

"No. I think I do know what you mean. Exactly what you mean, in fact." He watched me intently. I looked down, my face hot, searching for some way to change the topic. "Where did you get that flower?" I asked finally, gesturing to the bloom in his hand.

"Oh, I found it in the jungle. Actually, I wanted to give it to you."

I blinked in surprise, my face burning even more. "Me? What for?"

He stepped closer, reaching for my face. He tucked the flower behind my right ear, twisting the stem gently into my hair. "There. It matches your eyes." He put his hand gently under my chin, guiding my head back and forth so he could see how it looked. "Really pretty," he announced.

I was grateful he probably couldn't see my coloring in the semi-darkness. With my complexion, my blushes usually weren't very visible, but I suspected this one was. "Thank you," I said softly.

"Hey," he murmured, taking his hand away from my face but not stepping away from me. "How are you feeling? After today? And everything else this week? I know it must all be a shock."

I let out a deep breath, angling away from him slightly. "It was at first, but after I thought about it more, the less surprising it started to feel. We knew something must have happened to our settlers. We just hadn't anticipated *that*. But I already knew the Liberator was interfering with the System. This was just one more layer of his deception. One more thing I'll have to face when I get back to Iamos."

"It's okay, Nadin. You're not alone."

I smiled, looking at the broken stonework emerging in jagged pieces between trees and from underneath crawling vines and wide-leafed plants. More parts of the city—New Home, Ipilchan—that the archaeologists here had yet to excavate. More of my people's story to reveal. "You said that before. In Elytherios."

"I meant it then. And I mean it now." I turned back to him, standing so close. His voice so earnest. "Wherever you have to go—to whatever time—I'll go with you. I won't leave you. I promise."

My breath stuck. I looked up at him, meeting his warm brown eyes.

Old feelings fade, and new ones grow.

He bent close to me, and the thrill I'd felt from his proximity instantly turned to panic as his face almost brushed mine. I jerked away involuntarily, my mind suddenly far away, reliving the unpleasant sensation of lips on lips, a hot tongue in my mouth, and the absolute refusal of my body to allow that to happen again. I'd wondered once, briefly, if maybe the problem had been Ceilos. That maybe things would be different with someone else. But now that this was upon me, I knew otherwise. It didn't matter that it was Isaak. I still couldn't bring myself to want this. This was me.

And that's okay. You know it's okay. It's okay. My brain repeated it over and over, a panicked mantra.

"Nadin, I'm sorry," Isaak stammered as I stepped away from him, my heart pounding erratically, jagged breaths tearing from my throat. "I didn't think—I shouldn't have. I thought maybe you... That is, not all aces..." He trailed off helplessly, watching me. "Never mind. I'll go. I'm sorry. I'll—"

"Wait," I burst out as he started to turn away. "Don't go. Please." I squeezed my stinging eyes shut for a moment, trying to steady my breathing.

It's okay. You're okay. You are you, and it's okay. Everyone's different, but it's all normal. You're okay.

Isaak watched me silently.

"You said before—back in Hope Renewed—that you wouldn't want to"—I hesitated, struggling with the words, trying to remember how Tamara had said it in English, wanting to make sure I got this right—"to kiss or... or have sex... with just anyone. But if it was the right person, you would. Someone you cared about. Someone you loved." Tentatively, I stepped closer to him again. I didn't want him to think I was pushing him away. I just wanted him to understand. "But what if that person didn't want to? What if she loved you... more than *anything*... but she still didn't want to do those things?"

Isaak stared at me for a long, quiet moment. I waited for him to move, to say anything. I twisted my ring anxiously, looking for its comfort. Its reassurance. Hard and cool between my fingers. *Normal. Normal. Normal.*

It's okay.

Then he took a step closer as well, closing the distance between us. Slowly he lifted his hand, gently placing it on my cheek. "That would be fine," he murmured. "I can live without those things. Truly. As long as she loved me, that would be enough."

His words from back on Mars echoed in my ears. "*I'm not that different, you know. You don't have to explain to me.*"

I swallowed hard and threw my arms around him. He wrapped his around me, drawing me close, holding me tight. I buried my face in his chest, feeling his warmth envelop me.

This. This was what I'd longed for. What I craved. And what

Isaak was willing to give.

I closed my eyes, breathing him in, as my heart swelled with feelings I didn't want to name yet. Not just yet.

But soon.

Hours later, everyone in the tent was asleep except me. The flap to the outside had been closed, but I could still feel it there, just outside. I could feel it as strongly as if it were staring at me through the canvas and mosquito netting.

At last, I crept out. Overhead, Earth's moon was full. Its roundness hovered directly above the pyramid's top in the small opening between the trees. In its silvery light, I moved silently, around the far side of the pyramid and up the rickety wooden stairs.

I held still until my eyes adjusted to the darkness of the stone chamber. Then I crept to the wall with the engraving, feeling around for it in the shadows. At last, my hand closed over it—the earpiece I'd tossed aside this afternoon. Professor Espinoza had forgotten to retrieve it.

I slipped it into my ear, closing my eyes as my mind adjusted to the static. Then, when the dizziness subsided, I opened a System panel. Something so simple, but something that had been out of reach for the colonists in Achillios' party. Because sometime between then and now, the System had come back online. It had been waiting. Waiting for the Simoi to come to Mars.

Ten minutes later, I crept quietly back into my tent and over to the cot where Henry lay curled, asleep. I felt bad waking him. I knew he was exhausted. But this couldn't wait. I put a hand on his shoulder, shushing him when he jerked at my touch, sitting bolt upright. I gestured for him to follow me outside. He nodded and quietly stood.

"What's up, Nadin?" he whispered when the tent's flap was closed behind us.

"Henry, you did much work with the System, did you not?" I murmured. "Enough to have a passing knowledge of how it functions, how to use it?"

"Yeah, enough," he said, stifling a yawn. "I could probably do more if I had some guidance."

I nodded. Good. That was all I needed.

"I need your help with something, one last time," I whispered through the dark.

CHAPTER 31

- i s a a k -

EVERYONE WAS QUIET AS WE ATE BREAKFAST THE NEXT MORNING. I couldn't help but feel overcome with déjà vu, like we'd done this all before. This morning felt too reminiscent of the day we'd left Elytherios—had it only been two months before? The quiet. The stillness of the morning. The feeling that everything we'd worked for had come down to this moment, and now it was time to sink or swim.

"It's going to be different this time," Nadin said quietly to me as we started up the wooden steps to the pyramid. The chamber we'd entered yesterday was about two-thirds of the way from the top; a second set of stairs led the rest of the way, to the postern. "When a stable connection is created between two posterns, it's like opening a door between two rooms, rather than an instantaneous portal. We won't have to pass through to see what's on the other side."

"Are you saying we should hold back?"

She didn't answer. She was chewing on her lip. Her anxiety was making me anxious. The memory of the explosion as we passed through the postern kept replaying in my mind. Had it been a figment of my imagination? Nadin had felt it, too—it had made her lose her balance, stumbling into me, and made Ceilos lose his grip on Nadin's hand. But what could have caused it?

We stood, together, on the top of the pyramid. Here we were high enough to almost see over the tops of the surrounding trees. The sky seemed wider up here, blue in the early morning light, hot and humid already. I stood beside Nadin, Henry and Tamara to my left, Scylla and Lizeth to Nadin's right. Senghas, Espinoza and Abuelo stood behind us, watching curiously, eager to see what would happen when Nadin brought this ancient technology to life.

"Are you ready?" Scylla asked Nadin.

Nadin took a shaky breath. "I'm as ready as I'll ever be."

She removed Achillios' medallion from the pocket of her shorts. The key we'd brought from Elytherios was already in her hand. She clicked the medallion into place, and the key opened, unfurling outward and outward into the shape I couldn't name.

In front of us, the postern began to glow. Brighter and brighter, light filling the archway, outshining the sun overhead.

I took Nadin's hand, ready to step forward, but she held back. "Wait," she murmured in Iamoi.

She wanted to see what was on the other side before she went through.

The light burst, and the door opened onto chaos.

Elytherios was burning. Smoke billowed out of the postern as if it were pouring from an open door. I coughed at the overpowering, acrid smell. Around us, the others stepped back. I distantly heard Tamara ask if we should move away or close the door, but I was riveted in place.

Beside me, Nadin's face was unchanged. Firm and expressionless as a stone statue.

The smoke began to dissipate, and through the shadows, figures began to take shape. Slowly, I began to pick out their silhouettes. Three people. I breathed out in relief as I recognized them—Emil, Gitrin and Ceilos. They were safe. They hadn't been lost between dimensions.

But then the others behind them came into view, and my blood ran cold.

Eos. Marin. Surrounding them, restraining them in place, Enforcers. And, stepping forward coolly to face us, two unmistakable figures: Nadin's parents.

The *geroi*.

They'd found Elytherios. My knees felt weak, and I had to struggle to maintain my footing.

"Nadin," *Gerouin* Melusin said smoothly. She quirked her eyebrow, taking her in—her strange clothes, her dark hair. "What in the world have you done to yourself?"

Nadin didn't answer. Her voice was cold as death as beside me, in Iamoi, she said, "You tricked me. Everything that happened before I left Hope Renewed—it was calculated. The assignment you gave me to prove myself, that was just a ploy, wasn't it? You knew Gitrin was involved, and you wanted me to lead you to her. That's why you told the medic that Gitrin wanted me to talk to Isaak. So that I'd look for her to find out why. You knew that if I found Gitrin, it would lead you to Elytherios."

Melusin's eyebrows arched in surprise, and she looked over at Antos. "My, my. Perhaps we underestimated you, Nadin."

"You underestimated her in a thousand ways," I spat.

They ignored me. Still looking at Nadin, Melusin said, "This tutor led you astray for years. We'd suspected for a long time that she had connections to the rebels. After you failed your evaluation and she vanished, we knew it had to be true. She'd wanted to lure you to their side all along. The only way we could prove it, though, was to let you lead us to her."

"We found the message Gitrin left in her apartment," Antos added. "We knew there had to be more to it. A System protocol of some kind. But we were certain it would only play for you. So we needed to encourage you to look."

"Are you the ones who pretended to be the Liberator?" I asked. "Are you the ones who kidnapped Ceilos?"

"Ceilos has been valuable to us in more way than one," Melusin said, glancing over to him with a smirk. He stood beside the Enforcers, not looking at Nadin, a miserable expression on his face.

"Ceilos, you were part of this?" Nadin asked, her voice thick with an emotion I couldn't quite define.

"I'm sorry, Nadin. They said if I cooperated with them, they would overlook your—our evaluation scores. That our partnership wouldn't be dissolved."

Nadin looked stricken. Her shoulders slumped. Her usual expression of defiance was gone; now she looked utterly defeated. I reached over to her, touching her elbow gently.

"We will hold to that bargain," Melusin said, "but only if you return now."

"No," Nadin said, shaking her head. "I won't be part of this. What have you done to Elytherios?"

"The rebels have been taken prisoner. Their hive will be destroyed."

"You can't!" Nadin cried. "Did you not see it? Their technology has the power to heal Iamos, *gerouin*! You cannot destroy it!"

"Nadin, these people are traitors. Anarchists. If you side with them, you will be a traitor yourself. We will not show you leniency again," said Antos.

"I have traveled thousands of years into the future to deliver salvation to our people," Nadin snapped. "And you call me a traitor?"

As soon as she said it, I saw. Movement through the smoke behind them. Enforcers. A whole platoon of them.

They were stalling. Keeping Nadin standing here, arguing with them—leaving the door open.

They were going to come through. With all the force of the System and possibly even their neurotoxin at their backs. They were going to attack. And there was no one here to stop them but a handful of archaeologists. Even with machetes, we'd be no match for the sheer number of Enforcers standing just beyond this door. They'd overwhelm us, and then they'd have all they needed to invade both Earth and Mars.

"Nadin," I started, but she'd seen it, too. In an instant she'd whirled on me, shoving the key into my hands.

"Don't open it again," she whispered urgently in English, her fingers gripping mine. "Not this door."

Before I could react, she popped the medallion from its slot in the key with her thumbnail. It skittered across the flat stones atop the pyramid. Tamara dove for it, catching it just before it rolled off the edge.

The postern glowed blinding white as it began to close. There was a flash, as bright as a supernova.

Then the light disappeared. And Nadin was gone, too. She'd hurled herself through the door just before the connection broke, her form disappearing into a thousand glowing bits of glittering stardust.

She was back on Iamos. And I was here, holding the key. The only means to return to this exact place and time sat right here in my hands.

She'd saved us all. But what would happen to her?

"Nadin!" Scylla cried, running to the arch, but she just passed through it. The postern was closed. There was nothing but empty air between the stones now.

I felt cold. Numb. She was gone.

"Damn it!" Scylla screamed, kicking the side of the postern, her voice echoing over the trees. In the distance, birds flew into the sky above the canopy, startled from their perches.

I looked over at Tamara, still kneeling at the pyramid's edge, holding the medallion gingerly between her fingers. "She saved us, didn't she?" she asked quietly. "Without the key, they won't be able to come back here."

"And we can't get to her," I said, my voice coming out louder than I meant it to. I felt like I was going to be sick. It didn't matter that we still had the posternkey and Achillios' medallion. If we opened the door again, it would just replay this moment over and over. It was useless to us. They were all dead now. Nadin, Emil, all the people in Elytherios... They were as good as dead in the hands of the *geroi*. We were never going to see them again. *I'm never going to see Nadin again. Ever.*

"We can't just leave her with them," said Scylla.

"But what can we do?" Tamara asked. "She told us not to open the door again."

"Not this door," Henry said.

I turned to look at him, my mouth agape. It was the first he'd spoken all morning.

"What did you say?" I asked.

"Not *this* door," he repeated. "That's what she said, right?" When I nodded, he grinned and reached into his pocket, pulling out a small object. The corroded earpiece. The one Professor Espinoza's expedition had uncovered.

"What is that?" Lizeth asked, looking at the small thing in Henry's hand with narrowed eyes.

"Nadin had a feeling something like this would happen. So she gave me this last night."

"What is it?" Tamara said, getting shakily to her feet and coming over.

"Instructions. Datapoints. All the stuff we need to reprogram the key."

He looked at me, his grin wide and his eyes bright. I stared numbly at him, unable to get my mouth to form words. Unable to process any of this. Unable to believe that maybe it wasn't over after all. That all of them could somehow be saved.

That *Nadin* could still be saved.

Henry laughed at my expression. "Now you get it." He looked around at the others, holding the earpiece up to the light of the morning sun as if it were made of gold.

"Yeah," I said, my voice barely more than a whisper.

"We can make another door."

ACKNOWLEDGMENTS

Well, here we are again. First and foremost, I want to thank all my wonderful readers for being so incredibly patient with me on this book's *long* journey to publication. I know it's been an unforgivably long time since the release of *Fourth World* (and even the release of *Different Worlds*), and I truly hope it was worth the wait. I also truly hope the gap between this and the final book of the series will be shorter! Your support of me despite all the delays and your well-wishes for my myriad health issues has been truly appreciated. You all are the best.

Thank you to my family for your unending support. I don't know how to elaborate on that without it turning into another novel, so I'll leave it there. :-) ♥

Thank you to everyone who helped make this book a reality. Particular thanks to my editor Rose Anne Roper; my cover designer, Najla Qamber; Elise Marion and everyone at Mosaic Stock; Meagan and Jorge for lending your faces to the covers of my books; Pan Z and the others in #writing for your brainstorming help; RoAnna Sylver for helping me find my spoons; and to my dear friend Nikki Prudden for designing so many logos for me, and in particular the GSAF crest and the emblem for the Stateless (which you will get to see in *One World!*).

Thank you to the Asexual Visibility and Education Network (AVEN) for permitting me to quote their definition of asexuality within the book.

Thank you to everyone at Snowy Wings Publishing for being the best pub sibs and the best support group for indie authors in the world.

Thank you to my wonderful patrons on Patreon!

Thanks to everyone who has supported this series and recommended it to your friends, to fellow readers, and to schools and libraries. Seeing my words have an impact on so many people across the globe has been absolutely surreal—and wonderful.

And, of course, thank you to the Leopards for starting it all.

ABOUT THE AUTHOR

Lyssa Chiavari is an author of speculative fiction for young adults, including the critically-acclaimed *Fourth World* (Book One of the Iamos Trilogy) from Snowy Wings Publishing, and *Cheerleaders from Planet X*, a quirky sci-fi romance published by The Kraken Collective. Her short fiction has appeared in *Ama-gi* magazine, *Wings of Renewal,* and *Brave New Girls: Tales of Heroines Who Hack.* She's also the editor of the anthologies *Perchance to Dream* and *Magic at Midnight.* When she's not writing, you can usually find her exploring the woods near her home in the Pacific Northwest and dating every villager in *Stardew Valley.* Visit Lyssa on the web at lyssachiavari.com.

BOOKS BY LYSSA CHIAVARI

the iamos trilogy

Book One: *Fourth World*
Book Two: *New World*
Book Three: *One World*

Different Worlds – An Iamos Novella

other novels

Cheerleaders from Planet X

anthologies

*Perchance to Dream: Classic Tales from
the Bard's World in New Skins*

Magic at Midnight: A YA Fairytale Anthology

PRAISE FOR FOURTH WORLD
book one of the iamos trilogy

"*Fourth World* is a gem. Exciting and interesting while covering the span of archaeology, time travel, government conspiracies, overcoming diversity, individualism, and friendships that defy odds, Chiavari paints us a vivid colonized Mars with such beauty it's effortless to believe."

- Brenda J. Pierson, author of JOYTHIEF

"Striking characters evolving in a beautifully-described Mars, coherent and entrancing world-building, a mystery that builds relentlessly, one question after the other..."

- Claudie Arseneault, author of CITY OF STRIFE

"This book fires perfectly on all cylinders."

- Jaylee James, editor of VITALITY magazine

"The world-building of both the Martian colony and Nadin's world, Iamos, is nothing short of spectacular. Full of mysteries, intrigue, and fantastical new discoveries, *Fourth World* is the kind of book that's hard to put down."

- Mary Fan, author of STARSWEPT

Printed in Great Britain
by Amazon